Redstone Station

Photo: Carole Kurz

One of nine children, Therese Creed grew up in Sydney. After leaving school she worked as a teacher for several years before deciding to take a break and ride a horse from Victoria to Queensland. During a pit-stop on the ride she met and fell in love with Cedric Creed.

After marrying Cedric, Therese became involved in the running of his family's cattle station and had a crash course in – amongst other things – fighting fires, driving tractors, shoeing horses and fencing. Therese now divides her time between bringing up her four young children and helping out on the station.

THERESE CREED

Redstone Station

ARENA
ALLEN&UNWIN

To Murphy, my faithful packhorse

First published in 2013

Copyright © Therese Creed 2013

All rights reserved. No part of this book may be reproduced or transmitted in any form or by any means, electronic or mechanical, including photocopying, recording or by any information storage and retrieval system, without prior permission in writing from the publisher. The Australian *Copyright Act 1968* (the Act) allows a maximum of one chapter or 10 per cent of this book, whichever is the greater, to be photocopied by any educational institution for its educational purposes provided that the educational institution (or body that administers it) has given a remuneration notice to Copyright Agency Limited (CAL) under the Act.

The characters and events in this book are fictitious. Any similarity to real persons, alive or dead, is coincidental and not intended by the author.

Lyrics from 'Could I Have This Dance' copyright © Wayland Holyfield.
Used with permission.

Arena Books, an imprint of
Allen & Unwin
83 Alexander Street
Crows Nest NSW 2065
Australia
Phone: (61 2) 8425 0100
Email: info@allenandunwin.com
Web: www.allenandunwin.com

Cataloguing-in-Publication details are available
from the National Library of Australia
www.trove.nla.gov.au

ISBN 978 1 74331 333 6

Set in 12/17 pt Minion by Post Pre-press Group, Australia
Printed and bound in Australia by Griffin Press

10 9 8 7 6 5 4 3 2

The paper in this book is FSC® certified. FSC® promotes environmentally responsible, socially beneficial and economically viable management of the world's forests.

Chapter 1

The mob was strung out but moving in the right direction. From his position on the wing, Sam Day squinted ahead through the heat haze and buffalo flies at a group of calves. They hadn't 'mothered up' and their erratic, bat-eared movements stood out as they worked their way to the front. If they managed to bust out of the mob, they'd head for the thick band of gidgee suckers at the eastern end of the paddock and be nearly impossible to find. It wouldn't be the first time. Relaxing back into his saddle, he stopped worrying. Alice was onto it, and so were the dogs.

'Steady now,' he muttered under his breath, watching the overzealous kelpie, Lydia, make a beeline for the small group of delinquent calves. Alice's 'Stop!' came at the perfect moment to drop Lydia in a key position. This left the more sensible collie, Kitty, in charge of doing the blocking. Her small black and white form circled out wide, applying just enough pressure to make the calves tuck back into the mass of bellowing red bodies and think about finding their mothers. Meanwhile, Lizzy worked up and down the wing behind Alice, more insecure than the other dogs but fastidiously neat.

Sam's wife, Olive, had thought it ridiculous when their granddaughter had named her dogs after the Bennet sisters from *Pride and Prejudice*. Redstone Station in sandy Central West Queensland certainly *was* a far cry from the green manicured world of stately English manors, and there were even fewer parallels between the dusty-haired, wiry little canines and the buxom, bonneted and beribboned Bennet sisters. But *Pride and Prejudice* was Alice's favourite book, and she'd insisted on continuing the tradition by naming her horse Bingley. However, even Alice had started to wonder if it had been wise, when the first Lizzy ate a 1080 dingo bait, Mary died from snakebite and Jane turned out to be a useless 'Gold Coaster', with a flag-like flying tail and ridiculous lolling grin. During the last extended dry, Sam had put his foot down. 'We have enough *useful* animals that are hungry without having to feed such a waste of space.' So Jane, too, followed where Lizzy I and Mary had gone before her, though Sam's heart smote him when he replaced his rifle and returned to the house to hear the sobs coming from behind Alice's closed door.

Now, Sam looked again towards where Alice was perched on her nuggety chestnut horse. Yes, she was really home. Alice had changed quite a bit in the two years she'd been away at agricultural college in Longreach. Except for a few day at Christmas, she hadn't come home during that period, her holidays fully booked up with stock work at some of the properties close to the college.

In the time she'd been away, her petite, girlish form had taken on the confidence of a woman. Her dark eyes had a frank directness that hadn't been there before, and this had startled Sam on seeing her again. Her dark brown hair was longer than he'd ever seen it and was confined in a plait down her back. Her cheekbones and narrow jaw line were more defined, having lost any childish roundness, and her shoulders had a new squareness, the result of many hours of physical labour. She was truly beautiful now.

Bingley, happy to have his mistress back, walked eagerly, a spring in his step. His ears were pointed forwards, towards the cattle, except for an occasional flicker back in response to an invisible signal from Alice.

Stretch, the tall, impossibly thin old ringer, and one of the three regular mustering contractors Sam employed, growled as a cloud of dust erupted beside him and his skittish young horse shied. Two monstrous bulls, former friends, were now locked in combat, head to head, competing for the testosterone title. The ripple they caused reached the calves at the front, and the impulsion shot them forwards again, and out to the side of the mob. At the same time, Stretch cracked his whip to break up the fight, setting his horse off on another crablike scuttle. The calves made their break and a chase ensued, with two more ringers, Mushgang and Dan, in pursuit. The group of calves split like water and headed for the gidgee.

But Alice had anticipated this chain of events and already sent her dogs. The three Bennet sisters were victorious, managing to get between the calves and their intended refuge. Thwarted, the bleating youngsters whirled back into their own little mob. The two experienced ringers had the sense to call off the chase and allow the calves the freedom to choose between their bellowing mothers and the waiting wolves in the grass.

At last they were all safely through the sagging wooden double gates into the adjoining paddock. Out of familiar territory, the mob gave no further trouble and filed like lambs into the open side enclosure or 'cooler' of the solid old ironbark yards.

§

Seated at the dinner table that night, in the wide, old-fashioned timber-panelled kitchen, Alice watched her grandfather chew slowly, relishing his last bite. Then, just as she knew he would, he chased a tiny droplet of gravy round the rim of the plate with his finger. His hand was halted on its way to his mouth by a stern look from her grandmother, and he wiped it instead on the pale green cotton serviette. Alice smiled to herself. Nothing had changed.

'I'm glad to have you home, Alice.' Sam smiled. 'Everything will work smoothly again now.'

Alice basked in her grandfather's lavish appreciation. She hadn't realised until now just how much she'd missed him. Encouraging words of any kind had been fairly rare during her time at ag college. She'd come to recognise how different her grandfather was from other station managers. He never made her feel inadequate. The fact that she was female didn't concern him, or affect his faith in her capability. As a result, she'd never doubted herself, or questioned her suitability for any job.

The regular contractors who came to Redstone were all around her grandfather's own vintage; over the years they had grown out of their egos. They were all a little rickety and she easily pulled her weight alongside them. She'd never detected anything disrespectful or patronising in their attitude towards her. In many ways Alice had been very sheltered. Life could be so different for girls and women on the land with opportunities and respect for their ability not always there. This realisation had been one of the biggest shocks for her at college and on the various stations she'd worked.

Alice looked down at the remains of her meal on the familiar old china dinner plate. Everything around her seemed to be welcoming her home. After the musters, the branding had gone well today. Stretch had ceremoniously handed over to her the role of castrator, presenting her with his old pocket knife. The wooden handle was polished smooth with use, and felt warm as he pressed it into her hand. 'I sharpened it for you', was all he'd said.

Alice had examined the solid little weapon, its shining blade lethally sharp and true, then looked up to argue, but Stretch had silenced her with a wave of his rough old hand.

'I won't be needing it no more. I only do work for your pa these days and I guess I'll be out to pasture before long, now that me back's shot.'

Alice, aware of what this concession had cost him, hadn't been able to find the words to thank him.

The slight change to their usual routine had slowed things a little at first while they settled into their new positions. Stretch had taken Alice's old spot on the calf race, bringing the calves up one at a time. Mushgang, the youngest and strongest of the men, still handsome with his green eyes keen and bright in his bronze tanned face, kept his usual job of catching each calf as it emerged through the narrow little door at the end of the race. He invariably managed to choose the right millisecond for closing the cradle; this meant that the calf was held firmly between the steel jaws before it could hurt itself by struggling. Then the steel cradle was swung on a hinge onto its side, buffered from its fall to the ground by an old tyre.

Next came a blur of activity – a needle in the skin fold at the neck, brand on the rump, dehorning, earmarking and castration. For Alice it was like taking part in a well-known dance: each of the workers had their own part to play, weaving in and out with their chosen instrument – pocket knife, needle, ear pliers, hot brand, dehorner. The calf was the central figure around whom they revolved. No one ever collided and no one rushed, yet it was all over for the stunned calf in less than a minute.

Making the incision with the knife, Alice was clinical and confident. She could feel her grandfather watching proudly after he'd placed the smoking brands back in the furnace. She squeezed gently, so that a testicle emerged from the opening. With one quick flick of the knife she'd cut the sinew to which it was attached. She repeated the process for the other one and threw the balls into the tin bucket that was being eyed with anticipation from afar by the waiting Bennet ladies. Then the branding cradle was opened, the calf helped to his feet with a pull of the tail, and he was darting out the gate to the next yard.

Alice appreciated the easy cooperation of the workers in the yard as she never had before. Some of her recent experiences of yard work on other stations had been far from harmonious. In this setting, family tensions that were often just under the surface tended to erupt, triggered by the heat of the roaring furnace, yapping of dogs and bellowing of calves. When conditions were ripe, shouted arguments and criticism could become a usual part of the process.

The calves, reunited with their mothers, had rested until late afternoon in the shade of the immense old kurrajong trees growing beside the yards. Taking them back to their paddock was always Alice's favourite time. This was when the other men 'called it a day' and only she and her grandfather were left to accompany the mob back to their patch. The cattle, more than happy to return to the familiarity of their paddock, would walk on ahead, and Alice rode alongside her grandfather, the sting gone out of the sun and its rays turning the floating dust to gold. The dogs, with only half an eye on the cattle, were free to take a meandering course, inspecting all the smells and sounds among the trees, grass and rotting timber.

This evening there had been a slight breeze as they rode. They had passed through a camp of young box trees and the shiny round leaves had made the coarse, unearthly whisper that Alice loved. It always seemed to make time stand still. She'd felt again the ancient power of the land and the tingle of goose bumps on her skin. Now, at the dinner table, feeling satisfied and sleepy, Alice remembered.

She studied her grandfather's face thoughtfully. Sam had always been tough in his expectations, but fair and encouraging. He'd expected her to be able to perform any task that he undertook himself. Mistakes were never a disaster, just something to learn from. Never in a rush but always plugging away, her grandfather had taught her that with animals and physical labour, patience saves time in the end, and slow is often fast. Perhaps it was his age, but he was always reminding Alice not to 'bust a gut'.

Still, there was an unrelenting streak in her grandfather's gentle nature, and in his book laziness was the most deadly sin of the seven. Greeting him with a hug upon her return to Redstone three days earlier, Alice had realised with a jolt that he was an old man. And this afternoon she had noticed him struggling with fatigue. For the first time it had seemed that he wanted someone else to take charge. And there was a new concern in the way her grandmother looked at him, a kind of anxious tenderness.

Alice could feel her grandmother's gaze on them both now. There was a tightness to Olive's lips, and she burst their bubble, saying, 'Can Alice solve our problems with the bank, dear?' Alice suddenly wondered if the unspoken connection between the two of them had always irritated her grandmother. Did that closeness make Olive feel superfluous? Sam's face fell into the familiar old creases of worry and Olive's remorse was evident. She turned to Alice and spoke more kindly, 'Still, it will certainly be brighter around here now you're home, Alice. And . . .' she paused with great ceremony, 'I mean to start showing you the books later this week.'

As with the handing over of Stretch's knife, Alice understood the full honour of this concession. The books were sacred, and until now they had been her grandmother's special domain. Alice recalled the common affliction she'd seen among her peers at college, their hurt and frustration at their parents' domination. The older generation's refusal to allow their children any responsible or active role in managing their operations. Ag college had added insult to injury: there they had learned daily about new methods and skills they wouldn't be allowed to employ any time soon on their home properties. On so many stations it was a case of 'the old bull versus the young'. Perhaps this was why so many of her classmates had felt the need to blast their brains to oblivion with alcohol at any opportunity.

By contrast, Alice had been given so much freedom already. Now she was being welcomed home in a way characteristic of each of her grandparents. She hoped she was worthy of their trust. Yes, she recognised the gravity of her grandmother's offer to show her the books. She smiled at her.

'Thank you, Ma.'

Chapter 2

'Fencing with two is five times faster than fencing alone.' Sam made this observation as he put his hands on his hips and arched his back to stretch it. Alice knew it was true. A lone fencer had to walk kilometres back and forth between the vehicle, the tractor, and from one end of the fence to the other. Having two meant they could work at opposite ends. Also, one could drive the machine while the other worked the shovel or manoeuvred the post into place.

Alice and her grandfather took turns at operating the post hole digger and cleaning out the holes with a shovel, neither of them outstandingly strong. They did the same with 'boring' the holes in the wooden posts with the electric drill, the roar of the generator ringing out across the paddock. The breeze cooled the sweat running down their faces as they worked. Alice paused to look at her grandfather and felt a sudden rush of affection for him. He'd always been a smallframed, wiry man, and even in his old age he was agile. His thick, coarsely curled hair had been sandy-coloured, and as he aged it had simply faded a few shades to a dusty steel. He was always impeccably clean-shaven. His eyes were a pale amber-brown, similar to that of a grey kangaroo's; his long curling eyelashes and thick eyebrows added to this impression, and were a great source of annoyance to Olive, who had hardly any of either.

Alice strained the last length of wire for the day. She and Sam stood and surveyed with satisfaction the neat new fence stretching away down the paddock.

'I've been thinking, Pa, that we could split some of these bigger paddocks into four. Then we could rotate the stock and spell the grass. It would also force the cows to graze the scrubby bits that are going to waste at the moment.' Alice looked tentatively at her grandfather. He was still regarding the new fence, now with a slight frown. She went on cautiously, 'There'd be less unused grass to go rank and we might not need to burn so much. We could plant some legumes then, and they'd have a chance to get established.' She eagerly searched his face.

He suddenly looked tired. 'You're a glutton for punishment. You enjoy fencing then, do you, Alice?'

Alice said no more.

Driving home past Eagle Tor dam, she spotted a solitary red form standing near the water. When they got closer they saw it was a forlorn calf, not much more than a scrap of red hide stretched over a skeleton.

Sam sighed. 'Another bloody poddy.'

Olive was feeding three poddy calves already. As much as she complained, they knew she liked this job; otherwise, with the cost of the calf milk, they were hardly worth saving. This one was so weak that Alice was able to run him down on foot. They tied his feet and hoisted him into the ute.

'Did all the grown-up poddies from last year go to the meatworks?' Alice asked.

'I kind of lost track of them again,' Sam answered guiltily.

'Pa, no one breeds from poddies! Most people don't even save them.'

'Yes, I know.' He looked sideways at Alice. 'Only two of them were heifers,' he added hopefully. 'It won't happen again now that you're home, Ali.'

When they got back to the house, Olive whisked the poddy away for urgent ministration with electrolytes and water. Alice took herself out into the garden to do some watering and cool off. As she strolled here and there with the hose she saw the familiar mouse holes in the soil around the roots of the gnarled old mandarin and bush lemon trees. She placed the nozzle into one and was pleased to see the chooks streaking across the garden: they still remembered the ritual. The guinea fowls that her grandmother kept to deter the snakes began their automated squeaking.

There was a moment of suspense, then telltale rustles in the grass nearby. The mice were evacuating out of the escape holes. The chooks were ready, transformed from chuckling old ladies into ruthless predators, their beady eyes resembling those of their raptor ancestors. Each victorious hunter would run, drumsticks pumping, with her victim dangling from her beak, closely followed by a string of cackling friends; the mouse, too big to swallow whole, would eventually be torn to shreds between them. Alice would wait until all the action had died down before choosing another hole. Sometimes, in the aftermath, an offended cane toad would emerge from a hole and hop clumsily away.

Alice loved the Redstone homestead. It had changed very little in half a century, the only obvious addition being that of a slanting white satellite dish, perched up on the roof next to the aged copper weathercock. Olive had insisted Redstone have access to the internet.

Everything about the house spoke of enduring strength. It was a large, rambling, solid timber structure with open airy rooms and a generous veranda all round. The veranda was bordered by small decorative shrubs and herbs that her grandmother conscientiously managed to keep in good health, even during the driest times. Alice could almost feel the house embrace her as she wandered in for dinner. She paused on the veranda to pay her dutiful respects to King Henry the Ninth in his tall cage.

King Henry the Ninth was an ancient sulphur crested cockatoo who had been in her grandmother's family for longer than anyone could remember. None of his Elliot owners had ever had the cheek to shorten his name. Before coming to Redstone, he'd lived with Olive's bachelor brother, Eustace Elliot, whom she'd loved dearly. Olive now kept King Henry the Ninth out of loyalty to him. He had none of the clichéd vices of talking cockies, such as swearing or hurling insults. He never said 'pretty boy' or asked for a cracker. But he did on occasion feel the need to produce a loud, rattling smoker's cough. Sometimes this performance was topped off with a throaty gagging, concluding with the distinctive sound of phlegm being brought up and spat out. Eustace's slow death from emphysema had obviously scarred the elderly bird, and he hadn't as yet moved on. So Eustace's cough was his legacy, living on after his death. Alice, who loved most animals, had for some reason never taken to the bird, and she was certain that the feeling was mutual.

§

At dinner that night, Sam told Olive how good it had been to have help with the fencing and how glad he was that nothing dreadful had happened to Alice while she'd been away at college.

'I hope you can stop worrying yourself silly now she's home,

Samuel,' Olive said so sternly that Alice had to hide a smile. 'I don't know why you have to be so melodramatic. I'm sure you never wasted a thought on poor Lara when she went away.' She placed a wedge of apple pie in front of him.

'Well, it's a funny old world out there,' Sam said, looking apologetically at Alice. 'Wasn't sure how you'd go, Ali.'

She smiled at him to show she'd taken no offence.

'You don't seem too much the worse for wear,' Olive added drily.

Alice laughed. 'I'm fine. Longreach was alright – quite safe. Not exactly the big smoke. But I'm so happy to be home.'

'You look like you definitely need a bit of decent home-cooked food,' Olive put in.

Alice nodded obligingly. It seemed to her that, unlike her grandfather, her grandmother had barely aged during the last two years. She was still a robust woman, a little younger and a fraction taller than her husband. She was broad-shouldered with a heavy bust, but her hips and legs were slim. This gave her a top-heavy, sometimes overbearing air. Her clothing was always ironed, in spite of Sam's insistence that it wasn't necessary out in the paddock, and in defiance of the ubiquitous red dirt she persisted in wearing light colours. Most often she was in a dress, and she always wore an apron in the kitchen. Her thin hair had once been silky straight and blonde but now it was always curled and rinsed a shade of pale ginger. Her eyes were expressively large and blue and could alter in mood at lightning speed. She spoke with a definite, decisive manner; without ever raising her voice, she possessed the knack of making herself heard by anyone in the vicinity.

Sam fiddled with his dessert spoon, drawing circles on the tablecloth. Alice could see he was building up the courage to say something, and she waited for him to speak. Anything that could delay his apple pie had to be serious. Finally he launched into a pre-considered spiel, speaking in a quiet monotone.

'I know you must be bursting with ideas on how to improve this place, Alice. Like your idea about splitting the paddocks today. New you-beaut techniques and technology. And I know I must seem like a bit of a dinosaur. I want you to know that I'll do my best to listen to your ideas, and we'll even try some, as long as we won't be throwing the baby out with the bathwater.' His message delivered, he exhaled with relief.

It was the longest utterance Alice could ever recall him making and it had clearly been an effort. She looked fondly at his lined, weather-beaten face. How could he always read her so well?

Keeping her afloat during her time away, ideas and strategies for Redstone had been building in Alice's mind. They had come not just from what she'd learned at college but also from her weekend and holiday stock work on various properties around Longreach. In spite of how unpleasant some of these experiences had been, they'd served a double purpose: not only had she been able to cover a large portion of her college fees with the money she'd earned, but she'd also had the opportunity to quietly observe a full and varied array of property operations.

Was her excitement about all these possibilities for Redstone so obvious? Or was it just that her grandfather knew her so well? All her life he'd been able to read her thoughts and emotions by merely glancing at her face. As a result, Alice had never felt the need to explain herself to him. Today she'd been afraid of insulting the old man, of making him feel inadequate by suggesting changes to the way things had always been done. Realising this, and always the true gentleman, he'd given her an opening. She picked up his knobbly old hand and squeezed it gratefully.

§

Olive watched Alice take Sam's hand and felt the familiar twinge of jealousy. Thick as thieves, the pair of them – always had been. Alice was Sam's little girl. But she was nearly an adult now, and her personality, though unobtrusive, was beginning to emerge. Looking at her granddaughter, Olive noticed the same new self-assurance that Sam had seen. How very different she was from their own daughter, Lara. With a tremor, Olive realised that Alice was almost the same age as Lara had been when she'd come home from finishing school and dropped a bombshell: at nineteen and unmarried, she was pregnant.

Chapter 3

Olive Day prided herself on her ability to remain composed and in control in the face of almost any challenge (the only exception to this was her extreme and paralysing fear of snakes, which she had been unable to conquer). Her resilience had been well tested over the fifty-one years of her marriage, by the many trials accompanying a relatively isolated life on the land.

Sam had inherited Redstone from his own father, George, at an early age. The older man had been killed suddenly, falling off a horse when Sam was still in his teens. Sam had no memory of his mother, who had died in his infancy; his maternal grandmother had arrived at Redstone to fill the void. The old woman had remained there until her own death, less than a year after George's.

Redstone was then a well-known and respected property of one hundred and ten thousand acres. It was widely renowned for the quality of beef it could turn off because of the mineral-rich soil that made up a large part of its area. Olive was eighteen when she first danced with Sam at a local ball; direct and forthright as she was even then, there was something about Sam's steady gentleness that won her heart. Her wealthy and refined local family thought it an ideal setting for their daughter.

But once Olive had come to live at Redstone, it became clear to both her and Sam that she had few skills and little knowledge that would be of any practical use on the land. Instead she'd been groomed for a role as a lady of the 'landed gentry'. However, in the nineteen fifties this regal breed was close to extinction. The profitability of beef had declined, unpaid labour was outlawed, and extended dry seasons had ravaged the land. Redstone was no exception, and Sam had discovered upon inheriting the place just how badly things had been allowed to slip. There were also exorbitant death duties to pay. Other than selling up, he'd had no alternative but to go into debt.

So both Olive and Sam soon discovered that things were not at all as they had envisaged before exchanging their vows. Life was difficult, but they were in the first flush of love and back then everything seemed like an adventure to Olive.

After several meetings with the local bank manager of the day, Olive discovered she had an (untrained) aptitude for figures and business. In no time, she'd organised an efficient set of books to keep track of the operation. She insisted on tighter records of cattle numbers and began to chart incoming and outgoing funds. Using this information, she developed a tight budget to which she made sure they slavishly adhered. In hindsight, Sam had acknowledged that Olive's number-crunching had been more instrumental in saving Redstone than anything she could have done with a crowbar.

Once she'd grasped the gravity of their circumstances, Olive herself had immediately refrained from any unnecessary spending and put aside the lavish habits she'd grown up with. She learned how to milk a cow and grow vegetables. She taught herself how to cook and did it with style: her chutneys, jams, pickles and sauces soon became the envy of the local Country Women's Association. Sam always expressed admiration for his wife's uncomplaining acceptance of the situation, and Olive found that being useful appealed to her practical nature.

Lara was their beloved, miracle baby who came to them after fifteen childless years. An exceptionally attractive child, she had large, winning eyes of an extraordinary blue, and her pale gold hair was curly and silky soft. Long lashes and a full, pink mouth added to the angelic impression. Olive adored and doted on her.

From an early age, Lara discovered that she could use her beauty to great effect. The combination of her innocent face and some well-timed tact proved very difficult for most people to resist and she almost always got her way. Olive was aware of this, but her desire for Lara's happiness overruled any qualms and she could never bring herself to chastise her for it.

Pampered, treasured Lara: nothing was too good for this cherished child. Olive dressed her in pink and white, like a little lady. Sam bought her an expensive fine-boned white pony called Dove, which she used for pleasure rides close to the house. Watching Lara at pony club each week, Olive would glow with pride. It was an ideal opportunity for Lara to display her beauty and outshine the other bush kids on their more common, stubborn, scrubbing-brush varieties of pony.

Worried about the rough talk of the stockmen and the possibility of accidents, Olive never allowed Lara to go mustering or working with Sam. He began to complain to Olive that he couldn't understand their daughter and that he was at a loss when it came to disciplining the headstrong girl. As Lara approached her teens, Olive noticed Sam begin to withdraw, leaving the raising of this fairy-like female completely to her. The older Lara grew the more defiant she became; Olive searched for any common ground between Sam and their bewildering daughter, but it had been left too late and the distance between them continued to widen.

It wasn't long before Lara discovered she had the attention of all the local boys; alarmed, Olive sent her away to board at a reputable Catholic girls school in Brisbane. She returned home for part of each holiday, but always brought a friend with her and spent the rest of each vacation away, visiting in return.

Lara was academically gifted and had inherited her mother's mathematical brain. Once she'd graduated from year twelve with excellent results, she returned home to Redstone for a break before choosing a career path. There, she threw her energies into toying with the hearts of the local young men, and playing them off against each other. Olive tried to steer her in the direction of a few wealthy and respectable boys from church, but nothing pleased Lara more than doing the opposite of what was expected of her.

At that time, Sam had in his employ an exceptionally charismatic and talented young ringer called Benji Wilson. Benji had an affinity with animals the likes of which Sam said he had never seen before. In the three years that he was at Redstone, musters and yard work flowed without a hitch. Horses and dogs would bust themselves to please Benji. Apart from his occasional alcoholic benders, during which time he'd disappear to town for a few days, even Olive had to admit that his character was impeccable. As a rule, although she was ashamed to admit it, she didn't take kindly to Aborigines. But this young stockman was an exception.

However, Lara objected to Benji because he was the only young male she knew who didn't admire and adore her. She did her utmost to gain his attention and when this failed, resorted to taunting and joking. But still, Benji remained disinterested. Olive knew that her daughter was perplexed by this, but thought that the influence of someone who didn't simply fall at her feet every time she demanded it, might do her good.

With her high school studies completed and no useful occupation, Lara began to show up at the yards whenever Benji was breaking horses or working weaners. She sat by him in the shed and handed him tools when he tinkered with the machines. When he went on checking drives, she began to tag along too. At the time, Olive saw no real danger in this, despite the fact that Benji was the complete antithesis of the respectable matches she'd picked out for Lara. It was impossible for her to believe that a blackfella would be of any real interest to her daughter, handsome though he was. Sam seemed to have total trust in Benji, and because of this, Olive dismissed any slight concerns she had about the situation. So when she discovered them in bed together in the early hours of the morning after Lara's nineteenth birthday party, her shock was complete.

Olive immediately dismissed Benji, and Lara was packed off to a pricey finishing school in Brisbane. After that, Olive thought the whole unfortunate incident was over and that they would never need to mention it again. And then, four months later, Lara had returned to Redstone to defiantly deliver the unwelcome news.

§

The first time Sam held Lara's child, it was dawn and he'd driven through the night over corrugated roads to get them all safely to the hospital in Emerald. As the baby girl rested her large eyes on his face, he suddenly felt as though he'd heard an elusive line of music or tasted sweet cold water coming out of rock. In that instant the tiny creature had pierced his soul and taken possession of him. Sam said nothing, but Lara noticed his pale, wide-eyed expression as he looked at her baby, and immediately assumed he disliked the child.

Olive, on the other hand, didn't hesitate to speak her mind and Sam winced at her bluntness. 'She's pinker than I thought she'd be. She's not so terribly dark after all. In fact, she could almost be taken for a white child.' Olive looked hard then at the child and Sam saw her receive the same penetrating gaze in return. A little taken aback, Olive continued on nonetheless, saying, 'Her eyes are rather big for that tiny face, but I'm sure we won't have any trouble adopting her out.'

At this, Lara protested, as she always objected to her mother's well-meant plans. Sam wondered whether adoption was in fact exactly what Lara intended to do, after a respectable battle with her mother. But he was still tingling from the look the child had given him and there was no way he'd allow it. He spoke simply, his voice firm and final. 'This child belongs at Redstone, Olive. We won't hear another word about adoption.' It wasn't often that Sam opposed Olive's wishes.

Lara's mouth fell open to speak and then closed again. Sam could see she hadn't counted on an ally in her half-hearted bid to keep her child.

So Lara returned to Redstone with the baby, her spirits low. On the baby's tenth day of life as a nameless child, Sam began calling her Alice. Lara scoffed at the name, saying that it sounded like a house cow. She trialled some others – Juliette, Felicity and Sophia – but somehow Alice stuck.

For a while, Sam's greatest concern was Olive. He knew she was feeling heavily the assumed disapproval of the church and Country Women's Association ladies. She stopped holding morning teas at Redstone. She believed that their family's 'disgrace' was the talk of the town, and of course it was, for a little over a week. But Sam knew that the public interest was mainly due to the fact that Olive had always prided herself on being so proper; as a result, people were enjoying her downfall. He knew that life would move on and the ripples of the next small local scandal would soon wash over the insignificant disturbance that the arrival of Lara's baby had made in the ordinary flow of life in the town.

§

For almost a year, Lara tried fitfully to mother the scrawny infant. But there was something knowing in its serene gaze. It was almost as though it looked right through her and saw the absence in her of any maternal feeling towards it. Lara saw in the depths of those dark eyes an inescapable recognition and acceptance of her own shortcomings. Her inherent selfishness, usually so well disguised by her charm and beauty, couldn't be hidden from this tiny person who couldn't yet speak. For the first time, Lara's certainty of her own perfection was shaken.

Still she tried her best to love the little girl. She cuddled and kissed her, dressed her with care and even tried singing to her. But she resented the fact that Alice's presence made her doubt herself. And the brown-skinned baby was a constant reminder of the man she still felt so strongly for and knew she needed to forget. Eventually, she decided that Alice was better off without her, and enrolled in accountancy at university in Brisbane. She spent quite some time wondering how to break to her parents the news that she would be burdening them with her child.

So she was a little affronted when they both hailed the idea as a good one. Her father was positively encouraging in his monosyllabic way, and even her mother seemed in favour of the idea of her leaving. Lara felt indignation rise at their lack of opposition.

'You want me to leave!' she said accusingly. 'You're ashamed of me and want me out of your lives.'

'That's rot,' her father retorted in exasperation. She knew by his tone that he thought her impossible to please. But she also knew he was right when he said, 'Your heart's not in this place. It's about time you found out where you want to be.'

To add insult to injury, her mother put in, 'Of course we don't want you to leave, darling. But we love you and know what's best for you. In Brisbane you'll be able to put all this behind you.' At 'all this', Olive made a slight motion with a flour-covered wooden spoon towards the baby on the floor.

Lara followed her mother's gaze and looked down at her daughter. The child was examining a dying beetle. Transfixed, she poked it with a minute forefinger, as if trying to rekindle the life within it. At the break in the flow of heated conversation, Alice looked up. All their eyes were on her. She looked first at her grandmother, seeming to shrink a little as though sensing the older woman's patronising pity. Lara suspected that her mother was noticing Alice's skin, which had darkened in the last few months. Next Alice looked at Lara and sucked in a tiny breath. She seemed to feel the sting of resentment. Lara quickly tried to soften her expression. But Alice looked away, her little face calm, her hurt betrayed only by a slight tremble of her bottom lip.

Then Lara watched the baby's features light up as she shifted her eyes to her grandfather's face. As Sam returned Alice's gaze, Lara saw the child enveloped in a warm protectiveness that she herself had never seen in him. He was Alice's kindred in a way she'd never be. Reassured, the baby blinked up at him and then, with a subtle, conspiratorial smile, returned to her beetle.

Chapter 4

Alice was straining under the ironbark rail, holding it in place while Sam drilled the hole. His back was aching from holding the heavy tool at an awkward height. Once done, he hurried to thread the wire through and fasten it tightly in place with a Cobb and Co twist. It was their third day of yard building and Alice had been doing all the heaviest jobs. The dogs lay stretched out contentedly in the shade nearby.

'Have a blow, Alice.' Sam stretched his back.

'I'm fine, Pa.'

'Well, I'm knocked up.' He sat down on a drum, defeated.

Alice sat cross-legged on the ground and looked up at him with concern in her dark eyes. 'Let's head home. I've still got to work the weaners. We've done enough here for today.'

'Ali, we're gonna have to put someone on. We need some extra help.' Sam's exhaustion forced him to broach the subject at last.

'Can we afford it?'

'I think so. Especially if some of these ideas of yours help to increase productivity as you keep promising.' He smiled at her. 'And as you've been saying, we've got to spend money to make money. I want to get this place up to scratch before . . . while I'm still able. Anyway, we don't have a lot of choice.'

Over the weeks that followed, Sam asked around about a potential full-time stockman for Redstone. However, he soon discovered that suitable candidates were few and far between. Eventually it came down to three possibles, none of whom he was entirely satisfied with. When he'd made his choice he realised there was nothing for it but to break the news to Olive. There were fireworks at afternoon smoko that day.

As he'd expected, Olive didn't take the news very well. 'He's a rowdy drunk, Samuel! Sue's at her wits' end with him. Why can't we employ one of the other O'Donnell boys instead? I haven't heard anything terrible about them. Jeremy's a bad egg. Surely you remember the steeple climbing? And he didn't even make it to the end of year ten – the boarding school sent him home. You've no idea the things I've heard about him at CWA. Really terrible.'

'I have a pretty fair idea.' Sam was cynical.

So Olive elaborated. 'Coral's daughter made the mistake of getting tangled up with him. And so have most of the other girls in town, from what I've heard. Have you thought about Alice? I'm surprised you could even consider having that drunken lout around here after what happened with Lara at nineteen. Almost the same age!'

'This is a completely different case. Alice is nothing like Lara. And Jeremy's a good worker – more than half handy, switched on. He's been doing fencing contracting with Wayne Matheson for two years now. And he can turn his hand to anything. Everyone says so – even Brian admits that.'

'Maybe he's a good worker, but only when he's sober, which isn't very often. Don't think I don't know that Wayne has been threatening to fire him if he turns up to work hung-over again. Betty told me that weeks ago. In fact, Wayne probably *has* fired him, and now we're expected to take him.'

Sam spoke patiently. 'Liv, Brian wouldn't have suggested we take him on if he wasn't going to pull his weight.'

'Well, you can tell Brian from me that if he's failed at teaching his son some discipline and respect, an old softy like you won't get far in trying to reform him.'

Sam looked up in surprise and Olive continued triumphantly, 'Don't worry, I know all about your secret men's business. Faye overheard Sue telling Kathy that Brian was going to ask you to take him on. Get him away from town and clean him up. I think you're both dreaming. As if we didn't have enough to worry about without looking after other people's delinquent sons.'

Sam stood up slowly and faced Olive. He gently placed his hands on the table. 'Well, there isn't anyone else. All the young fellas that aren't working at home have gone to the mines. I've been asking around for weeks. We need some help here. I'm getting old. Stuffed.'

'You always say Alice can do anything.'

'And she can. But we're handing her a raw deal. The place is run-down. We have enough work for ten men.'

'Mushgang, Dan and Stretch have always been good enough until now. Why can't we just give them more hours?'

'Dan and Stretch are buggered, same as me. And Mush isn't far behind with his arthritis. I've let things go, Olive. And I have to face it. Alice can't fix everything on her own. She's just a blooming kid.'

'Just so long as you know I'm not happy about it.' Olive sniffed.

This statement usually ended all their disagreements. In favour of Olive's wishes. But today, Sam stood his ground.

'I'm going to give him a go. Who are we to write off a young bloke? You just never know what's under a hat.' Sam folded his newspaper, pushed in his chair and walked out onto the veranda.

§

Olive listened to the hollow thudding of Sam's boots on the stairs. When she saw he'd left his cup of tea and Anzac biscuit unfinished she knew that this time he wouldn't back down.

So Jeremy O'Donnell was given a starting date. After a few days of getting used to the idea, the thought of reforming a lost soul began to appeal to Olive, although she'd have died before admitting it. She'd make sure there were strict conditions. Jeremy could come, but on her terms: no trips to town, and no alcohol or girls on Redstone. Right up until the Saturday evening before Jeremy was to arrive, she continued to act disapproving of the plan, with lots of martyred sighing for Sam's benefit whenever Jeremy's name was mentioned.

Half an hour after lunch on the Sunday, Jeremy O'Donnell's noisy old ute pulled up next to the shed. Olive noted with pleasure that he wasn't brash enough to park closer to the house. A good sign. She peered out the window and saw him climb out of the cab. He was tall with an athletic build. She could see, even from here, that he'd grown into a fine-looking young man. She'd seen him often as a small boy in church with his family. Out of the six O'Donnell boys, he'd been the one who was always wriggling in his seat or fooling around. But in recent years they hadn't crossed paths.

'The handsome ones are always the worst,' she said to herself grimly.

§

From the stockyards, Alice heard the ute pull up. It sounded old, with a muffler in urgent need of attention. She hurried the group of weaners through the gate, closed it behind them and brushed some of the dust off her shirt. When she rounded the shed and walked towards the ute, the first thing she noticed was a dog chained up in the back. The stocky creature appeared to be a large blue heeler with a dash of something more box-headed thrown in.

Her grandfather had emerged from the darkness of the shed and was shaking hands with a tall, broad-shouldered man in his mid-twenties. The last time she'd seen Jeremy O'Donnell he'd been a teenager, but Alice recognised him straight away. Jeremy looked around and she walked closer, smiling at him in greeting.

She noticed he'd become very good-looking. The bright blue of his eyes was enhanced by heavy black lashes. His jaw was square and his hair was thick and a rich brown. Even his slightly crooked nose, which had obviously been broken on at least one occasion, only added an interesting charisma to his face. He returned her smile with what, she could tell, he believed to be an irresistible grin.

But Alice found she was immediately sceptical of the smile. She heard her grandmother's voice inside her head saying, 'Handsome is as handsome does.' Alice was a primarily intuitive being. Even as a small child she'd discovered that a person's exterior had little effect on her. Perhaps she'd learned this through her contact with Lara, when as an infant she'd longed for a mother who would truly love her. This early relationship had given Alice an immunity to any sort of charming wiles and an innate wariness of anyone who attempted to use them on her.

Now she could see that Jeremy was expecting her to go weak at the knees. 'Well, if it isn't little Alice Wilson, all grown up. Last time I saw you, you were a scrawny kid.' He raised his eyebrows at her.

Unperturbed, Alice replied, 'Hello, Jeremy. Last time I saw *you*, you were a clown.' Jeremy laughed good-naturedly at the memory, and Alice was relieved to see that his smile was genuine this time.

After showing him to the worker's cottage, set between two large gums, a stone's throw from the main house, Alice returned to the yards to finish working the weaners. The paddocks at Redstone were large, and some of them were rough or scrubby: cunning cattle had plenty of places to hide and opportunities to break away from the herd if they were that way inclined. By working the young cattle each day for a few weeks after weaning, Alice was addressing this problem before it even arose, ensuring that once they were 'bushed' they would be easier to muster and quite comfortable with the prospect of returning as a mob to the yards. With her dogs she was yarding them in small groups, then teaching them to flow through gates and along the race. Their reward for doing all this was a feed of copra meal. Each day they were becoming quieter and more cooperative. The panic had gone from their movements and they were responding well to the dogs. For these youngsters, the yard was no longer a place to be feared.

But that afternoon, she carried out the task mechanically, her mind on the newcomer. Things would be different now that it was no longer just her and her grandfather. Her mind went back to the last day she could clearly remember seeing Jeremy.

She'd been home from boarding school for the Easter holidays, and on the Sunday she'd gone to church with her grandparents as usual. The opening hymn was just finishing, and the last warbling notes of the electric organ echoed and died. Father Callaghan began the opening prayer, everyone giving him their full attention this early in the piece. Suddenly there was a series of loud thumps and clatters coming from above. The priest faltered a little, then continued on as though nothing had happened. Birds often made strange noises on the roof at this time of year.

The congregation sat down and prepared themselves for a session of listening to the Word of God, daydreaming or examining each other inconspicuously, whatever the individual case might be. The noises came again, this time closer to the steeple section of the roof.

'That's a mighty big bird,' Father Callaghan observed into the microphone pinned to his robes. Mr Allen, the acolyte who had been standing sentinel-like on the altar, strode importantly down the aisle and out the double doors to investigate.

Two sentences into the first reading, a flustered Mr Allen reappeared at the door. 'Someone will have to telephone Aaron at home. He won't be at the police station today.'

'Phone Aaron? Why on earth? What's happened?' asked the old priest.

'There's a couple of young clowns on the roof trying to climb the steeple.'

'Good Lord, this is something new!' Father Callaghan sounded intrigued.

Alice waited with the rest of the congregation for the priest to start down the aisle, before they all followed closely on his heels. As they emerged from the church and squinted up into the sun, there was unanimous surprise. The pair on the roof really were clowns. Two agile youths, fitted out in multicoloured suits, complete with frilled collars, wigs, and face paint, had hitched a rope over the sturdy cross on top of the steeple and were shinnying up. Their floppy shoes stuck out ridiculously to each side. Alice stifled a giggle.

'Get down at once!' Mr Allen had taken charge. 'The policeman's on his way.'

The lower clown swore and loosened his grip on the rope, sliding back down to the roof. The other wasn't far behind. Then, unexpectedly, rather than climbing down at the front of the building where the roof was low they clambered around to the back of the church and jumped off, landing heavily on the grass below.

The two entertainers bolted for freedom across the neatly mown lawn, the first clown leaping the low brick wall with agile grace despite his floppy shoes. The second wasn't so adept. Forgetting to allow extra clearance, he hooked the toe of one shoe on the edge of the wall; what followed was a spectacular nosedive into the dust on the other side.

There was a gasp from the congregation and a moment of suspense while they all waited to see if he was alive. He jerked to life and half rolled onto his side, a winded grunt issuing forth. Alice's heart went out to him.

'Michael!' Mrs Gibson, who'd been fiercely disapproving moments before, recognised her teenage son under the disguise, and motherly instinct took over. She rushed to his side. 'Michael, darling, are you alright?'

'He won't be once I get my hands on him.' It was Michael's mortified father who now arrived at his side. Michael's mother glared at her husband and extended protective arms over her son.

Michael began to moan with more volume now that he was getting his wind back. More people gathered around and a quiet babble broke out. Meanwhile, the other clown, noticing the absence of flopping footfalls behind him, had stopped and looked back. When he saw how it stood, he swore in frustration at his friend's clumsiness, hung his head and flip-flopped back to face the music.

Alice saw Father Callaghan, who had been too dignified to rush around the church in his long vestments, arriving on the scene. 'Who have we here?' No one answered. 'Well, if it isn't young Michael Gibson, and let me see now . . . Jeremy O'Donnell. Haven't seen you looking so pretty since your christening day.'

'Oh Jeremy, how could you?' Sue O'Donnell dissolved into tears onto the shoulder of the nearest old lady.

'There'll be a consequence for this, son.' Brian O'Donnell spoke with deadly control in his voice.

'Has anyone telephoned Aaron yet?' fretted Mr Allen.

Father Callaghan seemed to decide it was time to preside over the scene. 'Now hold on,' he said. 'We are always joyful when young people choose to join us for mass. Who are we to judge them on their exterior, or on the manner in which they come? Think of the Prodigal Son! Michael, can you walk, boy?'

Michael's mother helped him to his feet, and Father Callaghan nodded approvingly.

'Come into our church, boys, and take the seat of honour, right up the front.' The priest took a clown on each robed arm and escorted them to the middle of the very front pew. Returning to the altar, he smiled down on them benevolently and was seated to listen to the readings.

Alice discovered later that Michael, a newly initiated bullfighter, had 'clowned' at his first rodeo the evening before; he had been instructed by Jeremy, already a seasoned rodeo clown who had trained Michael up with all the tricks in his bag. It had gone off brilliantly, and Michael's antics in the ring had successfully distracted the raging bulls from the fallen riders. But more importantly, the crowd had gone wild. Afterwards, the two boys had partied all night. How and when they had decided to climb the steeple, Alice never found out.

The time came for the sermon. It was nearly Easter and the reading for the day was about Lazarus, the dead man whom Jesus had raised to life. Father Callaghan spoke about shedding the 'darkness of sin' that drags humankind into a state of 'living death'. He spoke about hearing the voice of Jesus calling everyone to come out of the tomb. 'His call is made in many ways, and people answer it in many ways.' He gestured at the clowns. 'Just as the people rejoiced at seeing Lazarus alive, we, too, should rejoice when our fellow man comes out into the light. We should embrace him, no matter what he has done in the past.'

Alice noticed Mr Allen still standing to attention on the altar. Up until this point, he'd been glaring disapprovingly at the clowns. Now, at hearing the old priest's words, he looked down at his polished black shoes and seemed unsure what to do with his face.

Father Callaghan paused. The two clowns looked up and he smiled at them again. Michael looked stricken. His plastic red nose dangled under his chin, dented beyond repair. On the side of his face that had hit the ground, the white paint had mixed with red dirt and some blood to make a ghastly ochre. Alice could see him wringing his curly wig in his hands, apparently overcome with shame and remorse. Jeremy, on the other hand, was smiling up at the priest with what looked like genuine regard for the old holy man.

'Cocky bastard,' Brian O'Donnell muttered through gritted teeth, but Father Callaghan didn't seem to be affronted by Jeremy's expression.

Alice was surprised when the priest gave communion to the clowns first. She could see some of the old ladies whispering among themselves, outraged at this mark of respect to the delinquents. When the recessional hymn was sung and mass concluded, Alice noticed with amusement that Jeremy genuflected on one knee towards the tabernacle, his rubber shoe folding up under his toe.

But the punishment wasn't over. Alice watched from the tea table set up outside, as the clowns came out the door, lagging a little behind everyone else. Father Callaghan wasn't going to let them just slope off; he greeted them with open arms and escorted them again, one on each side of him, towards the tea-sipping churchgoers.

§

Jeremy approached the tea table, looking at Alice curiously. She was helping her grandmother and another woman serve out the tea. Last time he'd seen her up close was at the primary school Distance Education camp years ago. It had been her first year of primary school, his last, yet he could still remember the tiny Bambi-like creature who had barely spoken to the other kids.

He'd gone away then to boarding school and they'd both grown older. 'She must be fourteen now,' he thought. 'Pretty.' He smiled at her with his monstrous red mouth and was about to ask her for a 'coffee, white with two', when her grandmother edged in front of her and handed him a cup of black tea, piping hot. The look Olive gave him warned him not to even ask for milk, let alone sugar.

Jeremy and Michael stood to one side of the crowd, sheepishly sipping their tea while Father Callaghan loudly discussed the dry weather with a few of the parishioners. Jeremy tried to avoid the flinty glares being shot at him by his parents. Mrs Allen, the acolyte's other half, was walking around with a platter of Arnott's biscuits; after offering them to everyone else, she swallowed her pride and approached the clowns. Jeremy was just about to take a Monte Carlo when she intercepted his hand, passing him instead a plain Milk Coffee biscuit.

Michael saw what had happened and shook his head. 'No, thank you.'

As the people started to leave, Jeremy plodded around collecting a few stray cups and delivered them back to the tea table. He gave them to Alice, her grandmother safely out of the way at the sink.

'Thanks,' she said and smiled. She made him forget he was a clown, her smile so beautiful, friendly and unself-conscious.

The clowns hung around until everyone had gone, waiting for the lecture they knew must be coming to them from the old priest. But all he said by way of dismissal was, 'Hope to see you back again next Sunday, boys.' Then, with a smile, he turned and disappeared into the church, off to the sacristy to change out of his vestments. Just a tired old man again.

Chapter 5

Olive could see that Sam was surprised when she agreed so easily to let Jeremy eat with them on his first night at Redstone. She supposed he'd been expecting her to insist on him eating alone in his cottage. But she had her reasons. Once they were all seated with their meals, she said, 'Before we say grace, I have something to say.'

'Bloody hell, a welcome speech!' exclaimed Jeremy, lowering his fork.

'Not exactly, although you are welcome here, Jeremy.' Olive had decided that a little kindness to start with wouldn't hurt. 'While you're working for us, there are a few things we expect.'

'Old Ma calls the shots here does she?' Jeremy looked at Sam in commiseration. 'Same at my place when I still lived there. My old lady's always worn the pants, but she lets Dad think he's running the show.'

Olive's face was stony. She'd played this scene out repeatedly in her imagination. In her mind's eye, Jeremy had listened demurely. Sam shifted uncomfortably in his seat and Alice shot Jeremy a warning glance. He seemed to realise he'd pushed his luck. 'Righto. I'm all ears. Fire away.'

Olive regained her composure and decided to launch into it with no gentle preamble this time. 'Firstly, we always say grace before meals. No one swears at the dinner table. There will be no drinking of alcohol or smoking while you're at Redstone.'

'Shi—... struth, a dry camp! That sounds serious. A bloke's gotta run amok every now and again otherwise his work suffers.' Jeremy winked at Alice.

Olive continued coldly, 'Girlfriends will not be welcome here. And there will be no weekend trips to town. I hope you can cope with those few conditions, Jeremy, as we do hope you can keep this position.' She finished off with a little sniff.

Jeremy looked at Olive with a direct, not unfriendly expression. 'The way I see it, Ma, is this. Beggars can't be bloody choosers. I know I only got this job because there wasn't anyone else.' He paused, challenging her to deny it. When she said nothing he continued, 'On the other hand, I could go to the mines tomorrow and get a starting wage four times the pittance I'll be getting here. All my mates have gone that way. But the truth is, the stinking mines make me sick. I'd rather work for a bloody septic sucker than go there.'

Olive had gone pale and was holding on to the sides of her chair.

Jeremy went on, 'But about your rules, I'll stick to 'em when I can. I'm not making any promises.' He looked at Sam. 'Better to be upfront about these things.'

Sam nodded in agreement and then withered under Olive's glare. 'Liv, let's just see how things pan out, shall we?' he suggested reassuringly.

Olive was thoroughly crestfallen. So far the reformation wasn't going according to plan. 'Well, the least you can do is call me Mrs

Day. We're accustomed to some respect around here, and none of our other workers have ever had a problem with that.'

'Can do. I can cop that. Any day, Mrs Day.' Jeremy chuckled. 'And you can call me Jed. Jeremy was my Pommy great-granddad.'

There was a brief silence as Olive considered how to respond. Sam jumped into the opening with unusual alacrity. 'Let's get started – food's getting cold.'

Somehow after all that they missed saying grace. As she washed up after Jeremy had gone back to his cottage Olive clashed the pots in mortification. She felt a sense of rising panic. Sam and Alice didn't seem overly concerned; Alice was calmly drying up and Sam was poring over the funeral notices in the paper. Olive wanted to say something to shake them up as she'd been shaken. But Jeremy's cheerful unconcern had made her feel unusually powerless. She finished tidying up and went to bed without doing any of her crochet.

The next morning, after breakfast, Olive watched from the window as Jeremy, Sam and Alice walked to the yards. She began to puzzle again over her new problem. How would she fit another man's wages into their already stretched budget? Should she ask Lara for help? But Lara's life now seemed to revolve entirely around her husband, Conrad Harradine, and their three children. Lara had met Conrad not long after leaving Redstone; the older brother of one of her university peers, he was now a successful barrister in Brisbane and Lara's life seemed to be complete, without the worry of her Redstone connections. Olive knew that the Harradines weren't short of money and were in fact often on the lookout for new ventures to invest in. But did Lara still care enough about the future of Redstone to consider money spent on it an investment?

Olive asked herself what would have happened if she'd listened to Sam and kept Alice at home instead of sending her away to boarding school. The money they'd laid out on school fees would certainly have come in handy now.

Alice had hated that boarding school and then wasted the opportunity by leaving in year ten. It had seemed outrageous at the time, as the quietly spoken girl had been awarded an academic scholarship for years eleven and twelve. Olive had fought hard to convince her to stay but Alice had been unusually stubborn, and Sam, to Olive's frustration, had sided with the girl. In the end, Olive had agreed that she could leave, but only on the condition that she furthered her education at ag college.

Through the primary years Olive had diligently taught Alice herself with Distance Education. With quiet pride she'd noticed that her own aptitude for maths had continued down the maternal line. Alice loved to read, too: novels, but also Sam's history books with their black and white photos of bullock teams, timber cutters, drovers and packhorses. Newspapers, farming magazines and farm production guides were always whisked away to Alice's room upon arrival.

But then the time had come for high school. Olive remembered the night she'd argued with Sam about sending Alice away. 'Alice must have a chance to make something of herself. She's very clever, Sam.'

Sam was strongly opposed to the idea. 'She has that chance – here. Redstone is her future.'

Olive had a trump card up her sleeve. 'Lara insists. She's going to pay all the fees. It may be that she wishes to get to know Alice after all when she's in Brisbane. We can't stand in the way of a mother's wishes.'

But Sam had made it clear that he was doubtful of this from the very first.

Still, Olive got her way, and Alice had made the journey to

Brisbane to start at the same reputable Catholic girls high school that Lara had attended. When she came home for her first Easter holidays, it seemed that Sam's fears had been warranted. Alice had seen Lara, Conrad and their two young children only once during her term in the city and had suffered horribly from homesickness. Sam had spoken accusingly to Olive. 'She's pining. Looks like a little wilted flower.'

Still, Olive had imagined that things would improve in time. Lara had loved boarding school and Olive was convinced that Alice would grow to like it too.

§

Alice didn't share all the details of her first term with her grandparents. She'd encountered the bullies before she'd found anyone she could call a friend. Subtle girl bullying. Quiet taunts and exclusion. The ringleader, daughter of the local member of parliament, was tall, beautiful, Jacinta Foster. She'd targeted Alice on the first day, sweetly commenting on her great 'tan'. Alice had explained that her father was Aboriginal, to which Jacinta had responded by asking whether she'd been adopted by a civilised white family.

By the end of the first week, having failed to ruffle Alice, Jacinta enlisted a gang of followers. Their secret conferences often involved glances towards Alice and a great deal of muffled tittering. While most of the other girls would have gladly been friendly with Alice, they were too afraid of attracting Jacinta's disapproval and generally avoided the lonely country girl.

It soon became obvious to all that Alice had brains. Mrs Parsons, her eccentric, middle-aged English teacher, clapped her hands in delight at reading Alice's first essay on the themes of *A Midsummer Night's Dream*. Mr Ferrari, the handsome young maths teacher, took a special interest in Alice and began bringing her extra problems to solve each week.

Jacinta, seething with envy, had intensified her mission to make Alice's life a misery. One day, while the class was waiting for Mr Ferrari to arrive, she'd called across the room to one of her friends, 'Hey, Bianca, what's worse than a dumb Abo?'

'What?' Bianca giggled stupidly, before the punchline.

'A smart Abo. Because they know they can get everything they want just by being black!'

Poor Alice, whose entire world until now had been contained within the boundaries of Redstone and the calm, orderly ways of her grandparents, found herself utterly disorientated and bewildered by the ruthless teen social dynamics of the city boarding school.

However, those high school years had toughened her, and she'd managed to keep her chin up and make the best of a bad deal. She'd been sent to learn, so learn she did. This attitude, and the promise of one day returning to her beloved Redstone, were the two secret weapons that carried her through, term by term of school and also the following years at ag college.

§

Now Olive, using the benefit of hindsight, was filled with an uncharacteristic regret for the part she'd played in the decision to send Alice away for schooling. Her hopes that Lara would take the opportunity to get to know her daughter had amounted to nothing, and Lara's continued indifference had been a source of secret sorrow to Olive over the years. In addition, Lara had never followed through on her promise to pay Alice's school fees, and Sam and Olive had been too proud to ask for the money.

The day of Alice's return from ag college, some weeks ago now,

Olive had searched the girl's face and figure for some resemblance to her mother. Lara's pretty features were there, in a darker shade. But not the eyes. And none of the essence.

Sam had been right: Alice was nothing like Lara. The girl's heart was truly embedded in this place, and had she been allowed to stay, Sam may have managed things a little better at Redstone.

'What's done is done,' Olive said matter-of-factly, out loud, to reassure herself.

Chapter 6

Jeremy took the veranda stairs two at a time. He wolf-whistled at King Henry the Ninth on the way past and only avoided a scolding from Olive because the kettle was boiling and she didn't hear. Just in time, Jeremy remembered to take off his boots; once inside, he started off on the right foot by commenting favourably on Olive's cooking.

'Oh ripper, shepherd's pie!' he exclaimed as Olive was serving up the meals. She didn't acknowledge the comment, but he noticed her surreptitiously add another spoonful to his plate. Then, with his mouth full of his first forkload, he said thickly, 'This is even better than Mum's! But don't let on to her I said that.'

Olive sniffed haughtily in response. But shortly afterwards, apparently addressing Sam, she revealed the existence of vanilla rice pudding for dessert.

'Fair dinkum?' Jeremy said. 'I'm liking this place more and more. Good company,' winking at Alice, '*and* beaut tucker!'

During dinner, Sam told Jeremy a bit about Redstone. He explained that the hundred-and-ten-thousand-acre area was divided into thirty-five paddocks of varying sizes and the country was a combination of gidgee scrub, cleared and virgin forest country, and small patches of brigalow. Among the distinctive features of Redstone were the stony ridges with red rocky outcrops from which the station had got its name. The back half of the property boasted an unusually high elevation for land in the western region, and bordered on two hundred thousand acres of national park where the land rose steeply in a mass of rocky outcrops that were visible for hundreds of kilometres around. It was the weathered remains of a volcanic mountain range.

In years with good rainfall, the national park was full of springs where the solid rock forced groundwater to the surface. Some of the spectacular deep rock gorges that were born in the thickly vegetated park ran into Redstone. There were also some natural cliff boundaries along a section of the border. Every fortnight, Sam explained, three full days had to be spent checking waters and fences on Redstone.

'I do the checking most of the time,' he said. 'Suitable job for a crippled-up old fella like me. My eyes are some of the only bits of me which still work.' He chuckled to himself. 'But just for this week, I'll take you along so you can see the lie of the land. While we're at it, you can get a bit of a feel for what needs doing.'

'Righto, boss,' said Jeremy, who had been listening attentively.

'Fencing is a high priority in many of the paddocks. And we have six sets of yards, all of them old, so we'll need to get stuck into fixing them this year. Then there's the open bore drains which Alice hates, and seventeen windmills.' Sam looked at the younger man apologetically. 'Afraid they all need some attention too.'

'Righto, Sam. Getting the picture. Good thing I'm a strapping young lad with plenty of go in me,' Jeremy said brightly. Alice seemed surprised at his enthusiasm.

Sam looked immensely relieved. Then, glancing at Alice, he went on, 'If Jeremy comes checking with me the next few days, that will free you up to look at the books with Olive. She's been hounding me for a while now to have an uninterrupted session with you in the office.' He looked warily at his wife.

'Lucky Alice.' Jeremy's eyes twinkled and Sam laughed guiltily.

'If you're planning on doing some long days of driving, Sam, I suggest you eat your pudding and go to bed quick smart,' Olive said. 'That cold of yours is sounding worse tonight.'

'I'll help him out with his pudding if he's not feeling up to it,' said Jeremy obligingly.

§

The pair of men greatly enjoyed the next two days of checking. As Olive observed to Alice wryly, they seemed to be 'getting along like a house on fire'. Jeremy quickly developed a liking for the gentlemanly old man, and admired his wealth of knowledge. He was keen to pick the older man's brains and took every opportunity to do so.

However, by the third morning, Sam's head cold had got worse. At breakfast, Olive had news for him. 'After you've eaten that, you're going straight back to bed.' She looked at him sternly, braced for his protest.

Sam sniffed and said blearily, 'I'm perfectly able to drive a car. Don't even have to get out for the gates with Jeremy there.'

'A day of complete rest is what you need. Do you want that cold to go to your chest?' In a more threatening tone, she added, 'If it gets any worse I'll have to take you back to Dr Wong. He wanted to check up on your heart again soon anyway.'

Sam glared at his porridge. Then he looked up pleadingly and said, 'What about you two girls? I thought you were busy in the office.'

'We're all up to date now, thanks, Pa,' Alice said.

'Well, I guess you'll have to take Jeremy out to check the back country then, Al. I was planning to take some gear and see if we could work out why the Red Gully mill isn't pumping properly.' Sam sounded disgruntled.

'Jeremy and I can do that. You rest up and get on top of that cold.'

Twenty minutes later, after packing the ute with the necessary equipment and with lunch in an esky, Jeremy and Alice set off. Jeremy discovered, to his confusion, that he was pleased to be heading out alone with Alice for the day. He was also a little nervous, and couldn't work out why.

Alice explained that the back country was her favourite checking circuit and he could tell she was proud to show it off to him. As they drove, he was suitably impressed by the towering piles of rock and the richness of the volcanic soil. They drove through all the bullock paddocks and past the western kurrajong trees that had been lopped for fodder during the last extended dry. They'd had some rain over the last fortnight, so the country was looking fresh, the box trees and other gums thick with shiny new tips and the dense bauhinia trees a mass of dark red pods. Flocks of budgerigars lifted in chattering clouds out of the grass and shrubs as the ute passed by.

They stopped at the Red Gully windmill and Alice went to check the water tank while Jeremy checked the float in the trough. Tank empty, Alice returned and began to hunt around in the tray for the windmill oil and grease. But Jeremy was one step ahead and had already taken them out.

'Oi.' He brushed the grimy oil container lightly against Alice's ear. She spun around.

'If it was a snake it would've bit ya.' He laughed. 'You know how to oil windmills?'

'I'm the Redstone windmill greaser,' Alice said. 'With me away at college the last two years, they haven't been done.' Then, in Sam's defence, she added, 'Pa's balance isn't too good anymore.'

As was generally the rule with windmills, a gust of wind arrived on the scene just as they were ready to climb up.

'The head hasn't turned into the wind,' Alice observed.

'Turntable needs oiling,' put in Jeremy. 'If we're lucky, that could be all that's wrong with it. That, and those trees that have grown up right in the line of the easterlies.'

Alice took the oil out of Jeremy's hand and started up the ladder on the tower.

'I'm coming too. Don't wanna miss out on the view.' Jeremy laughed wickedly, looking up at Alice's jeans-clad bottom which was just above him.

Once they were both up on the narrow square platform, Alice found that, as Jeremy had suspected, the little oil bath on the turntable was bone dry. She topped up all the other baths first, then filled the one for the turntable. She watched as the little woollen wick drew up the oil and began to feed it into the cavity where the steel ball bearings were housed.

The wind had dropped again, and Jeremy and Alice, neither of them shy of heights, stood shoulder to shoulder surveying the bird's-eye view.

'Not a bad place, this Redstone,' Jeremy said, not bothering to hide the pleasure in his voice.

Alice tilted back her head to look up at him from under the big brim of her hat. The sun illuminated her brown eyes with golden warmth and she smiled. 'Struth, what a smile!' Jeremy thought, then grinned back.

'I'll give those she-oaks a bit of a trim up,' he said. 'That'll make all the difference to this mill.'

The mill groaned slightly as a soft gust of wind began to turn the head.

'Good-o.' Jeremy nodded approvingly and they shuffled further around the platform, away from the slow-turning wheel. They were now facing west, away from the sun. Below was a wide plain, the rugged rusty backdrop of the range contrasting with the yellow-green of the grass. Alice pointed out an enormous old-man kangaroo in bounding, slow-motion flight. He looked as though he'd been carved from the red stone of the range and brought to life. Jeremy watched her watching the roo. He could tell she felt a deep bond with this land and for a moment he was jealous. A place to put down roots. A family that valued her. Lucky bugger.

They made several more stops to check waters and tighten some sagging fences with a star picket or two. Jeremy was impressed by the unique 'native well' at the dead centre of Cliff paddock. It consisted of an eight-foot-deep rectangular hole carved in a large flat surface of rock. It was nearly full of mineral-rich blue water which Jeremy tasted curiously. At one end were some roughly hewn steps going down into the water, an escape route for any incautious beast that happened to topple in.

'Pearler of a skinny-dipping spot,' Jeremy commented. 'Bet you've had your share of swimming starkers in this little spa, eh, Ali?'

'Whatever you say, Jeremy,' Alice answered evasively, turning back to the car.

Late in the afternoon, Alice stopped the ute abruptly alongside a nondescript section of fence line on the boundary with the national park.

'Why are we stopping here?' Jeremy asked, looking at her curiously.

'Come on, I'll show you.' Alice motioned into the park with her head. 'Wasn't going to, but I've decided I will.' She grinned conspiratorially at Jeremy then opened the ute door to jump out.

'Holy hell, you've got my attention now!' Jeremy flung open his door and followed Alice's departing form.

She walked a little further along the fence and held apart two wires for Jeremy to step through. Once on the other side he did the same for her, then pointed questioningly to a narrow pad winding away into the bush. Alice nodded and stopped to hang her hat on the fence, while Jeremy started off along the track.

They walked for a while through open forest country until, quite suddenly, the bush became thicker and damper. Dark green scrub trees, figs, broad-leafed creek trees and even palms began to appear between the gums. The land on either side of them began to rise, and soon they were hemmed in on both sides by rocky ridges. Jeremy could see some spectacular outcrops of weathered red rock through the trees.

The incline of the gully itself slowly became steeper, and the vegetation was so dense with vines that they couldn't see much on either side of the track. Jeremy noticed that the temperature had dropped considerably. The moist air was full of tangy smells that were new to him. He also noted that the track looked quite well used; as he clumped along with large strides in his heavy workboots he stepped on a large stallion pile. Horses had been through this way.

'Do you come here much?' he called back to Alice, who was a little distance behind.

She hurried up to him and grabbed his arm. 'Shh!' She made the sound urgently. 'Sometimes there are brumbies up here. Go a bit slower and try not to thump along so heavily!'

He looked down into her eager face. Without the big hat she always wore he could see her properly. Her usually serious features were alight with the pure delight of anticipation. Some wispy sun-bleached curls had escaped from her loose plait and her eyes shone. He gazed at her in amazement and felt a little shaken.

'Are they the scrawny inbred type with oversized heads?' he asked, trying to regain his composure.

'Shh!' Alice said again, and shoved him on with a little brown hand in the centre of his back.

Jeremy suddenly realised that his own heart was pounding with excitement. It was ridiculous. Alice's mood was so infectious that he was getting worked up over the possibility of seeing some feral nags that wouldn't rate for dog meat.

The gully became very narrow and the rock walls closing them in were now sheer. Their track merged with a pebbly creek bed; at its centre was a fast-flowing trickle of cold, clean water. They rock-hopped for a short way and then the dense vegetation ended quite abruptly. They stepped out into a natural stone amphitheatre formed by the head of the gully.

The sides were all of the same red rock, with moss, lacy ferns and small hardy shrubs sprouting out of the face directly before them. Water seeped and dripped from numerous cracks and crevices, the rivulets joining forces with the main flow, which also appeared to be issuing from solid rock. It then ran down over several step-like layers before freefalling into a wide shallow pool just below.

There were no brumbies, but plenty of evidence that they frequented the place. With a flash of iridescent blue, a kingfisher darted across in front of them, alighting on a tiny branch of one of the scraggly bushes growing out of the rock face. Turning its glossy head and bright beady eye, it regarded them with curious suspicion, poised for flight. They watched it in silence until it shot away and out of sight.

Alice flung out her arm with the air of a princess displaying her palace. 'What do you think?' Her face was glowing as she looked at Jeremy.

'Never knew there were places like this so far west.' Jeremy looked around, trying to avoid the intensity of her gaze. She was so alive here. She'd spoken more to him in the past ten minutes than she'd done in the last two days.

Whether it was some ancient power that emanated from the place, the higher concentration of oxygen or the sound of running water, Jeremy couldn't tell, but he was suddenly finding this girl overwhelmingly enchanting. He bent down to scoop up some water, which he threw over his head. He hoped the cold dousing would return him to his senses.

'Blackfellas would've prized this joint,' he observed.

Alice looked at him thoughtfully. After a moment, she revealed that she'd found several tools here: grooved grinding stones and a variety of left- and right-handed stone axes. She'd also found other special places such as this on Redstone itself.

'You wanna keep that to yourself,' Jeremy warned.

'I don't usually tell people. Pa's paranoid they'll turn Redstone into a sacred site.' Alice's eyes opened wide and Jeremy laughed.

'Your secret's safe with me.'

'I know.' She nodded at him.

Jeremy was surprised. 'Alice, I reckon I haven't done much to earn your trust. I would've thought you'd be a bit nervous coming to a place like this, on your own, with a bloke of my reputation.'

Alice looked at him quizzically. 'I never take much notice of reputations. I saw straight away that you had a kind eye.'

'A kind eye? Like a horse?' Jeremy asked, raising his eyebrows.

Alice nodded. 'Or a bull. It's exactly the same thing.'

He laughed. 'Heck, I've never had a girl say that to me before. You must be trying to butter me up.'

'You can take it as a compliment if you want to. I was just answering your question.' Alice's tone was matter-of-fact.

'You're too kind,' Jeremy answered, feeling bemused.

'I suppose we'd better head back.' Alice looked around longingly.

Watching her face, Jeremy was suddenly aware of the immense significance this place held for her. He felt humbled and honoured that she'd chosen to bring him here. His gratitude sounded in his voice as he said, 'Thanks for showing me, eh, Alice. This place is awesome.'

Unexpectedly, Alice dazzled Jeremy with a smile of genuine pleasure, completely disarming him. Fortunately, she started off down the gully before she was able to observe the effect she'd had on him.

Once they had climbed back through the fence, and Alice had once again donned her battered hat, the spell was broken. The tantalising, nymph-like creature was gone and in her place was only quiet little Alice Wilson. Jeremy exhaled in relief. He'd have to be more careful from now on.

Chapter 7

Over the next week Sam's cold worsened and went to his chest, so he was again confined to bed despite his protests that there was some urgent late branding to be done. Alice and Jeremy spent a few days tordoning tree suckers to thin out the overgrown area of Summerlea paddock. In recent years many of the Redstone paddocks were becoming less productive as thick stands of saplings and woody shrubs began to monopolise large areas of former grazing land. Mustering in these overgrown paddocks was also becoming increasingly difficult.

Alice was thinning out the clumps of smaller weedy trees so that only the larger timber remained. It was a physically taxing job that required continuous walking over rough ground and plenty of axe work, and her grandfather had been putting it off for some years. But Alice and Jeremy were knocking a hole in it, and she knew that while he was laid up, her grandfather would be relieved to think that there were two young and energetic bodies on the place.

Sam had scheduled the branding for the Tuesday. Their last round of mustering had been done just before Christmas, when Alice had arrived home for good. At the time, a mob of more than thirty calves had been overlooked; they'd been hiding with their mothers in the suckers at the western end of Top Cedar Tree paddock. Since then, Sam had been watching these cleanskins grow bigger by the week, and the prospect of branding the monsters was daunting for the tired old man.

On Tuesday morning, Alice went to his bedroom with his breakfast on a tray. She sat at the foot of the bed and smiled encouragingly at him.

'I'm sorry, Alice,' he said irritably. 'Been worse than useless this last fortnight. Have to put off those bloody calves again.'

'Actually, Pa, I was going to suggest that we still do the branding. I think Jeremy and I might manage, now that the dogs are working so well.'

He shook his head. 'Recipe for disaster, Ali. Those Top Cedar Tree cows are sly old snakes. That's why we missed 'em, even with the three old fellas helping.'

But Alice wasn't put off. 'Jeremy's keen. I've just spoken to him. It'll be good to get it done so you can rest up without worrying about it anymore.'

He still looked dubious. 'I reckon you'll just blow it and reinforce their bad habits. There's a few rogues in there that have escaped one too many times already.'

Alice's face fell in disappointment. Her grandfather softened his tone a little and went on, 'It's your call, Alice. You make the decisions around here now – you don't need my permission.'

'Don't be silly, Pa. Of course we won't do it if you're worried. There's always the endless amount of tordoning to do instead.'

Just then Alice heard Jeremy's cheerful voice in the kitchen. He was baiting her grandmother with some kind of nonsense and she was biting back. She looked at her grandfather and his eyes twinkled with amusement.

'Others having a secret meeting?' she heard Jeremy ask after a while. 'Hey, Alice, I've loaded the ute and saddled the horses,' he called. 'What's keeping ya? I'm keen for a bit of galloping.'

Alice looked apologetically at her grandfather. He winked at her. 'Looks like you're going mustering.'

Alice drove the truck with the horses on board to Cedar Tree stockyards, and Jeremy followed in the ute with the branding gear. The air was already hot on their faces as they rode out into the paddock with the dogs trotting along behind.

'We'll split up here, Jeremy,' said Alice, reining in Bingley. They had reached a thick stand of tall poplar box trees, the closest cattle camp to the yards. 'I'll go towards the dam – that's where most of the cattle should be at this time of day and I'll have the dogs.'

'I'll have Ace, but!' Jeremy exclaimed. 'Don't underestimate my stumpy offsider.' He glanced fondly at his tubby blue dog, who was busily sniffing Lydia's bottom.

Alice looked too, unconvinced. 'First, could you ride around to the southern corner? There are often a few head sheltering there in the creek. Come along through the suckers near the back fence line, and make a bit of noise so any cows hiding there will run this way. Then work your way back towards the dam where I should be holding the main mob.'

'Righto, boss. Sounds like a plan.' Jeremy saluted and cantered off.

When Alice came over the small rise behind the dam, she was pleased to see a large number of cattle in the vicinity. Some had already come to water and the others were feeding their way towards it. They were still quite spread out so she sent her dogs out wide and descended slowly towards the dam on her horse. It didn't take long for the cows to notice the dogs skirting them at a distance and they began to mob up at the water's edge. As soon as Alice saw them begin to move she stopped her dogs where they were, still a fair way from the cows. The dogs knew that their job now was to sit motionless until further notice. Alice, too, stopped her advance and Bingley dropped his head to nibble the grass.

While she waited for Jeremy to come in from the back of the paddock, Alice found her thoughts returning to her grandfather, as they had frequently in recent weeks. On Alice's return from college, her grandmother had gently informed her that he'd been having chest pains on and off for several months. She wondered whether he was giving up, now that she was home and Jeremy was there to help. It was a terrifying thought. Redstone without her grandfather at the helm would be like a boat without a captain.

Sooner than Alice expected, Jeremy's approach was heralded by the distant yapping of Ace. She cringed. She hated dogs that barked at the cattle. The sound was coming nearer quickly, suggesting that the cows Jeremy had found were running. If they came thundering into the middle of her nice settled mob at the dam all hell could break loose.

Alice rode a little way back up the rise and soon spotted a fast-approaching cloud of dust. There were about thirty head and she could just see Jeremy behind them, galloping flat out on poor old Rita. He managed to get alongside them, obviously with the intention of overtaking and slowing the mob before they reached the dam. But a few of them broke out on the opposite edge, heading off at a tangent. Alice recognised a brindle cow with one horn leading the deviants away – she had given them trouble last time.

Ace was onto them and succeeded in making them go faster. Alice winced. The rest of the cows and calves were now veering off course to follow the escapees. Jeremy was after them again; by galloping out wide, he managed to get around in front. The animals slowed and spun before taking off in the right direction again. Ace was on their heels, yapping, and they were approaching fast. Alice steeled herself for action but the brindle mono-horn had no intention of playing the game. Off she went again, this time out in the opposite direction. The little mob dispersed and half of them followed her, the rest continuing towards the dam.

Alice signalled to her dogs to stay with the herd at the dam, then she headed off towards Jeremy and the troublesome bovines. This time he went after One Horn and was soon racing alongside her. Once he'd edged in front he suddenly jerked on Rita's head with the intention of bringing her around to block the brindle beast. But the old mare wasn't accustomed to such heavy-handedness, and as she spun, her feet slid out from under her. She came down hard on her side, just as Alice arrived on the scene.

One Horn continued without altering her course, and the rest of the cows mobbed up again and followed her. Jeremy was back on his feet before the mare, having rolled free of her as she came down. He was too busy swearing at the unfortunate horse to hear Alice's concerned enquiry. 'Jeremy, are you alright?'

Rita clambered to her feet, her sides heaving and her foamy lather of sweat caked in dirt on one side. Jeremy jumped straight back into the saddle, with the clear intent of continuing the pursuit.

'Wait!' Alice called. 'I'll get them. You go and hold the mob at the dam.'

'Not bloody likely. I'm not letting that fat brindle—'

Alice interrupted him impatiently. 'Jeremy, it's just a cow, don't take it personally. Rita's knocked up.'

'Give me your horse then.' Jeremy was glaring after the departing cows and calves.

'Never. Just go to the dam and wait.'

'You reckon you'll do better than me?' He looked at her challengingly.

'Yes.' Alice met his eyes frankly.

He clearly hadn't been expecting such a direct reply. He raised his eyebrows at her and his aggressive posture relaxed. 'Righto then – in that case, I'd better do what I'm told.'

Alice started off after the departing cows at an easy canter, slowing to a trot, then a walk. She was in no hurry. The Bennet sisters saw her moving off and silently deserted their posts to go after her. Alice knew the cows would be heading for the shady camp that she and Jeremy had stopped at earlier that morning. The little mob was a long way off now, strung out in a line and still going at a decent pace. The last thing they needed was more pressure from behind. As she'd expected, once they reached the clump of trees they pulled up in the shade, blowing heavily. Alice turned off to the side, her plan to go in a wide semicircle rather than approaching them directly.

As she rode slowly towards them the cattle lifted their heads to watch her warily. She stopped where she was and cast her dogs to skirt wide around behind the little mob. When they were still a long way out from the cattle, she made them drop. Girl, horse, dogs and cows remained stationary for several minutes. The cows eyed the stealthy dogs in the grass and shifted nervously before turning their attention back to Alice. Once she could see that all eyes were back on her, Alice turned and began to ride back towards the dam.

§

Jeremy had shaken his head in disgust as he watched Alice's time-wasting tactics. After all his hard work the silly sheila was going to lose them. Eventually she'd disappeared from sight. He'd obviously have to go and bail her out shortly. He walked Rita back towards the dam and the waiting mob.

A short while later, he turned and stared in amazement. Alice was in the lead with the cattle a short distance behind her. The dogs were bringing up the rear. There was no noise and all of them were walking in an orderly fashion. But what Jeremy found most astounding was that the leading cow was none other than the brindled she-devil One Horn. Alice led the cows over the rise and then veered off to one side. The little mob began to trot as they descended to join the bigger herd, causing only a minor ripple as they were absorbed into it.

Alice signalled to Jeremy to wait while the cows settled again. He didn't think much of all this waiting, but as he watched the small, self-assured figure on horseback on the other side of the mob he wondered whether perhaps there was something in it after all. At last, she nodded across at him and set off in front of the cows towards the yards. There was nothing for Jeremy to do but follow along at the tail with Ace, and with the busy Bennet sisters skirting around him, he almost felt as though he was in the way.

With the cows safely yarded, Jeremy and Alice sat in the shade for a cup of tea and some of Olive's chewy chocolate walnut slice. Jeremy examined Alice with a new respect as she sat stroking Kitty's head, an absent-minded frown on her face.

'What're you stewing over?' he asked.

She looked up quickly. 'Oh, I'm just thinking about Pa. I hadn't realised until just lately that he's an old man.'

'It's a bugger, eh, old age.' Jeremy sipped his tea then continued, 'Here I was thinking you were wondering how much you'd impressed me this morning with your cow-charming act. You made me look like a right duffer.' He couldn't keep the admiration out of his voice.

'Oh.' Alice looked slightly surprised. 'I wasn't trying to impress you,' she said simply. 'They were going to get away.' She went back to stroking her dog.

Jeremy regarded her closely and saw that what she said was true. Unlike all the other girls he knew, Alice had little concern for what he thought. She didn't want or need his good opinion. She was amazingly self-contained for a chick. He found her strong-headedness both fascinating and unsettling. It seemed she was largely immune to the power of approval or disapproval from anyone but her grandparents.

Looking at her balanced so lightly on the log, with such quiet authority over her dogs, Jeremy was intrigued. He was visited by a sudden ridiculous vision of one of the bikie gangs that occasionally roared into town for lunch at the pub. They sported matching black jackets with the slogan Free Spirits emblazoned across their backs. The bold white script was bordered by feathery angel's wings. Jeremy looked sideways at Alice again. Free spirit.

Then she spoke, jerking Jeremy back to reality. 'Never mind about the cows, Jeremy. I had the advantage of knowing where the camp was. And I had the dogs. Branding's next and you can have the pleasure of outdoing me there – by a long way.' She looked at him, her pensive expression replaced suddenly by her unpredictable smile, and he felt his face redden. Blimey, he thought in dismay, it'd been years since he'd blushed.

Chapter 8

As the week drew to a close, Jeremy decided to head into town for some serious partying. He left in the early afternoon on Friday, taking the time to drop in to the kitchen to wish a stony-faced Olive a personal farewell.

'Don't lie awake worrying about me, Mrs Day. I'm a big boy now.' He flexed his muscular arms at her and grinned before bounding out the door, whistling at the cockatoo as he thudded down the veranda steps.

It was the first weekend since he'd been employed at the station that Jeremy had gone to town, and the three Redstoners all found themselves thinking how quiet it was without him. None of them admitted it out loud, and the word Olive used to describe it to herself was 'peaceful'. But they all realised that in the short time he'd been at Redstone, Jeremy had somehow become an important part of the place. By Sunday, Sam was eagerly awaiting his return, and even Olive was feeling more kindly towards the useful larrikin.

In the early hours of Monday morning the roar of an unfamiliar engine shattered the pre-dawn tranquillity of Redstone. It wasn't his ute but Jeremy was driving. He swerved and pulled up roughly near the big old house; as he did so, there was a woody clunk in the back, followed by a groan.

'Yep, that'll be his head,' he told himself brightly. He bounced up onto the dark veranda like an excited schoolboy and yelled, 'Surprise! Rise and shine!'

A tirade of indignant muttering issued forth from under the navy-blue-and-white-striped flannelette cover on the tall birdcage. King Henry the Ninth had been rudely awoken and was highly affronted.

Seconds later the veranda light came on and Alice appeared in her cotton pyjamas. 'Jeremy, you're not doing yourself any favours by—'

'Not so fast, Ali Baba, not so fast. Check out what I found on the side of the road.' He nodded towards the dented ute stopped on the edge of the veranda light, its huge spotlights reflecting beams back at them.

'That's not your ute,' Alice said suspiciously. Then, seeing the bunch of dingo scalps drying on the kangaroo rack, she added, 'It belongs to the travelling shooter Pa gets when he's in the area.'

'Fair dinkum? You mean Sam lets him come here? That useless piece of pig bait?'

'Maurie always rings to let us know before and after he's been. Pa says he does a good job.'

'Too bloody true! Have a squiz at what's in the back.'

Jeremy followed Alice as she walked tentatively over to the vehicle and leaned in to look past the empty dog cage. Lying on his side, looking up at her, arms and legs tied together with rope, was Maurie the shooter. He was wedged between the tailgate and one of two clean-skin calves that were tied in a similar fashion. Alice gave a little squeal and jumped backwards.

'That one drew the short straw,' said Jeremy, indicating the calf that was pressed against Maurie. 'Your shooter here don't smell so good. What do you think of my catch?'

'Pa will be so upset!' Alice sounded shocked. 'I'm glad you caught him though.'

Jeremy enthusiastically accepted the praise. 'That saying's so true – you know, the one about getting your biggest catch when you ain't even hunting? I usually use it for women, but it applies in this case too.' He laughed at his own joke but Alice was frowning distractedly.

'What is it now?' barked Olive, striding out onto the veranda.

King Henry the Ninth began clearing his throat. Olive had taken the time to don her floral dressing gown and put a hairnet over her curlers.

'Where'd you spring from, Curly?' Jeremy greeted her. 'We're just admiring the roadkill here.'

'Roadkill?'

'Well, he's not *completely* dead ... yet. He might even be well enough to appreciate all the effort you've gone to with your appearance.' He grinned and Olive flushed angrily.

'Whatever it is, you had better hope it's worth waking the household over. I told Sam to stay in bed. He's been having a terrible night with his back. And as I expected it's nothing important, just you coming home from a drunken orgy.'

'I don't think you wanna use that word no more, m'lady. It don't mean what it did in your day.'

'Oh, shut up!' Olive had lost her cool and the cockatoo was beginning to cough.

'Righto then.' Jeremy held up his hands. 'Just trying to save you from future embarrassment. And I s'pose if this isn't *important*, I'll just untie our furry poddy-dodging friend and let him drive away. Shall I get the calves out of the back first?'

'Get me out of here, you bastards!' A forlorn plea came from inside the shadow of the ute tray.

Olive's eyes widened. 'I'll go and get Samuel.'

'No rush, he ain't going nowhere.' Jeremy chuckled as Olive hurried back inside.

He looked at Alice. In the dim light her messy hair reminded him of a bird's nest. Or a halo. He could see the imprint of a fold of linen on her cheek, and the slight silvery trace of a bit of saliva. He wanted to kiss her, she was so beautiful. But instead he said, 'You wanna take a leaf out of your old ma's book. She must've learned at finishing school, you gotta check your face for dribble before rushing outside after a sleep.'

'Very funny.' Alice felt around her mouth for the telltale line.

'Here, let me help you.' From his pocket Jeremy produced a filthy checked hanky with a J embroidered on it and spat on the corner.

'You come near me with that and I'll clobber you!' Alice backed away with her fists up.

'What, I got germs or something?'

'Probably. How do I know what you've been kissing over the weekend?'

Jeremy detected a note of genuine disgust in Alice's voice and it stung him. She turned and walked away towards the door to meet Sam who had finally surfaced. The old man was half bent over with his hand on his lower back.

'Fuzzy's in for it now,' Jeremy said, his tone foreboding.

'Are you drunk, Jeremy?' Sam asked, pain from his back sounding in his voice.

'No, Sam.'

'Good lad. Tell me what's going on.'

Jeremy explained, loudly enough so the captive in the back of the ute could hear it all too. Driving home in the starlight, with only his ute's parking lights to illuminate the road, Jeremy had encountered Maurie coming from the opposite direction. They had met on a bend and the edgy Maurie had swerved, overcorrected and then locked up his wheels on the bulldust. 'Damaged the poor old-man ironbark,' Jeremy concluded.

'So what then?' Sam asked.

Jeremy went on and Sam's expression became increasingly grave at the description of what had been discovered in the back.

'I could have told you he was a bad bugger if you'd mentioned it to me,' Jeremy said gently. 'It's pretty common knowledge around town.'

'Maybe among *your* associates,' Olive said defensively, taking Sam's arm.

'So the whole time . . .' Sam left the sentence unfinished.

'I think you'll notice an improvement in your calving rate from now on.'

Sam hobbled slowly over to the ute and looked down at Maurie sorrowfully. Jeremy could see that he was more upset about having to lower his opinion of someone he'd trusted and liked than about the crime committed against him.

'Soft old codger,' he thought to himself. 'If they were my calves I'd wanna snig the bloke out back and chuck him down the well.'

'What shall we do with him?' As always, Olive was was concerned with the practicalities.

'Morning's not far off. And the stock squad should be here by lunchtime. I say leave him where he is,' suggested Jeremy.

'Sam, get me out of here! I swear I won't cause any trouble. Please!' Maurie begged in his reedy wail, staring pleadingly at Sam.

But it was Jeremy who answered him. 'Things have changed round here, Fuzzy Chops. Not everyone on the place is in bed by seven thirty anymore. Hell, I'm so unreliable you could find me on the road at any time of night. Especially if I've been entertaining a lady. And as you saw for yourself, my headlights are dodgy, so I'll see you long before you see me.'

'It won't happen again, I swear! I'll never set foot on the place again. No need to dob a man in, is there? Just get me out of this agony!' Maurie appealed to Jeremy this time.

'I wouldn't piss on ya if you were burning, mate.' Jeremy turned to the others and continued, 'I reckon we'll leave him here to do a bit of penance. Give him a gutful of his own medicine.'

'Nooooo!' Maurie strained on the rope.

There was a short silence. 'He can't stay in that position for too much longer,' Alice observed compassionately.

Taking up the suggestion, Jeremy asked Maurie, 'Would you like a change of position, mate? You've done the calf thing – I could hang you like a roo from your rack? I'd scalp you if I could get ten bucks for your fluff. But I don't think anyone'd be keen.'

'Please, Alice, I'm dying here.' Maurie made his best puppy-dog eyes at her.

But Jeremy answered again. 'While you're there, Fuzz, you can think about how many poddies you've lifted from a trusting old stick that was doughy enough to believe you were doing him a favour.'

'I'm sorry!' Maurie groaned.

Then, looking at Alice's troubled face, Jeremy unexpectedly produced his pocket knife and cut the old piece of rope that was binding Maurie's ankles. Next he swung the weedy little man onto his feet. Maurie tottered there for a moment before crumpling to the ground with what looked like a severe attack of pins and needles.

King Henry the Ninth was coughing in earnest now. Maurie looked around for the source of the rattling cough, and his eyes rested disbelievingly on the covered birdcage. The coughing episode reached its climax at last and the phlegm was brought up. Silence fell again. The Redstone folk were all still looking down at Maurie. He looked pathetically weak and thin, his moth-eaten whiskers sticking out on each side of his face.

'What're you doing with all that stolen meat anyway, Fuzz?' Jeremy asked. 'Not eating it yourself, that's for sure. Need a good worming, I reckon.'

'No! Please!' Maurie looked up from where he was still writhing on the ground as the blood returned to his constricted limbs.

'What?' Jeremy laughed incredulously. 'You think I'd waste a dose on you when there are useful animals around that need it?'

Before Maurie's pain had completely subsided, Jeremy marched him over to the shipping container next to the shed, used for the storage of dry feed and other matter that needed to be protected from moisture and marauding mice. Untying his wrists, Jeremy deposited the unhappy man roughly onto some empty bags and paused for a moment before closing him in. 'Stock squad'll be here after a bit, old mate. Best get some rest. Build up ya strength. Although there'll be plenty of time for that once you're inside.'

Just before Jeremy banged the heavy door shut, excluding the dawn light, he caught a final glimpse of the poddy dodger. Maurie looked so completely down and out: Jeremy horrified himself by feeling a fleeting pang of something like pity.

§

They let Maurie go at midday. He was babbling and falling over himself with gratitude that they hadn't called the cops.

'Get going, you snivelling idiot,' Jeremy said disgustedly. Out of respect for Sam, he'd become more creative with his insulting names and curses since coming to Redstone. 'We'll take care of our own vermin from now on. Including you, if you ever show your whiskers round here again.'

They stood and watched him drive away.

'What goes around comes around,' said Olive decidedly. 'He'll have to pay for his wrongdoing one day.'

'Yeah – today,' said Jeremy. 'The little nest egg he had in his glovebox will do nicely.'

They all stared in amazement as he produced a thick roll of cash from his chest pocket.

'Well, I suppose that will cover the cost of some of the calves he stole,' said Olive doubtfully, clearly trying to work out whether Jeremy had been right or wrong in taking it.

'You're joking, aren't ya?' Jeremy exclaimed. 'This is my commission. I'll be using some of it to wine and dine Alice on Valentine's Day.'

'We'll see about that,' said Olive as they walked inside for lunch.

Alice buttered the bread while her grandmother carved the corned beef. Then the older woman looked up at her and spoke ominously. 'I'll need you in the office after lunch. Remember, the bank manager's coming Wednesday week and I want us to be ready for him.'

Jeremy piped up, 'While we're making bookings, Alice, can I borrow you for a bit this evening?'

'What for?' Alice and her grandmother asked in unison.

'Ladies, ladies, keep your cottontails on! I just need a lift to my ute. And a drum of fuel. The needle had been below empty for quite a while when I ran into old Fluff Balls. He saved my, er, skin. Would've been a long walk home. Poor fella will never know.'

'The Lord works in mysterious ways,' Sam chuckled.

Chapter 9

Alice and Jeremy bumped along the road in the late afternoon sun and looked out at a world washed with warm golds, pinks and browns. The harshness of the dried-out land was softened by the slanting rays of the setting sun, and hidden hues emerged in the landscape that was largely bleached of colour in the full daylight. The two spoke little as they drove, the long blue shadows of the trees and termite mounds lying across their way.

'Could do with some bloody rain,' was all Jeremy said for the first five kilometres.

The only radio station that the ute could pick up crackled in and out of reception, at times startlingly clear. But Alice wasn't listening. The facts and figures she'd spent the afternoon perusing with her grandmother were swimming before her eyes as she stared ahead at the road. Profit and loss, overheads, direct and indirect costs were running through her mind and she frowned slightly. With her grandmother's blessing, over the weeks since Alice had returned she had added onto the computer ingoing and outgoing cattle numbers for each paddock. It had involved a great deal of ruffling through her grandfather's haphazard pocket record-keeping books. Alice now intended to begin recording calving percentages for each paddock and to develop a table for predicted weaning and branding times. She'd also been working on some files of her own, listing new ideas and ventures for the property.

She came out of her reverie and looked across to see Jeremy watching her as she drove. He smiled at her and she felt surprisingly comforted and reassured.

'How did your secret women's business go today?' he asked, as though he'd read her mind.

Suddenly Alice found herself spilling out her thoughts to him. All her dreams and plans for Redstone. Jeremy listened with his head slightly cocked, unusually quiet.

She told him about her plan to introduce seasonal mating. This would mean that instead of keeping bulls in with the cows all year round, they would be given a season to do their work with the cows, then removed to rest and recharge their batteries. Initially it would mean fewer calves, as the cows that had calved at the wrong time the previous year would fail to cycle when the bulls were on hand. However, after a few years the cows would be synchronised, and those that weren't would stand out as the less fertile and be culled.

She confided in Jeremy her concern that her grandfather was only focused on the short term. It was understandable: while *she* was thinking twenty years down the track, Pa, at his age, was concentrating only on surviving a day at a time. He had the bank manager breathing down his neck and regular interest payments to meet. Anything that meant a reduction in calf numbers, even in the short term, appeared madness to him. But Alice had done her homework. She'd calculated the exact figures using the worst-case scenario. There were losses in the short term, yes, but when all the calves were born at the same time the cattle workload would be cut by more than half, with only one annual round of branding and weaning for each paddock. Until now there had been haphazard branding and weaning all year round; there was always a drizzle of multi-sized weaners needing to be taken off at any time, and a drizzle of musters to match. These small mobs of weaners didn't get proper handling before being sent bush. As a result, they were flighty, slower to gain weight, harder on fences and difficult to muster.

Realising how long she'd been talking, Alice stopped and looked at Jeremy, but he just nodded for her to go on.

Alice explained that with perdictable numbers of a uniform size she believed they would be able to meet forward contracts for beef orders. Transporting bulk loads, less often, was a huge saving for a station as out of the way as Redstone. Of course, any plans were always subject to the weather, and extended dry spells were part of life at Redstone. But from her time at ag college Alice knew all about feed supplementation; loose dry-powder licks and molasses-urea wet licks were genuine options. Yes, another cost, but one that would pay for itself tenfold as the breeding cows would no longer need so many months to return to fertility after every dry.

They reached Jeremy's ute, and Alice pulled up behind it. But they continued to sit in the cab while Alice, her face shining, described her strategy of splitting the larger paddocks and starting rotational grazing. 'I'm sure we could nearly double our carrying capacity,' she said eagerly.

'It will mean loads of fencing, and new watering points,' Jeremy observed. 'But don't get me wrong, I think it's a top idea. The way to go. My brother John has been trying to convince Dad to do the same thing for a few years now.'

There was a short pause and they sat, listening to the hum of the crickets. Alice was pleased that Jeremy approved of her ideas, but she was still troubled by the thought of hurting her grandparents. Redstone was their home. What right did she have to tell them how to run it?

Looking across at Jeremy again, she explained her dilemma. 'They've done so much for me. More than grandparents should ever have to.'

'Excuse me for saying so, but I think it's paid off for them in spades if you know what I mean.' Jeremy looked at her, his eyes smiling.

Alice felt herself relax a little. Some of the weight had lifted from her shoulders with the relief of having confided in someone.

They climbed out of the ute and Alice examined the damaged ironbark while Jeremy refuelled his vehicle from the drum. Bits of Maurie's paint were embedded in the splintered bark of the tree. The farm ute radio was still playing. It sounded tinny and out of place in the isolation. The presenter was talking about fungal infections. He finished his spiel and then both Alice and Jeremy recognised the opening notes of the soppily romantic seventies hit, 'Could I Have this Dance'. Jeremy hurled the empty fuel drum into the back of his ute and bounded over to Alice.

Before she knew it, she was firmly in his arms and he was waltzing her in an exaggerated slow dance, their feet making patterns in the bulldust. He mouthed the words while Anne Murray crooned, '... Could I have this dance for the rest of my life? Would you be my partner every night? When we're together it feels soooo right ...'

After a slight struggle, Alice laughed and allowed Jeremy to manoeuvre her. She couldn't help being aware of the strength of his arms holding her. She could feel the life and energy humming inside this man. Her forehead rested for a moment on his chin and a tingling warmth travelled from his body into hers.

The spell lasted as long as the song, then the presenter's conversational voice irreverently cut off the last few notes, still talking about tinea. Jeremy released Alice and they stood looking at each other in the fading light, breathing quickly. The stress of her afternoon in the office was forgotten. She even wondered if, in another time and place, they could have loved one another.

But Alice was well aware of the kind of man that Jeremy had become, and all too familiar with his kind of girl. Jeremy had no place in her own special country. Hers was a solitary world of the outdoors, peace, and simple, rugged beauty. She had no use for Jeremy's life of rodeos, egos, drunken revelry, and promiscuity. And this world had claimed him. She'd been invited into it repeatedly at ag college and had consciously withdrawn from it. Alice knew that she didn't fit Jeremy's life any more than he fitted hers. As much as she liked him and enjoyed working with him, she had no intention of becoming another notch on his belt.

§

Jeremy, standing opposite Alice in the dusk, was experiencing a disconcerting absence of the self-assurance he usually felt around women.

'Are you blushing under that tan?' he asked hopefully.

'No,' Alice answered, and he knew that it was true.

There it was again. Jeremy marvelled at the strange absence of self-consciousness in this girl. She was so certain of herself. None of the usual rules applied here. His typical moves were obsolete; Alice was so different to other girls.

'You're lucky that wasn't "Eagle Rock",' he joked, trying to ease the intensity. 'You know the tradition for *that* song.'

She smiled up at him, then looked down, her eyelashes concealing her thoughts from him. There was another silence while Jeremy panicked inwardly. He wanted to kiss her, but some dormant instinct inside him rose up in warning against that course of action. He was surprised when, looking up at him again, it was she who broke the silence.

'Thank you for the dance, kind sir.' She spoke with dignity.

He realised that she was gently concluding the incident and relieving him of the option of any further action. On an impulse, he took her small brown hand in his big rough one and kissed the back of it.

And then it was all over. They climbed into their vehicles. Alice waited to make sure Jeremy's engine started and then followed him, keeping a distance behind to avoid his dust. Jeremy squirmed in his seat and swore quietly, cursing the uncomfortable turmoil he was experiencing. He'd really stuffed up big time. This girl had got under his skin; and yet she hadn't seemed like the dangerous type. Becoming involved in a serious relationship was something he'd resolved against doing long ago. He decided he'd soon get over her. If not, he'd have to shoot through. But the truth was, Alice's description of her plans for Redstone had excited and stimulated him. At last, it was something he could really sink his teeth into.

It was dark when they crossed the grid before the homestead. Jeremy honked loudly at the sight of Olive's fretting face in the kitchen window. He swept past much too quickly, skidding to a halt in the shed. Alice pulled up alongside. After a brief goodnight, she disappeared into the house.

Chapter 10

After that evening, Jeremy became Alice's ally in convincing Sam to consider some changes to Redstone. He wasn't constrained by the same fear of offending the old man, so he was tougher on Sam than Alice was prepared to be.

Another unexpected ally came in the form of the bank manager, Phillip Kift, who arrived at Redstone the following Wednesday in his maroon and silver four-wheel drive. In her careful preparations, Olive had outdone herself and her scones were so light that they looked as though they could float off the platter. She'd timed them perfectly and they were still slightly warm, but not enough to make the cream go runny.

However, Mr Kift initially refused a scone on the grounds that he was dieting, and Olive feared they were off to a bad start. She looked despairingly at the ample pile of cream and jam heaped on each. A dieter's worst nightmare. She couldn't have got it more wrong if she'd tried. Next, the important man asked if there was any fresh fruit, but the mangos had finished and Olive's last trip to Emerald had been three weeks earlier. It was the very thing she was completely out of.

'Tinned peaches?' she suggested hopefully.

But Mr Kift shook his head. 'No, thank you, a cup of coffee will be fine.'

Olive looked in horror at the huge pot of tea she'd just made and scurried over to reboil the kettle. 'Milk? Sugar?' She smiled sweetly.

This time he nodded. 'Skim if you've got any. I've brought my own artificial sweetener. Learned from other property visits. Not a staple in the bush.' He chuckled.

Olive laughed more than the bank manager's joke warranted, meanwhile panicking inwardly about the skim milk. Sam had just stirred the milk in the jug with a fork and the thick layer of cream floating on top had dispersed. The house cow made particularly creamy milk.

While she was still deciding what to do, the bank manager, eyeing the cream-laden scones, relented. 'Oh, what the heck, maybe just one.'

The tide had turned. As he chatted genially, Mr Kift ate scone after scone, opening the floodgates for Olive to confidently serve his coffees with the rich creamy milk. The more scones he ate, the better his mood became, and Olive noticed triumphantly that he stirred a heaped teaspoonful of sugar into his third cup of coffee. But it was clear that Sam wasn't enjoying himself. He'd never developed the art of idle chit-chat. And where were Alice and that larrikin of a Jeremy? They'd promised to be back in time for the bank manager's visit.

At last she heard the rattle of the paddock ute driving into the yard. Soon after, the two came up the stairs in a hurry. 'I'll teach that mangy cocky to swear if it's the last thing I do,' she heard Jeremy saying as he pulled off his boots outside the door. Then the young pair burst into the kitchen in their sweaty socks.

Olive looked at Alice in dismay. She was wearing one of Sam's shirts and her baggiest pair of jeans. Curls had escaped from her single plait and stuck out madly below the hat line, above which her hair was flat and plastered to her head with perspiration. Olive Day's granddaughter had come to meet with the bank manager wearing soiled men's work clothes and with hat hair.

Alice ran to the sink to have a wash before shaking hands with Mr Kift, who stood up in greeting.

'She could grow potatoes under her fingernails,' Olive noted.

Alice began by apologising profusely and explaining the delay. They had been trying to chase a fence-crawling bull back into the right paddock when the ute had become well and truly bogged.

'Did you get him back where he belonged?' Mr Kift wanted to know.

'The bugger got away on us,' Jeremy answered. He sat down without washing his grimy hands and picked up a scone. After putting the whole thing into his mouth he went on thickly, 'The horny old rogue liked the look of those young heifers through the fence too much. Not too stoked about being shoved in with those clapped-out old breeders where Sam put him. Can't say I blame him.'

Olive clasped her hands in horror. How had Jeremy O'Donnell ended up at their meeting with the bank manager? But Mr Kift gave a hearty bellow and sat back down too, picking up another scone.

Olive spoke quickly to prevent Jeremy from elaborating further on the bull and his desires. 'Well, you're here now, Alice, so let's get down to business. I'm sure Mr Kift doesn't want to be stuck out here all day.'

'Bet he does.' Jeremy used the back of his hand to wipe some cream from the side of his mouth. 'Reckon it'd beat being stuck in some carpeted office shuffling blooming papers.'

'You're quite right there,' Mr Kift agreed.

Olive looked from one to the other in surprise. Incredibly, Mr Kift was responding positively to Jeremy.

'However,' the important man went on, 'I do have to drop in on two other stations today, so Mrs Day is correct, we'd better get on with it.'

Mr Kift moved his plate and cup aside and opened his laptop on the table. The others waited with an anticipation that was slightly tense. Even Jeremy kept quiet. Mr Kift studied the screen with a frown and cleared his throat.

'Ah, yes. Redstone.' He looked up at Sam, his face serious. 'Mr Day, the bank has tabulated the performance of this station over the last five years, as well as we could with the limited statistics you've given us over time. It seems that this station is, er, struggling to remain profitable in today's climate. We need to look at some possible strategies to improve its performance.'

'You mean you're going to drop us?' Sam's voice trembled a little.

'Now, Mr Day, don't go jumping the gun. This is just a review. We'll give it another six months, and then I'll need you to come and touch base with me in Emerald. Six months after that, I'll come back out here again.'

'Holy hell, the bastards are gonna be on your case from now on.' Jeremy looked sympathetically at Sam.

'Mr Kift,' Alice spoke up, 'we've been working on a whole host of new ideas for Redstone. If you have the time now I'd like to run through them with you. I'm confident that we can greatly improve the productivity of this place.'

'Yes, Alice, but you forget that all these blooming plans of yours are gonna cost a bomb.' Sam's voice had a high note of despair. 'We need more expenses like a hole in the head.'

'Not necessarily.' Mr Kift spoke quickly. 'The bank may fund certain developments if they're needed for the long-term viability of one of our investments.'

'*Your* investment? Is that how you vultures look at it?' Jeremy snorted.

'We're a bank, not a charity, Jeremy,' Mr Kift said calmly.

'Well, we're not a charity case,' snapped Olive.

Alice got up and went into the office, where they heard the computer start up.

After a session in the office of looking through Alice's calculations and lists, Mr Kift appeared well pleased.

'Here's a printout of everything for you, Mr Kift. It includes all the projected figures as well.' Alice handed him a crisp manila folder and he gave her a congratulatory smile.

'I have a strong feeling that Redrock is on the road to recovery,' he said.

'Red*stone*, mate,' put in Jeremy. 'Better get it right before you bleed the place some more.'

Alice elbowed him in the side and Olive glared at him. 'I'm sorry about the manners of our employee, Mr Kift,' she said sternly.

'Don't apologise, Mrs Day. If what Mr Day says about him is true, then he's worth putting up with.'

'Jeez, that's bloody decent of you to say so, sir.'

'You two young ones will have your work cut out for you over the next couple of years.' Mr Kift waved his hand at the computer screen, then turned to lead the way out of the office.

Jeremy followed close on his heels. 'You're not wrong there, mate. It's just lucky that Alice here is such a bloody good sort, otherwise I'd've thrown in the towel by now.' Jeremy winked at Olive, who had gasped involuntarily, and Mr Kift roared with laughter as he walked back out into the kitchen.

Olive gave the bank manager a corned-beef sandwich and some more of the scones for the road. He drove away with a wave and a smile. Sam excused himself and went to lie down, while the others went about their various tasks with a spring in their step for the remainder of the day.

Chapter 11

Jeremy pulled up sharply in front of the main house, a load of gidgee fence posts he'd cut that day in the back of the ute. The cloud of dust from his tyres drifted up the veranda steps and made its way into the kitchen, where it hung for a while in a shaft of late afternoon sunlight. Olive frowned in annoyance as she watched the particles settle on the floor, which was still damp from a recent mopping.

Sam, sitting at the table with his paper and cup of tea, eyed the full load of posts through the open door with pleasure. 'He's a hard worker, that kid.'

'Well, for someone who was in such a hurry when he pulled up, he's managed to find the time to stickybeak.' Olive could see Jeremy still sitting in the ute, looking over to the yard where Alice was engaged in conversation with a young man.

'Why don't you sit down to chop those onions, Liv. Give your old legs a rest.'

'My legs are fine, thank you, Samuel,' Olive snapped.

'Nothing wrong with your eyes either,' Sam muttered, turning the page of his paper as Olive leaned forward to peer again at the pair near the yard.

A cocky tread on the wooden steps eventually heralded the entrance of Jeremy. He stood in the doorway looking extremely grubby. 'Afternoon, all.'

'Come in and sit down, mate. There's tea in the pot. Good effort for one day's work.' Sam indicated the gidgee posts with a wave of his cup.

'Cold beer would go down nicely.' Jeremy grinned at Olive's disapproving face. 'Don't worry, old girl. I'm taking off me boots.'

Sam poured him a cup of tea and pushed the biscuit jar towards him.

'Ta.' Jeremy dunked his ginger biscuit, took a bite then started to speak with his mouth full. 'I see Clive Lonergan's truck over at the yard. New bull come today?'

'Yep.'

'Thought you were picking him up tomorrow.'

'That was the plan, but Clive rang this morning to say they'd deliver.'

'Bit out of their way, isn't it? Is that one of his ringers talking to Alice?'

Olive jumped in. 'No, that's the Lonergans' eldest son, Walter.'

'What, Wingnut Wally? Is he old enough to drive?'

'He's nineteen. Six months older than Alice.'

'So, is he doing a line for her or what?'

'They often have a chat after church. He seems quite keen on her. Not that it's any concern of yours.' Olive continued with her chopping.

'Bloody hell, a bible-bashing bull breeder with big flappers. Not a feature you wanna breed on in your great-grandkids.'

Sam's newspaper shook with silent mirth, but Olive turned to glare indignantly. 'At least Walter has some manners. And he's very handsome, even if his ears are on the large side.'

'Good old Ma, make the best of a bad job. Might go along with extra-good hearing, I guess. That's always handy in the bush.' Jeremy winked at Sam.

Olive halted her chopping, turned to face Jeremy and put her hands on her hips in exasperation. 'I'll have you know that Alice is more interested in what's inside a person than what's on the outside. *She* knows not to judge a book by its cover. What is it you always say, Sam? You just never know what's under a hat.'

Jeremy was unabashed. 'Well, we all know what's under his, they bloody stick out like dog's bal—'

But Olive cut in, with a sharp edge in her voice, 'I think you'd better go now, Jeremy.'

'Good idea, I'll go and give my regards to Wing . . . Wally.' Jeremy sculled his tea and stood up.

'How about you leave that young pair alone, and go and shower off before tea?' Olive was now heartily regretting making him leave.

'Hell, do I stink that bad? Hey, do you reckon Wally's in with a chance?'

Olive sighed, the fight gone out of her. 'With Alice, who would know? She's a dark horse, that one.'

'Tell me about it. I have to work with her. But there's no need to be racist. You of all people, Mrs Day.' Jeremy shook his head melodramatically as he left the room, picked up his boots with a sweeping bow and walked down the stairs in his holey socks.

'Don't say *anything*, Samuel.' Olive returned to her onions and began to chop again with gusto.

§

Jeremy's weekend jaunts to town continued despite Olive's fierce disapproval. But as Sam explained to her, they had no right to hold him there over the weekend. As long as he showed up for work on a Monday at the usual time, it was none of their business what else he got up to. And show up he always did. Sometimes he arrived home late Sunday night and at other times not till dawn on Monday morning. As a rule he was quieter and paler than usual for that day, but he never shirked his duty or avoided pulling his weight. This pattern continued as the weeks went by. Only once did he try to invite Alice to accompany him to town. On Valentine's Day.

As the day approached, Jeremy was well aware that many of the girls in town were nursing a hope that they would be his chosen companion for the special evening. He decided to solve the dilemma by asking Alice. *She* certainly wouldn't be expecting it. He wanted to boost her self-confidence and show her how to have a good time. Jeremy visualised her coy acceptance and her grandmother's mortification. He could also picture the amazement of all the other girls in town when instead of going to the pub to select his chosen one for the evening, he took only Alice for a quiet bottle of wine next to the river.

On Redstone, the day itself passed without fanfare. Jeremy and Alice spent it converting another of the open bore drains. Sam had surrendered to this idea of Alice's relatively easily, having been aware in the back of his mind for some years of how wasteful the open drains were. These structures spilled groundwater continuously into long trenches using the natural pressure from underground. They became overgrown with prickly bushes and roly-poly burr and were a playground for feral pigs. Jeremy and Alice had been systematically replacing them with valved troughs and poly pipe, which meant that the water was refilled only when needed.

Late in the afternoon, dirty and tired, they pulled up in the shed and started to unload the ute.

'Alice, do you know what the date is?' Jeremy began, mysteriously.

'Not sure,' she answered. 'Ask Ma, she always keeps track of it.'

'It's Valentine's Day, you duffer.' He looked at her significantly.

'Oh, I guess you'll be trekking off to town tonight then. Ma *will* be pleased!' Alice laughed.

'Well actually, I thought I might take you with me, Ali. Will you be my valentine?' He waited for a blush and smile, but she didn't even skip a beat in her unloading.

'Very funny, Jeremy.'

He was a little taken aback but not at all put off. They were nearly finished in the shed now and she was about to head over to the house.

'You think I'm joking? Don't think much of yourself, do you, Alice? I'm serious, I want *you* to come with me tonight.' He was more insistent this time.

'So I can sit and watch while you and your friends drink yourselves into a stupor?' She stopped to look at him.

He patiently explained his romantic river plan, at which her voice softened a little. 'That's really sweet of you. But I'm going straight to bed as soon as I've had tea.'

Jeremy wasn't overly concerned. He should have known she'd be all prim and proper to start with. So all he said was, 'I'll pick you up in forty minutes.'

At the stated time, instead of waltzing in through the open kitchen doors as usual, Jeremy went around to the front door, which no one but the bank manager and stock agents ever used. He knocked smartly, wondering if Olive would open it to lecture him on Valentine's Day protocol. After a pause it swung open, and there stood Alice, comfortably clad in her pyjamas, her hair wet from the shower. She reminded him of a sleepy child, looking up at him with her large eyes, little wet ringlets in front of her ears. She looked a little guilty.

'Jeremy, you didn't really think I was going to come with you?'

'Well, yeah, actually, mug that I am.' He looked at her sulkily. Then he added, 'I can wait if you wanna chuck some clothes on.'

'I meant it when I said I was going to bed.' She spoke quietly but firmly.

Jeremy felt a wave of hurt anger go through him. The fact that he knew it was unjustified only made him more annoyed. 'Do you realise that I could ask any other girl in town and they'd fall over themselves to come out with me?'

'That's good then. Why don't you go and do that, and let me go to bed?' She smiled up at him kindly.

He was flabbergasted. To ease his indignation he replied roughly, 'I'll tell you what I'm gonna do. I'm gonna get pissed, and then I'm gonna find meself a gorgeous sheila.' He stopped to assess the result.

Alice was examining his face with a musing, distant expression, her head slightly cocked as though studying a portrait. Jeremy tried to read the expression. It certainly wasn't the shock he'd been hoping for. He had a horrible suspicion she was actually pitying him. This girl was maddening.

'A real hot sheila with a set of nice hooters,' he added for extra effect.

With this final sting he looked down at Alice's flat chest under the faded purple of her thin cotton pyjamas. All at once he was reminded of the swathes of winter mist that used to cling to the small conical hills he'd seen from his bedroom window as a child. Unearthly.

'Now I'm really losing the plot,' he cursed himself internally.

Alice followed his gaze and looked down at her own chest. 'Good,' he thought. 'I've hit a sore point.' He searched her face again for the hurt he expected to see there. But as she raised her lashes, he was startled to see eyes dancing with laughter.

All she said was, 'I'm surprised you wanted *me* to come out with you then.'

Her amusement was infectious and he found himself grinning stupidly. Her absence of vanity baffled and disarmed him.

Then all at once he found himself looking at the faded ornate timber design on the outside of the closed door. Soundlessly she'd gone. She was infuriating. Bewildering. Enough to drive a man to drink. A man – or a foolish boy? Why did she make him question his manhood and feel like an insecure child? King Jed, renowned rodeo clown, life of the party. Hunky Jed, every girl's favourite. And he'd been turned down by shy Alice Wilson.

Chapter 12

It was mustering time at Redstone. Weaning and branding were a little late this year. With Alice and Jeremy both there, Sam had been concentrating on replacing large stretches of fencing and repairing the many sets of yards.

Alice could see that her grandfather was more pleased by the day with Jeremy's ability to turn his hand to whatever was required. In particular, his knowledge of machinery was an enormous boon for the place. Working with machinery wasn't Alice's strong point, and her grandfather had never been keen on it either. Consequently, the maintenance on the Redstone equipment had often left a lot to be desired.

Jeremy was also an excellent welder and knew how to wield an oxy torch. Clearly feeling deprived of most of his usual pursuits, he'd begun to use his spare time tinkering in the shed and getting the tractors, grader and dozer back up to scratch. Sam decided to give some of the funds they would have usually spent on call-out mechanics to Jeremy as a bonus. It took a lot of persuading to make Olive relinquish the money, convinced as she was that he'd blow it all on grog or worse. But Sam was adamant.

They were all finishing off their bread and butter pudding at the big old kitchen table when Sam handed Jeremy an envelope with a few crisp fifty-dollar notes inside and explained what it was for. Alice saw Jeremy flush with surprise and embarrassment.

'Jeez, folks, thanks,' he stammered. 'Not a bad reward for a bit of fiddling with boys' toys.'

'You're a real asset to this place, Jeremy.' Sam looked at him earnestly. 'And it's only right you should know that.'

Alice waited for a boastful wisecrack from Jeremy, but it never came. Instead he flushed again with pleasure at her grandfather's words and fiddled awkwardly with the envelope in his hand.

'He's never been praised before,' thought Alice. 'At least, not for something that matters and by someone he respects.'

§

Alice had been right in her assessment. Jeremy's father and older brothers had never been overly encouraging. It wasn't the culture of their family to give praise. Silent lack of criticism was the best to be hoped for, as it indicated that no mistake had been made. To make matters worse, Jeremy's cocky, upbeat nature had always annoyed his father, who believed that for his own good he needed to be regularly brought down to size.

At Redstone, away from his father's criticism and negativity, Jeremy had discovered that he felt much more motivated. Sam was so grateful for everything he did and impressed each time he discovered a new skill that Jeremy possessed. The long-overdue maintenance jobs he'd been doing with Alice were giving Jeremy enormous satisfaction: there was variety in the work and a great deal to show for it at the end of each day. And Alice's quiet companionship was like a balm on his lively nerves. With Alice, Jeremy could relax and excel.

But by late March the mustering couldn't be delayed any longer. Alice had noticed weeks before that some of the weaners were nearly as tall as their mothers. The day after Jeremy received his bonus, he and Alice shod the horses and loaded the utes with all the branding gear. Dan, Mushgang and Stretch were lined up for the duration and they arrived in Mushgang's truck in the late afternoon.

Alice met them at the yards on the motorbike, her dogs greeting the trio excitedly. Stretch groaned as he lowered himself gingerly out of the truck.

'Back still no good?' asked Alice sympathetically.

Stretch shook his head. 'Getting shook up in Mushgang's bloody old rust bucket doesn't help,' he said crankily. He lit up a roly cigarette and leaned on the gate while the other two led the horses out of the truck and into the small night paddock next to the yard.

Alice noticed a new horse along with the regulars. She stood next to Stretch and watched the horses as they walked the boundary then dropped their heads to crop the grass. All except for the new mare, who paced up and down the eastern fence line, head and tail high and nostrils flared.

'Mushgang's.' Stretch nodded his head towards the newcomer. 'S'posed to be a nutcase.' He puffed contentedly.

'Why did he bring her?'

'His mate Wazza was gonna shoot it, but he paid some shonky dealer three grand for it. Supposed to be a registered Arabian. Sire is some endurance champion from the United Arab Emirates. Got papers, the whole works. Mushgang said he'd take her and try her out.'

'Has he ridden her yet?'

'Not yet. Had enough caper just getting her on the truck. He's got rocks in his head. Needs to face up to it: he's past it. We all are.'

For a moment Alice continued to watch the shapely dark brown filly repeat her agitated course. She looked to Alice like a sculpture in motion. Turning back to Stretch, Alice said, 'Being strong and fast isn't everything. Who says you're past it? I don't know of anyone with more experience in cattle work than you.' Alice had always loved Stretch. He often reminded her of a Russell Drysdale painting in his dusty clothes, with his weight so insufficient for his height. Looking at him now she noticed the old man seemed even more dishevelled than usual. Also, it wasn't like him to be down in the dumps.

'Well, I'm giving it away after this muster.' He forced out the words.

'Oh, Stretch, what will you do?'

'I don't need much money now that the missus has shot through. The kids are all set up down south, they don't need me no more. Henry Finlayson wants me to caretake for a while at Blackwood Downs. I'm still plaiting whips and there's a demand for the smaller roo-hide ones, for kids and that. Don't go worrying about me, Alice.'

'Has Jill really gone for good? She's done this before, hasn't she?'

'Ain't coming back this time, love. She's found another fella and they're – what's the blinking word? – grey nomads.'

Alice patted his arm comfortingly, her eyes full of the sorrow she felt for him. And at the thought that this would be his last muster on Redstone. She'd miss old Stretch. For the first time she wondered what his real name was. She was on the point of asking when her grandmother rang the dinner bell on the veranda and everyone headed towards the homestead.

§

It was breezy and cool the next morning. Alice was out of bed before dawn.

'Good day for branding,' her grandfather commented at breakfast.

They were starting with the paddocks closest to the house so they set out on horseback from the yards. Alice looked at Mushgang's new horse doubtfully. Before they had gone half a kilometre the Arab mare had shied repeatedly, spun and finally bucked in earnest. Mushgang rode the buck until his brittle old girth strap snapped and he was flung several metres, landing hard in the dust, still seated in the saddle. Its tail high, the fiery creature thundered away and out of sight. Alice leapt off her horse and ran to Mushgang. Although in his sixties, the ringer was still an exceptional horseman, trained as a boy by his father's Aboriginal stockmen. His real name had been forgotten long ago and he had taken instead the one given to him by his Murri nanny. Alice had always thought of him as an uncle, and knew that in recent years he had been suffering greatly from arthritis. Now Alice sat with him and made him have a drink from her saddle bag.

'I'll be fine after a bit of a blow,' he insisted, resting in the shade while Jeremy trotted back to the yards to get the ringer's other horse and a spare saddle. Once he was mounted again, although his face was still a ghastly grey, his usual good spirits returned and the rest of the day went without a hitch.

§

Despite complaining about Rita, the 'pensioner' horse he'd been given again to ride, Jeremy thoroughly enjoyed the day. It was very different to mustering with his father and brothers, which always involved a lot of shouting, galloping, barking dogs and cracking whips. By contrast, the four old men and Alice hardly raised their voices at all except to communicate with the dogs. The only yapping came from Ace.

However, the stout canine soon discovered that barking wasn't the go on Redstone and hung insecurely near Jeremy.

Jeremy watched Alice with admiration. She was in her element. She rode lightly and didn't appear to be giving the horse any aids. Yet Bingley changed direction or speed exactly when required. With an uncanny ability to predict what the cattle were going to do, Alice was always in position or sent a dog before any real trouble occurred. Back in the yard, too, the cattle flowed smoothly and the men weaved around each other without conflict. There were no flying accusations or arguments.

'So what do you think of my new employee?' Sam asked the three ringers at morning smoko. They were all sitting in the shade of some kurrajong trees on the far side of the yards, away from the bellowing of the calves that had just been weaned.

'Hope old Sam's paying you double,' Dan remarked by way of answering, lifting his hat and wiping his sweaty bald head with his handkerchief.

'Knew what he was doing when he took you on, I reckon,' Mushgang added.

'Yeah, I can retire with a clear conscience now, thanks, mate. Worth three of me – on one o' my good days,' said Stretch.

They all laughed and Alice beamed her congratulations at Jeremy. It was her smile more than anything that made his chest swell with pride, and he couldn't help grinning back.

'Stop it, the lot of you,' he said. 'All this talk'll swell me noggin. I wanna be able to put me hat on again before we go back out in the sun.'

They munched on Anzac biscuits and sipped tea in silence for a few minutes.

'What're you gonna do about your filly?' Dan asked, looking at Mushgang.

'You mean that cow of a horse or me missus?' They all chuckled again. Mushgang went on, 'She can keep running to China for all I care. I'm just glad she ditched my saddle, otherwise I might've bothered to try and track her down.'

With smoko over, Jeremy went to fix one of the slide gates while Alice and Sam took the first lot of cows back to their paddock. He watched them leaving with a smile. The Bennet sisters had their work cut out for them. A few cranky cows repeatedly tried to break back to their weaned calves, which were still locked in the yard. Ace, who had tagged along, came into his own at this point, showing the Bennet ladies how to use a bit more clout.

On their return to the yards half an hour later, Alice and Sam were trailed by the disgraced filly, who seemed to be trying to look inconspicuous. Mushgang ran her through the gate on his other horse.

'Hey, Jeremy, you're the buck-jump rider. Why don't you have a crack at her?' he suggested.

Jeremy suspected that Mushgang was joking, but he wasn't one to refuse a challenge. By the time Dan and Stretch were mounted again, he'd cornered the animal and saddled her.

He hunted her round and round the small forcing yard, then mounted her and bulged her some more. The others watched, and Jeremy noticed that Alice was looking dubious. Eventually, on Jeremy's signal, Mushgang opened the heavy wooden gates and the pair exploded from the yard. The agitated filly had already developed a lather of foamy sweat on her dark belly and flanks, but by the time she'd finished bucking she was wet all over and trembling. However, she hadn't been able to shake Jeremy. They all set off for the next paddock to be mustered, Jeremy still on the Arab mare. Now she walked like a zombie, completely dominated.

They mustered Hazelbrae, and Jeremy was on top of the mare at every moment. His heavy-handed control kept her in line and they yarded the cattle smoothly. While they were eating lunch, Sam told them that he wanted to draft some fat, 'empty' cows out of the mob waiting in the cooler. Anything that wasn't in calf had to be culled. Jeremy and Alice went to get their horses, leaving the older men sitting in the shade.

Bingley was loose in the little side yard, but the mare was tied securely; judging by the state of the reins, she had obviously been pulling back. She stood frozen and rigid as Jeremy approached, then, fast as lightning, spun her rump towards him and kicked out, high and hard, double-barrelling with her rear feet. He felt the wind of her hooves passing his ear as he jumped back out of the way. The second time he approached more warily, a short piece of poly pipe in his hand, but she attempted nothing further.

She saved her next bucking session until they were out in the cooler trying to draft off the fats. Again she was unsuccessful, but even once she'd given up on trying to dislodge Jeremy, her erratic, jerky movements stirred up the cows. This made Alice's job of blocking all but the required cows at the gate nearly impossible and the drafting process took longer than it should have.

By mid-afternoon the last little calf had been branded and the last big calf weaned from its mother. The sound of bellowing was deafening as the cattle called for their lost loved ones. Sam left Alice and Jeremy the job of returning the cows to Hazelbrae, and the four old men hobbled from the yards back to the house, each nursing his own set of aches and pains. Alice watched them go, a look of disappointment on her face. She explained to Jeremy that the slow dusk ride had been her and Sam's special tradition. She'd never done it without her pa before.

'Jeez, and I'm not much of a replacement,' Jeremy said.

They mounted their horses for the last time that day, Jeremy back on Rita. Both rode in silence, enjoying the satisfaction that comes from a good day's work. They had mustered, branded and weaned two paddocks in one day, a feat that hadn't been accomplished in recent years. Jeremy was aware of a bursting feeling of happiness such as he'd never experienced before. He tried to put his finger on it. Was it from the encouragement and praise he'd received today? The feeling of being valued? Was it the acceptance he felt here at Redstone, without the pressure to perform and entertain? Was it the quiet company of four true old bush gentlemen? Or was it the presence of the girl who was riding alongside him?

He decided he didn't need to diagnose the cause, and broke out instead into a cheery whistling rendition of 'Yellow Submarine'. Alice smiled at him as he finished mid-verse. He smiled back at her and felt his heart pounding in his chest. Alice seemed to shrink a little under the intensity of his gaze and called to Lydia, who was rolling on a dead thing.

'How'd you learn to ride like that, Alice?' Jeremy was genuinely interested.

'Like what? I barely got out of a walk today. I should be the one asking you.'

'You know what I'm getting at. I know a fair dinkum horseman . . . woman when I see one.'

Alice grinned, openly showing her pleasure at his praise. 'It was Eddy.'

'That your dad's name? The rogue stockman?'

'No, Eddy was my first pony.' Alice laughed, then added seriously, 'I've only spoken to my dad once. But Pa says I get it from him – my way with animals.'

'Sounds like he would've been worth meeting. Where is he now, your old man?'

Alice's face fell. 'I don't know. I wish I did.' She looked away and there was a note of sadness in her voice as she went on, 'There's so much I'd like to know about him. Pa says he was amazing.'

Jeremy decided it was time to change the subject. 'D'you train your own dogs? They're bloody rippers. Poor old Ace was out of his depth there today.'

'Those dogs are born knowing what to do,' Alice explained modestly. 'All I do is attach commands to their natural instincts so that I can tell them when and where to do it.'

'I've never had much to do with kelpies and collies. We always had the boofhead kind at home.' He threw Ace a disparaging look. The blue dog had his head poked into a hollow log which was lying on the ground, his chubby hindquarters wriggling with excitement. 'Goes with the type of owner, I guess.' Jeremy tried to keep the bitterness out of his laugh.

'Now, what about you?' Alice asked. 'You were the one doing all the stunt riding today.' She turned in her saddle to look at him and waited expectantly. Jeremy was a little reluctant to explain, but after a pause said, 'My dad's rule was, we only got a saddle once we'd stopped falling off bareback.'

'Wow.' Alice raised her eyebrows.

Jeremy continued, 'And . . . you know how it is. Big brothers think it's a laugh to put their smart-arse baby brother on horses that are way too goey for him. A few broken bones later, you learn how to ride.' He spoke in a flat, matter-of-fact tone.

'Or get killed,' said Alice disapprovingly. She knew Jeremy's five brothers by sight but had never had much to do with them.

Jeremy shrugged. 'It was all worth it, but. If I hadn't known how to stick on a beast I wouldn't have won my most prized possession in the calf riding when I was ten.'

'Oh?'

'Yep. My little leather riding boots. All carved with patterns and that. I loved those boots like nothing on earth. It nearly broke my heart when I grew out of them.'

The cattle flowed through the gate into Hazelbrae and meandered away, some of them stopping just inside the gate to eat. The older, wiser cows had already forgotten their weaners, but the first-calf heifers still looked around anxiously, occasionally bellowing, before eventually dropping their heads to graze as well. Once the cattle were all safely in the paddock, Jeremy and Alice rode home in silence, enjoying the evening glow on a landscape tinctured with colour that it lacked by day. They listened to the soft thudding of their horses' hooves in the dust and the low musical chatter of birds settling down for the night.

§

The old trio, Mushgang, Dan and Stretch, stayed for three weeks, during which time they helped to wean over a thousand calves. From the second day of mustering onwards, there was extra work in the afternoons to deal with the swelling mob of new weaners, who had to be worked through the yards in small groups to be quietened. Round hay bales had to be replaced regularly, and to make their first experience of the yards a pleasant one, Alice also insisted on giving them just a smell of copra meal. By the time they had weaned the large sappy calves and branded the few out-of-season ones, the old men were usually well and truly done in, so most days it was left to Alice and Jeremy to return the cows to their paddocks and work the weaners in the late afternoons.

After the first few days, Alice began to let some of the weaners out into one of the four 'weaner fields' at daybreak each morning. Her grandfather argued that it was too early for them to be out and that they'd break fences to get back to their home paddocks. But Alice had worked them thoroughly in the yards and was confident that if she yarded them again at nightfall, they would benefit more from the tailing and dog work in the paddock than they would from being confined in the yards.

'Happy cattle gain weight faster, Pa,' she said. 'It's been proven.'

The three old ringers stayed on for a few days after the mustering was finished and spent a good deal of time yarning on the veranda with Sam. Before they left Redstone, Mushgang asked Jeremy if he wanted the Arab filly. Alice pricked up her ears immediately. She'd been watching the horse closely over the last few days. The filly looked nervous, yes, but also highly intelligent. Alice suspected the little mare could be full of potential and wondered what had been done to her in the past.

Jeremy suggested that he could get a good price for her as a buck jumper at the rodeos. But before Mushgang was able to consider Jeremy's offer, Alice surprised them all by asking if she could take the unwanted animal. Mushgang hesitated, and Alice could tell he was worried.

After some discussion, it was decided that he'd take the mare home again for his son Troy to work on for a while. Alice was pleased; she knew Troy well, they were almost the same age and had been childhood friends. She knew he'd be gentle with the filly. Troy had been away at the mines for six months, but the talented young horseman had been utterly miserable there; Mushgang had told Alice that Troy had come to the conclusion he'd rather be broke and happy than cashed up and caged in. He'd just arrived back in town.

'Troy wouldn't be too impressed if a horse of mine harmed *you*, Alice.' Mushgang winked at her. Alice felt the same awkwardness she always did when Mushgang mentioned Troy's feelings for her, and pretended she hadn't heard.

But Jeremy hadn't missed the insinuation. 'Bit sweet on old Ali, your Troy Boy?'

'Oh, just a bit.' Mushgang chuckled.

Chapter 13

Alice's favourite event of the year – the bush run – had come around.

When Sam was a boy the national park that backed on to Redstone had been Crown land. The land had since been preserved because of the patches of rare forest, the spectacular rock cliffs and gorges, and also because of the existence of several sacred and significant Aboriginal sites. But sixty years ago it was in the interest of the government to allow Sam's father to release weaner cattle into the untamed region. The grazing kept the dense bush accessible and helped to control the enormous fire hazard that the area presented. Each year in late April a group of riders and packhorses would venture into the rugged terrain to collect the cattle again. George Day and his Aboriginal stockmen had built four rough huts and holding yards at strategic points throughout the area. The 'bush run' had become a treasured yearly ritual and the nights by the camp fire were filled with yarns and song.

Once the area was declared a national park, however, this all changed. The cattle were forbidden entry and the land grew a huge bulk of weeds and fuel. For ten years it was a constant worry to Sam, then a young farmer, and the firebreaks on the Redstone boundary had to be constantly maintained. Wild dogs, goats, brumbies and pigs also bred up in numbers and began to make their presence felt. Sam repeatedly sought permission to burn areas of the park near his boundary, but for reasons he couldn't fathom it was never granted.

Eventually the bushfire that Sam had been dreading occurred. The national park, the plants and animals were cooked by a fire so fast and hot that it created its own whirling storms of flame. In spite of his firebreaks, Sam lost kilometres of fencing and the winter feed from a third of Redstone.

After this fire, Sam had demanded a meeting with the National Parks department. Another young ranger, higher up the ladder than the one Sam usually dealt with, came to Redstone. He was a practical and sensible man and had experience with fires, having grown up in the high country of New South Wales. He indicated to Sam that if some of his cattle were to 'unofficially' wander into the national park, as they had done in the past, he'd not be prosecuted. So the bush run was reborn, and had continued ever since. It was one of the things Alice had missed the most during her absence from Redstone. Stretch, Mushgang and Dan had done the bush run with Sam during that time, but it was hard on their ageing bodies and now they gladly handed over the honours to Jeremy and Alice. In preparation, Sam oiled the old military packsaddles and checked all the canvas bags and tarps. Alice packed all the provisions and ran in from the Brigalow paddock the two hairy ponies that they used as packhorses.

Alice could tell that the excitement she and her grandfather were feeling had even infected Jeremy, when, on a sunny morning in late April, they opened the gate in the boundary fence and headed into the national park. He was quieter than usual, and Alice wondered whether he was pondering the privilege of his inclusion in the long-held tradition.

The first day they made for the nearest watering points, and it wasn't long before they had gathered a small mob of cattle. Each time they spotted more tracks and manure, Alice sent her dogs, who would swiftly disappear from sight. Once each bitch had found a little group of cattle, she'd begin to bark, holding the cattle there until Alice or Jeremy arrived to pick them up and drive them towards the main mob. Meanwhile, Sam and Ace stayed with the herd and the packhorses. Jeremy commented to Alice on her grandfather's intricate knowledge of every rise and fall of the land, and his ability to predict where the cattle would be found. He was also impressed by the Bennet sisters and the way in which they performed their role as scouts.

The first night's camp was up a deep gully. As they rode towards it, Alice looked with fondness at the familiar spot. There was no hut or yard here but they could push the cattle up to the head of the gorge where water seeped out of the hill most of the year. They set up camp below the cattle, effectively holding the mob in the enclosure made by the steep rock sides. Alice strung a rope high between two trees and tied Rita to a ring attached to it. This allowed her to walk freely along the length of the rope and reach just low enough to graze without getting tangled. Alice 'nightlined' one of the ponies in the same way, then turned the other horses loose. They wasted no time dropping their heads to crop the sweet untouched clumps of kangaroo grass.

Jeremy, who had built a fire and was collecting some bigger timber, stopped and looked at Rita on the nightline. 'Did my nag draw the short straw?' he asked Alice.

'She's the boss horse,' Alice explained. 'As long as she's here the others won't try to go anywhere.'

Sam looked up from where he was attempting to open a tin with a rusty tin opener and added, 'Mares are a problem if brumbies are about. Stallions can lure them away. They have no use for geldings. Usually kill them.'

Jeremy nodded. 'Dad lost one of his best mares that way when I was a kid. She was spelling in one of the back paddocks and she went off with some brumbies that'd broken the fence during the dry to get to water. He's still looking for her.' He poked Alice in the shoulder with a stick. 'See, Ali, even lady horses like a bit of rough stuff.' He trailed off to find more wood.

Sam shook his head in disgust and went back to his tin.

After a few nights, the smell of camp-fire smoke had permeated all their clothes and gear. Alice loved it. It was the special aroma of the bush run. As night came on, they sat around the fire and talked in soft voices. Alice had always noticed that her grandfather spoke more by the fire on the bush run than anywhere else.

On the first night, Jeremy had produced a flask of rum, swigged on it, sat back and sighed, 'This is the life.' But when no one would share it with him he'd put it away, complaining that it was no fun drinking alone.

On three of the nights they slept in the rustic log huts, herding the cattle into the rickety old holding yards. Alice spent some time alone in her favourite hut. It was a gum slab construction, with a tiny fireplace protruding from one end and a rusty tin roof. Carved into the walls and beams were old initials and words that she traced with her finger. Then she noticed to her surprise some brand-new carvings, and on inspection discovered Jeremy's and her own initials, etched on either side of a love heart. Despite the silliness of the joke, Alice felt goose bumps rise on her skin at the sight of it.

The fourth hut and yards had burned down, so that night and the next, they took it in turns to watch the cattle.

They had mostly fine weather, warm by day and cool by evening. Alice loved listening to the noises of the night: the throbbing song of the crickets and the double hooting note of the mopoke owl, the whirring and screech of bats and the hurrying rustles of the tiny night creatures as they bustled on their way. She felt completely safe and satisfied with the companionship of all the life forces around her and the warmth of the dogs' vibrant little bodies pressed against her. The ever-present munching of the horses in the dark was like a lullaby to Alice, and it was with this sound that she always gave herself up to sleep.

At dawn, the first bird call would slice through the darkness and chill of fallen dew. At this signal, Alice would get up and walk a little distance from the slumbering forms of Jeremy and Sam, and watch for a few minutes as the stars changed shift with the first glow of light in the east. Then she'd share in the exultation of all the singing feathered creatures as they exploded with the joy of the new day.

But then it would be a buzz of activity, rolling swags, stoking up the coals for breakfast tea, saddling the horses and loading up the ponies. By day the bush was full of life as well – they saw kangaroos, wallabies, shuffling echidnas and even the odd koala. Alice revelled in the smells and sounds around her as they travelled the familiar route. The bauhinias were covered in reddish-brown pods that contrasted with the bright splashes of white and pink made by the Major Mitchell cockatoos. Every now and then, one of the riders would intrude into the middle of an extended family of zebra finches gossiping in a patch of long grass.

One day, while she was answering Lydia's summons, Alice witnessed the capture of a wallaby by an enormous wedge-tailed eagle. It swooped out of nowhere and pounded the small marsupial with the weight of its wings to stun it. Then it picked up the immobilised creature in its talons and lifted off again. The sound of the bird's almighty wings beating reached Alice where she watched. On another occasion, her grandfather pointed out a kookaburra with a wriggling snake in its beak; they heard the thud, thud of the snake's body as the bird belted it on a branch.

It was Sam's ritual to read aloud of an evening from Henry Lawson or Banjo Paterson. His quiet voice took on a mellow expressive quality, rising and falling with the pattern of the words. Jeremy complained at first, but Sam told him to count himself lucky that it wasn't Jane Austen.

One night when Sam had just finished reading 'The Ballad of the Drover' by Henry Lawson, Jeremy commented disparagingly, 'Must have been a bit depressed, that fella – the stuff he writes.' He added, 'Needed a good drink, I reckon.'

'He was an alcoholic,' Alice said wryly. 'That's why he died so young.'

'Well, let's have some more of Banjo then. This stuff's getting me down.'

Alice and her grandfather looked at him with amusement. 'Pa, I do believe King Jed is requesting some poetry.'

'It's not as if there are many alternatives out here,' Jeremy chuckled good-naturedly.

A few times, when Sam was really relaxed, he produced an old dented harmonica and played some tunes. Alice found herself becoming teary as she listened to him. Looking at her grandfather in the firelight gave her a sense of time slipping away and of the preciousness of the days that they had left together.

'Normally Ali sings,' Sam explained to Jeremy on one of these occasions. 'Voice like a nightingale. Don't think she will with you here, though. Bit shy.'

'You guessed right,' Alice said in confirmation.

'I sing when I'm tanked,' Jeremy revealed. 'Not sure how good I am, though. Anything seems good when you've got a few rums under your belt.'

'Maybe we shouldn't ruin your delusions by letting you hear yourself sober,' Alice suggested. Sam spluttered on the tea he was sipping and Jeremy feigned disappointment.

On the second-last night, Sam groaned as he sat down near the fire. 'I'm getting too old for this sleeping-on-the-ground caper.'

Alice looked at him with concern as she handed out some plates of tuna, rice and surprise peas. 'I'll give your back a rub after tea,' she promised.

'Alice and I might have to come on our own next year then, what do ya reckon, Ali?' Jeremy said enthusiastically. 'You've taught *me* about Henry Lawson. I might teach *you* a thing or two next time.'

Alice knew it was a harmless jest and didn't rise to the bait. But then she noticed the look on her grandfather's face.

'You shut your smutty trap, boy!' the old man growled, in a voice so unlike his own that Alice jumped in surprise. For the first time she could recall, Jeremy looked chastened.

Then, less aggressively, Sam added, 'Sometimes you go too far with your rot, son.'

As usual, it was always with a sense of sadness that they returned to everyday life two days later. The days of the bush run always seemed somehow enchanted: for a little while the riders would step out of ordinary time and join with the scores of other bush travellers who had ever wandered the vastness and slept under the stars. The ordinary worries of everyday life seemed to fade to insignificance beside both the tiny and the immense rhythms of nature.

Chapter 14

Olive had some unwelcome news for the three weary riders when they returned from the bush run. They sat down at the kitchen table for a late lunch that Olive had prepared. They began to eat in silence; looking around, Olive could see they were all lost in thought. All three of them exuded a contented glow, and she felt excluded from the secret lingering magic of the jaunt. To her the vast reaches of the bush run represented a foreign and uninviting realm and she'd always felt that their special knowledge of this territory was an exclusive, unspoken understanding that Sam and Alice shared. And she could lay no claim to it.

They always returned from that cursed bush run with a dreamy, dangerously starry look in their eyes. Every year, without exception, they seemed so regretful to be returning to *her* world, the comfortable, predictable homestead that was Olive's domain. A primarily social creature, Olive always disliked her solitary week in April, which for the others was the most anticipated event of the year.

And now, just when she was aching for some decent conversation, they all had the hide to sit there quietly, their minds still roving free, back in that unruly, overgrown national park. This time Olive had been relying on that loudmouth of a Jeremy to have something to say, but even he was silently and absent-mindedly devouring his roast beef and pickle sandwich. Well, there was nothing for it but to say something that would bring them back to reality with a thud. She hadn't intended on telling them so soon, but petulance loosened her tongue.

'Samuel, two men from one of those huge mining companies came while you were away.'

Sam's eyes focused suddenly on Olive's face and she saw with a mixture of satisfaction and shame that she'd won his attention. Putting down his cup he swallowed and took a moment to consider her words.

'Mining company?' he said at last. 'What did they want with us?'

'They want to do some exploratory drilling on Redstone, and next door at Eden Station and Glenorchy. There's supposed to be a huge coal deposit under us.' Olive watched as Sam took a sip of his tea, and noticed that his hand was trembling slightly. Now she felt guilty for upsetting him. Alice's eyes were huge with horror as she waited for further details.

'I hope you told the marauding bastards to ping off,' Jeremy said vehemently.

'Well, I did try,' Olive said. 'In more appropriate language, of course. But they said we have no choice. I refused to deal with them on my own. They left, saying they'd be back next week with some paperwork.'

§

The intervening week passed slowly and anxiously for all the folk at Redstone. Then, at mid-morning on the appointed day, a new-looking dark silver four-wheel drive pulled up at the Redstone house-yard gate and two men wearing blue shirts, moleskins, R.M. Williams boots and spotless felt hats climbed out.

Olive made them tea and radioed Sam, Alice and Jeremy, who were replacing one of the cracked concrete troughs in Brigalow. The two men stood politely to greet the three when they came into the kitchen a little while later, their clothes soiled with dark mud. Sam shook hands with them, his eyes full of suspicion. They introduced themselves as Lionel Schuster and Jason Bamph.

They shook hands with Alice, then turned to Jeremy, who put his hands in his pockets.

'No point trying to come over all friendly, fellas, wearing those blooming cowboy outfits,' he said. 'Kicking cow cockies' arses is what you blokes do for a living, isn't it? We all know that's what you're here for. You lot and the government won't rest till you've sent all us farming buggers to hell.'

'Mr Day, is this your grandson?' politely asked Lionel Schuster, the older of the two men.

'No, Alice is my granddaughter, this is Jeremy O'Donnell, my head stockman,' Sam answered.

'Bloody hell, Sam, you never told me I'd been promoted!' Jeremy roared with laughter.

In spite of themselves, the remainder of the company smiled cautiously at one another and sat down at the table.

Jeremy spoke first. 'So what's your game, Shyster? Spit it out then, and you can cut all the fancy talk.' Jeremy had started the ball rolling.

The younger man, Bamph, looked uncomfortable and shifted in his seat, but Schuster calmly ignored Jeremy and looked instead at Sam. 'Mr Day, as we explained to your wife last week, the government has given our company permission to do some exploratory drilling in this region of Queensland. Nine of the holes we need to make are on a coal seam we believe to be running under this property.'

'My property. It's called Redstone.' Sam was burring up now.

Schuster was unfazed. 'Yes, under Redstone.'

'And what if I say no? What if I refuse you access?'

'I'm afraid you can't do that, Mr Day. I'm sure you're aware that under Australian law the minerals under this land are government property. We are legally entitled to do the exploration. The holes are small and inconspicuous, and we will carry out the operation with as little inconvenience to yourself as possible. You're more than welcome to be present at the drilling sites.'

'Crikey, Sam, they're inviting you onto your own place!' Jeremy turned back to Schuster. 'You lot are above all the rules the rest of us have to work under, eh? Poor old Stuey Hammond at Clermont there, got busted for clearing five acres out of an eight-hundred-acre paddock of virgin scrub – wanted to build some yards there two years ago. The fine he got nearly broke him. And now he's been kicked off his place: whole thing'll be a whopping black pit soon. Virgin scrub can go to buggery now they've found coal under it.'

'Outrageous,' agreed Olive, who was replacing the empty teapot with a full one.

'What happens if you find what you're looking for?' Sam spoke softly and slowly.

'Well, at this stage it's only exploratory work. For coal to be suitable for mining it has to be of a particular grade, depth and accessibility.' Schuster paused. 'Mrs Day, I must say I have enjoyed this most delicious cake. I can't recall tasting any better.' He smiled at Olive, but for once she wasn't affected by praise of her cooking and only nodded sternly. Schuster went on, 'We don't want to take up any more of your precious time this morning. We just require you to sign some paperwork, Mr Day, and then we'll be on our way.' Moving his plate and cup, he lifted a portable file onto the table and pulled out a thick sheaf of neatly stapled sheets and an expensive-looking black pen, which he slid across the table to Sam.

Alice had remained tensely silent up until this point, but now she addressed the older man coldly. 'Why does my grandfather need to sign paperwork? You said we have no choice about the drilling, therefore you don't need our permission.'

'You tell 'em, Alice. Bloody good point.' Jeremy sounded impressed.

'Alice, I see you're not just a pretty face,' Schuster said, his smile unwavering. 'But as you say, we don't need permission to drill and this is just a formality.'

Alice looked at him directly. 'If it's so insignificant, then I'm sure it won't matter if my grandfather doesn't sign.'

Schuster looked back at Sam. 'Mr Day, refusing to sign this document will hold things up a bit. You may have this business hanging over your head for longer than is necessary. It doesn't have to be a drawn-out process at all – with your cooperation it can all be finished in a fortnight from today. So if you'll just sign here—'

'Alice's dead right, why the bloody hell should he sign?' Jeremy snatched the paperwork out of Schuster's hand and scanned a few pages. 'You call this English? Here's an idea, why don't I take this wad and use it for—'

'Jeremy, give it back to the men,' Sam interrupted just in time. 'I have no intention of signing anything.'

For the first time, Schuster's smile began to slip. 'Well, I'm afraid we can't leave here today until we've completed all the necessary paperwork. We may be imposing on you a little longer than expected, Mrs Day. Is there any more of that most excellent cake?'

'I won't be signing, not today or any day,' said Sam. 'So it looks like you pair will be sticking around for quite a spell.'

There was a short pause while Schuster considered his next move. Bamph looked back and forth from Sam to his boss. Finally, Schuster spoke again, his tone confidential. 'I'll let you in on a little secret, Mr Day. Your neighbouring landholders have been far more obliging. As a result, I was able to offer them one thousand shares in our company at no charge, in return for their cooperation. I was hoping to be able to make you a similar offer.'

'This old stick is just like Father Christmas, eh, Sam? Just needs a fluffy white beard.' Jeremy sniggered at his own joke.

'I don't want shares in any damn coal company.' Sam's tone was becoming more hostile.

'Perhaps you're unaware of the value of a share in our company, Mr Day?'

But Sam answered only with a stubborn glare.

Schuster went on, 'Alright, I'll make a special concession just for you. It's going to delay things a little, though. I'll leave this form here for you to peruse at your leisure – I don't think you'll find anything of concern there. Next week our drill team will be on Eden Station to commence drilling. Someone will drop in to pick this up from you then. Please trust me when I tell you that you're not doing yourselves any favours by holding up the process.'

The two men stood up, thanked the Days for their hospitality and departed. From the window, Olive watched them drive away, and shook her head. More worry. Just what Sam needed.

§

Early the next morning, Sam took the paperwork into town to the local solicitor, Fred Campbell.

Fed up with the pace of city life, Fred had come to the area ten years before, bringing his family and business with him, and was now a valued member of the little community and a trusted source of advice. The old cattleman sat silently sipping tea while the portly solicitor perused the fourteen pages of fine print. Towards the end, Fred found what he was looking for.

'Ah yes.' He nodded slowly, then continued to read until the end. At this point he sat back and took off his glasses to look at Sam. 'Most of this is harmless waffle. But here, I've found the sting.' Fred indicated a small paragraph on page twelve. 'By signing this you would be giving the company unlimited access to Redstone without prior notification to you for a period of nine months from the date of the signature. Don't sign. You're not legally obliged to, and without this they'll be required to notify you each time they enter your property if they want to return for follow-up work.'

Sam's eyes were wide as he listened. 'Struth, Fred, I'm glad I came to you.'

'I would also suggest insisting that they obtain a council certificate of proof that any machinery and vehicles they bring onto your place have been thoroughly cleaned of seeds and foreign soils. It's not much, but it's just a little something that you're legally entitled to do. Making it slightly more difficult for them will show them that you're not a pushover.'

'I will certainly do that,' said Sam, getting up and shaking hands with the lawyer. 'Many thanks for your valuable advice, Fred. I'll be bringing you an esky of meat on Sunday.'

'Any time, Sam. Let me know what happens, eh? And refer them to me if they keep pestering you to sign.'

§

During the next few weeks, two separate employees of the mining company were sent to collect the signed documentation. Both eventually left empty-handed. Finally, Fred Campbell contacted the Australian head of the company in Sydney with a complaint, only to be told that the firm had been unaware of the situation.

At last, once the company had obtained council certificates, a small fleet of foreign machinery marched across the face of Redstone. There were two utes, a backhoe, and a large drilling rig pulling a dog trailer. The small gang of men set about boring deep holes at strategic points across the property, and digging shallow pits to contain the water that was extracted from the holes. Jeremy and Alice were required to open gates and move cattle in the path of the drilling crew.

Sam was withdrawn and surly for the six days of the invasion. When at last the geologists declared themselves satisfied with the samples they had obtained, it was with a sense of great relief that all the Redstoners watched the rig departing. In their wake, though, they left a lingering anxiety. Despite all Jeremy's best efforts at inducing them to talk, the drilling crew had been cagey about what they were finding and a fortnight later there was still no word from the coal company. Sam telephoned Lionel Schuster.

The man greeted him urbanely. 'Ah, Mr Day, you'll be pleased to know we're not planning any further drilling in your region for the time being. The coal was very "dirty" – in other words, low grade. It's more suitable for sequestration than mining. Also, the site is too remote to be of any practical interest to us in the short term.'

'The "site" you're talking about is our home and livelihood.' Sam's voice was full of quiet fury. 'My family have worked this land for over a century, Mr Schuster. The Day family settled this spot. This bit of soil turns off some of the best-quality bullocks in the country. Make for better eating than your blooming black gold. You fellas eat beef, do you?'

'Yes, well, as I said, we have no further interest in the property for now. We'll be in touch if anything changes.'

'That's bloody comforting, that is,' Sam said vehemently. 'We have plans for this place, Mr Schuster. Alice has a list of new developments longer than your arm. So do we go ahead, busting a gut trying to improve this place, or are you fellas going to pull the rug out from under us a few years down the track?'

Schuster sighed patiently. 'There is absolutely no cause for panic. We have numerous other sites more attractive to us for development at the present time.'

'Some other poor bugger has been given his walking ticket then. I can only hope that by the time you're ready to dig us up, Australia might've woken up to the fact that they aren't making any more food-producing land. By then, so much of it will have been sold off to foreign investors that a few people might be starting to go hungry. Maybe then they'll back off and let the few mugs that have stuck at this game alone.' With that, Sam hung up.

That night, when Sam went to bed, he lay awake thinking of the 'chosen ones', all the farmers who were unfortunate enough to be situated over 'suitable sites'. The old man's pillow was damp with angry tears when at last he drifted off to sleep.

Chapter 15

It was Sunday morning and Jeremy had woken up clear-headed. It was all wrong. He should have been feeling like death warmed up after a night of partying. And so he would have been if it wasn't for that new bugger of a senior constable.

The long-serving town policeman, Constable Aaron Hill, had recently moved away. A fair-minded and friendly middle-aged officer, Aaron had known when to bend the rules to common sense. His replacement was one Senior Constable Justin Glover, a tall stern man in his late twenties and a stickler for the rules. He had no interest in gaining friends in the town, and Jeremy reckoned he was using his remote placement merely as a stepping stone to greater glory.

Within his first fortnight, Glover had had Jed O'Donnell earmarked. He easily identified Jeremy's weekend drinking routine and habit of heading back to Redstone early in the morning, once he'd sobered up. It wasn't long before Jeremy had lost his driver's licence for being slightly over the limit, three times in a row. He knew Senior Constable Glover would be on the lookout to catch him driving again, so things were looking grim.

Olive was clearly pleased; Jeremy supposed she was happy to have him confined to Redstone and safe from the evils of town. She lectured him about the 'wholesome' forms of entertainment that had been popular when she was a girl. Many homesteads still had the remains of makeshift tennis courts, usually consisting of a fenced rectangle with a playing surface of crushed termite mound. These days, the Redstone tennis court was used as a nursery for the poddy calves, the old netting fence keeping them safe from dingoes. Olive also told him how the young men of her day had ridden their horses for hours, sometimes days, to attend dances at the local halls. Then there were Sunday cricket matches, where batters and fielders ranged in age from the very young to the very old. Some of the high-society ladies had even tried to hold English-style garden parties, complete with bone china cups and saucers and polished silver cutlery.

'Jeez, I wish I was around when you were a girl, Mrs Day,' Jeremy had responded cheekily.

For a few weeks Jeremy hadn't minded the change to his routine. He certainly didn't miss the start-of-the-week disease. But everyone seemed to be occupied on weekends except for himself. Alice was always busy poring over the books in the office, or handling her animals. Sometimes he helped her work the weaners, but she and her dogs seemed to have some sort of telepathy, to the point where he and Ace often felt they were intruding.

Sam had adopted the habit of resting more on weekends, dozing at the table or stretched out in the old squatter's chair on the veranda; Jeremy didn't like to wake him. And, of course, Olive was always busy with some consuming task, doing the books, cleaning, sewing or cooking.

To while away the time, Jeremy began to do some solitary weekend fencing. He also tinkered with the machines in the shed, and even tried doing the morning milking for Olive on Saturdays and Sundays. But the house cow always seemed miffed at the sight of him and never let her milk down properly. Sometimes he went hunting for pigs and other vermin, but these occasions lacked the thrill of his wild pig-chasing weekends with beer-drinking friends. He also began to miss the attention of his girls, his adoring fans who were always so easily impressed.

This Sunday, as he lay there thinking of the day ahead and listening to Alice hosing the windscreen of the 'town car' in preparation for the weekly pilgrimage to church, he came to a decision. He jumped out of bed and pulled on some jeans and a shirt. He'd catch a ride to town. There was bound to be someone still about.

Alice drove and Sam sat in the back with Jeremy. Sitting in the front passenger seat, Olive worked on her crochet, and sniffed with disapproval when Jeremy asked to be dropped off at the pub.

'Come in and get me when you're ready, Alice,' he called happily over his shoulder as he headed for the dilapidated building on the main street.

He swung the heavy door open wide. The Swiss cowbell on the lintel announcing his arrival, he walked in like a conquering hero returning from a crusade, and was greeted as such by a mob of hungover youths who were partaking in the hair of the dog. It was their usual Sunday morning service, and Jed hadn't been keeping the Sabbath. A few of them cheered and he received several congratulatory slaps on the back.

In no time he was seated on his usual barstool with four shouted drinks lined up in front of him. He gulped down two immediately, trying not to notice how dingy the smoky room looked to him now. The place was a dive.

Jeremy sat for over half an hour listening to his mates talk and doing his best to join in. Somehow their usual mindless chatter didn't interest him today. He downed another drink. Nothing worse than being sober in a mob of drunk people.

'Where's Hammerhead?' he asked, looking around for old Martin Hammerli, the Swiss publican. The sight of the calm old man and his quizzical smile was always reassuring. Then he remembered. 'What am I thinking? He never works Sundays.'

The most attractive of the girls, Brandi Hogan, soon began trying to get his attention by kissing the back of his neck and running her fingers through his hair. When this failed, she used the rung of the barstool like a stirrup to mount him. Straddling his lap and facing him, she engulfed him, wrapping her arms around his neck. Then she kissed his forehead, presenting him with her overflowing cleavage.

Then Brandi leaned back unsteadily and put one hand on Jeremy's cheek. The other pressed a cold can onto the nape of his neck. She giggled as he half caught her, preventing the backwards topple. Lurching back towards him, she breathed hot rum and smoke into his face and he looked at the caked and smeared make-up that obscured her naturally pretty features. Her almond-shaped blue eyes were bloodshot. She screeched and wobbled again, then, suddenly serious, looked into his eyes seductively.

'I've missed you, Jeddy.'

Unable to honestly return the sentiment, he said evasively, 'Yeah, it's a dry old camp out at Redstone.'

All the company laughed excessively at his weak jest.

Brandi tossed her long blonde hair and threw back her head, taking a large slurp of her drink. Then, the alcohol still in her mouth, she kissed Jeremy, prising his lips apart with her tongue so that some of it spurted into his mouth and dribbled down his chin. They all cheered.

'King Jed's back!' announced Wombat, triumphantly, raising a beer with his chubby sunburnt hand.

Jeremy half stood, helping Brandi back onto her feet, then bowed to his fans.

'What, you and Brandi leaving already?' Glen asked in mock outrage.

'Don't be too tough on him, mate. I reckon he's been through a bit of a drought out there.' It was Spook, one of Jeremy's boarding school mates. 'Only two geriatrics and that half-black piece.'

There was more laughter, but for once Jeremy was lost for words. The ridiculous irony of it took his breath away – these fools were mocking someone like Alice.

'Who says our Jed hasn't been getting some?' Nev piped up from where he was sitting at the far end of the bar. 'That Alice's pretty hot for a Murri chick.' Melissa and Brandi tittered.

'Don't get me wrong, mate,' grinned Spook. 'I wouldn't turn her down.'

Jeremy remained silent so Spook tried again. 'But Jed could have every girl in town if he wanted, I reckon.'

'Already has, hasn't he?' It was Max, another rodeo clown; Jeremy knew Max resented the way he always stole the show.

'All the *good* sorts, at least.' Wombat elbowed Brandi in the ribs. Brandi laughed along with all the others, giving Wombat a special flirty smile.

Then Max spoke again. 'You're not saying much, Jed. Look at his face. I reckon he's had her! Needed a bit of spice in your life, eh, Jed?' Jeremy could see Max was thoroughly enjoying himself now.

They all roared with laughter again, and Jeremy did his best to smile along with them, but he found he was suddenly nauseous. He sat back down again, trying to look unperturbed. This was all Alice's fault, he told himself. He couldn't even enjoy himself out with his mates anymore. And he was disgusted with himself for not having the guts to defend her – he, Jeremy O'Donnell, the bloke who feared nobody, who said whatever he liked. Jed the fearless was being gutless.

His train of thought was suddenly interrupted by the cowbell over the pub door and there was Alice's silhouette, the daylight flooding in around her little frame. She peered into the gloom, blinking at the sudden contrast.

'Speak of the devil! Hey, Jed, it's your boss!' Max really was in fine form today.

'How was church?' Melissa addressed Alice, giggling.

'Have your ears been burning, Alice?' Brandi asked.

'Can't tell by looking, she's pretty dark all over!' Max roared at his own joke.

'Can't see anything properly anyway in this dim pisshole.' Jeremy's voice was testy.

Alice looked unruffled. She stepped lightly inside and the heavy door banged shut behind her, the cowbell clanging wildly.

'Come and join us for a drink,' Melissa said invitingly. Jeremy saw Brandi run her eyes over the newcomer.

Alice spoke with quiet self-assurance. 'I just came to tell Jeremy that we're heading home now.'

'That's my summons!' Jeremy drained his glass and stood up.

Brandi clung to his arm like a limpet. 'Don't go, Jeddy! Mel and me will drive you back this arv.'

'Thanks for the offer, Brand, but it's two hours each way.'

'We feel like a drive, don't we, Mel? Anyway, there's gotta be somewhere out there where we can crash for the night.'

'Yeah, in Jed's bed!' Spook exclaimed.

They all laughed, except for Brandi, who looked close to tears, and Alice, who was looking out the window.

'Afraid not, Brand. Against house rules.' Jeremy pried her fingers off his arm.

'You've got to be kidding me!' Brandi screeched.

Wombat was sympathetic. 'How much longer do you reckon you'll stick it out?'

'Dunno, mate. Might see you fellas at the rodeo. If not before.'

There was a chorus of raucous goodbyes and another busty embrace from Brandi. As he walked towards Alice, Jeremy was aware that all eyes were on them. He opened the door for her, then stood aside to let her pass through, before following behind her. It was the least he could do.

Chapter 16

Alice and Jeremy were bumping through the paddock on Bald Hill, looking for a bull they had treated some weeks ago for tail rot. At the time they had cut off his tail well above the infected section. Since then, the offended creature seemed to have disappeared, and they were concerned about whether the infection had spread up into his spine.

As they drove, Alice told Jeremy that her school friend Bonnie was coming to Redstone for a long-overdue visit; she promised him that this event would be certain to liven everyone up a little. In former years, the extroverted and slightly eccentric Bonnie had been a regular presence at Redstone. She'd made a tradition of spending a large part of every school holiday at the homestead. During these trips to Redstone, Bonnie had been patiently tolerated by Olive and Sam for Alice's sake. However, during Alice's ag college years, Bonnie hadn't come to stay, and the two old Days had suddenly realised how much they had come to take her visits for granted. Sam even went so far as to say that he missed the crazy girl.

When Alice arrived home from college they had all believed that a visit from Bonnie would be imminent. Unlike Alice, Bonnie had stayed on at boarding school until year twelve and was now launching herself into a course in social work. In true Bonnie style, she'd also committed herself to hours of volunteer work with drug-addicted youths, and as a result she hadn't been able to get away until June.

Now, at last, the long-awaited arrival of Bonnie was on the cards. When Alice told Jeremy, he was immensely pleased. 'A young single bird rocking up at Redstone? Best news I've heard all year! You never let on to me whether she's a good sort?'

'Bonnie is the best and most beautiful person you could ever meet.' Alice answered him without taking her eyes off the rough cattle pad along which they were driving.

'This is sounding better by the minute.' In celebration, Jeremy began to whistle 'Here We Go Round the Mulberry Bush', then paused suddenly, an idea occurring to him. 'Hang on a tick, she's not that hefty red-headed thing I saw in town with you a few years back?'

'Bonnie has red hair.' Alice took a moment to eye him coldly. 'But she's certainly not fat.'

'Not fat, no, but if I remember right, she was built like a brick sh—'

'Jeremy!' Alice interrupted. 'I won't have you criticising Bonnie. And I'm amazed that someone as intelligent as you insists on placing so much importance on what people look like.'

'Hold it right there – did you just call me intelligent or was I hearing voices?'

'You've completely missed my point. If you're rude or inappropriate to Bonnie in any way during her stay, you'll have me to answer to.' Alice glared at him fiercely.

'Oooh!' Jeremy leaned in towards her, grinning and raising his eyebrows infuriatingly. 'I reckon I might like that!'

Alice shook her head in disgust and returned her attention to the track.

He went on cheekily, 'Anyway, I guess I gotta allow for a chance that your red-headed mate could've improved with age. Might've grown into her shoulders a bit by now. I'm not one to judge before I've even eyeballed a lady.' To his disappointment, Alice maintained a dignified silence.

A few moments later, they both spotted a large form lying in the grass about two hundred metres away. 'That'll be old AWOL,' Jeremy said.

But as they came closer, they saw that it was only a cow. Alice parked the ute and they walked over. At first the animal appeared unharmed but the stench of rotting flesh told them otherwise. The cow was still alive, but very weak. On closer inspection they discovered she'd been attacked by dingoes. The only part of her body that had been bitten was her udder, which had been almost completely torn away.

Alice was so overcome with pity for the cow that she failed to notice Jeremy, whose face had turned distinctly green. She looked up to see him striding a short distance away, retching violently and finally vomiting. She hurried to join him. 'Jeremy, are you alright? I'll get you some water.'

'Bastards.' Jeremy spat some saliva into the grass. 'The least they could do is finish her off and eat her. Must've just been pups playing, to maul her like that and go away.' He took out his checked hanky and wiped his mouth. Alice handed him the water bottle and looked at him in surprise. She hadn't expected him to be so affected by something of this sort.

Without further delay, they got the rifle from the ute and shot the cow. Then Jeremy, breathing through his mouth, used his large hunting knife to cut off some slabs of meat for the dogs.

They climbed back into the ute and continued on their way through the large paddock. Just as they were about to call off the search, Alice spotted the bull standing in among some prickly currant bushes down in a gully. He was all on his own. As they drove down towards him, Jeremy groaned. The bull's rear end was a mass of black blowflies. The infection had obviously taken hold and crows had cruelly pecked his wound and enlarged it beyond repair. Alice climbed out and hurried over. The bull let her come quite close and she spoke to him soothingly, her eyes filled with tears. Jeremy came over with the rifle and shot the unfortunate creature between the eyes. They stood looking down at the enormous body of the bull, limply distorted in death.

Alice sighed, relieved that the bull was out of its misery. 'He was a good bull, that one,' she said. 'Nice quiet temperament. We've only had him for a couple of seasons.'

'Better cut some meat off him then, too,' Jeremy suggested. 'Might seem less of a waste to the old bloke if the dogs get some burger meat out of him.' Alice watched Jeremy work. She had seen a new, more compassionate side to him today.

§

As Bonnie's visit approached, Alice was filled with a growing excitement. Over the last few years she'd sorely missed spending time with her best friend. Bonnie had always been such a source of strength for Alice. The night before Bonnie's arrival, she lay awake thinking back to her schooldays with the enthusiastic red-head. It was only when Bonnie had arrived on the scene that boarding-school life had become bearable for Alice.

Following that nightmarish first term in Brisbane, thirteen-year-old Alice had found it very difficult to go back after the short Easter respite at Redstone. Her grandfather had driven her to meet the bus at Emerald, his own heart bleeding at the sight of her serious, resigned face and dejected posture as she walked towards the waiting coach. If only Alice had known at that moment in time that she was about to meet Bonnie.

Bonnie was the new girl, a little newer than all the rest. She arrived on the first day of term two, amid rumours that she'd already been expelled from another reputable private school. Their form mistress stood with her at the front of the class and introduced her as Bonita Russell. She was tall and squarely built with frizzy ginger hair and a laughing open face that flushed red at the slightest provocation. Standing there before all those staring faces Bonita had looked around defiantly, as if challenging anyone to disapprove of her. Finally her green eyes met Alice's brown ones and Alice gave a quick reassuring smile. The affinity between them was forged instantly.

Their first class together was English, and Bonnie plonked herself down next to Alice saying, 'I hear you've got brains. Maybe I can copy your work?'

They both laughed and Alice felt a stirring of warmth in her frozen little heart. But the happy moment was interrupted when in walked Jacinta Foster and her entourage.

'Well, look what we have here. Bouncing Bonita is hoping to catch some of little Brownie's tan. You want a bit of colour on your pasty freckled face?' Jacinta grinned around at the others.

In one fluid motion, Bonnie stood up and swung a punch. Jacinta found herself on the floor with blood streaming from her nose.

'Nice to meet you too,' was Bonnie's cheery reply as she sat back down. 'Have some colour for *your* face.'

Bianca fussed over her friend, pressing a clump of tissues onto Jacinta's nose and inadvertently muffling her cries of 'Assault!' and

'I'm suing!' Jacinta quickly pushed away the tissues and shrilled, 'I want something done about this! My dad will make sure that you're expelled!'

'I didn't see what happened, did you?' said one of the other students, a girl called Melody. (Alice had helped Melody with her homework on more than one occasion.)

'No, neither did I,' piped up Gabby, seated at the back of the class.

'Me either,' called Chloe, beside her.

Jacinta's face screwed up in fury as she felt the tide turning against her. She stamped her foot and glared around angrily from behind her tissues. She looked so comical that Alice had to stifle a laugh. This didn't escape Jacinta's notice and her face turned pale with rage. She dropped her tissues and flew at Alice, kicking the front of the old-fashioned desk where she sat. It went crashing over onto Alice's thighs, the heavy steel edge cutting into her muscle.

'Black bitch!' Jacinta screeched, and fresh blood began to flow from her nose. Bonnie leapt out of her seat to confront Jacinta again.

'No, Bonnie!' Alice grabbed her friend's arm.

'It's not worth getting expelled over,' Melody warned quietly.

Nearly blind with rage, Jacinta glared around the room. Bianca hurriedly began shepherding her towards the door. 'I'm going to sue!' the furious girl was still sobbing as she disappeared from view, her face a mess of congealing blood. Strangely, though, the incident passed with no consequence more serious than a severe lecture for both girls in the principal's office.

Over time, Bonnie's antics gained her the admiration of all. She was hot-tempered but courageous, fair and loyal. She liked and was liked by almost everyone, regardless of their standing in the ruthless social hierarchy of the all-girls school.

When Bonnie came to Redstone for holidays she was like a

whirlwind rushing through the quiet establishment. She relished Olive's shocked looks and horrified exclamations and only bear-hugged her in response. She exchanged good-natured winks with Sam and told him wild, far-fetched yarns about the city. She was always inflicting congratulatory slaps on the sinewy backs of the stockmen and telling them how clever they were.

Early in their friendship, Bonnie had revealed to Alice the details of her upbringing. She'd been the unwanted result of a short-lived marriage, and her mother had gone on to have two more children with her second, more suitable, husband. 'My mum doesn't like me all that much,' Bonnie had confessed to Alice during their second lunch break together. 'Can't say I blame her. I'm an absolute cow to her and that anal-retentive husband of hers. That's why I'm boarding even though they live just around the corner.'

Alice was listening sympathetically, aware of the parallels between their situations.

'Even if I was a goody-goody she'd still hate me, though,' Bonnie continued. 'She says I look exactly like my dad. Probably act like him too, judging by her description. Can't say I've ever met the man.'

Bonnie's openness was refreshing for Alice, and the opposite of her own guarded reserve. As time went on, they began to influence one another: Alice found that she was able to steady Bonnie when her temper threatened to erupt. And Alice's personality, withdrawn since coming to Brisbane, began to unfold again under the influence of this vibrant, encouraging friend. With Bonnie by her side, she found new courage to face the daily trials of boarding-school life.

At times Alice wondered whether the special connection she felt with Bonnie also came from the similarities in their family backgrounds. Bonnie, too, had a father who apparently didn't want to know her, as well as a mother who had subsequently married, had more children and would rather she'd not been born. The day that Alice had enlightened the other girl about her own family situation, Bonnie had suggested joyfully, 'Hey, Alice, our mums should meet. I reckon they'd hit it off!'

But over the years that followed, an important difference in their circumstances became apparent: at holidays, Bonnie had to return to a home which held no warmth for her, while through her grandparents, Alice always experienced stability and love.

Now, as a young woman taking on the responsibility of the family property, Alice was beginning to realise just how much she continued to rely on this love and support. And recognising the fact that her grandparents were getting old had only made her cherish them all the more.

Chapter 17

'So *you're* the great Bonnie.' Jeremy was the first to encounter Alice's best friend, as she stepped out of her little green car. She'd pulled into the Redstone shed and parked next to the tractor he was servicing. To Jeremy, the tiny, flimsy-looking car seemed strangely inadequate to contain the life force of the unruly-haired creature that had just emerged from it. He held out his grease-covered hand in greeting.

Bonnie took it without hesitation and shook enthusiastically. 'Yes I am. But there's no need to throw my size up in my face!' They both laughed and Bonnie went on, 'And you must be Mr Solve-Every-Problem Jeremy.'

The two studied each other with the particular curiosity of people who know a great deal about one another, but only through the accounts of a common third party.

'Is that what Alice's said about me, then?' Jeremy asked, intrigued at the thought of Alice talking about him.

'Oh yes, she's always singing your praises. She never told me you were so hunky though.'

Jeremy, although well aware of his good looks, was a little taken aback.

Bonnie saved him from having to reply by rattling on, 'Then again, we all know looks never rate a mention with Al. Seems you've brightened her up a bit. She can be such a serious, dedicated little thing. Needs someone to loosen her up, teach her to enjoy herself. I've been so worried about her, 'cause that was always my job and I haven't been round much in recent years.'

'Alice *does* have plenty of fun in her own way, I reckon,' he said, strangely compelled to defend her against the slight note of criticism he thought he detected in Bonnie's comment. 'It's just that her idea of a good time is a bit different from most people's. And she doesn't always let on when she's having a laugh.'

Bonnie regarded Jeremy with interest. 'Hey, don't get me wrong – Alice's the only reason I'll ever amount to anything. And Mr and Mrs Day, of course.'

'Yeah, they seem to have that effect on people,' Jeremy said quietly, more to himself than to Bonnie.

They were interrupted by the sound of thudding hooves, and a moment later an elated Alice was hugging her friend. Both girls were teary and babbling and Jeremy felt as though he'd suddenly become non-existent. Without paying him any further attention, the two girls left the shed and he returned resignedly to his machine.

As it turned out, Bonnie and Jeremy got along like a house on fire. They egged each other on, taking the Redstone mealtime conversations to formerly unknown levels of outrageousness. Olive became thoroughly worn out with trying to maintain some level of decorum. During her ten-day stay, Bonnie was a constant, exuberant presence at every job they undertook, keen to pitch in and get her hands dirty, but not always using the caution required.

When the weekend arrived, Jeremy invited Bonnie to drive him into town in his ute for some Saturday night action. He was still disqualified from driving, so his motives were a little selfish, and he also faintly hoped to induce a trace of jealousy in Alice by taking Bonnie out on the town. To his disappointment, Alice seemed to entirely approve of his offer to provide some evening amusement for her friend. She waved them off happily, wishing them a wonderful time.

Once in town, he took her to the usual destination. The Swiss cowbell tinkled as usual when Jeremy opened the pub door for Bonnie and ushered her into the din. It was a smoky, merry rabble that met their eyes. Behind the bar, Hammerhead looked up and gave Jeremy a nodding grin. Brandi, Melissa and Veronica stood up in greeting, and Brandi trotted to meet them, taking Jeremy's arm.

Wombat yelled hospitably for two rums, and Spook clapped Jeremy on the back as he pulled up chairs for himself and Bonnie. Brandi promptly perched herself on Jeremy's knee.

'Aren't you going to introduce your friend?' she asked, looking sideways at Bonnie. The group eased their chatter and looked on expectantly.

'Everyone, this is Bonnie. Alice's best mate, up from Brisbane.'

Bonnie waved. 'Hi, everyone.'

The hum started up again as they quietly discussed the newcomer. Nev quizzed her on how she liked Redstone.

A few minutes later, Max sauntered over, his dark eyes curious and a half-smile on his angular face. Jeremy looked up suspiciously.

'Bonnie, I'm Max.' He held out his hand.

She shook it. 'G'day.'

'You don't sound much like a city chick.' He smirked around at the others.

Bonnie jumped to her feet and held her body in an exaggerated posh lady stance. 'You *soooo* need to clarify that comment!' She was speaking in a fast, slightly American, clipped, inner city, career woman accent. 'I think we need to touch base and have some dialogue on this? I can see you have issues. Let me know when is good for you. You can page me 24/7.'

The onlookers whooped and applauded appreciatively, Jeremy loudest of all. Bonnie curtseyed and sat back down. She looked up at Max, who was still standing there, the mirth gone from his expression.

'Come to Brissy sometime, pal. I'd be happy to show a baffled bush boy some back streets.'

'That's the best offer *you've* had in a while, Max,' sniggered Glen.

'Yeah, thanks, don't hold your breath.' Max wandered away.

A few more people had pulled up chairs and were soon enjoying the lively banter with Bonnie and Jed at the centre. Jeremy thought they made a great team, spurring each other on. The wit was flowing freely. Hammerhead threw in his two cents' worth every now and then. The pub was alive and the old barman was in high spirits.

They fell quiet at last and sipped their drinks. Brandi spoke up. 'So you're Alice's best friend?'

'Love her to death. Went to school together. Only passed my exams thanks to Al,' Bonnie gushed.

'Really? I never knew she was smart.' Brandi's voice was sweetly innocent. Jeremy shifted uncomfortably under Brandi's weight, tipping her off his knee.

Then Glen commented, 'Not many of 'em are smart. Only just bright enough to find their way to the grog shop or the servo for some petrol sniffing.' A few people laughed obligingly. Jeremy noticed that Bonnie had started to change colour.

Then Veronica spoke up honourably. 'Glen, not all Murris are like that. I'm sure Alice's no different to us.'

'Oh, she's different to *you* lot, I can assure you of that!' exploded Bonnie.

'Anyway,' Melissa said, 'why didn't she come with you two? We aren't racist or anything. Blacks *are* allowed in here if they're not too feral.'

'Yeah, 'specially the girls. The pretty ones anyway.' This time it was Wombat's attempt at humour. He was rewarded with some hearty guffaws.

Bonnie put her hands on the table and stood up slowly. She looked around at the smiling faces. At the sight of her, some of the closest conversations ceased.

'Is this pub called Redneckville or what?' she blurted. 'Exactly which century are we living in here?' Then she turned and looked at Jeremy, saying clearly, 'You know, Jeremy, I've noticed it's always the scum of the earth who feel the need to really bag the blackfellas. It's the only way they can fool themselves that there might be someone even more pathetic than themselves.' She paused for effect and waved her hand around. 'Look at these useless bits of debris here that you call friends – perfect example. They think they can slam someone like *Alice*. It's hilarious. One day when it's full, someone should roll a grenade into this hole you call a pub, do the world a huge favour.'

'Are you hearing this, Jed?' Nev asked incredulously.

Jeremy felt everyone's eyes on him. He swallowed. 'Yeah, mate, and I reckon Bonnie's about spot on.' He pushed his chair back and stood up beside her. 'Only wish it could've been me that said it.'

There was a stunned silence while the gang processed what had just happened. Jeremy suspected they were more shocked by his single comment than by anything Bonnie had said. But he didn't regret it one bit. Instead he felt a huge sense of relief.

The silence was soon followed by an angry mutter rising to a loud babble as comprehension dawned. Beside him Jeremy felt Bonnie bracing herself to face the angry mob and their flying insults. He could see she was prepared to take them all on single-handedly, and her bravery humbled him.

He grabbed Bonnie by the arm. 'I reckon we might just nip out for some fresh air.' He had quite a battle getting her out of the pub. She resisted, stopping every couple of metres to turn and hurl back obscenities which, Jeremy had to admit, were even more creatively foul than the ones she was receiving.

Once outside, Jeremy pulled Bonnie a little distance from the pub, just in case anyone had the motivation to follow them out. They sat at a rough wooden table at the dark end of the little courtyard. Jeremy listened patiently while Bonnie continued to rant and fume. Finally she paused for breath and to look at a mob of muscled youths who were arriving on the scene. The athletic-looking crew had just carried a half forty-four-gallon drum to the well-lit end of the courtyard and set it down.

'The Warrigals – local rugby team,' Jeremy explained quietly. 'Heading home from the charity match at Longreach – do it every year. Money goes to the Flying Doctors. They'll be dropping off some blokes from here on their way through. This'll be the initiation for the rookies. "Flaming Arses", I'd say.'

Bonnie clapped her hands in delight, all her fury forgotten. They watched while the drum was stuffed with newspaper and sticks. One of the team poured on some fuel and the igniting was accompanied by a hearty cheer. For a minute or two, Bonnie and Jeremy were illuminated with fiery light.

Some of the boys looked up and yelled greetings when they saw Jed. 'Hey, it's King Jed! Didn't join us this year, mate? We were a couple short too.'

Jeremy nodded in greeting at the coach. 'G'day, Webber. Not this year, mate. Done my time.'

The big man shook an accusing finger at Jeremy. 'Bloody shame. Still, can't stand here crying all night. Got things we need to be doing.'

Bonnie and Jeremy watched while a group of six of the youngest and greenest-looking boys were shoved into the middle of a rough circle formed by the others. Each was presented with a tightly rolled piece of newspaper. Then, on the command, they obediently dropped their pants and stood in readiness. They were shuffled into place around the burning drum, their backs facing the flames and their faces staring wide-eyed out into the darkness. The coach told them good-naturedly, 'You can wait for one of us to do it or you can stick 'em in yourselves.'

The boys unanimously chose the latter. Bending forwards slightly, each youth inserted one end of his paper roll and waited.

'Now!' On the command, the rookies backed cautiously towards the flames, jostling each other a little to light up the far end of their newspaper cigars. Then they were off, bare-bottomed silhouettes bounding and whooping in all directions, lighting up the darkness around the pub with leaping flame. As each paper torch burned closer to the sensitive region, the cries became more shrill, before merging with the triumphant cheers of the rest of the team. Bonnie was yelling along with the loudest of them, banging her hands on the wooden table.

The Warrigals milled around with much back-slapping and jubilation, and the newly initiated six eventually returned to retrieve their pants and go inside. The darkness around the pair still sitting at the table seemed extraordinarily quiet in the aftermath. The odd flicker of light was still issuing from the smouldering drum.

'Now *that* was worth seeing.' Bonnie sighed in satisfaction.

'Hasn't been all bad then, our night out on the town?' Jeremy asked.

'Bad? It's been great so far!'

'What about your little blue with my mates in there? Didn't spoil your fun?'

'Hey, there's nothing better than a good blue! Did you see how mad they got? I was just getting warmed up when you dragged me away! I'll do even better next time if I get half a chance.'

Jeremy laughed in admiration. 'You're blooming different, you are. I can see why Alice thinks so much of you.'

'Aw shucks!' Bonnie laughed.

They heard a roar from inside the pub, followed by clapping. Someone was performing for the footy team.

'Where to now then?' Jeremy asked. 'I was thinking I should go in and see old Hammerhead about getting some cheap leg opener and giving it to ya, before we head off somewhere more private.' He looked at Bonnie curiously, awaiting a reaction. But she didn't arc up.

'Nah.' Her tone was flat. 'Don't think it would work – for either of us. What you *really* want is some sort of potion that would transform me into Alice. I can't imagine Hammerhead has anything that sophisticated. And cheap leg opener wouldn't do it for me either. Not when I know you're so wrapped up in my best mate.'

Jeremy was astounded. He stiffened up, concentrating all his energy on trying to look nonchalant. How much could Bonnie see in the dark? This chick was a bloody wildcard.

'Don't bother trying to deny it, King Jed. Anyway, I don't blame you one bit. It's the one thing I've observed about you that proves you've got some brains after all – you falling for her.'

There was a short pause, then Jeremy gave in. 'Righto then, Miss bloody Psychic, do you reckon you can tell how she feels about me?'

'Ah, now that's a different story. My loyalty's not that easily compromised.'

'Might have to go and see Hammerhead after all, to get some cheap tongue loosener,' Jeremy suggested.

Bonnie laughed. 'Won't do you any good either, buddy. I can read Alice better than most people can, but this one's got me stumped. I'm not sure she even knows herself.'

'Knows what? If she likes me?' He was dismayed.

'Whether she should allow herself to or not. Whether she even wants to. That girl's got the strongest head of anyone I know. Don't be deceived by her docile appearance. She's bloody stainless steel when she makes her mind up.' Bonnie spoke with admiration in her voice.

Jeremy slumped in his seat. 'You reckon I should give up on it then?'

'That's your call, mate. Depends how badly you want her. How long you're prepared to keep on trying. Has she taken you to the Brumby Spring yet, in the national park?'

'Yeah. Why?'

'That's a good sign. She has some weird cosmic thing going on with that place.'

'She took me there in my first week at Redstone.'

'Really?'

'She said she trusted me 'cause I had a kind eye.'

'Yep, that sounds like Alice logic.'

They sat in silent thought for a time, then Bonnie went on, 'If it's any comfort to you, I know how you feel. Been besotted with a fella called Brad for the last two years now. He thinks I'm a good laugh, but as far as taking me seriously goes . . . He'd sooner throw himself at these delicate, brain-dead types. You know – the skinny, giggly ones with nice teeth.'

'Hell eh, Bonnie. That sucks.'

'Yeah, it does.' She sagged a little.

'Hold on for a bit, I'll go and see Hammerhead.'

An hour later the pair were parked at the riverbank, incoherently oblivious to their problems. They were sitting in the tray of the ute, Jeremy with his arm around Bonnie, swaying from side to side. They alternated between singing snippets of every sad song they could think of and erupting into bouts of hysterical laughter. They toasted Alice, they toasted Brad, Jeremy's father and Bonnie's mum. They toasted all the people they could remember who had ever caused them pain.

§

They woke the next morning snuggled up together in Jeremy's swag stretched out in the back of the ute. They were covered in dew and sour condensation from the inside of the canvas cover.

'Have I got my clothes on?' Bonnie's words were slurred and dull.

'Yep. And my belt's still done up.'

'Good-o.'

Jeremy made a fire and boiled the billy in silence while Bonnie went to wash her face in the river. He hugged his knees close to his chest as he squatted, staring into the flames. It wasn't just the hangover that was making him feel lousy. Having acknowledged his feelings for Alice, he couldn't go on denying them to himself. And he was shocked at how powerful they were. When had this happened? Hadn't he just wanted to have a bit of fun with the shy little bird?

While Bonnie drove the first few kilometres out of town, Jeremy scrabbled around valiantly trying to find his sense of humour and crack a few jokes. When he was spent, Bonnie made an admirable effort in return. In the end, two grey faces exchanged sickly, defeated smiles and fell quiet. With the glare of the morning sun behind them, they drove on towards Redstone. Jeremy's sore head registered every nauseating bump in the road. But at least they had some time to recover. As they sped along, he gradually began to feel the astringent peace of the dry landscape flowing over him. He lowered his shield for a while and the two of them indulged in unspoken, mutual misery. And were firm friends.

Chapter 18

Alice had never gone in much for rodeos. Her love of animals and aversion to loud raucous noise took away from the excitement of the spectacle. Rather than admiring the amazing skill of the riders in the sandy ring, Alice became transfixed on the provoked bull or terrified horse trying to dislodge the predator it believed to be attacking it. So she wasn't absolutely sure why she offered to drive Jeremy to a local event.

Alice knew that for a few years now, 'King Jed' had been the most renowned bullfighter in the region, and was highly sought after by all the rodeo committees of remote central and western Queensland. At one time, his popularity had risen to such a height he'd become one of the main drawcards at various events. But since starting at Redstone, it seemed that Jeremy's priorities had changed a little and he had only clowned at a handful of closer rodeos. Also, now that he'd been deprived of his driver's licence, it appeared that many more rodeo-goers were set to suffer the disappointment of the absence of King Jed. Alice knew that her grandmother saw this as a positive development, and the older woman didn't hesitate to tell Jeremy so. They were discussing the approaching local rodeo one afternoon smoko.

'It's about time you grew up and stopped taking part in that ridiculously dangerous caper,' Olive stated.

'I'm here for a good time, not a long time, Mrs Day,' Jeremy retorted.

'None of us are really here for a long time,' Sam observed quietly to himself.

Jeremy explained that he'd been booked up for this particular rodeo for many months and, as he put it, a man had to stick to his word. Alice also suspected he'd been secretly hankering after the adrenaline buzz and ego boost that he derived from his combat with the fiery beasts and the adoration of the rodeo crowds. So she offered to be his driver for the occasion. She'd given it some thought and decided that it was the least she could do for Jeremy, after all he'd done for her family and for Redstone.

So one sunny winter Saturday, Alice found herself on the rodeo scene. She'd always felt out of place with this crowd: she didn't possess the necessary look, walk or talk. She seated herself high up on a rail with a bunch of leggy sunburnt kids and listened to their running commentary with a half-smile on her face.

The first two bulls, Black Jack and Executioner, came and went, their riders failing to cling on for the necessary eight seconds. The two rodeo clowns hovered around the sheltering barrel in the middle of the ring and attempted a few token tricks. But once rid of their riders, the bulls hung on the fence without much fight left in them. There were a few lethargic cheers, and a faint spattering of applause. A disgruntled murmur rippled through the crowd at the lack of action. Rodeo audiences could be ruthless. Luckily it was time for the two new clowns.

The third bull, Red Weapon, put on a better show with his rider, a twelve-time champion. When the gate rope was pulled he exploded out of the chute, the cowbell clamouring wildly on the leather kicker under his belly. Red Weapon was a grotesque cross-bred scrubber; he must have been newly brought in from someone's back country and saved from the meatworks for this special purpose. He had a cork-screwing motion, deadly to ride out. Sudden turns and spins added sting to his repertoire. The kicker flew off after the first few bucks but that didn't pacify him. The rider lasted an admirable six seconds before he was flung off to the side, landing heavily and much too close to the whirling back end of the Weapon. The enraged bull swung around to attack.

Enter King Jed. The crowd burst into applause at the sight of their favourite. He was dressed in a proper clown suit, excepting his footwear, which was spiked football boots to give him purchase on the sandy ground. He had an orange curly wig and thick face paint. In one hand was a ridiculous glittering walking cane, and tied to the wrist of the other were two neon yellow pompoms which his arm movements sent bouncing every which way.

With a high-stepping run he approached the bull from the opposite side to the unseated hero and poked him hard in the ribs with the glittering cane. Instantly the bull snapped around to face this new attacker, but was blinded by the pair of huge fluffy pompoms. Snorting into them, he lowered his head and charged. He headed in a straight line away from the rider in the sand, and past Jed's outstretched arm. The other rodeo clown rushed to guard the fallen rider.

Jed cartwheeled then to another part of the ring, where he performed a quick somersault and righted himself, shaking the pompoms and whooping to attract the bull's attention. The bull spun to face him again, gathering his muscles for another charge. Jed turned, dropped his braces, pulled his baggy pants down and bent over, flashing an outrageous pair of stripy bloomers and looking between his legs at the bull. The crowd showed their raucous appreciation. Meanwhile, two more men rushed to the fallen rider and dragged him away.

Jed straightened up, hooked up his braces again and jogged on the spot while the bull ran at him. He waited until it looked as though the bull would surely knock him down; then, at the last possible moment, he dodged to the side, sending the bull careering into the rail. Alice gasped along with the rest of the crowd, before everyone applauded madly. Crazy now with the pain and confusion, the unfortunate animal swung around again and took a few moments to locate the clown.

Jed was taking an exaggerated circular walk around his hand, which was leaning on the glitter cane planted in the sand. His other hand was on his hip, the pompoms bobbing erratically. The crowd roared with amusement and the bull bellowed and charged again. This time, Jeremy had lined himself up with the gate and was through it like a shot, the bull on his heels. Once through, he leapt the side rail and the bull disappeared from view into the adjoining yard. There was an explosion of applause and several cries of 'King Jed!'

Alice felt quite awed at the sight of Jeremy's familiar form in this different persona. She was stunned by the easy talent and athletic grace that shone through the ridiculous capering act. She clapped as loudly as anyone.

More bulls came and went, and Alice's eyes, like those of everyone else, anxiously followed Jed. He became funnier and more reckless with each one, endlessly taunting and dodging. Alice had never seen a bullfighter with less regard for his own safety, or more willing to risk his neck simply for the pleasure of the crowd.

At one point, her heart was in her mouth when a rider who had been bucked loose was still caught by his hand in the strap. His body flopped around dangerously, dangling to one side of the bull while his running feet tried to reach the ground. Jed dived into the whirlpool and somehow released the strap so that he and the rider were flung free. He rolled dramatically, over and over in the sand, seeing that the bull had moved to a safe distance to wait.

At that, a hysterical Brandi initiated a screaming Mexican Wave. It was enthusiastically taken up, and travelled noisily around the ring of spectators. This spurred the bull into action again and he careered around the fence. Twice Jed narrowly dodged a charge, pausing only to blow an exaggerated kiss up at Alice with his horrible red mouth.

The kids beside her, who had previously given no sign that they were even aware of her existence, now looked at her in sudden wonder and admiration. Feeling slightly dizzy, she clasped the rail tighter and tried to subdue the heady emotions she was experiencing. Surely it was just the buzzing atmosphere that was getting to her. And she was certain that it could only be pride that she was feeling for her workmate.

The bulls were followed by the bronco riding. Exhausted from the suspense, and not overly keen on seeing the horses perform, Alice climbed down. She wandered a little distance away from the ring and crowds, towards a clump of trees at the edge of the rodeo grounds. She looked back curiously, viewing the scene from afar and musing over the strange activities of human beings.

She hadn't been there long when Brandi and three companions that Alice didn't recognise appeared. Brandi, obviously tipsy, greeted Alice like a long-lost friend, throwing her arms around her and lurching with all her weight onto Alice's slight frame. She righted herself and stepped back when she felt Alice's resistance to the hug.

'Frigid little thing, isn't she? Murris aren't usually so picky.'

The three others giggled. Alice felt the familiar sinking sensation of her high school days. She prepared herself for what she knew was coming.

'Don't look so sour, Alice, we just came over to ask you to come and sit with us. You look like such a loner. I'll even buy you a drink.' Glancing at the others, who were laughing again and leaning all over each other, Brandi added, 'Yes, I swear I will!'

Alice smiled benignly. 'Thanks, Brandi, but I'm perfectly happy here. I actually came to get away from the noise.'

'Oh my God, would you listen to the girl?' It was a meaningless comment but the gigglers were more than satisfied. 'I even said I'd buy you a drink!'

'I'm driving home after this and I'm not a big drinker, but thanks anyway,' Alice answered politely.

Brandi's mouth fell open in mock horror. 'An Abo who doesn't drink? I never met one like that before.' The girls were nearly wetting themselves now.

'Maybe that has more to do with where you meet them, Brandi,' Alice observed quietly.

This really provoked the busty blonde. Brandi's smile disappeared and she lurched at Alice again, pointing her drink can at the tranquil face. 'This black slurry's really up herself.' She spluttered the words, and Alice felt droplets of rum-laced saliva spray her face. 'You think just because you got Jeddy by the short and curlies that it makes you worth something? Do you really think he's interested in you? He's just ginning around with you for a bit of variety.' Brandi glanced proudly at her friends to see whether they appreciated her cleverness. 'Look at her!' she continued. 'She's so thick, she can't even understand what I'm saying!'

Alice was looking over Brandi's shoulder at Jeremy, who had

removed his costume and was walking towards them, now dressed in his normal clothes. She looked back at Brandi and explained, 'I understand your meaning perfectly, Brandi. I'm not overly concerned, though. You seem to think your opinion is of some significance to me. In that you're quite mistaken.'

Brandi gaped like a fish. 'Did you hear her? Significant! Mistaken! Who in hell talks like that? Who the hell taught a Murri to talk like that?'

'Jane Austen,' said Alice, saying the first thing that popped into her head.

Brandi was nonplussed. But by now she'd spotted Jeremy approaching, so she reduced her volume and her tone became more conversational. 'Jane who?'

'Jane Austen,' Alice repeated.

Jeremy was within earshot now and his face broke into a surprised smirk at what he assumed was their topic of conversation. 'G'day, all. Talking about Jane Austen? Moving up in the world, are we, Brand?'

Brandi looked baffled. 'Is she that posh chick from Willow Tree?' she asked uncertainly.

'No, she's not from around here,' Alice said quite seriously.

'Thank Christ for that, she sounds like a stuck-up cow,' Brandi concluded.

Jeremy exploded with laughter and slapped Brandi on the back. The blonde was elated. Her friends were laughing too. She glared triumphantly at Alice, but she had already turned to go.

The confrontation over, the tipsy girls meandered away to the covered pavilion with Jeremy. Alice had declined his invitation to join them and instead sat down on an upturned drum to take off her boot and straighten out an annoying fold in her sock. She found that

Brandi's attack hadn't really upset her as it would have done when she was younger. She smiled to herself about Jane Austen – 'that posh chick from Willow Tree' – and listened to the dull roar of music and voices coming from the pavilion.

§

Troy looked up from his beer to see Alice Wilson wandering reluctantly into the babbling throng. Her eyes met his and her face flooded with relief on sight of him. As she approached, he jumped up and pulled a plastic chair over to where he and Mushgang were sitting.

Troy hadn't seen Alice since he'd returned from the mines. And although he thought about her often, he really hadn't had much to do with her for years now. But the two of them had spent many hours together as children when Mushgang had been working with Sam on Redstone. Those times were some of Troy's happiest memories.

The youngest of Mushgang's children, Troy had been a surprise to his parents, conceived when all his siblings were in high school. He was very close to Mushgang, who often told him that he was the only one of his children who would ever amount to anything. This always made Troy laugh, as his brothers and sisters had all made successful careers in the city, while he was just a messer with horses.

Troy had been a quiet, passive child who'd had a strong affinity with animals even as a toddler. To outsiders his life had apparently been settled and stable, without any major hiccough. But he took small things to heart and was often a victim of his own deep emotions. Now he grinned to himself, recollecting the time when as children he and Alice had been so upset over a dead kingfisher they'd found; together they had performed an elaborate funeral for the little bird.

Alice sat down and smiled her smile at him. She certainly wasn't any less beautiful. He had so much he wanted to tell her, so much to say, but Alice was seeking tidings of the Arabian filly who had dumped his dad in the dirt. Troy had been so busy working horses for other people that he'd had little time to spend with the mad horse.

'I don't think she's gonna come good,' he said quietly to Alice. 'Hate giving up on a horse like that but I reckon I'd be wasting my time.'

'Will you let me have her then?' Alice asked eagerly. Troy frowned and glanced at his dad. Alice looked at the older man too. 'Mushgang, please?' She spoke imploringly.

'Struth, Alice, those bloody eyes of yours are hard to refuse. But Sam would never forgive me if that filly hurt you.'

'Please, just let me try. I'll deal with Pa. It'll be on my own head.'

'Yeah, that's what I'm worried about,' Mushgang laughed.

Alice laughed too. 'I promise, if I don't make any progress, I'll get rid of her.'

Mushgang tore open a packet of peanuts, looking thoughtful.

Troy noticed Alice watching Jed O'Donnell. He wondered if the rumours were true. Somehow he couldn't picture Alice with a loud bloke like that. He followed her gaze. Jed was sitting not far away, surrounded by all manner of females. They had jostled to buy him drinks and drape parts of their bodies over him. It looked like Troy's worst nightmare.

Apparently enjoying himself, Jed looked across and winked at Alice. She smiled but then turned back to Troy; to his relief, she didn't appear to give Jed another thought. They continued to talk about handling touchy horses.

Nothing had changed. He still felt the same way about Alice and he couldn't imagine wanting anyone else.

§

At eight o'clock Alice felt a tug on her plait and turned to see Jeremy standing beside her. 'Ready to go?' he said. It was much earlier than she'd expected he'd want to leave. Some of the girls had followed him and clung to him stupidly, lamenting his intention to go.

'Settle down, ladies,' Jeremy said. 'There are plenty more fish in the sea. What about young Troy here?'

The shy eighteen-year-old looked terrified and braced himself to make a quick getaway. But the simpering girls had eyes only for Jed. Without further ado, Alice stood up and farewelled Mushgang and Troy.

'I'll ring you about it tomorrow, Ali,' Troy called as she and Jeremy left.

The caterwauling procession trailed behind them, and Alice walked briskly ahead to the car park, freedom in sight. She waited patiently in the driver's seat for the girls to make their repeated farewells, lavishing Jed with hugs and kisses. At last he broke free and leapt into the ute, quickly slamming the door shut.

'Start her up, Alice,' he ordered cheerfully, and he blew a kiss through the protection of the wound-up window.

They drove in silence for several minutes, Alice concentrating on the road as she was unaccustomed to night driving. Suddenly she became aware that Jeremy was studying her profile in the darkness. She turned and smiled at him quickly, before looking back to the road.

'So did you have a blast?' he asked her doubtfully.

'It was very interesting,' Alice answered, nodding the affirmative.

'Interesting? Never heard *that* used to describe a rodeo before. That could mean bloody anything.'

'Your girlfriend doesn't like the way I talk much either,' observed Alice.

Jeremy chuckled at the memory, then became serious. 'Hey, they weren't giving you a hard time before I got there, were they?'

'Not particularly. Nothing out of the ordinary. But they do seem to think that you and I are . . . you know.'

'No, I don't reckon I get your drift. You better explain.' He turned his body in the seat and looked at her expectantly. She laughed and shook her head, keeping her eyes on the road.

After another short silence Alice noticed that Jeremy had slumped tiredly in his seat. The euphoria of the rodeo ring had clearly worn off at last.

'You were really amazing today, Jeremy,' Alice said. 'I'm not a rodeo expert, but I've never seen anything even close to what you do out there.'

Jeremy sat bolt upright again, his face shining like a chuffed schoolboy. 'Crikey, Ali, you reckon? Ta.'

'I can see why they wanted you to come so badly. You're the star attraction.'

'Now you're dribbling.' He shifted uncomfortably in his seat and looked out of the window into the blackness.

They drove on, Alice enjoying Jeremy's silent companionship after the din of the rowdy gathering. Then he spoke again. 'Looked like you were having a good old chinwag with Troy Boy back there.'

'Yes, I'm glad he came.'

'He's a couple of years younger than you, isn't he?'

'Six months younger. He's eighteen.'

There was another short pause while they both thought about Troy.

'What're you mulling over?' Jeremy asked suspiciously. 'About your secret talk with Troy Boy?'

Alice laughed. 'I'm surprised you even had a chance to notice what anyone else was doing.'

'Well, I was a bit worried about you. Thought you might be having a shocker of a time. Didn't take very good care of you, did I?' Jeremy looked at her apologetically.

Alice glanced at him in surprise. 'I'm a big girl now, I wasn't expecting you to look after me. Anyway, I could see that you were otherwise engaged.'

'Oh . . . righto.' Jeremy sounded strangely disappointed.

The Redstone veranda was lit up like a Christmas tree when they pulled in to the shed. Jeremy jumped out while the ute was still moving, so that he could rush around to open the driver's door for Alice. He bowed low as she stepped out past him into the chilly air. She pushed him lightly with her fist and started for the space between the shed wall and the front of the ute, but he grabbed her hand. She turned to look up at him.

'Thanks a million for coming, Alice. I was really stoked about having you there today.'

He gave her a quick hard embrace and she winced at the medley of women's scents that were still lingering on him. Then he held her loosely against him for a moment longer, their breath making clouds of vapour.

'Alice! Come in out of the cold!' It was Olive on the veranda, peering out suspiciously into the darkness towards the shed.

Jeremy called back brightly, 'Hang on a tick, Mrs Day, we're just getting up to no good here. We'll be finished shortly.'

They could see the old woman's silhouette stiffen as she leaned forwards and peered harder.

Alice was feeling tired after the two hour-long drive. How easy it would be to rest her cheek against Jeremy's warm chest, and wrap her arms around him as his were around her. But after the feelings she'd experienced that day, watching him in the ring, she wasn't game. She suddenly felt that she was venturing into dangerous territory.

'Night, King Jed.' She gently pulled free of his embrace and walked away. At the gate she paused to look back at him still standing at the shed, barely lit by the glow from the veranda, and gave him a little wave. Then she disappeared into the house with her grandmother.

Chapter 19

'Morning, Jeremy,' said Alice absent-mindedly.

It was the Monday after the rodeo weekend and Jeremy was trying his best to retain some of the essence of King Jed the Invincible. At least for a few days. Alice's distracted greeting as he swaggered into the shed wasn't at all helpful. She was clearly preoccupied with the task at hand, methodically packing the ute with all the gear that she and Sam might need checking the back country. Jeremy knew this process always involved the consideration of the time of year, the current conditions, the general state of the stock and the standard of maintenance of the fences, windmills and other infrastructure in the areas being checked.

He watched her sulkily for a short time, recalling the females who had been clinging to him on Saturday night. 'Why don't you ever call me Jed?' he demanded.

Alice paused for a moment and frowned at him. 'What?'

'It's always Jeremy.' He piped his name in a posh falsetto.

'I don't know. Jed doesn't suit you,' Alice said with quiet authority and then went about her business again. She'd dismissed him – just like that. Feeling annoyed now, Jeremy persisted.

'Everyone else seems to think it does.'

'Fine, I'll start calling you Jed then.' This time she didn't pause in her efficient movements, her mind clearly on more important things. Jeremy felt as though she was fobbing him off like a wilful child.

While they were waiting for Sam, Alice helped Jeremy add the final touches to two new steel gates that Sam had asked him to make to replace some badly rotted timber ones in Cliff paddock. As they worked, Alice called him Jed several times; Jeremy was sure she was saying his name more often than she usually did, and somehow managing to make it sound corny.

By 7 am Jeremy had begun to miss the sound of his real name on Alice's lips. Sam came across the yard carrying the esky. They loaded the gates into the ute and tied them down. Then Alice jumped into the driver's seat beside Sam.

'Thanks, Jed. We'll see you tonight,' she called.

Perhaps noting the unfamiliar name, Sam looked at Alice questioningly but wisely refrained from commenting.

'I'll keep working on the other new gates today, Sam,' Jeremy said in farewell.

'Thanks, son. Sixteen urgent. Twelve more need doing sometime soon.'

'Righto. Ta-ta then.'

'Have a good day, Jeddy.' Alice dazzled him with one of her rare, full-blown smiles and pulled away.

He swore loudly to himself and kicked a rock with the toe of his boot. It hit the iron wall of the shed with a resounding clang and bounced away.

Shortly afterwards, Jeremy stopped welding and lifted his mask to examine a small body truck that was pulling up at the loading ramp. Mushgang. On board was a single horse. Jeremy recognised the nervy creature at once and muttered to himself, 'Don't tell me that bloody lunatic is still kicking round.'

The truck door opened, but instead of Mushgang's crooked form, a young, lively figure sprang forth.

Jeremy squinted. 'Troy Boy.'

Troy unloaded the filly and she skittered across to the far end of the yard, where she stood on full alert, suspiciously eyeing Troy and then Jeremy, who strolled towards him.

'G'day, Troy. How'd you be?'

'Yeah, not bad, thanks. Ali about?' Troy asked hopefully.

'Sorry, mate, she headed off with Sam half an hour ago,' Jeremy answered. Troy looked crestfallen. 'Jeez, you must've left your place early,' Jeremy added.

'Yeah, before five. Bloody nippy too, I tell ya.'

'I reckon it would've been. Hoping to catch Alice, eh? Did she know you were coming?'

'No.' Troy continued to look downcast. 'She was coming to our place tomorrow to pick up this filly, thought I'd save her the trouble. Will she be in later today?'

'Not any time soon, mate. They've gone out to the back country. All day job.'

'Yeah, I know the one.' Troy's voice was full of undisguised disappointment.

There was an awkward pause, and Jeremy realised he and Troy were sizing each other up. Troy Boy didn't look too sure of himself. But Jeremy wasn't so convinced of his own advantage. The younger man had a slightly melancholy, artistic appearance to match his temperament. His soulful green eyes had slight shadows beneath them, and an unearthly quality that reminded him of Alice's own. In spite of his shyness, Troy had an undeniable air of dignity, and Jeremy knew instinctively that this young man was kin with Alice in a way that he himself could never be.

It was well known around town that Troy wasn't a big drinker, and his apparent lack of interest in girls had resulted in speculation among Jeremy's friends about his sexuality. But Jeremy knew that Alice had a great deal of admiration for the way Troy conducted himself; he'd heard her discussing it with Sam on more than one occasion. And her feelings about his own antics were no secret to him either. So he regarded the other man with an element of dismay mixed with grudging respect.

Jeremy broke the silence. 'Getting plenty of horse work these days?'

'Lots at the moment. Seems to be all or nothing. And people don't like paying too much to have their horses broken in.'

'Must make it hard to do a proper job,' Jeremy said with genuine sympathy.

Troy looked at him in surprise. 'Yeah, it does.'

'Not a miner then, eh? Couldn't hack it at the big black hole?'

'No, it was doing my head in.' Troy shuddered slightly at the memory. 'Like being the living dead. How's life at Redstone?'

'Yeah, bloody good.' Jeremy grinned. 'Best job I've ever had by a long way. Best boss a fella could have.'

Troy smiled. 'Yeah, old Sam's out on his own, Dad always says.'

'Too right. And you won't catch me whining about working for Alice either.'

'So I'd have thought.' Troy's smile disappeared and he looked Jeremy directly in the face. 'Not thinking of quitting any time soon then?'

'Steady on, Troy Boy – you got your eye on my job or some bloody thing?'

'Yeah well, if you're ever thinking of shooting through, let me know first, eh? Would've jumped at that job if I'd been about.'

''Struth I'm lucky then.' Jeremy exhaled with a whistle. 'They would've taken one of you over ten of me. Couldn't get any other bloke at the time. Old Liv still doesn't trust me as far as she can kick me.' Jeremy chuckled.

'That's not what I've been hearing,' Troy said generously.

'Fair dinkum?'

'Sam's been raving about you to anyone who'll listen.'

'What about Alice? What does she say about me?'

'I dunno, mate. I don't get to talk to her that much.'

Jeremy examined his face knowingly. 'You're a bit sweet on our Alice, eh?' His tone was gentler than usual. Troy blushed and looked away. 'I can't say I blame you. I'd hazard a guess that any bloke who had much to do with that little lady would end up more than half keen.'

Troy looked down, blushing. 'Known her since we were kids. Not interested in me though, is she.' It was more of a statement than a question.

'Poor bugger.' Jeremy shook his head understandingly. He tried not to look too pleased, and offered, in an uncharacteristic burst of humility, 'Well, mate, if it makes you feel any better, she doesn't so much as bat an eyelid at me either.'

'Yeah?' Troy suddenly brightened up. 'I reckoned so. She doesn't act like she's too keen on ya anyway.'

Jeremy suddenly felt defensive. 'Well, I reckon there's plenty more fish in the sea, digger.'

'Yeah, maybe for you. Do you think she's saving herself for Wingnut Lonergan? That's what he reckons anyway. He can't wait to get his claws on this place either.' Troy waved his hand around. 'Maybe I should try going to church. Small price to pay if it'd help.'

'To be honest, mate, I haven't the foggiest. She doesn't run off at the mouth like other chicks. And there's no point trying to get her drunk.' Troy smiled and nodded and Jeremy added fondly, 'Stubborn little princess.'

The two men shook hands more warmly and Jeremy slapped Troy on the back as he turned to climb up into the truck.

'Good talking to ya, Troy.'

'Yeah, you too. See ya round.'

Jeremy stood and watched the old truck rumble away before shaking his head and returning to the shed and the waiting gates.

§

That evening, Jeremy paused in his work and stretched as the paddock ute rattled into the shed. Alice parked it in the usual bay and sprang out. Sam eased himself stiffly from his seat and straightened slowly, hanging on to the tray.

'You still going, son?' he asked in surprise. 'Must've been a bloody long day.' Then, seeing the gates, 'Those there are a credit to you, son. Never seen the likes of you for working.'

Jeremy looked awkwardly at the gates, trying to hide his pleasure.

'You've done so many, Jeremy!' Alice exclaimed.

Jeremy looked at her and beamed, welcoming with relief the sound of his proper name on her lips.

Chapter 20

Alice stepped out of the shadowy church into the August sunlight with her grandfather. Her grandmother had already rushed off to the tea table to help serve. Walter Lonergan looked across and smiled at her from where he was chatting to an elderly grazier, Grant Finlayson. He soon excused himself and appeared at her side, at which her grandfather shuffled off.

She'd only had a few moments of small talk with Walter when some of the chatter around them died away and they both turned to look for the cause. Alice gasped in dismay as Jeremy walked towards her through the small groups of churchgoers, his face an ugly mess of early-stage bruising. One of his eyes was puffed half shut and seeping blood at the corner. His hair was wet; he must have tried to wash his face. He was clasping his shirt closed, and when she looked closer Alice could see that the buttons were torn off.

Alice saw her grandmother glance up from the tea table and a look of horror appear on her face. Mr and Mrs O'Donnell stood fixed to the spot. Stepping away from Walter, Alice walked towards Jeremy, looking around for her pa and some quiet conversation broke out again. Alice took Jeremy's arm and was about to ask what had happened when old Father Callaghan hobbled over. Walter sidled up again on Alice's other side.

Alice wished Walter would go away, but she was glad of Father Callaghan's presence. The old priest's ministering days were coming to an end but he still knew how to handle tricky situations. She hoped he'd make Jeremy feel sheltered from all the curious and unfriendly glances being directed his way.

§

Jeremy's heart was still pounding and he was beginning to feel the hits he'd taken to the head. Now that he'd stopped walking, the glare from the bright sunlight was making him feel light-headed.

'Hello, son.' Father Callaghan greeted him as though there was nothing unusual about the situation. 'Good to see you, as always. How are things with you?' They shook hands.

'Well, Father, I've had better days.'

'Me too, Jeremy.'

'Got meself into trouble again.' Feeling like a guilty child, Jeremy looked at his boots.

'So I see.' The priest laughed quietly. 'By the way, I've heard you're working miracles at Redstone.'

Jeremy looked up again and smiled gratefully. What a bloke. The old man's face was full of amused wisdom as his eyes met Jeremy's. He gave a quick nod before turning his attention to bent old Eileen Hogan, who was tugging urgently on the arm of his robe.

Ignoring Walter's challenging glare, Jeremy looked sideways at Alice. 'Can I see you for a tick, Ali?'

He was surprised to discover that, like the priest, Alice wasn't shocked by or ashamed of him. Instead she gazed up at him in concern. He wondered whether she'd worked out the cause of the fight. She said goodbye to the sulky Walter and led the way to where the town car and Redstone ute were parked side by side.

'Are you alright?' Alice's voice was full of compassion as she studied his smarting face. She made a small involuntary gesture with her fingers as though she wanted to reach up and touch him, then she stopped herself.

Stupidly, he felt a sudden lump of self-pity in his throat and couldn't answer. Perhaps sensing his momentary weakness, Alice went on conversationally, 'I guess you won't be wanting the extra time in town while I'm at the Collinses'. You can go home with Ma and Pa if you like. Or you can come riding with me and old Mr Collins. I've also got to pick up the branding cradle we bought from the Glen Dee clearing sale beforehand.'

His temporary lapse overcome, Jeremy found himself grinning. 'What a ripper of a choice. A drive in the country with Ma and Pa Kettle, or a pleasure ride with a prize geriatric.'

Alice nodded and smiled. 'The choice is yours.' She turned to open the ute door and locate the first aid kit behind the seat.

'I reckon I'll come along with you,' Jeremy said. 'I don't think your ma's too happy with me just at the minute.'

'Alright, good. You can help me lift Mr Collins onto the horse.'

'You beauty. Sounding better and better.'

Alice dabbed Jeremy's weeping eye with a medicated swab. She seemed unconcerned about the scrutiny of the small crowd that was still lingering outside the church. Then, using some small safety pins from the kit, she proceeded to pin Jeremy's torn, damp shirt closed at the front. He looked down at her with helpless longing.

Just a short time ago, he'd gone into battle with his own tribe – and it was because of her. Joining his mates at the tail end of a weekend bender might not have been such a good idea after what he'd said to them that night with Bonnie. Bloody Max. But he didn't care. He was glad he'd finally shown them how much Alice meant to him. More than the whole damn lot of them put together.

Still emotionally charged from the fight, he found the gentle touch of Alice's little fingers on his chest and stomach cruelly tantalising. She seemed to be sending tiny electrical impulses straight into his skin, causing his heart to race uncomfortably and his breath to quicken. He held his arms down stiffly beside his body, fists and teeth clenched with the effort it cost him to prevent himself from wrapping his arms around her.

As they drove away from the church towards Glen Dee, Alice told Jeremy a little about John Collins, a man that Jeremy knew only by sight. A drover for over forty years, he'd travelled most of the stock routes in the country. Now in his nineties and suffering from dementia, he lived on a few acres on the edge of town with his daughter Ellen, who was also quite elderly. Ellen had been complaining to Olive about her father's constant requests to be allowed to get on his horse. So Alice had offered her services. Ellen had told Alice that John was most lucid in the morning, so they wasted no time at Glen Dee, heading to the Collinses as soon as the cradle was loaded into the ute.

Ellen answered the door a few seconds after they rang the chimes.

'Oh, Jeremy, you're here as well!' she said, beaming. 'Goodness, how kind of you both, and on a Sunday too! He's been asking and asking to get on a horse. It will mean the world to him, you know.'

Politely refraining from commenting on the sorry state of Jeremy's face and clothes, she ushered them through the house and out onto the back veranda where a tiny, straight-backed but wizened old man was seated in a rigid-looking chair. He was chewing the stem of an old-fashioned tobacco pipe, but it didn't appear to be issuing any smoke.

'I try to make him sit in the squatter's chair, but he insists on that hard old thing!' Ellen pointed at his seat.

The old man took the pipe out of his mouth at the sight of the two young people, but stared only at Alice with eyes that must have once been icy blue. 'Lillian,' he rasped, 'that angel's here again. The one I've been telling you about. She's just walked out onto the veranda.'

'He thinks I'm Mum sometimes,' Ellen explained in a low voice.

'Don't think I can't hear you going on with your rot, girlie,' John said irritably.

'Dad, it's Alice Wilson and Jeremy O'Donnell. They've come to take you riding.'

'Take me riding? I've ridden round the world and back, old lady. I don't need no one to take me riding. That angel's here again. Can't you see her, Lily?' Looking conspiratorially at Jeremy, he added, 'Blind as a bat, that woman.'

'Dad, it's not an angel, just little Alice,' Ellen said patiently. 'Do you feel like going riding?'

John spoke again, addressing Jeremy. 'Does nothing but contradict. Whatever happened to love, honour and obey? That's what I'd like to know.' He drew on his unlit pipe and Ellen sighed.

Alice was just about to repeat the invitation when Jeremy piped up, 'You're not wrong there, old boy. Don't know their place, these women of today.'

'Right you are, Cedric – now you're talking sense.' John sat back in his chair with a wrinkly grin, looking pleased as punch.

'Barefoot and pregnant is how you want 'em.' Jeremy laughed to himself, warming up.

Alice elbowed him in the ribs. The old man rocked back and forth, choking with croaky laughter.

'With a house yard full o' prickles,' Jeremy continued.

John hooted with delight and held his belly.

'Everything went pear-shaped when they got the vote.' Jeremy was on a roll.

'You know, that's what I've always said!' the old man gasped. He paused for breath and took out a hanky to wipe his eyes.

'Don't encourage him, dear,' Ellen warned.

This made old John furious. 'See what I have to put up with? No respect. Has to throw in her two bob's worth. Blah blah blah. Women should learn to speak only when they're spoken to.'

Jeremy winked at Ellen then said, 'Should learn to save their breath to cool their pudding!'

This sent John off into more fits of laughter. When he finally calmed down, he looked up at Jeremy with watery eyes and said, 'Oh, I like *you*, mate!'

'Good thing too, old chum. If not, I'd have to flatten ya!'

'Jeremy!' exclaimed Alice.

'Don't I know it!' John slammed his pipe down on the table.

Jeremy shook a finger at him tauntingly. 'So watch your step, Johnno!'

'So you always say, you rotten coot!' John squeaked in a high strangled voice, and was then in stitches again, having a whale of a time.

But his laughter began to change into more of a splutter, then an almighty coughing fit. Ellen scurried over to him and started patting him hard on the back, while Alice ran inside to get a glass of water. But Jeremy picked up the pipe and shoved the stem towards John's mouth. 'Suck on that, mate,' he suggested.

Ellen missed a few beats in her patting to look incredulously at

Jeremy, but John clawed at the pipe, put it to his lips and inhaled. For some reason it worked.

'I'm not sure you're well enough to go riding, Dad.' Ellen was now rubbing his back. 'He seems to have forgotten about it for the moment, anyway,' she added, looking up at the young pair. 'Maybe we should leave it for another day.'

'Get your chubby hands off me, Lily, and get out of my way. I need to go riding.' John gripped the pipe stem in his teeth and, with his hands on the armrests, began to heave himself up out of his seat.

'That's the spirit, you old tiger!' Jeremy urged him on.

'Wait until I get your walker!' Ellen's voice was panicky as she rushed to the other end of the veranda. The situation was getting out of control. Alice ran around beside John and took his arm; he was still in the process of standing up. Ellen rolled the walker at top speed towards them and was edging it in as close to him as possible when Jeremy strode around to the back of John's chair and grabbed him under the arms, lifting him off his feet. Ellen issued a sharp cry.

'Jeremy, be careful!' exclaimed Alice.

Hanging there, Jeremy's hands easily supporting his withered old frame, John's body straightened out. Then Jeremy spun him into position and gently set his feet on the ground. He maintained his hold until John's hands were grasping the walker.

'Ready to roll!' Jeremy looked at Alice's stern expression and made his face go serious.

They all made their way around the veranda to a single step down to a pathway leading to the back gate. Beyond it was a paddock with four old horses and a timber shed. A wheelchair had been placed ready in front of the step.

'Who put that contraption in my way?' John demanded.

'It's yours, Dad.' Ellen sounded jaded. Aside to Alice she explained, 'This happens every time.'

John started to protest, 'If you think I'm going to—'

But Jeremy cut him off. 'Me first!'

He jumped excitedly into the wheelchair and performed a three-sixty on the spot by pulling the wheels hard in opposite directions. Then he went careering down the path, skidding to a halt at the gate. 'I've parked your chariot,' he called.

John leaned hard on Alice and Ellen, trying to launch himself down the step, walker and all. They guided him down the path towards Jeremy, who lifted him off his feet again and held him dangling until he'd let go of the walker. Then he plonked the old man down into the wheelchair, none too gently.

'I'll push!' Jeremy set off on the bumpy track to the shed with Ellen following close behind, looking flustered.

Alice jogged ahead to find some bridles. The door of the shed was difficult to pull open, and it was clear from the abundance of spiderwebs and the blanket of dust coating everything that it had been a while since anyone was in here. Alice found some crusty old bridles and a halter. She looked around for a saddle. John's old packsaddles were there, relics from his droving days, but a riding saddle was harder to find. Eventually she located one under some hessian sacks, but it had been partly dismantled, the stirrups, girth strap and saddle cloth all hidden in various places around the shed. Leaving John outside in his chair Ellen and Jeremy joined Alice inside the cluttered little building. While they were hunting, Ellen explained apologetically that her younger brother had moved John's gear in case the old man ever took it into his head to try to go riding alone. On hearing this, Alice exchanged an uncomfortable look with Jeremy.

By now the horses had wandered over.

'Marmaduke,' said John, indicating an aged half-draft horse with an incredibly long, shaggy mane and tail.

'How old is he?' asked Alice.

'Nine or ten, I'd say.' John spoke proudly.

'I think Marmaduke here has been voting for some time,' Jeremy observed quietly as he saddled the elderly equine. Alice put bridles on two of the others and attached a lead rope to Marmaduke's bit. Then Jeremy lifted the old man up into the saddle.

Alice had been having some serious misgivings, and seeing how stiff and unsteady John was when he'd clambered out of the wheelchair had done nothing to reassure her. But once in the saddle an amazing transfiguration took place. The frail old man sat comfortably balanced, confident and alert. Jeremy and Alice hopped on to the other horses bareback and Alice took the lead rope from Ellen. That was when John spotted it.

'What the bloody hell is that? I'm not a two-year-old! I've been riding since before you were a twinkle in the swagman's eye, girlie!' he fumed at Alice.

'Stockman. He was a stockman,' said Jeremy as he jumped down and unclipped the lead rope.

'What on earth are you doing?' Ellen squeaked.

'Stop worrying and give the poor old bugger some dignity.' Jeremy remounted. Then, looking back at Ellen's anxious face, he added, 'Only have to take one look at him to see he still knows what he's doing.'

John was a doddery old man no more. He had the seat of a drover and looked like an extension of the horse. He briskly picked up the reins and slapped them hard on each side of Marmaduke's monstrous neck. The ancient horse set off at a trot, and then the old man looked around at Alice and Jeremy impatiently, to see if they were keeping up. As she bumped her horse into a walk, Alice shot a panicky glance at Jeremy, but he was still sitting there, staring after the old man. She thought for a moment she saw tears in his eyes but she couldn't be sure, the one closest to her was so puffy and bruised. Jeremy was such an enigma: that morning he'd been brawling in the pub and now he was getting teary over an old man on a horse. The two sides of his character seemed so often to be at odds with each other.

In spite of more slapping from old John, Marmaduke soon slowed to a plodding walk. Alice and Jeremy caught up and rode one on each side of him. The loose horse trailed along behind. After a few laps of the paddock, Jeremy opened a gate out into some scrubby bushland. Alice looked warily at him, but he just grinned. Marmaduke went through it at surprising speed, John glancing around with bright eyes.

They rode into the bush in silence for a while, then the old man looked at Jeremy alongside him and started to speak. 'Ceddy, mate, did you hear that on our last leave Jimmy Costello spent his whole pay packet on a peach?'

'Fair dinkum?' said Jeremy.

'Reminded him of home, he said. From New South, he is. We all thought he was stark raving crackers. Reckon he must have had an inkling he was gonna be blown to smithereens that week.'

'Struth.' Jeremy looked shaken.

John went on, 'Enjoyed that blinking peach, he did. The bugger ate it in front of us, juice everywhere. Must remember to tell his ma if we ever get out of this hellhole.'

There was another short pause before John rambled on. His confused babble was punctuated with wartime anecdotes. Jeremy and Alice heard about the shortage of toilet paper and what the men had used instead. John made a jibe about the powerful smell of frightened Hughey's sweat, stronger even than the smell of the corpses.

He also threw in some morbid jokes, the kind that are born amid death and destruction in an attempt to pull through sane. As he spoke, a chill pervaded the innocence of the sunlit bush around them. The birds were chattering and an intermittent breeze was toying with the young gums, but Alice was touched by a creeping horror from a war long past. Something which had been little more than a story in a history book, half listened to at school, suddenly became sickeningly real.

Alice hadn't known that as well as his forty years of droving, old John had also been a digger in the Second World War. It seemed that the first of the two chapters in his life had been the one to leave a lasting impression on his worn-out old brain.

At last he fell silent. Marmaduke lagged a little and Alice pulled up and looked at Jeremy. 'I think we should head back.'

'Righto. Spooky old bugger, isn't he?'

Alice could see that Jeremy was trying to make light of what had happened, but she sensed that he, too, had been shaken by John's stories.

On the way home, John was calmer, and quiet. The rhythmic movement of the old horse, the fresh air and the smell of the sun on the leaves had worked magic. Marmaduke seemed to find a new lease of life now that they were heading back. The loose horse trotted on ahead.

They rode in silence until the open gate came into view. Then John suddenly pulled his horse up and looked around, bewildered. 'Where are the cattle?' He looked hard into Alice's face.

She smiled at him sadly, and Jeremy for once stayed quiet.

'They're gone, aren't they?' John said, looking around again, then staring back piercingly at Alice.

'Yes, Mr Collins, they're gone,' she answered gently.

'Damn shame,' he said softly, then thumped Marmaduke into a walk again.

Ellen insisted Jeremy and Alice stay for a cup of tea afterwards. A minute or so after sitting down in his hard wooden seat, John fell into an exhausted doze. Jeremy lifted him gently into the squatter's chair, and Ellen looked over wonderingly at the wilted sleeping form.

Alice and Jeremy spoke little on the drive home, both mulling over the events of the day. As she turned in to the Redstone road, Alice glanced at Jeremy. His face was a mosaic of multicoloured bruises and the knuckles of his right hand were swollen.

'Queer bloody day,' he said.

'That's for sure,' Alice agreed.

'You just never know about people, eh?' He looked across at her. 'You know, he just looks like a crusty old codger, and yet he . . .' Jeremy left the sentence unfinished. 'That thing your pa goes on with, about not knowing what's under a hat, well, he's dead right, I reckon.'

Chapter 21

While she worked with her young horse in the yard, Alice could see Jeremy loitering aimlessly around the shed, and she read slight dejection in his posture. It was Sunday and as usual she'd been to church that morning with her grandparents, but Jeremy had declined the invitation to accompany them to town. His bruises were almost healed now, but he hadn't been back to the pub since the fight. His reluctance to talk about it had more or less confirmed for Alice that she had been the cause.

This morning he'd gone instead to the Cedar Tree stockyards to replace some rotten timber. Now he was leaning against the ute, watching her handling the flighty Arab mare. Trying to win the suspicious animal's confidence was a painstaking process, and at times it seemed that for every step forwards with the nervy creature, there were two steps back.

It was when she was working with animals that Alice most wished she'd known her father. According to Sam, he'd been quite remarkable when it came to handling horses and dogs. It puzzled her that someone who cared so much about animals would have so little interest in his own daughter. Did he ever think of her and wonder what she was like? Or did he, like her mother, just consider her to be an unfortunate accident? How she wished she could pick his brains now.

Still, during the past week Alice felt she had made good progress. The mare now let Alice rub her all over, even inside her ears and under her belly. She could also pick up the mare's feet without fear of her kicking out, as she'd done initially if anyone had even bent to touch her hooves. And she was starting to lead beautifully. In the beginning, she'd furiously resisted any tension on the lead rope, pulling back and even rearing. But now she'd learned that as soon as she cooperated and moved closer to Alice, the pressure was removed. Alice believed the animal was extraordinarily intelligent, and this inspired her to persist.

But today Alice cut the session short and let the filly loose into the night paddock. It was clear to her that Jeremy was in greater need of attention than the horse. She carried her gear over to the shed where he was still lingering beside the ute. He looked at her sheepishly and explained, 'I was just heading back out to Cedar Tree.'

'Do you want a hand?' Alice offered.

He perked up immediately. 'You betcha! A Sunday date at the yards. Just you and me, baby!'

'Don't get too excited.' Alice hung up her gear and jumped in to the ute.

As they drove along the track, she observed, 'It can't be too exciting for you on weekends here. You'll be glad when you get your licence back.'

She waited for a witty confirmation. But all Jeremy said was, 'Hell, I can think of worse things. This old place isn't so bad. Can't complain about the company anyway.' He winked at her.

Most of the solid old ironbark rails of the Cedar Tree yards were still sound, but the gates had been made from planks of lighter timber and many of them were splintering or rotten. Last time Lower Cedar Tree paddock had been mustered, two more gates had been broken by weaners squeezing their heads through the gaps. For the past five years, Sam had been patching the gates with smaller pieces of timber and wire, and a proper repair job was now long overdue.

After the first ten minutes of work, the pair had a good system going. Jeremy was measuring the replacement planks and cutting them with the chainsaw. Alice fixed them in place with a G-clamp, drilled the bolt holes and reused the old bolts to fix them on. The recycled bolts were a bit rough and rusty, so Alice used a small sledgehammer to bang them through, before greasing them up and screwing on the nuts.

One bolt proved particularly stubborn, and after several bangs with the hammer she pulled it out again and bent over to inspect it. She made sure the two holes were properly lined up then replaced the bolt. She stood up suddenly and swung the hammer with more gusto than before. But on the backwards stroke, it hit something behind her, and Alice heard an agonised grunt.

She spun around in horror just in time to see Jeremy crumple and drop. He lay on the ground in the foetal position, issuing a groan.

'Oh no! Jeremy, are you alright?' Alice flung the hammer away and dropped to her knees beside him. She lifted his head onto her lap.

'Vicious bloody woman,' he moaned.

'Where did I get you?' she asked urgently.

'Fair in the family jewels,' he croaked, then groaned again.

'Oh Jeremy, I'm so sorry! I swung that hammer as hard as I could!' Alice stroked his forehead soothingly. 'Can I get you something? A drink of water?'

Jeremy looked up into her guilt-stricken face and suggested hopefully, 'Can you kiss it better?' He spoke in his normal voice this time, his eyes twinkling.

Alice instantly stopped stroking and pushed him roughly up into a sitting position. 'You seem to be recovering. I think you'll live.' She spoke wryly, to hide her immense relief.

'Cruel, hard wench,' Jeremy complained as he clambered to his feet.

'You're the cruel one, to scare me like that. Did I even hurt you?' She could now see he was absolutely fine.

'It did hurt a bit! You hurt my pride!'

'Well, I hope you got a thrill out of upsetting me so much,' Alice said accusingly.

Jeremy looked at her slyly. 'You *must* like me a bit then? To be so upset?'

'I don't enjoy inflicting pain on any creature,' Alice said calmly.

'Oh . . . ta. I'm honoured. You mean you'd feel no different if it was a cane toad you'd belted?'

She laughed out loud, any anger at his trick gone.

Jeremy hung his head in mock sorrow. 'You really know how to build a bloke up.'

§

As they drove home, Jeremy was still tingling from the sensation of Alice's fingers stroking his head and elated from the few minutes of lying in her lap.

'How are your family jewels now?' Alice asked as they pulled in to the shed.

'Right as rain.' Jeremy grinned. 'Not like I'll ever be needing 'em anyway. No chance of *me* having any kids.'

Alice looked at him questioningly.

'Marriage and kids,' he continued. 'You won't ever catch me falling into that old trap.' He spoke confidently, but his intention was more to convince himself than Alice. Since meeting her, his once-firm resolution against marriage had started to weaken, and this frightened him. His own experience of family life hadn't been a good one and he'd escaped it as soon as he could. Now he could do what he liked, when he liked, without answering to anyone. And he wanted to keep it that way.

'What were you doing there anyway? Right behind me?' Alice asked with a probing look.

Jeremy suddenly felt like a small boy who'd been sprung stealing cookies. 'Do you really wanna know? . . . You were bending over, and your butt in those jeans was just too bloody tempting. I came over to pinch it, then chickened out at the last minute.' He examined her face warily, not sure how she'd take this revelation. 'That's when you hit me.'

She laughed softly to herself before replying, 'Well, I guess you won't be trying that again in a hurry.'

Chapter 22

It had been an unseasonably wet winter. This, combined with the mild autumn and the good rain they'd had the previous summer, had resulted in a large build-up of dried grass and other plant matter. Hazard-reduction burning and the updating of firebreaks with the grader were two jobs that were on the cards for the near future. But after a particularly hot Wednesday in early spring, an out-of-season electrical storm took the crew at Redstone by surprise. Sitting at dinner, Sam looked out at the frequent flashes that were illuminating the range to the west, his face full of concern.

Sure enough, when Alice woke at dawn the next day, she was met with the acrid smell of smoke. She leapt out of bed and ran out onto the veranda in her pyjamas. Standing in the small yard at the front of his cottage, Jeremy saluted her. He'd been observing a billowing brown cloud in the west that was obscuring part of the range. He called out to her, 'G'day, mate. Better get your gear on. I'll fill up the slip-on fire unit and water trailer. Lucky the grader is already out at Red Gully.'

'It needs more fuel though,' Alice called.

'Righto, I'm onto it. Meet you at the shed in ten.'

Alice hurried back inside, where her grandmother could be heard scolding her grandfather animatedly from the direction of the bedroom. She poked her head around the door frame and found her grandfather struggling to pull on his overalls while her grandmother stood beside him in her dressing-gown, hands on hips. Olive looked stormily at Alice. 'Will you please tell this silly old man that his days of firefighting are over?'

'Liv, if I drive the grader it'll free up Alice and Jeremy to patrol the breaks,' Sam said determinedly.

'Did you listen to anything Dr Wong said about your heart? And what about that cough? I'm sure the smoke will do wonders for that.' Olive was furious.

Alice cut in. 'Ma, have you phoned Eden and Glenorchy?'

'Yes, of course! They'll be here as soon as they can. Alice, will you please back me up with your grandfather?'

'Ma, if we can stop the fire before it gets to the flat country, it will all be over quite quickly.'

'Well, if it gets away on you, send Sam home as soon as the neighbours arrive.'

'Oh, that'll look bonza, won't it?' said Sam sulkily.

Alice left them bickering and hurried back to her room to get dressed. Then she grabbed the two-way radios, filled some water bottles and threw them with some fruit and leftover quiche into a small esky, before jogging out to the shed where Jeremy was filling some drums with fuel. She loaded the rakes, chainsaw and the hand-held drip torches or fire bugs that they would need for backburning. Then she went to fuel up the motorbike.

Sam came out to join them, Olive tailing him in her floral dressing-gown, still berating him for his foolishness.

'Mrs Day, you look a picture,' Jeremy greeted her.

Olive frowned at him, distracted for a moment. He tipped his hat at her, leapt onto the motorbike and rode away. Sam had ducked out of sight into the passenger seat of the ute, but Olive's ranting face was in the window seconds later. Alice jumped in to the driver's seat and interrupted her grandmother mid-sentence.

'Ma, when people arrive could you please tell them to go straight out to Upper Bullock then head west from there? That way is longer but the road's much better and there are fewer gates.'

Her grandmother was glaring at her now, and didn't answer. Alice started the ute and set off, certain that the irate woman would follow the instructions. Ma always rose to the occasion in emergencies.

By the time they reached the grader in Red Gully, the distant smoke cloud had become ominously thick and billowy, as though it had reached the open grass of the boundary paddocks. Alice fuelled up the grader with the drums, a process which seemed to take much longer than usual.

'Bloody westerly,' muttered her grandfather, referring to the wind that was just starting to pick up.

As she tipped in the final drum of fuel, they heard Jeremy approaching on the motorbike. He pulled up abruptly. 'The fire's in Cliff paddock and most of it's staying up on top, but it's burned down the southern face and come through the fence into Top Boundary paddock. It must have happened in the cool of last night, because by some flaming miracle it's stopped at that overgrown road along the fence. But it's burned all the way along the break into Bottom Boundary.' He motioned with his hand in the direction of the fire. 'I only went far enough to see that it's jumped the break somewhere in there. That's where we'll need the grader, Sam. I'll leave the gate open for ya, and me 'n' Ali will try to find the front of it.'

Sam nodded and heaved himself up into the machine. Once they'd made sure the grader would start, Jeremy headed off in the lead on the bike with Alice close behind in the ute, towing the water trailer. As they came closer to Redstone's boundary she could see the fire burning up against the sky on top of the cliff.

In Top Boundary, she drove along the fence road. The fire had burned through the fence from the national park, and one side of the track was black and still smouldering in places. Sections of fence had been roasted. The slope of the land had been in their favour, though, as the fire had been burning slowly downhill when it hit the track and stopped. Had the ground been flatter, or had there been any wind behind it, the fire would have easily jumped the overgrown break.

Judging by the billowing smoke cloud ahead of her, Alice could see that the fire had advanced well into Bottom Boundary paddock. With the westerly behind it, the front would be travelling quickly now. She hoped they could block it on the downhill slope before it reached the grassy creek flats at the eastern end of the paddock. Otherwise, the fire would almost surely get away. In the heat of the day, the wind-driven flames would do extensive damage to pasture, trees and fences. After the good rain in the first half of winter there had been no early monsoonal storms, so there was no moisture about to protect the soil and plants from being cooked. All the gullies were bone dry and a raging grass fire like this one would jump them with ease.

The motorbike and ute entered Bottom Boundary at the corner gate; leaving it open for Sam, they headed along a cattle pad that veered away from the fence. Alice stopped and unhitched the thousand-litre water trailer so that she could drive across country. She'd have to take her chances with the six hundred litres in the slip-on unit.

The fire had jumped the old break along the fence and raced across the paddock in a narrow tongue to the east. The thin corridor had burned outwards then, so that by the time Alice and Jeremy arrived, there was a vast blackened V-shape, bordered by hungry flames. Alice knew they had to get to the foremost point of the fire and try to halt its advance before working back along the sides.

Jeremy had gone ahead and Alice was following the wing of flame, trying to see through the baffling smoke. The two-way came to life. 'Alice, I've found the front. We need the tank here, quick as you like.'

Before she had time to reply, Jeremy's silhouette loomed up out of the smoke and they moved around in front. Jeremy parked the bike where it would be safe on an area that had already been burned, while Alice started the engine on the firefighter unit to power the pump. Jeremy came to join her and unravelled the hose, then started blasting the wall of flame with water while she drove along in first gear.

After about twenty minutes they had managed to slow the advance of the fire at the very front, but it was still spreading outwards on either side. All at once there was a sudden gust of wind and the flames swept easily past them and continued their onward march. It was clear that Jeremy and Alice weren't going to be able to stop it on their own. Alice hopped out of the vehicle and jumped up in the back. Then over the crackle of the flames she heard the rumble of the grader and spotted it through the smoke carving its way across the paddock. She yelled to Jeremy and pointed. He nodded, retracted the hose and jogged towards his bike while Alice got back into the ute. They both bumped across the paddock towards the distant grader.

§

Sam had known from experience that the fire would be travelling fast, so he hadn't followed Jeremy and Alice through the corner gate. Instead, heading east, he'd come in at the far end of the paddock and was grading the old road across the centre. He gritted his teeth and peered through the grimy windscreen, trying to ignore the nagging tightness in his chest. Eventually he reached around and opened the door on the machine. The smoke couldn't be worse than the airlessness of the cab.

He saw Alice and Jeremy reach the newly graded line. Taking the fire bugs, they headed off on foot in opposite directions and set about lighting the grass on the western edge of the break so that a slow line of flame began creeping back, against the wind, towards the rapidly approaching fire front. Sam was gratified to observe how well they worked together.

It wasn't long before the graded break had been widened with the back-burn. Just as Sam had hoped they would, Alice and Jeremy began to light another strip fifty metres further in towards the approaching fire. These flames, pushed by the wind, raced to meet their slower counterparts near the graded track. The two lines of flame collided and soon extinguished one another.

Sam slowed the grader to a crawl. He was panting slightly, his fist on his chest. By this time the main fire front had arrived. He smiled with satisfaction at the sight of Alice and Jeremy standing shoulder to shoulder in the ash, watching the approach of the galloping wall of flame from the national park. It reached the smoking black corridor they had made and abruptly halted its advance.

§

Alice radioed her grandmother to let the neighbours know they'd blocked the fire in Redstone, and to advise them to head home again to patrol their own boundaries. While her grandfather finished off on the grader, she and Jeremy took off their sooty hats and sat down for a brief rest and drink in the shade. They regarded one another without speaking, and Alice noticed that the black smears on Jeremy's sweaty face made his eyes appear an even brighter, more intense blue than usual. They grinned at each other simultaneously. While they were eating some of the quiche, they discussed their next move.

Suddenly, Jeremy jumped to his feet. 'Oi, what's going on with the old bloke?'

Alice looked over to see the distant grader, now stationary, with its front protruding through a section of badly mangled fence. 'Pa!' she shouted.

They bounced over the grass in the ute and Alice jumped out before it had rolled to a stop. With relief she saw her grandfather's face looking at her sheepishly through the open door. He lowered himself down from the cab, gently pushing her hands aside as she tried to steady him. Jeremy stood by quietly while the old man caught his breath.

'Pa, you're pale,' said Alice. 'What happened? Is it your heart? Oh, I should have listened to Ma!'

'Settle down, Ali. I just gave myself a bit of a fright, that's all.' He examined the fence. 'Made a bloody mess o' that, didn't I?'

But Alice wasn't interested in the fence. She'd never seen her grandfather looking so weak and shaken. 'I'll radio Ma.' She turned to go.

'No you won't.' Her grandfather spoke sharply. 'She's already in enough of a flap as it is.' Then, more gently, he added, 'There's no need to worry her like that.'

'Well, then I'm taking you home right now.'

'I'll take myself home on the bike,' Sam said. 'Be a bloody waste of effort if this fire got away on us again now.'

In the end they convinced him to take the ute. Alice took over on the grader, as the breaks along the entire length of the boundary would need to be brushed up that day. Jeremy began the tedious task of patrolling on the bike the edges of areas that had already burned.

This involved continually stopping to throw pieces of burning timber back into the blackened country and also raking any smouldering cow pats away from potential tinder and into the ash. Mounds of manure were notorious for smoking innocently for many hours after a fire had passed, only to glow red with life again when fanned by a wind gust. With the chainsaw, Jeremy cut down several burning trees that were threatening to fall across the break and reignite the blaze. However, the cool of the late afternoon was their ally, and the danger for today had largely passed.

At dusk Jeremy doubled Alice home on the motorbike, leaving the gear under a singed tree for the following day. Every muscle in Alice's body was aching with fatigue, but the shock of seeing her grandfather so unwell had affected her far more than the physical exertion.

Until today, she'd believed that she was prepared for the time to come when her grandparents would no longer be able to run Redstone. She'd felt herself capable of taking on more responsibility as time went by, and had even pictured herself running the place. But today, seeing the greyness of her grandfather's face, she'd suddenly realised she was far from ready. Even if she did possess the skills and knowledge, without their strength and support how could she carry on?

Puttering home in the twilight, Alice was suddenly overwhelmed by the full realisation of everything her grandparents meant to her. And the thought of losing them filled her with terror. She put her arms around Jeremy's waist and pressed her cheek into his broad, steady back and felt comforted.

At this, Jeremy spoke. 'You did a sterling job out there today, Alice. Never seen another girl with as much go in her as you, even if you are little and weedy.'

'Thanks.' She laughed, relieved to be distracted from her painful thoughts. 'I'm sure you mean that as a compliment. You didn't do so badly yourself.'

'We make a bloody good team, don't you reckon?' Jeremy turned his head, waiting for a reply, but Alice only smiled. How she wished it were true for the long term. Jeremy went on, 'Been to smaller fires than that bastard, with three times as many people, all running round like chooks with their heads cut off and rattling away on two-ways, and they've still got away on 'em. Old Sam knows a thing or two about fighting fires, I reckon.'

The veranda lights were shining out across the yard in welcome, and a mouth-watering smell greeted them as they walked towards the house.

'Life's bloody good, eh, Alice?' Jeremy put his arm around her shoulders just to bother Olive, who had appeared a moment earlier at the veranda railing. The old lady frowned disapprovingly, and Alice, deciding that her grandmother had suffered enough anxiety for one day, ducked out of Jeremy's grasp and bounded lightly up the steps to kiss her on the cheek.

Chapter 23

The weather was getting hotter and it had been another long day. Dinner was quieter than usual. But the crew at Redstone had finally finished all the extra firebreaks and strategic burning they intended to do. Since the fire, they'd been so busy that Jeremy hadn't even had time to celebrate his newly reinstated driver's licence with a trip to town.

After completing the most urgent job of replacing the sections of burnt boundary fence, they had looked to further prevention measures. Each day for more than a fortnight, they had set off after lunch with fire bugs, rakes and a full tank of water on the ute firefighter. Late in the day, when the heat had gone out of the sun, they lit fires, using the direction of the wind to burn corridors back to the existing firebreaks. Much of the grass was still a little green from the early winter showers, which made it difficult to keep the flames travelling and required much raking of burning ashes to spread it.

Sam complained that it had been much easier in the old days when they could just 'light her up' in the afternoon and let a cool creeping fire burn its way through the old grass from one break to another.

But he could see the logic in Alice's argument that the old grass was important organic matter to be returned to the soil, and must be left to rot, or be eaten and deposited as manure. Her plan to start rotational grazing would help prevent the build-up of grass in the future, as most of it would be eaten.

For several months, whenever she found a bit of spare time, Alice had also been working her way systematically across Redstone dropping legume seeds. This had given her an opportunity to work the horses, too, her saddlebags loaded with seeds. At first there had been little evidence of the plants germinating, but as the months passed she'd noticed various members of the legume family appearing in greater numbers. She was fiercely protective of these fragile little weeds and determined to prevent them from being burned. The soil needed the nitrogen they could harness.

But now the team of three planned to have a few slower days before the next round of mustering. Tonight, Jeremy was lost in his enjoyment of the roast-beef dinner, totally focused on the food. To break the silence, Alice asked her grandmother whether the meeting in town that day had been a success. It had been a special occasion: the Country Women's Association and Rotary had condescended to meet in the same hall, at the same time, to work together on a problem facing a family in town.

'Little Keira has been given a fifty per cent chance,' Olive explained. 'The leukaemia is quite advanced apparently.'

'Oh no!' Alice exclaimed.

Jeremy looked up, jolted out of his reverie. 'What's happening?'

'CWA and Rotary are going to raise money to help the Mesitis,' said Olive. 'With all those kids, they'll never afford Keira's treatment, not to mention the travel backwards and forwards to Brisbane.' She glared at Jeremy as though it was all his fault.

'That's hard luck. How're you gonna get people to cough up?' Jeremy was interested enough to rest his loaded fork on the side of his plate, leaving his mouth temporarily empty.

'We haven't fully decided yet, but we thought that if Rotary held a community barbecue and CWA had a cent sale and a cake stall—'

'You should make millions!' interrupted Jeremy sarcastically, hoeing into his food again.

'Oh, and I'm sure you have a better idea!' Olive snapped.

'Wouldn't be hard to come up with one,' Jeremy said through his food. 'Ask me in the morning. I'll sleep on it.'

'I can hardly wait.' Olive sniffed.

Alice noticed that Jeremy was unusually quiet and distracted for the rest of the meal.

The next morning, as she was finishing breakfast, Jeremy came rushing into the kitchen with his boots on, waving a dirty envelope covered in his messy scrawl. He saw Olive's face and looked down at his feet.

'Oh, sorry, Mrs Day, but this is urgent!' He shoved the envelope at her and ducked back out to remove the offending boots.

'Do you expect me to be able to read this?' Olive was looking at the envelope distastefully when he returned.

'What? Your eyesight that bad, old girl?' He snatched it back again.

'Why don't you run us through it, Jeremy?' Alice looked at him encouragingly.

'Righto, boss.' Jeremy sat down at the table and cleared his throat theatrically. Sam folded his newspaper and looked attentive. Jeremy launched into an animated description of his plan, barely pausing for breath. When he'd finished speaking he looked around eagerly. Alice was gazing out the window with a slight frown of concentration on her face. Sam was nodding slowly with just the hint of a crooked smile. Olive was looking straight back at him, sceptical.

'Is that it?' she barked.

'It?' exclaimed Jeremy. 'Do you know how much sleep I lost over hatching that plan?'

'I think it's brilliant.' Alice smiled at him. 'I'll help.'

'One out of three,' muttered Jeremy, turning to look at Sam.

'I reckon you might have something there,' said Sam after a pause.

'Oh, this is lovely.' Olive sounded affronted. 'Fine then. I can see where your loyalties lie. Side with Jeremy.'

'Don't talk rot, woman – this isn't about you *or* Jeremy.' Sam looked exasperated.

'Ma, it's Keira we're thinking of. Anything that will raise some funds—'

Olive cut Alice short. 'We've already planned it! That's why I drove all the way to town yesterday!'

'Well, I reckon I'll phone around tonight, Liv,' Sam suggested. 'We'll have a brief meeting on Sunday after church. I'll let the Rotarians know and you can do CWA.' Olive glared at him sulkily, and Sam added, 'That is, if you want them to be involved.'

'Tell them the meeting's at the pub,' said Jeremy.

'Oh, this is improving by the minute,' said Olive, annoyed.

'Now, now, Mrs Day, keep your bloomers on. I happen to have good reasons for wanting to hold it there.'

'I'm well aware of your reasons for frequenting the pub, Jeremy,' Olive snapped.

He ignored her and went on, 'We'll need Hammerhead onside and some more locals I have in mind. I reckon I can talk them into helping if the conditions are right.'

'Righto, son,' said Sam. 'Pub it is.'

'Sam! Really!'

'Hammerhead can organise a liquor licence for the day itself,' Jeremy continued, thinking out loud.

'Sam!' Olive's voice was rising in pitch. 'Surely you'll back me up in saying there's no place for alcohol at a fundraiser for an ill child?'

It was Jeremy who answered. 'You bet there is, Mrs Day! That's the whole point – getting people sloshed enough to give away more than they can afford. Get 'em into the spirit of the thing, if you know what I mean.'

§

The Sunday pub meeting, while a success, wasn't without its fireworks. The hung-over crew of all-nighters joined in with the respectable elder community members, and not all of their contributions were helpful. Once his ideas had been approved by the majority, Jeremy outlined a long list of jobs that would need to be done before the big day. Alice wrote them all down on a sheet of butcher's paper and made sure that each person who offered to help put a signature next to a particular item.

CWA took the huge task of providing the food for the day while Rotary agreed to tackle the insurance and money handling. Gladys Hogan from the shop took on the advertising and Hammerhead was to organise the liquor licence and hire a jumping castle. And as they sobered up later that day, some of the youths realised with dismay that King Jed had also coerced them into volunteering for tasks to which they would never have usually agreed. Nev had 'offered' the use of his bobcat and truck and promised to supply a load of creek sand for the kids' digging area. Glen found he had agreed to repair the wooden stand and mend the yards at the showground with timber that Gyro had said he'd provide from his block of land. Wombat had been more than happy to cut it to size with his portable sawmill. And they would all be making themselves available to help set up the grounds before the big day. Justine, Melissa, Angela and Libby had promised to make sure all the boys had the necessary outfits for their 'frocka' match. Brandi was put in charge of rounding up one rugby team of fifteen girls and Alice was to find the other.

In addition, Alice announced that Redstone would be donating a weaner steer for a weight-guessing competition. At this, Walter Lonergan (after a brief consultation with his parents) declared importantly that his family would donate a quality breeding heifer. Everyone clapped politely and Jeremy gave Alice the thumbs-up.

The sight of this exchange induced an angry explosion from Mrs Coral Dart, president of the local Country Women's Association, who had been simmering quietly up until this point. Coral was one of several attendees at the meeting who objected to being organised by this town larrikin less than half their age. Now she looked around at her peers and said loudly, 'I find it strange that a fellow whose favourite pastime is preying on young girls is suddenly so interested in helping one. Is there an ulterior motive here?'

Sue O'Donnell looked mortified and Brian's expression turned sullen.

'Now steady on!' Sam retorted gruffly.

Olive also objected, saying indignantly, 'That comment was completely uncalled for, Coral. I don't like what you're insinuating.'

For a moment Jeremy was astounded at this support from such an unexpected source. Recovering quickly, he jumped to his own defence. 'If you mean your Genevieve, Mrs Dart, she's not so young. Has a good few years on me. And I'm not calling her a cougar or anything, but she was bloody keen.'

'I can vouch for that,' Hammerhead growled. (The old publican was usually in bed at this time on a Sunday.)

Mrs Dart began to change colour and rose out of her seat. She left quietly, along with a few others, accompanied by loud cheers from the drunks.

'Looks like we've got rid of some hangers-on,' Hammerhead commented, collecting their glasses.

§

As the big day approached, word travelled. Some of the local youths who'd gone away to the mines for work came home for the special occasion. Four of these were girls, newly toughened by their experiences in the harsh, male-dominated environment of the mines. They were keen to be involved with the women's rugby and signed up with Brandi. This completed her team, which was otherwise made up of the town's wildest party girls.

Bonnie arrived at Redstone on the Friday with two reinforcements for Alice's team. The two other girls were social workers from the government department where Bonnie did her voluntary work, and the three were excited at the thought of letting off some steam. Giovanna Mesiti, Keira's mother, was also determined to play despite her relative maturity. She and two of Keira's older sisters joined up enthusiastically. The rest of Alice's team was sourced from other high-school girls home for the holidays.

Ewan Webber, the Warrigals' coach, agreed to come north two days before the event to help Jeremy prepare the women's rugby and men's soccer teams for the big day. During the training sessions on the Saturday the sportsground rang with laughter, and all the players went home that night anticipating a day that would prove to be memorable.

Chapter 24

Dawn on the day of the Keira Mesiti Novelty Bash was chilly and clear. Olive had been lying awake for some time, wondering how on earth Jeremy O'Donnell had wound up in the position of chief organiser of a charity fundraising event. There was no other way of looking at it, she'd been wrong about Jeremy.

She got up and put some bacon in the grill; it was his favourite breakfast. Then she brewed some extra-strong tea. But when Jeremy came to the table, she noticed with concern that he didn't take any of the bacon, not a single rasher. Was it possible that King Jed was suffering from an attack of nerves? Olive watched him struggling to finish his single piece of buttered toast, and sympathetically topped up his mug.

§

Jeremy surveyed the scene before him as he walked over from the car park, still feeling a little queasy. It was only eight o'clock but a small crowd had already gathered at the showground. The jumping castle had been inflated and was crouched beside the canteen, whirring and ready for an invasion of small barefoot people. Over in the large mound of white creek sand that had been dumped there for the day, several children were already excavating with a variety of digging implements and toy machines.

The rust-coloured weaner steer from Redstone and the grey Lonergan heifer were standing dejectedly in one of the old gidgee yards to the side of the grounds. They were shifting warily, looking back at the people who were sizing them up.

By nine o'clock the crowd had swelled. Some were seated on the small grandstand while others were setting up camp on the grassy slope beside the oval. But most were milling around chatting or laughing and catching up on the local gossip. A convoy of caravans and motor homes driven by grey nomads had arrived in town on the Thursday, and had halted their journey westwards especially for the event.

Fred Campbell, the town lawyer, was commentator for the day. Preceded by some electrical crackling, his voice rang out over the ground, welcoming the throng. Jeremy was pleased to see that everyone was in high spirits. This was no ordinary day out. The community was feeling unified and purposeful, here to help a sick kid and have a damn good time to boot.

The first event of the day was the women's rugby match. As Jeremy had hoped, it turned out to be a true crowd pleaser. The menfolk of the town saw a new side to the women they thought they knew so well. It was a short match with only ten-minute quarters, but it turned out to be more than long enough for tempers to flare and suspense to build. Jeremy noticed that quite a bit of money was changing hands, in addition to that which was rapidly filling the circulating donation tins. People laid private bets as the two teams warmed up, and the favourites to win were most definitely the team he had coached, the Bobby Socks. Brandi's bunch of fifteen, comprised of the roughest girls around, certainly looked daunting. They were all dressed in black. Their fingernails, too, were painted black, and they wore short black socks to help distinguish them from the other team. As Jeremy led them through a series of muscle stretches, they were eyeing off the Long Socks aggressively and screaming random cries of challenge.

The other team wore multicoloured outfits and their stripy socks were long. They focused only on Ewan, calmly doing their stretches as if oblivious to the daunting rabble nearby. Jeremy battled to keep his mind on his team, but his eyes kept flitting across to Nancy, so adorable in her rainbow socks. Bonnie started chanting quietly, something about power and pride, brains against brawn, good over evil. Soon all the Long Socks had joined in, and the united monotone sounded impressively threatening. However, Kelly Miller, one of the high-schoolers, was suddenly overcome with nerves and rushed off to the toilet.

In the first quarter, during which time neither team scored, Jeremy was surprised to observe that the teams were fairly evenly matched. The first scrum was an ugly affair with the Bobby Socks defending. Despite their disadvantage, they managed to regain the ball in the scuffle. Jeremy was relieved they hadn't positioned Brandi or Bonnie as front rowers, as the two girls seemed to be taking things very seriously. Even so, there was a great deal of screeching, shoving, scratching and hair pulling. Bonnie was number eight for her team. Her effort equalled that of all the others combined, some of whom were nearly lifted off their feet from her rearward pressure in the scrum.

During the short interval one of the CWA ladies, Beryl Sawtell, scurried out onto the field with a platter of cut-up oranges. Puffing and red-faced, she insisted that all the girls eat a quarter of an orange before resuming play. Kelly Miller rushed to the toilet again and then it was time for the game to go on.

In the second quarter, the Bobby Socks scored two tries in quick succession, Libby kicking a goal after each. But they also earned two penalties for high tackles (one being more of a strangling). This gave Jenny Lonergan the opportunity to kick two conversions for the Long Socks. Another vicious and drawn-out scrum resulted once again in the Bobby Socks regaining the ball. Then Carrie Allen, one of the miners, nearly scored a third try for the Bobbies, dropping the ball just metres from the line. Things weren't looking good for the Long Socks. Jeremy, whose eyes kept following Alice, had to remind himself to be pleased with the score.

§

Alice was surprised by how much she was enjoying the game. At half-time, when Beryl bailed them up with oranges again, she looked around for Jeremy. He was engaged in a pep talk with the Bobby Socks, his face alight with enthusiasm. She smiled proudly to herself. Jeremy had impressed her yet again with this novelty bash. He wasn't making it easy to keep her feelings for him cool.

Ewan gathered the Long Socks together and told them to awaken their primal instincts and show some fighting spirit. 'Don't let them scare you with their dirty play,' he said insistently. He advised Bonnie and the social workers, the biggest and most assertive players in the team, to initially hold on to the ball and draw the opposition. Then they were to pass it via the high-school girls to Alice on the outside.

Bonnie drew them into a huddle and barked, 'Let's do it for Keira!' Starting soft and low, she broke into a mantra-like chant which rose in pitch and volume as first the Mesiti sisters, then all the other Long Socks joined in: 'For Keira! For Keira! For Keira!'

The huddle burst apart with a cheer and the Long Socks were fired up and ready to face the enemy.

During the third quarter, Alice came into her own. She was winger, and what she lacked in aggression and size she made up for in speed and agility. She scored two tries, and just missed out on another, when two of the miners blocked her near the tryline. They slowed her just enough to give an enraged Brandi the opportunity to launch her solid frame at Alice's darting one. It was more of a bodily charge than a tackle and Alice was flattened. Some of the crowd booed.

While Alice was recovering, Jenny kicked a penalty goal, making up for the ones she'd missed after Alice's tries earlier in the quarter. Jeremy ran some water out to Alice, then, picking her up like a baby, ran with her between the goalposts. The crowd roared appreciatively as Alice struggled to free herself and dart away. The third quarter closed with the score standing at fourteen to nineteen in favour of the Long Socks. They ceased play just long enough to eat more oranges.

When the game was underway again, Alice noticed with concern that Bonnie was on the warpath. Early in the fourth quarter, Brandi got the ball and Bonnie thundered towards her. She came in from the side, pushing away two of her own teammates in her eagerness to reach the blonde. As the gap between them closed, Bonnie roared, lowered her head like a charging bull and launched herself into Brandi's ribcage.

As Brandi went down, the ball was catapulted over the sideline. She was winded, but that wasn't enough to stop her from thrusting her fingers into Bonnie's wiry curls and twisting them cruelly. Suddenly they were wrestling, with first Bonnie, then Brandi on top. The crowd went wild with enjoyment and Alice could hear money clattering into the donation tins. Ewan attempted to separate the girls and had his face scratched for his trouble. The crowd was chanting, 'Fight! Fight!

Fight!', and it was only with the assistance of Jeremy and some of the other players that Ewan was eventually able to disentangle the two.

After this altercation, Libby earned three points with a penalty kick for the Bobby Socks, bringing them within two points of the Long Socks. Play resumed with only four minutes to go. Then, to the Bobbies' horror, after a few lucky passes Alice yet again gained possession of the ball. But this time, a number of them were hovering near her in readiness. She felt them closing in on her as she streaked towards the tryline. She twisted at the waist and flung the ball backwards at the nearest pair of long socks she could see.

It was Giovanna Mesiti; by some miracle, the older woman caught the ball mid-stride. The attackers slightly altered their course and continued to advance. Alice slowed to a jog and watched anxiously.

Giovanna issued a bloodcurdling war cry and ran straight into the fray, her face contorted into a grimace of reckless determination. The cluster of Bobby Socks engulfed her momentarily before she somehow burst through and out the other side, still hugging the ball. She pelted towards the line with the baying she-hounds close on her heels, before diving into a victory slide. She lay on the ground, elated, her nuggety little body heaving. Amid all the jubilation, no one noticed Jenny's final kick, which went wide and dribbled along the ground. Nonetheless, the Long Socks had won, twenty-four to seventeen.

§

After the game, the girls disappeared to change and the Country Women's Association ladies produced the first round of refreshments, which consisted of mountains of scones, pikelets, slices and cakes. Fred got on the microphone to remind everyone that the donation tins were circulating — an unnecessary reminder, as these containers were already a-clatter with coins in appreciation of the home-cooked food. Hammerhead and Mushgang had opened the bar as well, so things were well and truly underway.

Ewan pulled Jeremy aside, his mouth full of pikelet and another one in his hand. 'What a game, eh?'

'Yeah, I reckon!' Jeremy answered thickly through a mouthful of chocolate cake.

'That Alice's a hot little goer . . . Never noticed her before. She spoken for?' Ewan folded in half the pikelet he was holding and stuffed it into his mouth.

Jeremy gulped down his mouthful of cake before he'd finished chewing it. He took a large sip of beer to chase and soften the chocolaty lumps that were having trouble clearing his Adam's apple. Then he looked sideways at Ewan.

'Not exactly. I mean, there are fellas interested. Wingnut Lonergan for one. But she's . . . a bit of a loner, I s'pose you could say. High standards. Picky little wench.'

'Surprised you haven't hit on her yourself, mate. Dunno how you can stand it with her out there, just the two of ya. Drive me mad, it would.'

Jeremy laughed in answer, a little too jovially. Then a loud cheer captured their attention and they looked across to see Arthur Sawtell setting up the seniors tug of war. Fred Campbell announced the event, and the pot-bellied, bow-legged contestants posed and flexed their muscles in an impressive show of strength. However, it was all over a little too quickly, one side having the advantage of three men under seventy. Winners and losers fell in a heap, jumbled with the heavy rope.

Next the 'buggered hat' competition was announced and the crowd was directed to three trestle tables that had been lined up in wait. In a short time the tables were covered with a motley variety of hats, mainly felt, in various degrees of dilapidation. The contest for most battered headgear was going to be tight.

Meanwhile, at a signal from Ewan, Jeremy and most of the other young men disappeared off to change. It was time for the 'frocka' match. The boys soon reappeared, grotesquely attired in loud florals and gaudy prints; someone was even in sequins. Their muscled hairy legs and arms sprouted incongruously from the softly falling folds, and their faces glowed with that unique brand of elation that only the wearing of women's clothing can bring on in a man.

Jeremy was immensely proud of his outfit. He'd refused to show Alice his frock in advance, promising to dazzle her on the day. It was a hideous purple leopard-skin print, sleeveless, with a high waist and full skirt. He'd jammed the bust with two water-filled balloons that trembled erratically. A thick black vinyl belt was done up tightly underneath to hold them in place. His hair was covered with a small beanie, crocheted from some kind of feathery twine in the same ghastly shade of purple as the dress. All of Jeremy's teammates wore hats or head adornments of some kind to distinguish them from the opposition, who were bare-headed.

In spite of the absurdity of the costumes, the game was fast and furious. Keira's father, Nato, was referee. A fiery soccer fanatic, he seemed to forget the light-hearted nature of the game, presiding over the hairy damsels as though it were a World Cup final. There were a few nasty colourful collisions that appeared serious enough to briefly silence the crowd, but no injuries worse than a bleeding nose were sustained. The rodeo clowns, Jeremy, Wade, Michael and Max, incorporated some stunts into the game; their somersaults, leapfrogs and cartwheels were all well received and raucously applauded.

At the front of the grandstand, Jeremy could see Keira perched on old Gordon Mesiti's knee. The range of emotions displayed on her face reflected the twists and turns of fortune throughout the match. She watched her four strong brothers with a pride that transcended the ridiculous nature of the event. The hatless team were victorious, but the final score of one/nil belied the intensity of the game and the many thrills that the audience derived from watching the players in frills.

After the frocka match it was time for lunch. By now Jeremy's appetite had returned and the smell of the barbecuing meat and onions was tantalising. The tables were loaded with foil-covered dishes of potato bake, quiche, macaroni cheese and fried rice, again courtesy of the Country Women's Association. Several large bowls overflowing with salad had been added at the last minute, along with six huge cane baskets of warm buttered bread rolls.

While people were queuing for the food, Jeremy and Hammerhead set up a gold-coin-rolling contest on the undercover concrete slab. The target was a two-litre bottle of rum and the winner was the one whose coin landed closest to the bottle without actually touching it. Father Callaghan walked away with the rum after his one and only attempt. 'Here's to divine intervention!' he yelled, the bottle held high over his head in unpriestly jubilation.

Despite the size of the smoko a couple of hours earlier, everyone did justice to the delectable lunch spread. The donation tins were now being stuffed with five- and ten-dollar notes as the people (many of whom were tipsy) got stuck into the first-class tucker. Jeremy could see Senior Constable Glover hovering around like a thundercloud, silencing groups of chatting locals by looming up suddenly beside them. For a large part of the day he unknowingly sported a KICK ME sign, stuck onto the back of his perfectly pressed police shirt with electrical tape. No one dared to do as instructed by the sign, but nor did anyone remove it. And Gladys Hogan later swore black and blue that she'd seen him slip a couple of hundred-dollar notes into a donation tin when he'd thought no one was watching.

The ute-jumping competition was announced after lunch. This event was a matter of genuine pride, as station owners, ringers and trainers alike had the opportunity to display the athleticism and obedience of their working dogs.

At this point, everyone noticed an unfamiliar, well-dressed woman who had pulled up in an expensive four-wheel drive not long before. With her was a sleek, tan coloured greyhound on the end of a light plaited leather lead. They lined up along with the others.

More than half of the dogs were eliminated in the first round. Jeremy's Ace didn't even make an attempt to jump the adjustable horizontal pole in Gyro's ute tray. The shove the uncooperative animal received from Jeremy's boot completely failed to motivate him. Instead he ducked out of sight under the ute, much to the delight of the onlookers. Once the bar had been raised a sixth time, only the mystery greyhound could clear it. This slender, leggy creature leapt over it with ease, completely devaluing the effort of the other dogs. There was some half-hearted applause, followed by some resentful muttering when the mystery female greyhound owner promptly collected the prize and departed as suddenly as she'd come.

Fred's cheerful voice heralding the horse races soon took people's minds off the unknown marauder and any ill feeling was short-lived. In Jeremy's initial plan, there had been a real 'bush-style' horse race. But then the Rotarians had discovered how much this single event would blow out the cost of insurance for the day. Consequently, that idea had been scrapped and a horse race using human 'horses' had been decided on instead. Two of the Rotarians had put all the horses' names in a sweep, written on strips of paper. They were sold for twenty dollars apiece.

The 'horses' were lead-roped and lined up for display, while the crowd buzzed, discussing their form. Jeremy was mobbed by willing female jockeys and looked around hopefully for Alice. But he saw with disappointment that she'd already taken hold of Troy's lead rope.

'Righto.' Jeremy held up his hands. 'Which one of you ladies is the lightest?'

At this point Beryl Sawtell and Heidi Campbell decided to intervene and hurried over to lead each wandering jockey to a waiting horse.

At the starting line, the jockeys mounted piggy-back style and the horses crouched, waiting for Mushgang to crack his whip. Then they were off, horses straining and jockeys bouncing uncomfortably down the two-hundred-metre stretch. Jeremy was in the lead for the first fifty metres, until he and his jockey, Libby Cook, suffered a tumble. Michael Gibson, ridden by the petite Helen Mesiti, won by two lengths, and Wyatt Dart, with Kelly Miller as jockey, took out second place.

Then it was time for afternoon smoko and the Country Women's Association ladies produced yet another fine feed. Clive Lonergan took the microphone from Fred to announce the results of the weight-guessing competition: Gyro Edgson had won the steer, Olive Day the Brahman breeding heifer.

While everyone was still eating, some of the donated goods were carried up onto the stand. Barry Field, a saleyards auctioneer originally from the town, had come north especially to offer his services. Jeremy displayed the goods in his usual theatrical manner, and the crowd made bids. Barry had the knack of picking the right starting price, keeping it all rolling along rapidly, and knowing when to pronounce an item sold. People were caught up in the moment and more than a few ended up with goods they hadn't planned on purchasing.

When everything had been sold and Barry was wrapping the auction up, a highly intoxicated Carrie Allen screamed her request: 'How much for Jed? I wanna buy Jeddy!'

Barry immediately took up the suggestion, calling, 'How much for O'Donnell, Jed O'Donnell for a day – who'll give me three hundred?'

'Me!' screamed Carrie, and Jeremy looked decidedly disconcerted.

'Four hundred!' screeched Brandi, without waiting for Barry's prompt.

'Four-fifty, who'll give me four-fifty for a day with Jed?' Barry rattled.

'I WILL!' Carrie yelled.

'Five hundred!' Brandi was bouncing on the spot.

'You can't be serious?' Barry spoke into the microphone in his normal, non-auctioneer voice.

''Course she's bloody not!' Jeremy said loudly.

'Five hundred!' Brandi screeched again.

'Sold!' Barry concluded the session.

By now the sun was low in the sky and the novelty bash was drawing to a close. People dispersed a little and some started to head for their cars. Tired children were wailing and a few adults were becoming loud and unruly after several hours of drinking. Senior Constable Glover was visibly on alert and ready for action.

At this point Fred Campbell appeared on the stand to make a few final announcements and acknowledgements. Nato Mesiti came up to thank everyone, but became choked up with emotion, so Giovanna rushed to his side and forced out some heartfelt words of gratitude.

There was an awkward pause and then the band began to play. It had been set up on the back of Nev's truck not far from the bonfire, which Jeremy now lit for the stayers. The Long Socks, Bobby Socks and frocka teams had long since buried the hatchet and now grouped around the fire laughing and talking. Bonnie even went so far as to buy Brandi a drink.

Olive came and found Alice, who was sitting chatting with Ewan, Bonnie and Troy, to let her know she and Sam were leaving. Jeremy looked up from where he was sitting on the other side of the fire with a bunch of admiring high-schoolers.

'I'm coming too,' said Alice, standing up to go with her grandmother. Jeremy was secretly pleased. He'd been watching Ewan and Alice for some time, not sure of the direction in which things were heading.

But Ewan objected. 'Steady on, Alice, we're just getting started here! We've got some serious celebrating to do!' He took her by the arm. 'The best is yet to come!'

'Yes, that's what I'm worried about.' Alice smiled at him and unhooked his fingers from her arm.

Ewan jumped up from his seat and stood in front of her, grinning. 'You're not going anywhere.' Over his shoulder, he addressed Olive. 'You just head on home, Mrs Day. I'll take good care of her.'

Alice tried to push past him, first on one side then the other, but met with his solid chest both times. On her third attempt, he wrapped his arms around her just as Olive began to pound him on the back with the large rectangular Tupperware container she was holding. Bonnie and Troy looked on in amusement.

At this point, Jeremy jumped to his feet, overcome with a violent compulsion to flog the hell out of Ewan. 'Must be the rum,' he told himself. He struggled to suppress the urge and concentrated instead on the enraged old lady battering his friend's broad back. 'Now, now, Mrs Day. We haven't had a single brawl yet today. Everyone's been *so* well behaved. Please don't spoil it by starting a blue.'

'Jeremy, get this neanderthal away from Alice!' Olive demanded loudly. 'She's trying to come home!'

'Webber, mate, I wouldn't mess with Mrs Day. She might look like a sweet old biddy but, let me tell ya, she can be savage.'

By now Alice had broken free from Ewan's embrace and was facing him again, looking flustered. Jeremy looked at the glow of the fire on the contours of her face. A few curls had escaped from her plait and her eyes were large and entreating as she looked up at the big football coach. Jeremy wished intensely that *he* was the recipient of that look.

'Bloody hell, Ali! Don't look at him like that – he'll never let you out of here!'

'Too right I won't.' Ewan was grinning down at her.

Olive brandished her container in readiness for another strike, but the next moment they were all distracted by a small explosion nearby. Someone had let off a firecracker and it spun an erratic course across the grass, spewing colour as it weaved between the shrieking youths.

When Jeremy turned back, Alice had gone, though Ewan was still there and so was Olive, who was watching the commotion disapprovingly.

Ewan looked around wildly. 'Where'd she go?' he exclaimed in dismay. 'Bugger! Slippery little witch!'

Olive looked surprised then pleased to discover her granddaughter gone. Without further ado, she strode away, leaving Ewan and Jeremy standing there. In the fading light, Jeremy spotted Alice at a distance, walking with Sam towards the parked cars.

'She was fair dinkum!' cried Ewan disappointedly. Like Jeremy, he was unaccustomed to knockbacks. 'I just thought she was trying to stir me up, make me keener. It bloody worked too!'

'Tried to tell ya, mate,' Jeremy said. All his murderous feelings towards Ewan had evaporated. 'Not like other girls, our Alice.' He was smiling after her. Ewan eyed him suspiciously and shook his head before walking away dejectedly to get another drink.

Chapter 25

There was an unfamiliar smell in the air. Olive had been experimenting with a new recipe.

'Bit on the nose, whatever you're cooking, Mrs Day,' said Jeremy from the door where he was pulling off his boots.

Sam had just been on the phone to Arthur Sawtell, who had given him some statistics from Rotary to pass on to Jeremy. Counting the grey nomads, over four hundred people had attended the novelty bash, and Rotary had handed the Mesiti family a cheque for nine thousand, two hundred and twenty-six dollars. Sam relayed this information to those present in the Redstone kitchen and smiled warmly at Jeremy. Olive was as proud as any of them.

Alice put the plates of food on the table and after saying grace, they all examined the strong-smelling food. Even Olive suspected she may have overdone it. Jeremy, starving as usual, decided to dig in first.

'Holy hell, Mrs Day, this is horrible!' he announced after forcing down the first mouthful. 'Wouldn't give this to a dog I liked.'

'You mind your manners, you ungrateful sod,' Sam said, in the tone that he normally saved for a misbehaving animal.

However, Olive's response was unusually mild. 'It's curry. I guess none of us is used to spicy food. But it's good to branch out now and again.' Alice nodded in agreement and Olive continued, a little more sternly, 'I don't mind you telling me when you dislike something I've cooked, Jeremy, however there are less offensive ways of doing it.'

'Righto, give me a minute, I'll try again.' Jeremy stared at his plate for a moment. Then, looking up at Olive, he said, 'Mrs Day, I like you . . . but I don't like this.' He pointed at the curry.

Alice and Sam looked curiously from Jeremy to Olive. She tried to maintain a severe look but found that she couldn't. She gave a small snort and then laughed. 'I suppose I can cope with that.'

'Nothing to growl about on an ordinary day,' Jeremy continued conciliatorily. 'Best bloody cook I've ever come across, by a long way.'

Olive busied herself with the teapot, anxious to hide the pleasure Jeremy's words had given her. She changed the subject. 'Jeremy, I'd like to take this opportunity to congratulate you on the great success of the novelty day.' She paused. 'Well done.'

Sam and Alice made sounds of agreement but Jeremy was silent, so she went on, 'It was all your initiative.'

Jeremy looked up shyly from his plate. 'Jeez, that's real praise coming from *you*, Mrs Day. But I did have a bit o' help you know. I just handed out the jobs.'

'Yes, but it was all your idea. I was wrong to try to discourage you.' Olive spoke earnestly.

Jeremy looked bashful and stared at his curry again.

'And there's custard tart for dessert,' she added.

'You beauty! Worth every bit of effort for that!' Jeremy grinned like a schoolboy.

'Also, I'm giving you that Lonergan heifer.' Olive sniffed primly to show that she was serious.

The other three stared at her in amazement, but Sam and Alice made no comment.

'Holy f—... mackerel.' Jeremy fell silent. It looked to Olive as though he was scrabbling around for the right words. 'Thanks, Mrs Day,' he said finally, smiling at her with genuine humility.

She recognised it immediately and smiled back. 'That's my pleasure, Jeremy.'

With quiet determination and many sips of water, Jeremy forced down some more of the curry, with Alice and Sam following suit. Olive watched him, remembering Sam's comment at one time about 'writing off a young bloke'. They were making some headway in the reformation process, and at times she congratulated herself for it. But then, try as she might, she couldn't dismiss the sneaking suspicion in the back of her mind that perhaps Jeremy hadn't changed that much at all. Perhaps her new perception of him was simply a result of her beginning to know him at last.

After eating a large serving of custard tart smothered in thick cream, Jeremy appeared to recover from the unusually timid mood that had kept him subdued through much of dinner. 'Real nice type, that heifer. Show quality, I'd reckon.' He wiped his dessert bowl clean with his work-roughened forefinger and sucked it. 'Very decent of the Lonergans to donate her. Best not mention it to Wingnut, though, Ali. Don't think he'd be too stoked about me ending up with her.'

Olive tried to look grim. He was back to his usual self.

'Don't worry, Jeremy, I know when to keep quiet,' Alice answered.

Jeremy regarded her for a moment, then laughed. 'Couldn't be more different from me in that way,' he said. But he clearly wasn't going to waste time dwelling on that depressing thought. Instead he looked longingly from his squeaky-clean bowl to the remaining tart in the dish. Olive pushed it towards him, deciding that just for tonight, she'd go all out and bend the dessert rules.

'Ripper! Ta, Mrs Day.' Jeremy slid the wedge into his bowl and started into it immediately. Through his food he mumbled thoughtfully to himself, 'Best bloody heifer I've ever owned.' Then, more quietly, 'Only heifer I've ever owned.'

Sam looked up from his tart in surprise.

Swallowing his mouthful, Jeremy looked around at them all and announced, 'I'm gonna call her Olive.'

Chapter 26

Fencing with Jeremy was extremely productive. The three Redstoners were working on a seven-kilometre stretch that would divide Pandemonium paddock in half. They made a good team. Sam did all the tractor- and ute-driving jobs, Alice all the walking jobs, and Jeremy the tasks that required heavy lifting. It was an efficient combination.

After months of fencing on and off, at last they were realising Alice's dream of quartering all the paddocks of more than a thousand acres. The barbed wire was expensive and all the timber posts had to be first cut by hand, but they had already commenced rotational grazing in Top Cedar Tree, Mistake Creek and Hazelbrae. This meant that all the cattle were condensed into a quarter of the original area for a month or two, then rotated through the other quarters. The immediate improvement in health of the pasture in these paddocks had been enough to convince Sam that it was worth dividing the other large paddocks in the same fashion.

But fencing was a manual and often tedious job. With all the mustering up to date and no other urgent jobs presenting themselves, they had now been fencing for eight days straight. Despite Jeremy's best efforts to keep them entertained with his usual foolish tricks, the team were losing a little of their enthusiasm for the task.

Sam took a spell in the late afternoon shade, cutting plain wire ties with the pliers for attaching the barbed-wire strands to the steel pickets. Alice was standing at a distance, sighting the final ironbark strainer post for the day. Jeremy had just lowered it into its hole and was holding it in place. He was causing her great frustration by tilting it in the opposite direction to the way she was signalling it needed to go in order to be straight. Finally, though, she was satisfied and came to help him fill in the soil around its base, packing it in hard with the flat end of a crowbar. She was tired and her lower back was aching.

Perhaps sensing her exhaustion, Jeremy took hold of her crowbar and said, 'Here, mate. I'll finish this. You reverse the ute over so I can bore the holes.' The ute had the generator and post hole borer in the back.

Her fatigue made Alice sloppier than usual, and she swerved and overcorrected as she backed the ute towards Jeremy a little too quickly. When she could see she was getting close to the solid post, Alice slowed abruptly and was horrified by a loud bang at the back of the tray. How could she have misjudged so badly? Even worse, she'd just given weight to one of Jeremy's favourite theories, about women being unable to think spatially. But when she hopped out to inspect the damage, she saw that she'd stopped a good metre from the post. Jeremy, looking at her owlishly, banged the steel ute tray hard with the crowbar to repeat the startling sound. Snorting in disgust, Alice rolled her eyes and went to start the generator.

They were all relieved when at last the sun began to descend and it was time to head home for a well-earned dinner.

§

'Who would be so rude as to call at this hour? Right on teatime!' Olive said indignantly.

Alice had just placed a steaming dish of baked vegetables next to a roasted chicken at the centre of the table. Her grandmother was adding a jug of thick gravy and some steamed greens to the spread. Any meal that didn't contain beef was a rare treat at Redstone and the smell was tantalising. The three fencers were anticipating the meal with watering mouths. And then the phone had started trilling.

'I'll give them a piece of my mind,' Olive muttered as she strode towards the offending device.

But after a curt greeting and listening for a moment, her face relaxed and she said pleasantly, 'Oh, hello, Fred, I'm fine, thanks . . . Yes, it was a wonderful success, we were all very proud of Jeremy . . . Oh, they were extremely grateful, Keira is in Brisbane now with Giovanna. And is Heidi better after her little operation? . . . Thank goodness for that. Now, what can we do for you, Fred?'

Alice exchanged an amused glance with her grandfather at her grandmother's cordiality to the caller following her ominous threat.

But then Olive's tone sharpened. 'Alice? What do you need Alice for?' After a pause she said coolly, 'Oh well, if that's how it is, I'd better put her on then. Goodnight, Fred.'

'Can we start?' Jeremy made his request the second Olive lowered the phone.

Ignoring him, she looked at Alice. 'It's Mr Campbell. He has an important and *confidential* matter to discuss with you.' Her grandmother's emphasis on the word 'confidential' showed Alice how annoyed she was about being excluded from the secret. Looking apologetically at the old woman, Alice took the cordless handset and walked into the next room.

'Hello, Mr Campbell.'

'Call me Fred, everyone else does.' Fred Campbell's jovial voice came over the phone and she could picture his rosy, good-natured face. 'How's the town's best winger today?' he asked.

She laughed and Fred went on, 'Alice, I have some good news for you – of a sort. Your father has left some items of value to you in his will. As soon as you can get to town I'd like you to come and view a copy of the document and we can make arrangements for you to take possession of—'

Confused, Alice cut in, 'My father? He's sent you his will? Why?'

'A solicitor in Cairns sent . . . Alice, you *do* know . . . You've been notified, haven't you? Oh hell, didn't you know he'd passed away?'

Alice was silent. She suddenly felt as though the ground was slipping away beneath her feet.

Fred, his professional hat slipping, swore to himself in annoyance. 'Christ. Alice, I'm so sorry. The solicitor assured me that the family had notified you. What a damned awful way to find out.'

'It's not your fault, Mr Campbell. I didn't even know where he lived. Maybe they didn't know how to contact me,' Alice said, her voice expressionless.

'Well, I feel a right insensitive prat. Should've guessed something like this might have happened.'

Alice spoke firmly. 'Mr Campbell, I had to find out one way or another. And I don't really want anything. Tell his family to keep it.'

'Now, you need to come in and see me about all this before you go making any rash statements. Just take a little time to get used to the idea, then come and see me. Give Heidi a ring before leaving Redstone to make sure I'll be in the office.'

'But Mr Campbell—'

'Fred. And no buts. You sleep on it tonight. Talk to your folks.'

'Alright, I suppose so. Goodnight, Mr Campbell.'

'Goodnight, Alice. And once again, I'm truly sorry.'

Alice went back to the kitchen and replaced the phone. Her grandparents put down their cutlery and looked up expectantly. Jeremy didn't stop shovelling food into his mouth, but his eyes followed her with interest as she sank into her chair. Her grandmother was clearly keen to be let in on the secret, but Alice couldn't speak, her mind too paralysed to form any thoughts.

'Well? What's the big news? Mystery solved?' Olive prompted impatiently.

'My father died,' Alice said at last. She was looking down at her neat little hands, folded together on the red and white checked tablecloth.

There was a stunned silence. Sam's eyes opened wide and he shook his head. Olive looked decidedly uncomfortable.

Jeremy was still studying Alice. 'Bugger, Ali.' His voice was gently sorrowful.

She looked up at him. His eyes were full of sympathy, and she felt a sudden lump in her throat.

'That's rough luck,' he went on. 'Specially with you being so keen to meet up with him again.'

'Yes.' Alice breathed out the monosyllable as a regretful sigh.

'Were you? I didn't know that,' Olive snapped accusingly. Alice didn't react, knowing it was discomfort that made her grandmother insensitive.

Then Sam spoke up. 'Would've liked to see him again myself. Benji was a legend. The world has lost a remarkable man. It's a great shame.'

Alice felt numb. She wished they would all stop talking.

'How did he die?' her grandmother asked. 'Not coming off one of those wild things he used to ride?'

'Mr Campbell didn't say. Ma, can I please eat this tomorrow? I might just have a bath and go to bed.'

'You must eat something, Alice. You've been out working all day. What else did Fred tell you?'

'I have to go and see him about the will.'

'Will? What of value would Benji have ever had?' Olive demanded.

Alice stood up and went mechanically to put away her untouched plate and cutlery. She had to get away. Be by herself.

'Alice, you must eat,' insisted Olive. 'When does Fred want to see us?'

'Next time I'm in town.'

'Can you take a break from fencing? We could go in tomorrow.'

'Thanks, Ma, but I think I'll leave it till next week when I go to pick up those pallets of lick in the truck. There's no need for you to go to the bother of coming. It's something I'd rather do alone.'

'Without me interfering, I suppose you mean.' Olive sounded offended.

Luckily, Sam came to the rescue. 'Of course that's what she means, Liv. Leave the poor kid alone.'

A long time after going to bed, Alice lay wide awake, staring into the darkness with wide, dry eyes. Her exhausted body was held hostage by the sickening maelstrom of emotions whirling around in her brain. Any hint of drowsiness had been chased away. She searched the recesses of her memory for every detail of her one and only meeting with her father.

Alice found that she could clearly picture his face. She'd been fourteen, and the memory was still vivid. She and her grandfather were bringing the Summerlea breeders and calves in for weaning. As they approached the Redstone yards, through the cloud of dust the mob had raised she'd seen a man. She'd known him immediately.

He was balanced on the top rail of the old house yards and he sat up tall and waited. Alice felt her heart pounding. She was about to meet her father. Something she'd been longing for all her life suddenly seemed terrifying. When they came round the bend in the track, the rippling mob was moving quickly. Her two dogs circled the cattle, returning often to her side at the tail of the herd before venturing out again to push a beast in here, hurry one along there, or tidy up the stragglers at the back. Sam was out in the lead but Alice could see that Benji was searching beyond him, looking for her. As she came closer, Alice saw that his eyes were shining.

Her grandfather had seen him too; raising his hat, he yelled out in welcome as he passed. Once the cattle were yarded, her grandfather sent her to take the two horses to the back yard, where they would wait until they were needed later. From there, Alice watched her grandfather warmly shake Benji's hand and slap him on the back. The two men chatted for a minute, then looked in her direction, smiling. Alice swallowed nervously and waited until she saw her grandfather beckon. Then she trotted over to them.

She examined her father shyly. Their eyes met and she recognised an extraordinary gentleness in his gaze. Her anxiety drained away.

'Alice, this is Benji Wilson.' Her grandfather smiled at her encouragingly before looking back at the stockman. 'I'll just go on inside and tell Olive to boil the jug. You two come on in when you're ready.'

But as he started to walk away Benji called after him. 'Thanks, Sam, but I'll be keeping on my way after I have a talk with Alice.'

The older man turned back, disappointed. 'Oh, that's a mighty shame, Benji. Been great seeing you back here.' He held out his hand and Benji shook it again, firmly.

'You too, Sam. I wanna thank you for everything.' Benji looked significantly at Alice.

'It's been a privilege.' The two men smiled at one another and then, tipping his hat, Alice's grandfather turned and walked away.

Benji climbed back up onto the rail. He patted the timber beside him with his hand and raised his eyebrows at Alice. She climbed up too and perched alongside him, regarding him curiously.

'You're my father, aren't you?'

'Yes, Alice.'

She looked again into his eyes. They were her own eyes, lustrous and dark. It was an eerie feeling.

'Have you ever seen me before today?' Alice asked.

'No. I never knew I had a little girl. Never knew until a few days back. First time I bin back south since leaving here. Ran into old Stretch and he told me.' Benji paused, then went on, 'Had to come and see you for meself.'

'And what do you think of me?'

The frankness of her question seemed to please him. 'I think today I'm one lucky fella. I just can't believe that the best girl I ever saw is my own girl.' He bestowed on her one of his rare and famous smiles. The Benji Wilson Smile. Alice wondered whether it was this smile that had won her mother's heart. She'd never forget it. She tingled all over and smiled back, her face glowing.

Then, serious again, she asked, 'Are you going to take me away?'

Benji looked surprised and for a fleeting moment, elated. 'Do you wanna come?'

Alice looked away, suddenly afraid. She couldn't bear the thought of leaving Redstone. But at the same time, she wanted to get to know this man.

Benji studied her countenance with a half-smile. 'Don' you worry, Alice. This Redstone is your country. Sam and Mrs Day are your people. Not my country and not my people. I would never take you away from here. I'll go back to my own place. But it won't be the same, because now I know about you. My own girl. This has been my lucky day.'

Alice took his hand and squeezed it gratefully. He hopped down effortlessly and still holding his hand she alighted beside him.

'When's your birthday?' Benji asked.

'The twenty-first of April.' She beamed at him. It was the first thing she'd told him about herself.

He nodded slowly. 'I'll remember.'

Behind him, Alice could see her grandmother waiting impatiently on the veranda, hands on hips. Benji tipped his hat to the grim-faced woman then looked back into Alice's eyes. 'I'm not gonna forget about you.' He kissed her small hand and gently released it. Then, before Alice had a chance to say goodbye, he was walking away.

Alice stood numbly where she was and watched him go.

As Benji drove away she realised that she hadn't asked him when *his* birthday was. She watched the trail of dust rise along the road behind his departing vehicle and her vision became blurred with tears. Her mind was suddenly flooded with all the things she wanted to tell him. About her horses and her dogs. How much she despised boarding school and Jacinta. About the Brumby Spring and the bush run. She wanted to ask him about the strange shivery feeling that she often experienced when she was alone in the scrub. She wanted to share thoughts and ideas with him that she'd never revealed to anyone before. But she'd save all these things until next time. She couldn't wait to see him again.

Now, at age nineteen, lying in her narrow wooden bed, Alice was soothed a little by the memory of her father's smile. But there had been no 'next time', and she ached with loss. It was the same loss that she'd experienced every year since on her birthday. There had never been another word from him. She'd always intended to track him down, to go looking for him in 'the north'. But she'd missed her chance.

The strange feeling that she'd truly known Benji had to be merely a product of her yearning imagination. She hadn't known him, and he obviously hadn't wanted to know her. It was somehow easier to be angry than sad, so the relief that might have come to Alice had she shed tears of bereavement never arrived. She wouldn't indulge in such tears when she had no real claim to kinship with the man who had died. Dry-eyed, she fell at last into a light slumber just before dawn.

§

The following Wednesday, Alice drove the old truck into town, picked up the pallets of lick, then went to see Fred Campbell. He told her that Benji had died a little more than a month before, of lymphoma. He'd refused all treatment and the aggressive cancer had ended his life quite quickly. Apart from Benji's wife, a woman called Leilani, Fred couldn't tell Alice of any other family.

In the will, Alice had inherited a two-year-old Hino body truck, complete with a stock crate. She'd also been left two horses, of which there was no detail provided, a saddle and a dog. Alice felt pleased about the truck, but uncomfortable about the animals. Why had Benji left them to her? It seemed too personal a gesture from someone who had never known her. These animals had lived and breathed beside Benji. He'd handled them and probably taught them everything they knew. They would innocently carry a painful significance for Alice, and she wasn't sure that she wanted to be surrounded by these constant living reminders of her lost opportunity.

That night when they sat down to dinner, Alice gave her grandparents and Jeremy the news of her inheritance. Then, her duty done, she quietly set about eating her meal, leaving them to discuss and analyse what they had learned.

Her grandmother seemed dubiously pleased. 'Well, if it actually amounts to anything and this truck really exists, it will be a great boost for our budget. We're long overdue for a new truck and we can get rid of the old one at last.'

'Been a reliable old girl, that truck,' Sam observed. 'Might still come in handy for—'

'No, Sam,' Olive said. 'Vehicles cost money to maintain. Especially that one. It's definitely going, as soon as this new one materialises.' Always thinking of the practicalities, she added, 'How are we going to get all this down here from Cairns?'

'I thought I might take a trip up on the bus,' Alice said quietly.

'Hitch a ride with some grey nomads,' Jeremy suggested helpfully.

'But where is this truck? I mean, who has it now? What sort of people will you be dealing with?' Olive was beginning to get worked up.

'Well, heck, Alice's probably gonna find she's got a few dozen siblings up there.' Jeremy chuckled.

'Thank you, Jeremy. I can always rely on you to add stress to a situation.' Olive glared at his grinning face.

'Chin up, Mrs Day. No need to get your knickers in a knot. I could go along with Alice and be her – what's the word? – chaperone. I could make sure none of them little piccaninnies stow away in the crate.'

Olive looked at him uncertainly, as if considering the offer.

Alice resolved the dilemma. 'Thanks, Jeremy, that's really kind of you, but if I'm gone for a few days Pa will need you here.' There was a slight tremor in her voice. The visit, while exciting, would undoubtedly be one of painful discovery for her. By stepping into her father's world, she'd be exploring her own feelings in a way she'd always avoided, until now.

'Rejected again.' Jeremy sounded mournful.

'But surely you won't be staying up there though?' The old lady was alarmed.

'I don't know,' said Alice. 'It seems rude to just show up for the goods, then clear out again. And I want to find out a bit more about my father.'

'The less you know the better, in my opinion,' Olive said sulkily.

Sam couldn't let that go. 'Now, Olive, that's not fair – or honest. Benji was a capital fellow. He was well worth knowing. Just because Lara landed him in the—'

'Sam, how dare you?' Olive was going red in the face.

Alice jumped in. 'Please don't worry, Ma. I'm quite capable of looking after myself. It's something I feel I have to do. I may never get another chance.'

Chapter 27

Alice stood for a moment regarding the dilapidated wooden house set high off the ground on rough timber posts. It had welcoming wide verandas all round, rimmed with straggly little flowering bushes, frangipani and hibiscus. From behind these, a number of small children were peering shyly, their skins a variety of shades. A motley collection of dogs came running around the side of the house, barking to announce the arrival of a stranger.

It hadn't taken Alice long to find the solicitor's office in Cairns. The tidy young secretary had given her directions to Benji's former home, a small acreage not far out of town. Now that the taxi had driven away, leaving Alice standing at a short distance from the house, her swag hanging from one arm and her backpack on the other, the nerves that had plagued her for the entire length of the bus trip from Emerald had turned to nausea. She gritted her teeth and walked towards the house.

The dogs stood their ground, still barking, but the children melted into the darkness under the house. As she approached the front steps, she could hear muffled giggling coming from the safety of their secret domain. A woman came out of the front door and stood at the top of the steps beaming at Alice. She was small, thin and very black. Her head was covered with a mop of soft black hair with a slightly reddish-brown tinge at the ends of her curls, and she was wearing a baggy, light cotton dress in a large scarlet flower print. Alice guessed this was Leilani.

The older woman held her arms out wide as Alice started up the steps, greeting her with a hug once she'd reached the veranda.

'Alice, sweetheart. We've been expecting you any day now.' Leilani held Alice at arm's length and looked her up and down. 'Benji didn't lie about how pretty you were.'

Alice laughed in embarrassment, but she felt her anxiety fast subsiding at the genuine welcome she could see in Leilani's deep-set brown eyes. 'Hello, Leilani. I'm so glad to be here.'

'Not as glad as we are to have you, my love.' Leilani grabbed Alice's heavy swag with her skinny arms and heaved it inside. 'Come and have a cuppa.'

Sitting at a little wooden table, on mismatched chairs, the two women regarded each other with mutual pleasure as they sipped their tea.

'Benji was so proud of you,' said Leilani. 'He used to think about you all the time. Every day, I reckon.'

Alice longed to believe this was true, but couldn't help expressing her doubts. 'Why did he never contact me or tell me where you lived?'

'Oh, my love, when he saw you with your people he knew that you had been raised the white way. You were doing really fine without him coming to stir up trouble.' Leilani patted her hand. 'He didn't want to mix you up and make you unhappy. He knew Sammy Day was a good man. Sammy told him that one day you would be running Redstone. Benji thought he should keep himself out of it and not go interfering.'

'It wouldn't have been interfering. I just wanted to talk to him and get to know him. I could have learned so much from him, Leilani.'

'I know, baby. I thought so too. But Benji, he made up his mind. He didn't forget you. He used to ring old Stretch every year in April – your birthday month. Benji wasn't happy you had to go away to townie school. He said you needed to be in your own country, not in some noisy city. Stretch told him all about what you been doing. Deadly with horses. Deadly with dogs. Alice, love, he was so proud.'

Alice's eyes were full of tears; normally she would have attempted to hide them, but for some reason she didn't mind Leilani seeing.

'That's right, my love,' Leilani said. 'You go on and cry now. I always cry, every day. For a man like our man, who wouldn't?'

Alice wiped her eyes and smiled at Leilani. She took a calming sip of tea and then asked, 'Do I have any brothers and sisters? Were those kids I saw all yours?'

Leilani laughed. 'No, none of them really mine, sweetheart. Not from my own body. I got something not right downstairs. Never had a baby. Raised plenty but.' She laughed to herself again.

'Did Benji – my father have any . . .' Alice wasn't sure how to finish the question.

Leilani came to the rescue. 'Kids with other women? No, honey. He was a good man, my Benji. My good man.' Suddenly she began to wail loudly and covered her face. Alice jumped up and went to her. She bent down and put her arms tightly around the shuddering little body until Leilani's sobs eased.

Glancing up, Alice saw four little faces peeping around the door frame. She smiled and they disappeared again amid peals of laughter. Leilani chuckled through her tears.

Alice went back to her chair and sat down again. 'I'm not going to take the truck, Leilani. You can sell it, and the horses. I can see that you have a lot of people to look after here.'

'No chance, sweet. Benji left me pretty well set up. He wanted you to have those things more than anything. Would be rotten of you not to take 'em. Would be wrong to Benji too.'

The sound of a clapped-out car pulling in to the yard interrupted their conversation. An old red Ford station wagon stopped at the bottom of the steps, and a woman and some more chattering kids climbed out. The kids shot off around the back but the woman came quickly up the stairs. She stopped abruptly in the doorway, eyeing Alice narrowly. She looked worn and tired and, Alice suspected, older than she really was. Her face must once have been pretty but her sullen expression, drooping posture and straggly hair gave the impression of jaded exhaustion.

'Alice, this is Mary, Benji's sister,' said Leilani. 'She's your family too.'

Alice stood up and held out her hand, but Mary pushed past her and plopped down into another of the miscellaneous chairs. She continued to regard Alice with an unfriendly stare as Leilani went on.

'Benji has another sister, Ruby, but she gone north with her man to Lockhart. His brother Reuben died already too.'

Alice looked from Leilani back at Mary and smiled tentatively, sitting down. At this Mary spoke. 'Heard you showed up. Didn't take ya too long. Never come when Benji was alive, did ya? Or when he was sick. Jus' when he was dead.'

Alice drew in a sharp breath but Leilani was indignant. 'You shut your angry mouth, Mary. This little girl never knew. You know like I do Benji wouldn't let us tell.'

'What she come here for anyway?' Mary was still glaring at Alice. 'Jus' look at that coconut sitting there. Why don' you just get your stuff and go?'

Alice remained silent. After Leilani's warm welcome she'd let her guard down and now she felt shaken. But worst of all, she knew that there was an element of truth in what Mary said. She'd never made any effort to find her father. She'd waited until it was too late.

But Leilani spoke reassuringly. 'Don' you take no notice of Mary, honey. She's real sour. Sour old fish. She don' really mean it. She talks cranky to everybody like that. But specially you 'cause you're so pretty an' she's so ugly and sour.'

'You the ugly old sour one, Leilani. Don' know what Benji wanted with you. Not right in the head, I reckon.' Mary was scowling at Leilani now.

'See, sweetheart?' Leilani smiled calmly at Alice. 'Talks like that to me too.'

Mary sat there sulking while Leilani told Alice all about Benji. He'd grown up further north on a large station where his father had worked. As a teenager and young man he'd been employed on several stations around Queensland. Not long after leaving Redstone, he'd met Leilani in Cairns and decided to go out on his own as a contract musterer and horse breaker. They had married and Benji had worked in the Cairns area ever since. He was highly respected in the community, despite his well-known occasional benders. When he became ill he'd sold all his working dogs but one, and all his horses except for two.

'Reckon he loved those animals more than he loved me.' Leilani laughed quietly and rocked back and forth in her seat. 'Loved that truck too. Was like his baby.'

Later that afternoon, some of the kids condescended to let Alice play with them. Leilani brought out a cricket bat and some stumps obviously used only on special occasions. Mary seemed to have cheered up and the two older women sat on the veranda and cackled as they watched the game. The children were in ecstasy. After that, Alice had a permanent trail of kids behind her.

Three unspeaking men arrived just on dark and nodded to Alice before stretching out on the veranda. She rolled out her swag on the quieter side of the house and lay awake listening to the tropical hum. She thought first of her father, and found that the thought of him no longer made her angry; then for some unfathomable reason she thought of Jeremy and wondered what sort of a stir he'd have caused with these people had he come. Would they have liked him? To her surprise, she had a feeling that they would have. With the image of him uppermost in her mind, she drifted off to sleep at last.

§

The next morning, Alice found that she was first into the kitchen, so she made a pot of tea. Mary wandered in shortly afterwards, her wiry hair sticking out at all angles. She stood regarding Alice for a moment.

'Want a cuppa?' Alice asked, pouring her one. She'd noticed the day before that Mary had her tea black with two sugars. Alice handed it to her and Mary took it wordlessly and sat down, still examining Alice as she began to sip.

'You a good girl,' she said finally. 'Benji would've liked his girl.'

'Thanks, Mary.' They sipped their tea. 'Do you know any of the places where Benji worked? I would like to meet some of his friends.'

'Take you after breakfast,' answered Mary briefly.

So they spent all that day visiting in Mary's car. Mary, solemn and withdrawn, with two little boys hiding behind her legs, waited patiently at each property while Alice chatted to a variety of people about Benji. She saw horses he had broken in and dogs that he had bred and trained. As the day wore on she became aware of a growing warmth inside her, a building pride in her father, who had been so highly regarded by so many.

That afternoon they returned to Leilani's and ate sausages around the fire; this time the men spoke a little. Four more carloads of people arrived and another round of sausages and onions was put on to cook. The cricket set came out again and everyone from the very young to the very old joined in, playing until it was too dark to see. Alice was named 'man of the match'. Things went downhill when another, rowdy carload of people arrived bringing grog.

Alice disappeared inside before midnight to roll out her swag in a back room. She was thinking of the long drive ahead. However, not long after going to sleep she was awoken again when a few of the children, dragging blankets, came and nestled in beside her, accompanied by an old dog.

§

After breakfast the next morning, she loaded the horses and the dog onto the truck, somewhat mechanically. She hadn't really even looked at them properly yet. There would be plenty of time for that back at Redstone, and for the emotions it would no doubt arouse in her. Then she drove back over to the house to make her farewells.

By this time, the fire had been relit and the last of the sausages and onions were cooking. The mob gathered around and Alice was hugged, kissed and slapped on the back. The children hung on to her clothes while Leilani and Mary squeezed her and cried.

Leilani put the soft palms of her hands on Alice's cheeks and looked deep into her eyes. 'You let me know if you ever need anything, honey. I love you, sweetheart.'

And Alice knew she meant it, this tired little woman who already had too many people to care for. 'Thank you, Leilani. I will. You too.'

Mary walked with Alice to the truck holding her hand. As Alice hoisted herself up into the driver's seat, the children clung to her.

She drove down the dirt track honking the horn, a trail of squealing barefoot children pelting along behind her. The few men who were awake, standing by the fire, raised their hands in farewell salutes. Alice's face was streaked with tears. For the first hour that she drove, they flowed like two little salty streams down her cheeks, splashing onto her jeans. But she was smiling.

Chapter 28

It was nearly Christmas and Redstone was critically dry. The storms that sometimes came in October, bringing the first relief from the dry season, hadn't arrived. Then November had come and gone with unrelenting sunshine and skies that were endlessly blue.

If it hadn't been for the few unseasonal showers they'd had on Redstone through the winter, the grass would have been completely gone. As it was, it was becoming sparse and unpalatable for the cattle. The ground was baked hard and cracked in places. All the dams were low or dry and their boggy banks had become treacherous for the weakened cows. All the cattle were showing the strain, their bones visible through their hides; the lactating cows were doing it particularly tough, and their calves were stunted from lack of milk.

The dingoes were making their presence felt, coming in from the national park and killing or mauling the feeble calves. The cows, usually so protective of their babies, were too weary to put up much of a fight. Each day there were new grim discoveries, heralded by circling crows and eagles that could be seen from a distance. Wild brumbies, goats and pigs also began to break the boundary fences in search of water and feed. Checking became an even more vital and frequent duty than usual.

But as her grandfather admitted to Alice at dinner one night, the cows had hung on much longer this time before starting to 'crack up'. This could only be due to the mineral dry lick Alice had insisted they begin to use three months earlier. It had involved more expense, with small shelter sheds needing to be built, and replacing it regularly was time-consuming. But now, as significant numbers of cattle on the neighbouring properties began to die, the Redstone cows hung on.

In December, the time of the usual wet season, the clouds began to build. Each day, the sky taunted all the thirsty creatures inhabiting the parched country below. Starting mid-morning as almost invisible wispy tendrils of vapour, the clouds would accumulate throughout the day. By early afternoon the sky would be half full of a spectacular fluffy display that piled higher upon itself as the day drew to a close. But no amount of wishing, praying or gazing skywards would induce it to release a single drop of moisture, and by the next morning the clouds would have evaporated again. This pattern continued for a few weeks until the inhabitants of Redstone began to go about their business ignoring the empty promise of the clouds.

On her return from up north, Alice had turned the yearling colt from her father out into the Brigalow paddock with the pack ponies. She'd watched him gallop away with his tail held high and thought back to what Leilani had said when she'd taken Alice to see the horses: 'Benji sold all his horses and dogs when the sickness came. Except for two and one. The big grey mare he said you might not like. But 'e wanted me to tell you, she's strong and will get the job done. He was going to breed from her. The colt he said was the one for you. He knew you will like that horse.'

But apart from occasionally checking on the colt to make sure he was behaving himself, Alice hadn't given him a lot of thought since then. The liver chestnut was still at the gangly adolescent stage, but she could see he was a large part-Arabian. He had a perfectly sculpted head with a small nose, large flared nostrils and a deeply dished-out face in true Arabian style. His eye and manner were a little fiery and her grandfather had shaken his head ominously at the sight of him.

The grey mare was six or seven years old, judging by her teeth. Also visibly Arabian, she had a dash of something more solid – Sam thought perhaps even Clydesdale. Alice had ridden her once: she discovered that the horse was indeed willing and sound, but that she and the grey had nothing in common. The mare was a hard-headed man's horse. Alice gave her to Jeremy to ride and they hit it off immediately. She also gave him the honour of naming the grey, since she'd forgotten to ask Leilani what she'd been called. He named her Carmen, after a lesbian he'd once met and liked immensely. Strangely, it suited her to a tee.

Benji's pup had been living under the veranda, and to everyone's surprise Olive seemed to have taken a fancy to him. King Henry the Ninth was the only creature the old woman had ever previously admitted to any affection for, so why the ungainly pup was considered worthy of this special attention, Alice could only wonder. He was tall and long-legged, his bony frame covered by course medium length hair, mainly white, with a few large brown splashes. Clearly a cocktail of working dog breeds, he also had something of an overgrown terrier about him. Regarding the unrefined-looking creature, Leilani had said, 'That big ugly pup, Benji made us keep for you. He said don' be put off by his ugly head.' She'd chuckled then. 'He's real special, that pup.'

Alice still felt a strange ambivalence about the intimacy of inheriting her father's animals, and had so far avoided spending any time with the unattractive creature. She told her grandmother to choose a name for him; to Alice's dismay, Olive named him after Mr Darcy. Alice thought it a terrible waste to use the name on such a timid, badly proportioned mongrel.

§

Although she would never have articulated them to her husband and granddaughter, Olive had her reasons for her attachment to the pup. By being kind to Darcy she felt that in some small way she was making amends for her treatment of Benji. After all, the stockman had given them Alice, and while it had seemed a disaster at the time, life without Alice was now unimaginable. Olive could clearly remember the day Benji had come back to Redstone in search of his daughter. She'd been filled with apprehension, afraid that he had come to take Alice away. At that moment, she'd realised how deeply she'd come to love the fey little creature that was her granddaughter, and just how vital a part of Redstone Alice had become.

Olive had always considered herself an excellent judge of character. But just recently, her confidence had been shaken. Since Benji's death, she'd even gone so far as to wonder anew about Lara's actions leading up to Alice's conception. At the time, she'd laid the blame solely and heavily on Benji's shoulders, always maintaining that he'd taken advantage of a young, innocent girl. But now she wasn't so sure. Even as a small child, her daughter had never agreed to do anything unless she wholeheartedly wanted to do it. In recent years, with Lara always absent, Olive had been able to view her daughter's actions more objectively. In doing so, she had realised that self-interest was now, and probably always had been, Lara's prime motivation in life. She never contacted Redstone unless she needed something. She'd been back only twice since Alice's first birthday, and her three children were virtually strangers to their bush grandparents.

Then there was Jeremy. Sam had seen his potential from the very beginning, while Olive had blindly adhered to the bad impression she'd already formed, based solely on the stories and gossip of others.

'Well, it's never too late to learn,' Olive told herself one day, as she sat on the steps patting the pup.

§

For Alice, now wasn't the time to dwell on her father's death. She'd only allow herself the luxury of mourning for the father she'd have loved to know once it had rained and they were on top of things again. And only then, too, would she attend to the pup. With so many drought jobs to do, there had been little time to work with any of the animals.

All Alice's leftover energy was devoted to Mushgang's Arab filly. The animal's sensitive, fast responses and the speed at which she was learning thrilled Alice to the core. Her grandfather had always talked about the 'horse of a lifetime', the kind a person only encounters once, and even then, only if they were lucky. Alice strongly suspected that she'd found that horse.

But her grandfather was concerned. 'Horses like that filly can be killers, Ali. It's not just the bucking. I saw her double-barrel Jeremy that day. Once a dirty horse, always a dirty horse. Can't ever trust 'em.'

Alice had tried to explain that she and the filly truly respected each other and therefore she believed she had nothing to fear. But he wouldn't listen. 'Arabs are bad news, Alice. Spooky bloody things. Lunatics when they're fresh, which is most of the time. Your dad always had Arabs – now he's the only bloke I ever saw that could handle 'em.'

Alice was delighted with this piece of information, and Sam clearly regretted making the comment.

'Stick to what you know, Ali. You won't beat the old Australian stockhorse.'

'Pa, she's the most intelligent horse I've ever handled.'

'Oh, Arabs are intelligent alright, I'll give 'em that. That's their biggest problem. Too many brains and ideas of their own.'

'That's what people say about Brahman cattle, too,' Alice argued. 'You always say that intelligent animals are either the best or the worst kind, depending on how they're handled. I remember you telling me that if I was having a problem with a horse, to hop off and go inside for a good look in the mirror.'

At this her grandfather had chuckled. 'You're a good listener, Alice. But this horse is damaged goods. It's already made up its mind that it hates people. Very hard to reverse that kind of attitude.'

However, Alice continued to work with the filly in defiance of her grandfather, and she could feel the connection growing stronger by the day. Lately she'd noticed that at the sight of her the filly raised her head, pricked her ears and gently flared her large nostrils. Then she'd walk towards her, quivering her lips in a silent nicker. She came of her own free will: this was more than enough reassurance for Alice. The filly wanted to learn. She wasn't a fighter, but like any free spirit, she could become one when backed into a corner. The name on her papers was Desert Storm; Alice renamed her Desert Rose.

Late in November, with her grandfather spying anxiously from the house and Jeremy hovering in the shed nearby, she'd ridden Rose for the first time. As the site for the momentous occasion she'd chosen the open sandy side yard, with its dappled shade and a trough. Her grandfather had argued with her the night before, insisting that she should start in the tiny forcing yard. This would ensure that the filly would have to curve her body, making it harder to buck. But Alice knew that Rose needed breathing space.

Apart from breaking into an instant sweat, her body tight and trembling, the sensitive creature had behaved like a lady. Alice had mounted quickly and then simply sat, stroking the mare and talking softly for a long time. Then she'd dismounted and mounted again several times in quick succession before unsaddling Rose and letting her go. Jeremy had asked her later if she'd 'chickened out', but she assured him she'd achieved exactly what she'd set out to do for that day.

Since then, Alice had ridden Rose at every opportunity, usually at daybreak or sunset, but always within the safety of the yards. Alice could now turn her, stop her and move her with the slightest touch of a leg, twitch of a finger on the reins or shift in her body weight. In the paddock, Rose had mated up with Snoopy, her grandfather's old bay stockhorse. He was well and truly at the bottom of the herd pecking order, just as Rose was clearly at the top. Therefore, the two were no threat to one another and soon became inseparable.

One afternoon a few days before Christmas, Jeremy and Alice were home a little earlier than usual from 'pulling' a windmill. This was a greasy, strenuous job that involved hauling the pipe under the windmill up from under the ground, section by section, with a block and tackle type pulley, until the damaged length was found and could be replaced. They were having smoko with the old couple, who had been out checking on the back country. On this rare occasion, Olive had accompanied her husband, to keep his spirits up, Alice supposed. Sam was complaining about the way windmills always played up in the driest times when there was no surface water lying around to rely on for back-up.

'I'm going to take Rose for a ride outside the yard this afternoon,' Alice announced suddenly. 'Out into Summerlea, I think.'

'Why don't you go up the fenced laneway, Ali? Much safer. Jeremy, can you go along with her?' Sam said.

'If the lady wants my company I'd be honoured,' said Jeremy gallantly.

'Yes please.' Alice nodded. 'She'll be less anxious with another horse there.'

'Bugger. Here I was thinking you were wanting my company.'

Alice ignored Jeremy and went on, 'She'd hate the laneway, Pa. Too hemmed in.'

'That's the whole point,' Sam growled.

'Jeremy, could you please ride Snoopy? They're mates.' Alice smiled at him hopefully.

Jeremy made a face. 'Carmen would be better, female company 'n' all.'

'They hate each other with a passion. Even through the fence. Carmen wants to be top horse,' Alice explained patiently to the unperceptive males.

'Righto, I'll ride another geriatric. Snoopy's only a bit more than half dead. He even makes Rita look like a spring chicken. The things I do for you, Alice.' Jeremy shook his head.

They set out from the yard, the young horse and the old, the small woman and the tall man. Sam and Olive were watching from the window but Alice was entirely tuned in to Rose. All her uncertainty left her as she felt the filly relax and stretch out into a free-flowing walk. Yes, she was happy to be out in the open.

The dusty air seemed to shimmer in the late afternoon sun that was slipping under the cloud bank. Insects hummed and the stillness was oppressive. But Alice was oblivious to everything but her mare. Finally, she and Rose stopped. Alice smiled at Jeremy, acknowledging his existence; silently, he gave her the thumbs-up. She took her water bottle from the little pouch in front of her saddle. The mare shied and turned her head to inspect the movement and unfamiliar sound, so Alice rubbed her neck and showed her the bottle.

'I just need to get off for a leak,' Jeremy whispered.

Alice laughed. 'I've never known you to be quiet for so long.'

'Well, you touchy women put a man on edge, I can tell ya.' He dismounted and went to find a tree.

Alice took the opportunity to hop off too; her girth needed tightening. She pulled the leather strap up a hole. Rose rested one back leg on the point of the hoof, a sure sign of relaxation.

Something had been pricking the top of Alice's foot inside her boot, so she took a moment to crouch down and have a look. A splashing stream of urine sounded on the ground close behind her. Unperturbed, she continued with her mission, determined not to look around. But a sudden wetness on the middle of her back sent her leaping forwards in indignation. Rose lifted her head and lurched away, stopping after a few strides to turn back and investigate. Snoopy stood dozing as though nothing had happened. A disgusted Alice spun round to see Jeremy zipping up his fly and pointing her water bottle towards her. With relief, she realised that the spray of liquid hadn't been warm. Jeremy looked at her face and doubled over with laughter. It was hard for Alice to maintain the angry glare. Nor was there any point: she knew that Jeremy was incorrigible. Suddenly she found herself laughing too.

Chapter 29

'Sam! Sam! Snake!' Olive was bellowing from the little three-sided shed behind the house, where she milked the cow each morning.

Jeremy strolled in calmly from the opposite end of the shed. Olive stood on the milking stool pointing wildly at the large snake, which had frozen mid-journey across the dirt floor, tasting the air with its tongue. The milker was shifting anxiously, aware that all wasn't well but held prisoner by the head bale.

'It's a brown!' Olive screeched. 'Don't just stand there!'

Jeremy put one hand on his hip. 'What a whopper!' he said admiringly. 'Yep, he's a bad bugger alright.'

'Kill it!' Olive was almost hysterical by now.

Jeremy shifted his weight onto the other foot. 'You're forgetting the magic word, Mrs Day.'

'Please! Please, Jeremy, kill it!'

'What will you give me for doing it?' Jeremy taunted, his eyes twinkling.

'Just kill it! Immediately!'

'All in good time, Mrs Day, all in good time. I just wanna know what you'll do for me in return.'

'Sam! Help! Sam!'

'Will you cook golden syrup dumplings for dessert?' Jeremy suggested quickly.

'Yes! Just kill it!'

'Every day this week?'

At this point the snake decided it was time to unfreeze and depart, so without waiting for an answer, Jeremy grabbed the snake-whacking wire that hung on a hook near the door and struck hard across the middle of the creature's length. Olive let out a deafening scream and the snake writhed in the dirt, its back broken. Jeremy hit it again, closer to the head, and it lay jerking fitfully with its final muscle spasms.

'You are utterly infuriating, Jeremy O'Donnell! You're very lucky I don't have a weak heart.' Olive stepped down and plonked herself onto the stool, panting, her hand on her chest.

Jeremy sniggered as he hooked the limp body of the snake over the end of the wire, waved it at Olive, then headed for the door carrying it in front of him. He stopped and looked back over his shoulder at her. 'I'll be looking forward to those dumplings. You might be a cranky old sow, but you sure know how to make A-one dumplings.' Having said this, he departed.

Olive sat there a little longer, amazed to discover that she was feeling pleased. She scolded herself inwardly. It hadn't been a compliment — Jeremy had been outrageously insolent. He'd called her an old sow!

But she had to admit to herself that while Jeremy was cocky and disrespectful, he was also resilient. During this latest dry spell, Olive had noticed that everyone's spirits had remained high, and that must be at least partly because of Jeremy. Nothing seemed to have the power to dampen his everlasting sense of fun. He threw himself into even the tedious drought jobs with energy and enthusiasm, and his arrogant swagger, cheery whistle, ready jokes and tricks kept them all buoyed up despite the unrelenting dry. But Olive had been most struck by Sam's unusually positive frame of mind. She'd been dreading the onset of the usual brooding silence that characteristically gripped her husband during tough times. Jeremy's silly antics had succeeded where all Olive's solicitous concern had failed.

So, later that day, Olive made the golden syrup dumplings for dessert with extra-special care.

§

It was a depressingly dusty Christmas. In the morning, Jeremy stayed at Redstone to tinker in the shed while the others went to church. But nobody prayed for rain. They had worn out that request. Olive stubbornly cooked up a hot roast turkey and baked vegetables which they dutifully ate despite the hunger-sapping heat of the day. They struggled most with the hot plum pudding, except for Jeremy, who had three helpings.

At last, on Boxing Day, when even Jeremy had concluded that the clouds had forgotten how to rain, the sky suddenly opened. They were just finishing afternoon smoko after yet another day of dreary drought jobs. As usual, the clouds had been building throughout the day, but the Redstoners had gone about their business with little expectation of the sky delivering on its promise. Sam had been putting out molasses in the deregistered truck, which Jeremy had fitted with an old steel thousand-gallon tank for the purpose. Again, Olive had gone with him. Jeremy had noticed that despite his reasonably good spirits, the old man was slowing down. Jeremy and Alice had been erecting a temporary fence around Top Cedar Tree dam to keep the cattle away; over recent weeks, the pair had pulled seven stuck cows out of the boggy sides of this watering point. In their weakened state, the suction of the knee-deep mud was too strong for the miserable bovines.

But now, all at once, while they were quietly sipping their tea, the rain began pounding on the iron roof of the stately old Queenslander. The unmistakable sound filled the four at the table with instantaneous delight and they leapt out of their seats. Sam grabbed Alice and waltzed her across the kitchen. Jeremy noticed a flicker of jealousy cross Olive's joyful face at the sight of them. But it was short-lived, as he grabbed her chubby wrist and put his arm around her, jigging her around the kitchen table. She protested loudly but her pleasure was betrayed by her smile.

The frogs that had long been hiding in the few remaining damp places were suddenly resurrected. The exultant throb of their combined voices pierced through the roar of the rain on the corrugated metal.

Olive recovered quickly from her brief episode of elation and went to do the washing-up. Jeremy, Alice and Sam went out to stand on the veranda. Cracks in the ground had been transformed into miniature river systems that merged and broke their banks. The water had formed a shallow coffee-coloured sea, the surface of which was punctured by the fast-falling drops. The tangy scent of the rain on the earth flowed over and around the small group on the veranda. The falling water had banished the oppressive humidity and for the first time in weeks they felt cool. They revelled in the feeling of the tiny icy droplets that were bouncing onto them from the wooden veranda railing. As they gazed at the wall of falling water, Jeremy shouted over the din, 'Told ya it wasn't far off!'

'It's almost worth having the dry, for the feeling you get when it rains!' Alice spoke much louder than usual, but Jeremy still had to lean in close to hear her over the deafening roar. He was caught off guard by a sudden wave of emotion brought on by their close proximity. Powerless against the urge, he threw his arms around her in a crushing embrace. Briefly she hugged him back, while Sam looked out at the rain and pretended not to notice. Even when Alice extricated herself from Jeremy's arms, she let him take the liberty of holding her hand as they stood side by side. Sam turned towards them and they all grinned madly at one another. The rain had set in, and with it the kind of temporary insanity that affects all people on the land when a drought breaks.

In the week that followed, they had more storms and two days of continuous heavy rain. They also lost a few cows. As had happened in other years, after hanging on during months of dry, for a few unfortunate animals the sudden change in weather was the final straw. At first the rain brought only mud and pools of water. Then, like magic, an emerald-coloured film spread over the land. It was as though a semi-transparent green veil had been laid gently over the red dirt. The dormant landscape had been awoken. The sun came out again and the land exploded with growth.

The cattle cropped the rich sweet grass shoots; the manure ran from the animals like greenish treacle, their starved stomachs unable to process the too-rich feed. Within a fortnight of the first rain, the stunted calves visibly began to pick up, their dull roughened coats beginning to shine. The flocks of budgies returned and commandeered bushes and trees across the station, the mad chattering of their extended families jubilant. Dusk was a symphony of amphibious song, the trilling of cane toads carrying on the still evening air.

Then there were the insects. Having been strangely absent for the first half of the summer, they now made up for lost time, arriving in their millions. There was no point staying up after dark, as the unscreened house would rapidly fill with swarming winged things, drawn by the most insignificant of lights. Even the bluish glow of the computer screen was enough to lure the multitudes. Large green frogs also emerged from their daytime hidey holes to lurk close to the lights, the buzzing banquet an irresistible attraction.

§

For some weeks after the rainy period it was too wet to muster or fence. The yards remained a muddy bog and the road into Redstone was impassable for anything larger than a four-wheel drive, so carting cattle was out of the question. Alice knew that this was the time of year when they usually sold their first load of bullocks, but after weathering the extended dry, the older cattle weren't ready for the meatworks. Her grandfather now planned to try to offload some later, before the April bush run, to make room for the new ones they'd be bringing in from the national park.

Alice was concerned that due to their age once they'd reached the required weight, the bullocks wouldn't bring the price Sam had been hoping for. The meatworks would penalise Redstone heavily for the extra teeth the hefty beasts would have cut by April. The bank wouldn't be pleased, and neither would her grandmother. But the hold on mustering, as well as the abundance of feed and water in the paddocks, meant that for a short while everyone had more time on their hands. Jeremy began to restore an old Willy Jeep that had been rusting untouched in the shed for decades. It kept him happy for hours, and sometimes he was so engrossed that he forgot mealtimes and Alice had to go and get him.

For her part, Alice was able to work with the horses again. She wormed them all and took the opportunity to trim their feet while they were soft from the wet ground. She ran Benji's Arab colt in from Brigalow and put him in the night paddock near the yards so that she could spend a little time handling him each day. He was very touchy at first, with a tendency to rear at the slightest provocation, and had a high star-gazing head carriage. But once she'd earned his respect, he decided almost overnight that it was simply easier to toe the line. Like most males he responded well to lavish praise and was soon eating out of her hand.

Alice suspected that she'd merely reawakened in him the memory of some early lessons learned at the capable hands of her father. Benji had painted the sketchy outline of a masterpiece, and she was now faced with the delicate task of finishing it, true to his style. In some strange way, working with the colt seemed to begin healing the wound Alice had been carrying since the loss of her enigmatic father.

The dog, Darcy, had finally begun to grow into his head. He was still ugly, but now that his proportions were sorting themselves out he was less awkward looking and he had an air of patient wisdom about him. He began to shyly approach Alice and even follow her at a polite distance over to the yards. Perhaps he'd sensed that the time was right. Alice couldn't help but develop a fondness for the harmless creature with his wounded-looking amber eyes. She finally forgave him for being the unknown Benji's dog.

Before long he'd started to come with Alice and the Bennet sisters when she rode out from the yards on Rose. At first he was too timid to do anything other than trot along behind her, doing his best to be inconspicuous. When they came across cattle in the paddocks, Alice gave practice tasks to the bitches, instructing them to gather the mob, move them or block them. Darcy would watch longingly (or so Alice imagined), stock still, but every fibre in his body alert. One day, to the extreme mortification of the Bennets, Alice took only Darcy for the afternoon expedition. On reaching the first little mob of cattle, Darcy began to work. And from that day onwards, he never stopped.

Chapter 30

Valentine's Day came around again. While working on the Jeep, Jeremy had been giving it a lot of thought. Should he or shouldn't he? His pride had taken quite a dent the year before when he'd chosen Alice as his valentine and been unexpectedly turned down. He wasn't sure that he wanted to put himself through that again. He asked himself why he was even still thinking about Alice when there were any number of other, willing potential partners for the evening.

A few days before the fourteenth he decided he definitely wouldn't ask her, and was immensely relieved by the resolution. But somehow he didn't get around to making any alternative arrangements. No worries, he told himself, he'd just show up at the pub, same as last year. He'd have girls throwing themselves at him as usual, even the ones who had come with other partners.

But on the afternoon of Valentine's Day, Jeremy found himself experiencing a sense of déjà-vu. Alice came rushing into the shed where he was tinkering to tell him that Carmen had cut her hind legs badly; Alice thought she must have been fighting other horses through the barbed-wire fence. Despite the seriousness of her tidings, Jeremy was temporarily distracted by how lovely she looked. Her hair was escaping loose from a low ponytail and her clothing was spattered with mud and blood, but her smooth skin and fit little form were glowing with health. In the relative darkness of the shed her agitated eyes seemed luminous.

Seeming frustrated by his lack of response, Alice grabbed Jeremy by both arms and looked up into his face. 'Come on! I need some help. She won't stand still for me!'

Jeremy smiled down at her stupidly and received a thump in the chest in return. She jogged to the old broken refrigerator that they used as mouse proof storage in the shed, and rummaged around for bandages and antiseptic.

'We'll need to give her a tetanus shot,' she muttered, then, turning to Jeremy, added, 'Get a tetanus needle from the fridge inside, please!'

Once the wounds had been cleaned, Jeremy and Alice were relieved to find that although messy, they weren't very deep. They threw some lime powder onto the cuts and gave Carmen her needle. After being stubborn and difficult with Alice she behaved like a lady for Jeremy. He was tickled pink over this and explained that it was just his way with women. They let her out into the grassy holding yard where they would be able to keep an eye on her over the next few days. The pair stood shoulder to shoulder watching the big grey mare walk tentatively away.

Then, to his horror, Jeremy heard himself asking Alice if she knew what the date was. She gave him a wary sidelong look and didn't reply. Yes, she had noted the date, he saw. There was no backing out now.

'Are you busy tonight, Ali?'

'Jeremy, I—'

'Look, if another fella's taking you out I'll just—'

'No. No one is taking me out. But Jeremy—'

'Just a quiet night somewhere. By the river? Jeez, Alice, what's the big deal?' Jeremy looked at her imploringly.

She looked down at her muddy boots.

'Don't you trust me? I know I'm not Mr Perfect, but I'm not gonna force myself on you.'

Alice looked back up at him. 'I do appreciate you asking me, Jeremy. But I know that neither of us would enjoy it. And of course I trust you! I spend half my life alone with you.'

Jeremy felt hot indignation flare inside him. Why had he given her the opportunity to humiliate him again? This Valentine's Day refusal was becoming a ritual. He wasn't going to beg this time, at least. 'Righto then. Have a nice night. All alone. Hey, Ali, you should think about joining a convent. You'd make a great nun. Your skin would stay nice and pale under an old habit.'

'Thank you.' She was infuriatingly cheerful. 'Some of the most amazing people who have ever lived were nuns. Ever heard of Mother Teresa? Saint Mary MacKillop?'

'Reckon they still wanted someone to love 'em, but. Bet they were lonely in bed at night. Withered up. Craving love.' Jeremy looked at Alice, whose features were unreadable. How could she be so cold?

She turned and started to walk away, but he caught her hand.

'Please, Ali?' Yep, now he was begging. What in hell was he thinking?

'I'm sorry, Jeremy.'

Her expression was gentle. But now Jeremy was fuming. He dropped her hand. 'I reckon you got tickets on yourself, Alice. You're just a bloody snob. I dunno why I waste my time with you.'

Last year he'd made no impact. This time he could see he'd upset her, hopefully as much as she'd upset him. She was looking up at him, large dark eyes full of bewildered hurt.

'I never asked for your attention, Jeremy. Do you think I don't know that getting me to go out with you is just some sort of challenge for you?' Alice spun around and walked away, but not before Jeremy had seen tears spring up in her eyes. Before he could prevent it, he experienced a sharp stab of regret over his cruel words. He tried not to wish them unsaid: she'd deserved it, he told himself. Was Alice anything more than just a challenge to him?

He stormed over to his cottage to change, and resolved to head off now before his anger could cool. All the way to town in his ute, Jeremy filled his mind with noisy thoughts and blasted his eardrums with AC/DC. He wouldn't think about Alice. Impossible Alice.

That night he had a blast. He did everything that usually spelled a good time. And as always, he was the life of the party. But while his body drank and laughed, his mind drifted back to stately old Redstone and Alice. He found himself remembering her accusation and wondered if it was true. Jeremy didn't leave the pub with any of the girls that asked him to. Instead he drove home alone in the early hours of the morning.

§

Just after dawn, he came and found Alice at the yards where she was working with Benji's colt. He climbed through the rails and stood diffidently in front of her. She looked up at him, seeming surprised to see him up and about so early. As soon as he was sure he had her full attention, he started to speak.

'Ali, I wanted to say I'm real sorry for upsetting you yesterday. And mostly for those crook things I said.'

Alice examined him with her most probing gaze. Then her

expression softened and her eyes spoke compassion. Jeremy felt like a naughty child. In his hung-over state it was maddening.

'Forget it, Jeremy. I wasn't upset for long.' Alice smiled encouragingly.

Jeremy looked at her serene countenance and saw that what she said was true. 'Why not?' All his guilt had evaporated and he spoke testily. 'Why didn't I upset ya? Am I so unimportant? Like some sort of annoying little kid? I s'pose you couldn't care less what *I* think.'

'That's not it at all! I just knew you didn't mean those things you said about me. I know why you said them. I knew that I hadn't done anything wrong, so why be upset? I think a whole lot of you.'

He'd been expecting some kind of sulky, begrudging acceptance of his apology and had been prepared for a few weeks of making amends for the terrible offence he'd caused her. And here she was, feeling sorry for him. Worst of all, he'd needlessly caned himself with guilt for the last twelve hours. Even the rum had failed to anaesthetise the rotten feeling.

Alice reached out and touched his arm. He looked down into her earnest face and reconsidered what she'd just said. She thought 'a whole lot of him'.

'I hate arguing with you, Jeremy. Let's be friends again now that Valentine's Day is over for another year.'

'Righto then, Miss Wilson.' He gave her a quick, hard hug and she sighed in his arms, obviously relieved. He vowed to himself that he would never speak to her rudely like that again.

Chapter 31

The grass had shot away and Redstone was looking a picture. Good feed was now abundant and there was water trickling in all the gullies. The cows were shiny and healthy, their episode of starvation already forgotten.

In March, the Redstone weaners were taken off their mothers despite Sam's insistence that they were too small. But Alice was adamant.

'It's the breeders we need to think about now, Pa. If we don't get those weaners off, those cows will be too slow to recover from the dry, they won't cycle, and our calf numbers will be down again next year.'

The weaning went very smoothly. Alice's dogs were working so effectively that they almost compensated for the lack of manpower. Each afternoon, once her grandfather had disappeared inside to doze in his chair, Alice would saddle Rose and work the weaners. She was pleased to see that Rose was coming along in leaps and bounds.

Then, in April, it was time for the late bullock muster. Sam was strongly opposed to Alice's intention to ride Rose. This was a rogue generation of bullocks: they hadn't been worked as weaners, as Alice had been away at ag college. Sam warned her that there was no place for a green horse on this muster.

However, fate was in Alice's favour. The day before the bullock muster they discovered that Bingley was lame. Then Dan arrived with Mushgang for the four-day muster without his horse, having had to put the gelding down with a broken leg a few weeks before. Suitable horses were thin on the ground so Alice had her wish.

The first paddock they mustered was Pandemonium. When the riders entered at the eastern gate the main mob of bullocks was gathered at the trough. The nervous beasts got wind of the riders when they were still a distance away, and thundered off into the brigalow suckers.

'Cunning old coots,' Sam muttered. 'We'll let them run till they hit the back fence, then work them back around the long way.'

He sent Jeremy on Carmen to trot in one direction around the fence, and Dan in the other. The remaining three split up to canvass the brigalow suckers en route to the back fence, where they hoped the main mob would have pulled up.

Jeremy and Ace arrived on the scene first; at the sight of them, the bullocks began to shift uneasily in preparation for flight. Luckily, Alice arrived shortly afterwards, bringing with her several head that her dogs had flushed out of the suckers. She, Jeremy and the dogs positioned themselves at strategic points around the mob, at a respectful distance, in order to hold the bullocks where they were. When the three older men arrived, the cattle began to mill around suspiciously, looking for a weak point in the blockade. But the riders and dogs stayed in position for more than fifteen minutes, until the bullocks had settled down.

The task now was to move the mob along the fence, exerting just the right amount of pressure to keep them moving without startling them. Sam and Dan went in the lead, Alice, Jeremy and the dogs took the wing, and Mushgang stayed on the tail. They began to push the mob, and at first the large beasts travelled in an orderly fashion.

Then Ace disgraced himself when a hare bounded across his path too tantalisingly close for him to resist. He was off after it like a shot, baying like a hunting hound. Several touchy bullocks rushed forward in surprise, which made some others bust out sideways. Instead of going out wide the too-keen Lydia made an aggressive beeline for them, and the added pressure only hurried them on their way out into the paddock. Kitty and Lizzy went out wide to block them, but, overcome by the size of the galloping bullocks, the two little bitches backed down at the last minute. Next Darcy closed in on the cattle from the side; targeting the ringleader, he leapt at the monster's face and hung for a moment from its nose. The bullock spun around, disturbing the flight of his followers just enough to allow the other dogs to close in again.

By now Alice and Jeremy had arrived and between them they were able to turn the bullocks back towards the fence. But the whole mob began to rush. Sam and Dan were overtaken and in no time the bullocks were in full flight. They were moving fast, but in the right direction along the fence, so the riders' only option was to keep up and try to steer them into the fenced laneway leading to the bullock yards.

Jeremy managed to get close to the lead, and at this point Carmen truly came into her own, roughly shouldering several straying bullocks back into the mob. At Alice's command, Rose stretched out in full gallop, working her way to the front of the mob to help Jeremy direct them into the wing at the beginning of the laneway. Alice hadn't even paused to consider the effect of the unruly chase on her high-strung mount, and it was only once she'd slowed down and reached the safety of the laneway that it occurred to her how responsive and willing Rose had remained amid the confusion.

Once inside the fence, there was nowhere for the uncooperative beasts to go but along the laneway and into the yards. The bullocks slowed to a bellowing trot and the riders were able to drop back to the tail and relax. Once the solid double gates had been shut, they left the bullocks to mill around in the cooler. To give the stirred-up cattle a chance to cool their brains, the four men and Alice took a break for smoko.

Mushgang chewed slowly on a piece of Olive's date slice and looked sideways at Alice as though seeing her for the first time. 'I take my hat off to you, Alice. I thought I was pretty damn good with horses until today.' He shook his head. 'I had that filly well and truly written off. You've proved me wrong. Wait till I tell old Stretch.'

'I'm not as convinced as you, Mush,' said Sam disapprovingly. 'I wouldn't trust that mare as far as I could throw her. Flighty bloody thing that she is.'

'Well, Troy'll think I'm talking rot when I tell him. I reckon he'll be showing up here to see for himself.' Mushgang laughed quietly to himself.

At once Jeremy was on full alert. 'Troy Boy'll jump at the chance to come and see Alice,' he said tauntingly, poking her in the ribs with his finger. She pushed his hand away.

'You're not wrong there,' said Mushgang, chuckling. 'Been stuck on Ali here since he was nine.'

'Don't be ridiculous, Mushgang,' said Alice crossly. 'Troy would be horrified if he could hear you.'

'That's true too,' Mushgang agreed, still grinning.

'Poor fella. Better brace himself for some cruel knockbacks.' Jeremy shook his head sympathetically. 'Unless he has a secret weapon of some kind that I don't know about. He'll need some kind of magic to melt the Ice Queen.' He leaned forward and smiled provokingly into Alice's set face. 'Same as what he uses on those hot young fillies, maybe.'

Alice shoved Jeremy's shoulder hard before standing up to put her cup away in the esky. 'Must be time to draft,' she announced decisively.

'Aw, just when things were getting interesting,' complained Dan.

'Alice, you go on ahead with Jeremy and get started,' said Sam. 'Your eye for fats is every bit as good as mine these days.'

'And a fair bit better too,' added old Dan. They all laughed.

'But use my horse, please, Ali,' called Sam as they started to walk away. 'It'll be too much pressure for your green filly.'

'Pa, just let me start on Rose and see how I go,' said Alice. 'I've done a fair bit of yard work with her on the weaners. Please don't worry.'

Sam shook his head in concern.

'This I have to see.' Mushgang stood up and stretched. 'I'll help too.'

They drafted all the 'finished' bullocks out of the herd into a side yard. Darcy and the Bennet sisters were lined up along the fence, eyes riveted on Alice. She and the filly weaved quietly between the hefty beasts until she spotted a fine full-framed animal with well-covered loins. Rose seemed to sense immediately when Alice had chosen her beast: the agile little horse locked on to it and began a subtle, unrelenting pursuit. With quick, understated movements she started to block, advance, veer and retreat at the precise moment required to separate the bullock from the mob almost before it had registered what was afoot. She then became more assertive and entirely focused on the chosen animal as she directed it authoritatively towards the gate.

This pattern was repeated with each new beast. Rose rarely rushed at a bullock, but nor did she allow it time to stop and think. The sensitive filly seemed to be able to gauge the particular flight zone of each animal and to stroke its perimeter in order to achieve sufficient propulsion without panicking the beast. Most of the troublesome bullocks found that, once separated from their gang of brawny cronies by this small, dark, determined duo, it was simply easier to comply.

Alice was glowing with triumph when they finally finished. She'd discovered the filly's aptitude for this kind of close work when working on the weaners, but she'd been uncertain about how this would translate to the pressure of the bullock yard, with such large animals and other horses, men and dogs present. Rose had come through this test with flying colours.

They had a late lunch before returning the remaining bullocks to the paddock, and Sam hugged Alice with relieved admiration. 'You're a Wilson alright,' he said proudly.

'You taught her all she knows, eh?' Dan grinned.

'Wish I could make that claim,' Sam answered him seriously. He added quietly, 'What Ali's got can't be taught.'

Chapter 32

Alice's favourite month had come around again. April meant the bush run and her birthday; this year she'd be turning twenty. A few days before they planned to leave, she ran in the pack ponies from Brigalow, the Arab colt along with them. She noticed with concern that one of the hairy little workhorses had lost a great deal of condition, and on closer inspection, discovered an enormous abscess inside his mouth. She lanced it and gave him a penicillin needle, but the pony was in poor shape.

The result of this was that Alice was able to bring along her solid chestnut Bingley in his place. Even though he'd never carried a pack-saddle, he was such a compliant animal that she had no doubt he'd rise to the occasion. She was pleased with this development, as with all the work she'd been putting into Desert Rose she'd been conscious of neglecting her faithful old gelding. It would have felt like adding insult to injury had she excluded him from the bush run as well.

At the close of the bush run the previous year, her grandfather had announced that his aged bay Snoopy wouldn't be coming on the expedition again; the rugged terrain of the national park was beginning to prove too difficult for the old trooper. Now that Jeremy had Carmen, Alice assumed that her grandfather would be riding Rita. However, the day that they began the shoeing, the old man asked her to shoe up old Snoopy.

In answer to her look of surprise, he said, 'Yes, I know. Old Snoop was meant to be out to pasture before now. But somehow I'd feel like a right hypocrite if I left him behind. I'm a bloody sight more broken down than he is. We'll battle along together.'

Once most of the preparations had been made, Alice sewed a long calico case for a thin rectangular piece of soft foam. This she inserted into her grandfather's swag without his knowledge. She also packed some hot-water bottles. So far it had been an unusually cold April and the nights had been chilly: she knew that her grandfather's stiff old body would protest against long days in the saddle and nights of sleeping on the ground. As she made these preparations, Alice's usual joyful anticipation of the trip was disturbed by an uncomfortable inkling that this bush run would be her grandfather's last.

§

As they set out, Jeremy was almost as excited as the other two. He told himself that the thrill of the hunt was the main attraction for him. To some extent this was true: the daily stalking of shy mobs of young cattle hidden in hollows and up gullies was constantly stimulating. But without admitting it to anyone, Jeremy was also anticipating spending time in the wilderness with the two people he'd come to care about more than almost anyone else in the world.

This year, as a mark of respect to them, he joined in wholeheartedly with their traditional evening pursuits. He was a lively participant in cards and quietly tolerated the bush poetry. When they got yarning, he added to Sam's stories with wildly exaggerated tales of his own.

As it turned out, they were lucky with the weather. They had a week of mild, balmy autumn days and nights. The bush was a picture, abundant with new life after the summer rain. The gums, bauhinias, wilgas and yellow jack trees were dense with bright new leaves and tipped with warm colour. Little bubbling springs seemed to have been born in all the gullies, and crystal water was welling up from what appeared to be solid red rock. The animals and birds all seemed to be in a hurry, flirting, talkative and busy as they made the most of the last warm weather.

The quietest of last year's weaners had been selected for the national park; they had made good use of the abundance of soft grasses and were shiny, well covered, and large for their age. All Alice's work with them the previous year was clearly paying off. Upon discovery, they were mostly compliant and happy to join with the main mob. They respected the dogs, and some of them even appeared out of the bush of their own accord, joining the mass of slow-moving bodies. Several larger animals that had been missed on previous years had joined the mobs of quiet youngsters and allowed themselves to be collected at last. This was an unexpected bonus and Sam was pleased.

'I'll never again call what you do with those weaners and dogs "fooling around", Ali. You have my word on that.'

On the third evening, after Jeremy and Sam had exchanged some yarns, Alice ceremoniously produced a battered volume, her eyes shining in the firelight.

'I hope that's not what I think it is,' Jeremy said warily. He was lying back against his pack, his feet towards the fire.

'Now, Jeremy, you've grown to love Henry and Banjo.' Alice looked at him coaxingly.

'Did I say that? Sam, have you ever heard me say that?' Jeremy objected.

'Didn't need to, mate,' Sam chuckled.

'Jeez, thanks for the back-up.'

'And it's time for you to get to know Jane too,' Alice said decisively.

'Now, hang on a minute.' Jeremy pushed himself upright. 'Depressed alcoholic poets are one thing, but poncy English fellas in tights and mobs of lovely ladies in castles or some blooming thing, now that's something else altogether. That's asking too much of a man.'

Sam looked at him with sympathy. 'This'll be my second time, mate. It's actually not as bad as you think.'

Alice was indignant. 'I listen to all *your* tall stories.'

'Dumb dog that I am, thought you liked 'em!' Jeremy sounded genuinely hurt.

'And I do!' Alice exclaimed. 'You're a natural at yarning. But how do you know you won't like *Pride and Prejudice*?'

'Call it a gut feeling. Righto, you win. But don't wake me up if I go to sleep.'

After half an hour of listening to Alice's soft voice describing the faraway world of the Bennets and Longbourn, Jeremy found himself lying on his back again, his arms folded, looking at the stars, his heart throbbing with happiness. If Jane Austen was the worst thing about his life at the present time, things weren't half bad.

Chapter 33

Alice knew that Troy had been longing to visit Redstone ever since Mushgang had told him about the transformation of the filly. As it happened, not long after the crew returned from the bush run, a turn of events in his own life forced Troy to stop procrastinating and pay Alice a visit. It was afternoon when he arrived and found her over at the yards, working Rose. The little mare was a lather of sweat from the circle work they'd been doing. Alice was trying to improve Rose's balance in a collected canter and teach her to slide to a stop on command.

Engrossed in what she was doing, Alice only looked over and waved when Troy walked across to the yard and sat on the top rail. Then she kept working, barely aware of his presence.

At last she rode towards him, looking up at him sitting in the glow of the late afternoon sun, his usually subdued green eyes alight with emotion. She dismounted and, leaving Rose's reins to dangle loose, climbed up and settled herself beside him on the rail. All at once, she was vividly reminded of the time she'd met with her father.

He spoke admiringly. 'I've seen a few fellas with flash tricks in this horse game, Ali. But this here is bloody special. Knowing what a tough case that filly was – it's damn near a miracle.'

'We just understand each other, Rose and I, that's all. You know how it is when you really click with a horse.'

'If you say so – I'm not gonna be the one to disagree.'

Alice's rare musical laugh rang out in the evening air, her amusement at Troy's solemn manner showing on her face.

'You think I'm a real dill, don't you, Alice? You'll be glad when I'm gone.' Troy looked away then as though wishing the words unspoken. Alice could hardly bear it that she had the power to upset him so much; she'd hoped it wouldn't still be so. Troy was like a beloved brother to her. She'd often wondered why, when they were undoubtedly two of a kind, she wasn't in love with him, and had always imagined that one day she probably would be. But perhaps they were too similar. Just recently she'd become certain that she could never return his feelings. Why was she so sure? It couldn't be because of Jeremy: the realisation had merely coincided with his coming.

Alice squeezed his hand warmly. 'I think you're lovely, Troy. And what do you mean, "gone"? Where are you going? Not back to the mine, surely?'

'No fear. No, an opportunity's come up working for some horse guru bloke in the States. An old mate of Dad's has been working with this legend fella there for thirty years. Wants a young offsider.'

'Troy, that's wonderful! This could be a real breakthrough for you.'

'Yeah, well, if I'm serious about getting anywhere in this game I've gotta move on from the small-time stuff. Branch out a bit and try to make some sort of a name for meself. This job will pay pretty good too – this fella has some money to throw about, they reckon.'

They sat in silence watching the sun drop behind the jagged outline of the range. Alice wished they were kids again and everything could be simple and uncomplicated.

§

Troy, reluctant to leave, stood with Alice beside his ute.

'Troy, just think, you'll be getting some real recognition for your talents at last!' Her smile broke over him like a tingling wave.

He looked into her eyes and swallowed hard, thinking of how gladly he'd forgo all other recognition if he could only win hers. 'I'll miss you, Ali.' He forced himself to continue to meet her unwavering gaze.

'I'll miss you too. But I'm so happy for you. I really believe you'll have an amazing time over there.'

'Thanks. I hope you'll stay afloat here too. It's tough, I know.'

'We'll manage. Jeremy and I are slowly getting on top of things.'

'He's a good fella, no matter what anyone says. He's a bloody lucky one too if he's gonna end up with Alice Wilson.' Troy boldly searched her face for confirmation. Before coming out here today he'd been hoping that she'd be heartbroken to hear he was leaving for the States. He'd fantasised about her begging him to stay and confessing to strong feelings for him. But deep down he'd known how it would be – and sure enough, she had been thrilled for him, like a good friend or sister, no more. Now he needed to know how things stood with O'Donnell.

'Oh Troy, there's nothing going on between Jeremy and me. Surely you've seen the types he goes for?' Alice looked down. 'Luckily, a girl like me holds no attraction for someone like Jeremy. That's why we get along so well.'

'You fair dinkum?' Troy laughed incredulously. 'So be it.' He held his hands up in front of him. 'Not my place to interfere if the big fella hasn't let on any different.'

Alice smiled, but for a moment avoided meeting his eye.

At last Troy looked at his watch. 'Hell, time's got away on me. I'd better hit the road.'

They hugged. Alice kissed him tenderly on the cheek before releasing him. She held his shoulders and looked into his face. 'I can't wait to hear all about it.'

'Yeah, righto. But I'm not much of a letter writer . . . and, Ali . . .' Troy stammered, 'could you use a couple of dogs? I mean . . . I want you to have 'em . . . my dogs.'

'Troy, are you sure?'

He gave a quick nod. Then, looking at his battered boots, he added, almost inaudibly, 'Don't forget me?'

'Forget you?' Alice exclaimed in astonishment. 'As if I could! Think about me from time to time too, if you're not too busy having amazing experiences.' She laughed.

Troy looked at her helplessly, wishing that somehow he *could* find a way to stop himself from thinking of her.

At that moment they heard a metallic bang and a loud curse coming from the depths of the shed. It was Jeremy working on the grader. They both glanced towards the sound, then back at each other. Alice was smiling absent-mindedly. Yes, Troy was certain Jed would get her in the end. At least, he hoped so. It would be easier to bear than if it was Wingnut Lonergan. He studied her face, making a mental note of every detail.

As he drove away, Troy took a last longing look in the rear-view mirror at the fast-diminishing figure of his angel.

Chapter 34

Things were going unusually smoothly at Redstone. The wet season had been bountiful, the cattle were fat and the gullies still running with crystal streams. Over dinner one evening, Sam told Alice that for the first time in many years, he felt they were truly getting on top of things again. He said that thanks to her determination and drive and Jeremy's energetic assistance, many of their new plans were well on the way to being realised. There was a unanimous mood of positivity and enthusiasm in the old homestead.

Then the unexpected occurred. The eternally healthy Olive developed a persistent cough, which forced a rare trip to the doctor. The chest x-ray that followed revealed a fairly advanced lung cancer. But worse was yet to come. The cancer turned out to be secondary to one that had started in Olive's breast, and by way of her glands had successfully established itself in various locations throughout her body. According to the Brisbane oncologists, cure was out of the question, and Olive haughtily dismissed the option of buying some time with chemotherapy. She would spend her last days gracefully at Redstone. So home she came.

Olive's hacking cough was a constant reminder to the Redstone folk of her worsening condition. In commiseration, King Henry the Ninth began coughing with new vehemence. The bird had become virtually bald over recent months, his feathers having failed to regrow after his last moult. Crouched on his favourite knobbly perch, he reminded Alice of a large featherless hatchling. But despite his appearance and the increasingly sombre atmosphere at Redstone, the bird seemed to be more wickedly jovial than ever before.

Then, lifting his cover one morning, Alice made the sad discovery of his puckered little body, curled up stiff and cold on the floor of his elegant old cage. His remaining feathers were so sparse that his pink goose-bumpy flesh looked almost as though it had been plucked. Alice lifted him out gently, feeling a little guilty over the absence of any real sadness over the loss. She and the bird had never seen eye to eye.

However, her grandmother was excessively distressed over the ancient cockatoo's passing. She allowed herself to be overwhelmed by misery in a way that Alice and her grandfather had never witnessed before. Three days after the bird's death, Olive was still inconsolable. In the afternoon, Alice brought her a cup of tea and sat close beside her on the bed.

'I can't explain why I'm so upset about him,' Olive sobbed apologetically, holding tightly to Alice's hand. 'I suppose he's always been a stable presence in my life. My mascot for normality.' She took a deep breath and wiped her eyes before adding, 'I just never dreamed I'd be the Elliot who outlived him.'

In the face of adversity, her grandmother had always uncomplainingly put her nose to the grindstone. And Alice knew that her grandfather, who suffered more from low spirits than his wife, had found that during these times his wife had been a rock to which he could cling until the storm had passed. But now she seemed to be giving up, and Alice had never seen Sam so terrified. She made numerous attempts to cheer her grandmother and ease her grandfather's panic. But eventually, to everyone's surprise, it was Jeremy's disrespectful taunting and niggling that managed to rekindle the old lady's fighting spirit a week after King Henry's demise. 'Cheer up, Mrs Day.' He appeared beside her bed where Alice was also sitting. 'Now you have a guardian angel, white wings, yellow headpiece – the lot.' His grin was infuriating.

'Oh pipe down, Jeremy,' Olive said irritably, pulling herself up on her pillows a little.

'Righto then, I'll leave you in peace.' He turned to go, but in the doorway he stopped and looked back. 'In another time and place . . .' he paused, 'I know you'll hear that cough again.'

And then he was gone. And to Alice's great relief, Olive was laughing.

The illness took Alice's admiration of her grandmother to a new level. As the weeks passed and she became sicker and weaker, the elderly woman uttered not one word of complaint. Alice's role changed as time went by. Initially she continued to work outside on the station but came in regularly to check on her grandmother, bringing her things to occupy herself with, crochet, crosswords, and a variety of material to read. Soon, however, even these diversions tired the formerly inexhaustible woman. Olive began to require help even to shower and go to the toilet. So Alice spent more and more time at her side.

Olive never ceased to be a lady. When Alice gave her foul-tasting medicine or a painkilling needle, her grandmother would smile and pat her hand. When Alice dressed the weeping bedsores that had broken through the papery skin, or wiped her clean after she'd finished on the commode, her grandmother would say, 'Thank you, darling,' as brightly as if Alice had just handed her a cup of tea and a cupcake.

§

When it became clear that Olive was dying, Lara arrived at Redstone with her three younger children. She immediately dismissed Alice from her role as primary carer, saying, 'I'm here now, so you can go and look after Dad.'

But her bossy style of 'helping' grated on Olive's nerves, and the children were in and out of the sickroom, grumbling and demanding things from their mother.

Twelve-year-old Dante pined for his computer games. He wandered around sulkily or watched television, refusing all of Alice's offers to take him outside and show him the station. One afternoon she came in and heard him bellowing at Lara, 'They don't even have a proper TV! It hardly picks up any channels. I've never been so bored before. You never told me we were staying this long. I would've stayed home with Dad if I'd known.'

Chantel, the quiet, pretty little eight-year-old, floated around listening to the adults' conversations. She changed her clothes several times a day and gave the distinct impression that she must have been Scotchguarded at birth. Next to the little doll, Alice in her stained jeans and heavy workboots felt like a bunyip from the billabong. But after a few days, Chantel began to accompany Alice outdoors and worry less about 'getting dirty'.

Chantel liked Jeremy and batted her eyelashes at him when he teased her. She tittered at all his jokes, her hand over her mouth and her little head tilted to the side. Even when, on the third day of their visit, Jeremy told her that she needed a good flogging, she was overcome with hilarity and took it as a compliment.

The youngest, Theodore, worshipped Alice right from the outset, and wanted to go everywhere with her. Alice took the stocky five-year-old out checking with her in the ute and he enjoyed every small task, soaking up information like a sponge. On two occasions she rode out on Bingley to quieten the weaners with Theodore perched on the front of her saddle. Then Lara discovered that there had been no helmet, so any future sessions were forbidden.

One day, Alice and Jeremy took the little boy swimming in the creek, and all three of them had a wonderful time on a rope swing that Jeremy had rigged up over the waterhole. Alice was glad Lara wasn't there to see what Jeremy taught the sturdy little boy to do on the swing. He returned starry-eyed, wet and in seventh heaven. Lara was furious with Alice. 'If he gets a middle-ear infection, I'll know who to thank. And another thing, please refrain from calling him Teddy. You too, Jeremy. His name is Theodore. This is precisely what I was afraid of when we settled on that name. I warned Conrad at the time.'

At this Theodore spoke. 'I like being Teddy.'

Lara rolled her eyes, looking accusingly at Alice. 'This serves me right. The minute you let them out of your sight—'

'Poor kid'll get bashed at school with a poncy name like that,' Jeremy interrupted. 'Did you warn Conrad about that?'

§

As the days passed, Alice could see that Lara's care wasn't helping Olive's state of mind. Previously the old woman had been so calm and accepting, but now she began to moan in her sleep and call out for Sam. On the morning of the sixth day of her stay, Lara was being rude and short-tempered with everyone. Alice went into the sickroom and said, 'Mum, why don't you have a day off and spend some time with Pa? I'll look after Ma.'

Lara glared at her. 'Is that your way of insinuating that I'm not coping here?'

'Of course not, I just thought—'

'Do you think I can't look after my own mother?'

Chantel, who had been listening in the hallway, poked her head around the door to watch. At the same time, Sam stopped on his way out the door and came into the room.

'Lara, you're exhausting your mother with all your rot. Come out of here and leave Alice alone.'

This was like a red rag to a bull.

'How dare you, Dad? After everything I've done for Mum this week. Oh, I see how it is, Alice has become the favourite around here.'

'Dunno 'bout that, Lars.' It was Jeremy, through the open window, waiting out on the veranda for Sam. 'But for one thing, Ali has a bedside manner that leaves yours for dead.'

Chantel's head was swivelling back and forth excitedly, studying the face of each speaker in turn.

'Oh really?' Lara was seething now. 'Well, seeing as you're so precious, Alice, I guess it's a good thing that I didn't let them put you up for adoption at birth like Mum wanted to.'

At this, Olive started to whimper. 'Alice, my love, don't take any notice.'

Sam spoke again, quietly. 'You take yourself and your mouth away from here now, girl, and leave your mother in peace. Alice will do this from now on.'

'Mum should be in palliative care, in a hospital with people who are properly trained,' Lara stated authoritatively.

'You've said your piece, now get out before I give you a hiding.' Sam was shaking.

Lara looked at him disdainfully and swept out. Chantel trotted after her.

Olive was crying quietly now and Alice ran to her and stroked her forehead. 'It's alright, Ma, don't upset yourself.'

There were two more days of stormy silence from Lara, which everyone felt was a marked improvement. Alice stayed by her grandmother's side day and night, leaving only for a few moments every so often when her grandfather came in. Teddy stayed for much of the time too, listening to Alice's gentle voice reading poetry and singing to her grandmother. They played snakes and ladders, fiddlesticks and snap while the old lady dozed. Every now and then Jeremy poked his head in to break the monotony and crack a joke. But Lara stayed away.

§

'Alice!'

Alice woke with a start and glanced at the bedside clock. Just after 4 am. Her grandmother's voice had a note of panic in it. Alice jumped up from the bed that she now slept in, and hurried to her side.

'What is it, Ma? Do you need something for the pain?'

'Alice, I've never shown you love like I should have. Like you deserved.'

Alice, still waking up, blinked dazedly at the brightness of the bedside lamp. 'Don't be silly! You've been wonderful to me. Always.'

'No.' Olive shook her head fitfully on the pillow. 'I never looked after you like I did Lara.'

'Ma, Lara is your own child. Of course you should love her best.'

The old lady let out a deep sigh. 'So I've always believed. But just lately . . . the last few days, I'm not so sure. Things become clearer . . .' She stopped, out of breath.

'Shh, Ma, don't try to talk anymore.'

As much as she loved her grandmother, Alice had always been aware of a distance between them. She'd accepted it, but had sometimes longed for a closeness that never came. Now this distance was dissolving. With only days, maybe hours to live, her grandmother was closing the gap. Alice gently rested her head on the faded patchwork quilt covering her grandmother's wasted chest. She could feel the shallow rise and fall of her laboured breathing.

The old woman laid a withered hand on the back of Alice's head and stroked the soft curls. 'My dearest girl!' she whispered.

Just after morning smoko later that day, Alice stepped out through the double doors to the veranda for a breath of fresh air. When she returned a minute later, her grandmother's soul had flown.

Chapter 35

Towards four o'clock in the afternoon, Lara began to glance out of the window and up the road at regular intervals. Where was Conrad?

All the preparations for the funeral were complete. She had spent the morning making up a funeral leaflet on the computer and potting some sun jewels in terracotta basins to put near her mother's grave. The Country Women's Association ladies were taking care of the food for the wake and preparing the hall. Alice had been into town to meet with Father Callaghan and to help decorate the church. Lara had wanted to go too, but had supposed that she wouldn't be welcomed by any of them.

Alice had now arrived home and was having a cup of tea at the table. She looked exhausted. She'd been holding it all together for everyone else for just a bit too long. 'Doing what should have been my job, I suppose,' Lara thought bitterly. Why was it that just the sight of Alice made Lara feel guilty? It had been that way since the day she was born. Sitting at Alice's elbow was Theodore, quietly imbibing some milk through a bright green straw that Alice had brought home from town for him. How strange that he'd become so attached to his half-sister in such a short time.

Sam and Jeremy were working over at the little Redstone graveyard on the far side of the cattle yards. Shaded by the old kurrajong trees, they had been tidying up with the tractor and ute, and digging the newest grave. Lara was concerned about her father. He had aged a great deal since she'd last seen him, and looked very frail and unwell, especially these last few days since Olive died. If only he'd been easier to talk to, more approachable. How had Alice managed to grow so close to the old man?

Lara heard an engine and rushed back to the window, thinking it might finally be Conrad, but it was only the men returning. Alice jumped up to reboil the kettle. Lara stood and watched her father and Jeremy talking in the shed. Jeremy was gesticulating with his hands as he talked. He was always energetic, she'd give him that. She could see that her father was listening patiently, and she noticed how bent and tired he looked. Then the distant dust trail of an approaching vehicle caught her eye.

'At last!' she said. 'Conrad's here.'

'Just in time for a cuppa,' Alice commented and took an extra cup out of the cupboard.

Lara, Alice and Theodore went outside to meet him, and Lara yelled to the other two children, who were watching TV in the sitting room. Conrad's usually spotless silver BMW was caked in dust as he pulled up right in the centre of the turning circle. He climbed out and groaned. Lara gave him a kiss and he patted the children's heads. Then he turned to Alice and gave her a matter-of-fact smile and perfunctory greeting. 'How are you, Alice?'

'I'm alright thank you, Conrad. How was your trip?'

'Abominable. I don't know how you people tolerate the state of those roads. You really need to get onto the council about it.' He shook his head. 'And no mobile phone coverage if you get into trouble! Ludicrous!'

Lara turned to look at her father and Jeremy, who had walked over from the shed. The old man looked defeated. He waved and nodded at Conrad, then continued past into the house. But Jeremy, who'd overheard Conrad's comment, stopped to join the welcoming committee.

'You don't like our roads, digger?' He grinned in welcome. 'You're in the wild, wild west now, mate. You gotta like it or lump it.'

'Conrad, this is Jeremy,' Alice said.

'Oh . . . should I know you? You must be the head of the Redstone Executive.' Conrad snorted at his own joke. Lara felt slightly uneasy. She wished Conrad would refrain from baiting the young ringer. It would undoubtedly lead to trouble.

'Who, me? Don't be silly, I'm just middle management,' Jeremy answered, unperturbed.

'It's just that you sounded so . . . well qualified.' Conrad looked sideways at his wife. But Lara had already learned the hard way that it was a mistake to enter into any sort of banter with the ringer.

'Well, I can blow my nose without a hanky,' Jeremy said enthusiastically. 'I bet that's something you can't do.'

To Lara's horror, Jeremy proceeded to demonstrate, leaning forward, holding one nostril closed and snorting a stream of air and mucus out through the other one. It landed on the ground not far from Conrad's expensive casual shoes. The kids giggled. Jeremy then repeated the process with the other nostril. He stood back, his chest out and hands on his hips, looking expectantly at Conrad. Conrad looked back coldly. Alice opened her mouth to say something but Jeremy beat her to it.

'Lighten up, old mate. Oh . . . *I'm* getting the picture, you don't like anyone's jokes but your own, eh?'

Lara wished Jeremy would be quiet. Her husband never had much patience when he was tired.

'Surely there's something you should be doing?' Conrad asked.

'Bloody oath there is! I should be kissing Alice.' Jeremy grabbed hold of his workmate and swung her round. 'Should've done it yonks ago but she just won't let me . . . See?' He set Alice down again and winked into her exasperated face. The kids giggled again.

Conrad turned to Lara. 'Is there any necessity for us to be standing out in the heat, talking to this imbecile?'

'Well, your kids are getting a laugh out of it.' Jeremy launched into a monkey impression and the kids laughed louder.

'Come inside for a cuppa, Conrad,' Alice grabbed her stepfather's arm firmly and, to Lara's relief, steered him towards the house.

Jeremy did his monkey walk all the way back to the shed and dangled there from a beam, issuing chattering noises before finally disappearing into the shadows. Lara was shocked to find she had to suppress a smile. The kids, who had stopped to watch, looked disappointed to see him go.

§

Late in the morning of the following day, there was an unusual amount of traffic on the Redstone road. The funeral was over and Jeremy was driving the town car with Sam in the front passenger seat. They were leading the long procession of cars towards Olive's final resting place. Jeremy tried to ignore the sombre presence of the hulking black hearse in the rear-vision mirror.

Try as he might, he just couldn't seem to get his head around the fact that Olive had gone. She'd been so full of life for an old girl.

So much go in her still. He'd always imagined that dying old ladies would be quiet and weak. But Olive had been strong, brave and determined, right up until the end. It was a bloody shame. She hadn't seemed ready to go, somehow.

He glanced at Alice in the mirror. She was sitting in the middle between a swollen-eyed Bonnie and Theodore. She had her arm around the little boy and her face was calmly serious, betraying nothing. Bonnie had sobbed bitterly throughout the entire service, while Alice, statue-like, had shown little emotion of any kind. But Jeremy knew how badly she was hurting and wished he could go to her and comfort her. Why couldn't she just let herself have a damn good bawl?

Then Jeremy glanced at the hunched figure of Sam beside him. He seemed to have visibly diminished since Olive's death. The sight of the dignified old man brought the lump back into his throat. He decided it was time to speak, to break what had been a long silence. 'She wasn't such a bad old girl, your Olive. Pretty damn gutsy, I reckon.'

Sam looked across and nodded an acknowledgement of the comment. They drove on for a while longer, then Jeremy spoke again, more to himself than anyone. 'Wish I didn't give her so much curry. Hope she doesn't come back to haunt me.'

Alice gave a little gasp and Jeremy could feel her glaring at the back of his head. He hadn't meant any disrespect. He just couldn't believe that a feisty temper like Olive's could be extinguished, just like that, in one go.

Jeremy looked at Sam again. He was looking out the window at the ruddy landscape sliding by. Jeremy wondered whether it all looked different to him now that Olive was gone. His other half. He just couldn't fathom that sort of union with another person. Tied together for a lifetime.

Jeremy hoped he hadn't upset the old bloke. A moment later he was relieved when a slow rumbling chuckle shook the old man's frame.

Chapter 36

The Harradines were packed and ready to go. Alice, her grandfather and Jeremy came out to the car to make their farewells. For once, Jeremy was perfectly respectful, wishing them all a safe trip and even shaking hands with Conrad. Sam was brief and courteous, his mind on other things. Alice cuddled and kissed all the children and pecked Conrad on the cheek before turning to her mother.

Lara gave her a hug and a brisk kiss. 'Take care, Alice. Let me know if you need anything, won't you?'

'Thanks, Mum, I will,' Alice lied.

Suddenly she found herself thinking of Leilani. Why was it that she'd had no trouble feeling complete trust in Benji's wife, a woman she'd only known for two days? And would it hurt to give Lara the benefit of the doubt?

As they watched the low-set luxury car gliding away, she thought back to the evening before.

After dinner, Alice had taken her cup of tea out onto the veranda steps and into the quiet freshness of the night. She'd been craving some time alone. She had been so busy attending to the minute by minute needs of her grandmother, and then organising the funeral, she hadn't had a chance to stop and feel. She leaned back on her elbows and gazed up at the star-studded sky. One impossibly bright star had seemed closer than all the others, pulsating with white radiance. She wondered if her Ma could see her sitting there, and to her surprise, found herself smiling. Olive's suffering was over. She had run the race. And Alice would never cease to be inspired by the courage her grandmother had shown during her last days.

As well as the loss, Alice had found that a strange new peace had settled on her since that last talk with her grandmother. Ma had truly loved her, and this knowledge filled her with a warmth that helped to soothe some of her grief.

Then Alice had heard the boards creak behind her and Lara had sunk down beside her on the steps.

'Thank God that's all over,' she said. 'I'm thoroughly exhausted, but I'm guessing that you're even more tired than I am.'

Alice, a little surprised at the trace of compassion in Lara's voice, looked up and smiled. She felt her mother examine her face for a moment.

'You'll be alright, I suppose, you and Dad?' Lara asked.

'Yes, Mum, we'll manage.'

'It's not as if I can be much help anyway.' Lara sighed. 'I'm not exactly Dad's favourite person at the moment.'

Alice met her mother's eyes again. She wanted to say something reassuring, but Lara continued, her tone still more diffident than usual.

'Mum and Dad were always good to you, weren't they, Alice?'

'Yes, always,' Alice said emphatically.

Lara nodded. 'I knew they would be. They did a much better job raising you than I could have. I wasn't ready. You do understand that, don't you?'

Alice nodded too, and tried to read her mother's expression. Was she attempting to apologise? Was she trying to say that she had cared about her all those years? Alice decided that it was safer to remain unconvinced, and in doing so, avoid future disappointment. That way, anything that followed would be a bonus.

But then, unexpectedly, Lara took Alice's hand. For a few moments, neither of them spoke. The crickets throbbed and a cow bellowed to its calf somewhere off in the distance.

'Mum?' Alice said on an impulse.

'Yes?'

'There's something I've often wondered about.'

'Yes?' Lara said again, and Alice felt her tense up slightly.

'Why did you give me Benji's surname?'

Lara looked thoughtful for a moment before answering. 'Well, at the time, I told myself it was to get at Mum and Dad; prove I wasn't ashamed, I suppose.' She paused and looked at Alice, before adding wryly, 'Your paternity was hardly a secret, after all.'

'But now?' Alice prompted.

'Now . . .' she paused again, 'I think it was because of the way I felt about him.' Lara's eyes were large in the dim light. 'It wasn't just another crush, Alice.'

'Oh.' With a sudden thrill, Alice realised, her mother had truly loved Benji. Trying not to sound reproachful, she asked, 'Why didn't you tell him about me?'

'I couldn't afford to have him as part of my life,' Lara answered quickly, a slight edge to her voice. 'I needed him to stay in the past.'

Alice nodded, unable to speak.

'So there it is,' Lara went on, 'completely selfish in its motivation as usual.' She looked away.

'Thank you for telling me,' Alice said finally. 'It means a lot . . . knowing that you really cared for him.'

Lara shrugged, and her cool, matter-of-fact expression returned. Alice wondered whether she should release her mother's hand, but then Lara spoke again.

'While I'm in this unusually repentant mood, I want to say how glad I am that you and Mum were . . . so close.' Lara breathed out slowly before continuing. 'In a way, as my daughter, you compensated for me . . . my wrongs. Thank you.'

Squeezing her mother's hand, Alice smiled up at her. They had sat a little while longer, looking at the stars and feeling the tickle of an intermittent breeze.

§

With the visitors gone, and her grandfather tucked safely into bed, Alice took a brush over to the yards and called Rose in from the night paddock. The rhythm of the brush strokes over the mare's gleaming coat helped to calm Alice; as she worked, she leaned into the warm curve of Rose's neck and half closed her eyes.

Movement nearby brought her out of her trance, and she looked down at Darcy, who had sidled over from the house and was now standing by dejectedly. The poor creature had just lost yet another loved one. A minute later, he was joined by Jeremy, who wore a similar expression. Alice put down her brush, and she and Jeremy sat together on the grain feeder in silence for a time, Darcy sitting mournfully at their feet.

'How're you travelling, mate?' Jeremy said at last.

Alice only nodded in response, not meeting his eyes. She knew she was shutting him out, but she hadn't the energy to try to explain. Finally she said, 'It's Pa we need to think about now.'

'It's *you* I'm thinking of.' Jeremy put his arm around her shoulders. 'And I'm real sorry about your mum, Ali.'

'You mean my ma,' Alice corrected him.

'No, your mum. She's not much comfort to ya, eh? Your ma was a nosy old chook but she wasn't short on courage. I'll never forget the way she stuck up for me that day in the pub.' Jeremy shook his head. 'But your mum's another story. First-class bitch, I reckon. You deserve better.'

Alice felt tears sting her eyes; annoyed, she brushed them away, trying to work out why Jeremy's comment had upset her. The tears certainly weren't in defence of Lara. Perhaps she was mourning the complete absence of any feelings of loyalty towards her mother.

But Jeremy had seen her tears and was mortified. 'Hell, Alice, don't take any notice of me. Great big bloody mouth. I gotta learn to shut my gob. Anyway, luckily your dad's genes hammered hers. It's hard to believe she's even related to you. She'd fit right in with those Bingley sisters, I reckon.'

Alice gave him a watery smile and he looked relieved. He pulled her closer to him and they sat in silence. Jeremy was always such a source of strength. She suddenly found herself wondering how she'd have managed the last few months without him. She rested her head gratefully on his shoulder.

'I'll help you look after the old bloke, Alice. We'll muddle through alright.'

Alice nodded again and Darcy pressed his angular body against her legs. She looked down into the dog's adoring amber eyes and felt a stirring of affection for the awkward creature.

Chapter 37

Following a week of strong westerly winter winds, Redstone was visited by a severe dust storm. Fine particles of desert soil from the west were suspended in the air like brown fog for two days. From the homestead, the shed and yards were only just visible. Outside it appeared overcast but rather than grey the predominant colour was a dull beige and the sun looked like a distant, pinky-orange burning ball peering down through the gloom.

'Haven't had a dust storm this thick in years,' observed Sam. 'Always reminds me of Judgement Day. This is what it'll be like for the ones who get left behind.'

Jeremy made an expression of exaggerated panic at Alice. 'Struth, that'll be me!' he said.

The dusty air did nothing to help Sam's chesty cough. As always he didn't complain, but his quiet listlessness worried Alice. He seemed dull and distant, and Alice knew that during his waking hours he never stopped thinking about her grandmother. They shut up the house as much as possible and Sam stayed inside. The taste of dust was in everyone's mouth and they had the constant sensation of grit between their teeth. Jeremy and Alice blew brown smudges onto their handkerchiefs and their eyes were red and irritated. Every surface was blanketed with a thin layer of fine chalky dirt.

On the third day the wind changed and the air gradually became clearer. Alice wiped down all the surfaces inside the house and Jeremy did a hurried job of his cottage. The vehicles, saddles and tools in the shed were all covered in a thick pale layer, which was removed in stages as each item was used over the weeks that followed.

Then, in late August, winter inflicted its last bitterly cold spell for the year on Redstone. Making the most of the lingering coolness, Alice and Jeremy decided to spend the day fencing. Sam, under the weather again, had agreed to stay home and do some odd jobs around the house. Alice knew he was also planning to duck out and check the calves in Windlass Gully from yesterday's branding, to make sure they had all made it through the chilly night. Out-of-season calves always did it tough, and the old man had admitted to Alice at breakfast that he was beginning to see the logic of seasonal mating.

When Alice and Jeremy arrived home late in the afternoon, Alice was quietly concerned to see an empty spot in the shed where her grandfather's paddock ute should have been parked. While she yarded the weaners, she anxiously listened for the sound of the vehicle returning. It was after five when she finished and checked the clock. Her grandfather never stayed out so late anymore, especially when he was crook. She took the motorbike and let her dogs off the chains again to follow her.

She found two sets of tracks at the gate into Windlass Gully paddock. Her grandfather had been and gone. From where she'd pulled up at the gate, Alice could see the cattle huddled in the gidgee camp for the night; everything looked in order. On closer inspection, the treadmarks in the dust revealed that instead of going home, he'd headed west, away from the house. She rode in that direction but soon lost his tracks on the hard-packed dirt of the road. As she checked one paddock after another, Alice fought to control her rising panic. By now she'd left the dogs far behind and the sun was going down.

Finally she spotted the ute, its silver roll bar catching the rays of the setting sun. She'd ridden up to Eagle Tor to get a better vantage point. The ute was parked alongside a stretch of barely stock-proof fence line that her grandfather had been worrying over. While she squinted towards the distant vehicle, the idling motorbike engine spluttered and died. Out of fuel. She threw the bike down in disgust and started to run, her feet pounding the rocky slope as she descended towards where her pa must be.

She jogged until the ute came into view again and then slowed for a moment to a walk, trying to see her grandfather. In the dying light she spotted a sitting figure, slumped sideways onto a post further along the fence. With a strangled cry she broke back into a run. Well before she reached him, she could see that the life had departed from his worn old body. He looked so small and grey, like a withered scarecrow. His frail arm hung from the fence, hand still grasping the pliers that were partway through a figure-eight tie in the wires. Alice unclenched the pliers and gently prised his cold knobbly fingers from the steel handles. She folded his arms and, kneeling beside him, half lifted his body onto her lap. Then she cradled him like a big rag doll, rocking him and humming a soft croon of agony.

§

Jeremy found them there like that an hour later, the headlights from the old ute illuminating the scene with shocking brilliance. He dimmed the lights, left the engine running and walked over slowly.

'C'mon, mate, let's get you in out of the cold.'

He gently disentangled the two, then lifted Sam's limp form and carried it to the ute, placing it carefully into the tray. He took off his own oilskin coat and laid it over the old man's body. Such a small crumpled heap. Was such a man.

He walked back to Alice who was still sitting in the same spot, bowed over. He stooped and picked her up as though she were a child, then carried her to the ute. She grasped his shoulders with frozen fingers and buried her face in his neck. He held her for a while, just like that, before lifting her into the passenger seat.

'Where's Pa?' It came out as a sob.

'He's in the tray. You know him, always happy to ride in the back if a lady needs a seat.'

She nodded. Her face in the darkness frightened him. Her eyes so stricken and huge. He reached over and pulled her close to him as they drove away.

'Poor old bugger.' Jeremy's voice was husky. 'Just like him to pop off without causing anyone any hassle.'

Chapter 38

'Is this Campbell fellow really a practising solicitor?' Conrad said into Lara's ear in a low voice, but still loud enough so that Alice and Jeremy could hear. Alice's mother and stepfather had made the long trek to Redstone for the second time in the space of a few months, to attend Sam's funeral. This time, much to Alice's disappointment, they had left the kids in Brisbane with Conrad's elderly parents.

Now they were all sitting in the shabby waiting room of the only solicitor in town, and Conrad was looking around contemptuously.

'He's not a city toff like your lot, if that's what you mean,' Jeremy said genially in answer to Conrad's question.

Ignoring him, Conrad continued to address Lara. 'It just strikes me as bizarre that, having a barrister for a son-in-law, your father didn't use my services.'

'Shows he didn't trust ya, eh?' Jeremy observed.

'I don't think I'll dignify that with a response,' said Conrad.

'Bloody hell, I wasn't trying to sound dignified, poor dumb ringer like me!' Jeremy hung his head. Alice elbowed him in the ribs, starting to wonder whether bringing him along had been such a good idea. She'd wanted him there for moral support but she was now thinking that one of the ladies from church might have been better.

The plump middle-aged woman behind the desk had been listening with her lips pursed, but she took advantage of the brief silence to say, 'I think you'll be more than satisfied with Mr Campbell's standards. He is highly regarded in this town and an excellent boss too.' She glared at Conrad, then looked back down at the form she was filling out.

'Well, it would be a damn shame if *you* didn't think so, Heidi, being his wife 'n' all,' Jeremy piped up. 'And who's gonna tell you any different in this two-faced town?' He snorted.

'I'm sure *you* wouldn't hesitate to say so, Jeremy O'Donnell, if *you* thought any different.' Heidi had developed a red spot at the centre of each cheek and now Jeremy was being inflicted with the glare.

'Thanks for the compliment, Heidi – I mean Ms Campbell. Now, let's all just settle down. You need to keep up your professional front for these good people.'

To Alice's relief, the office door opened and they were ushered in by the jovial Mr Campbell. Alice noticed Lara looking with distaste at his pot belly and the redness of the burst capillaries in his cheeks.

They all sat in silence after the will was read. It was quite simple: everything had been left to Alice.

'I don't understand it.' Lara spoke bitterly. 'Dad must have changed it after Mum died.'

'They last updated it just after your mother was diagnosed with cancer,' Fred said gently. 'The date's here, next to their signatures.'

'But why? Why would they cut me out?' Lara's eyes were full of resentment.

Alice, who had been sitting there speechless with shock, now cringed as she felt Jeremy beside her prepare to speak.

'Maybe they just thought you were all sorted, down in the city with Conrad here,' he offered.

'What gives you the authority to comment?' Conrad said heatedly.

'Yes, what on earth would you know about it?' Lara nearly spat the words at Jeremy. 'Just because you're in with my daughter —'

'Mum!' Alice interrupted.

Jeremy let out a low whistle. 'Jeez. I should be so lucky,' he said ruefully to himself.

Lara looked incredulous. 'Do you really expect me to believe that you two aren't . . . ?'

'I know, it's rough on a man,' Jeremy agreed sadly. 'But no, I don't expect you to believe it. Not with your history.'

There was a brief stunned pause, then everyone began talking at once. Conrad jumped out of his seat and strode across the room towards Jeremy, but Fred Campbell quickly intervened and Conrad allowed himself to be persuaded to sit back down again. Alice felt utterly miserable. Jeremy, on the contrary, seemed to be thoroughly enjoying himself. Finally, a red-faced Mr Campbell managed to restore order.

Unbelievably, the silence was again broken by Jeremy. 'Anyone else have a theory?' he asked conspiratorially, looking around at all their faces.

'We don't need to hear any more of your base ideas, thank you.' It was Conrad, still on the warpath.

But Jeremy was clearly not intimidated. He shrugged. 'It's a free country after all. And I'll tell you what I really think, now you've pushed me to it.'

'Please don't!' said Alice weakly.

Jeremy stopped. There was a short pause before Conrad said, 'Carry on then, let's have it. I want to hear what this ignorant git has to say. I might need some amusement one day and I'll be able to think back to this occasion and have a jolly good laugh.'

'Righto, Conman old boy. Since you insist.' Jeremy cleared his throat importantly. 'I think Sam and Mrs Day finally twigged. A few crows came home to roost, if you know what I mean.'

'Chickens,' muttered Fred.

'Eh?'

'No matter,' Fred said hurriedly and Jeremy went on.

'Anyway, like I said, the old folks worked out, God bless 'em, that if Lara got Redstone, she'd sell up. They knew Alice lives and breathes the place, and they also knew that knowing that wouldn't stop Lara from cashing it in first chance she got. 'Cause she's never cared two hoots for Ali or lifted a bloody finger to help her in any way.'

There was another stunned silence. Then Alice decided it was time to speak. 'Redstone was your home just as much as it is mine, Mum. I think it's only fair that you should have a share in it. Just as long as you let me stay there to run it.'

'Yes, I think we should contest the will,' Conrad agreed heartily.

Jeremy made a noise of disgust in his throat. 'Course you do, Conman.'

'You've said enough, Jeremy,' Fred warned.

For a moment no one spoke, then Lara said, 'No. We'll respect their wishes. Leave it the way it is.'

'Good girl!' Fred clasped his hands and beamed at Lara but she scowled and looked away.

'Now, darling, we shouldn't rush into anything.' Conrad spoke in his most soothing voice. 'We need some time to think it over.'

'No, Conrad,' said Lara again, her tone slightly threatening. 'It's decided. Discussion over.' She stood up and walked over to where Alice was perched on the edge of her chair. She gave her daughter an awkward hug and a kiss on top of her head. 'I hope you will be happy at Redstone, Alice. I never was. They must have known that.'

Alice took Lara's hand and looked up into her face. 'Thanks, Mum.'

Chapter 39

The dust that had settled over the land like a grey-brown blanket in the dust storm before Sam's passing remained largely undisturbed for many weeks. The erratic breezes that came during September weren't enough to dislodge the dull gritty layer that had cemented itself to the light dew on the leaves and grass of Redstone.

The last decent rain had been in early April, but the grass had hung on well, thanks to the good moisture that had remained in the ground from summer's drenching. But now, at last, the pasture began to look spent and parched and the dust coating did nothing to improve the effect. The condition of the cows was also beginning to slip, and Alice and Jeremy had resurrected the molasses truck.

Since her grandfather's death, Alice had thrown herself into her work with unrelenting determination. It seemed to Jeremy that she was continually moving, always on her way to the next job or preoccupied. When she sat, it was only to analyse lists of important figures. Her smoko breaks were more often than not held in front of the computer. This was hard on Jeremy, who was an essentially social being.

He instinctively understood that she'd withdrawn into an inner world of grief and he tried repeatedly to draw her into conversation. But she continued to shut him out.

In an attempt to find some relief from the sombre atmosphere at Redstone, he started making more regular weekend trips to town again. However, he spent most of the time away thinking of Alice, all alone back at the station. He tried talking horses and dogs with her, and on one occasion he desperately resorted to Jane Austen. But even this topic failed to raise the slightest hint of a spark in Alice's solemn dark eyes. Next Jeremy turned to his old standby of taunting and teasing, but Alice reacted only with a patient tolerance that made him feel like a naughty schoolboy.

Just when Jeremy thought things couldn't get any grimmer, Alice got a call from the bank. The Redstone loan had come up for review. The new manager, Carl Trent, said he needed to arrange a meeting with her to discuss the future of the property. He confirmed with Alice that she'd taken up the station's management since her grandfather's death, and then checked her age and years of experience. After indicating that the bank had some new concerns about the size of the debt, he fixed a date for a visit the following week.

§

Alice's scones weren't nearly as good as her grandmother's and she'd made them at dawn, so they were quite heavy and cold by the time Carl Trent arrived. He was younger and more serious than his predecessor, Phillip Kift, and to Alice's disappointment he insisted on meeting with her in private; despite Jeremy's tendency to be inappropriate, Alice would have drawn strength from his presence.

The anxiety she'd been suffering over the prospect of the visit had taken its toll, she looked tired and gaunt and she was unable to put on a show of confidence. Carl seemed to sense her uncertainty, and commented, not unkindly, on how alone she was in the world. Looking at the figures, he pointed out the way they'd been stretched by Kift in order to maintain the loan. Even with Alice's grandparents at the helm, Redstone had barely been able to meet the repayments. He went on to suggest that, considering the circumstances, the only realistic course of action for Alice was to put the property on the market. The bright side, or so he said, was that even after the debt was cleared she'd walk away from the place a very wealthy young woman.

Alice quietly informed him that she had no intention of selling and assured him she'd continue to meet the repayments and oversee the improvements. 'Mr Kift was confident that with all the changes we are making here, Redstone will become profitable again in the future,' she explained. 'The innovations he approved were mostly mine. They are costing money now, but it won't be long before they start to pay off.'

'Perhaps,' Trent said doubtfully. 'But it may reach the point where the decision is taken out of your hands, Alice. I'm certain that in a short time you'll come around to my way of thinking. A station of this size is an enormous concern for someone like you to handle alone.' He drained his cup before adding, 'It's not what I'd call feasible.'

Then, assuring her that he'd be in touch again soon, the bank manager departed. He had barely touched his scone.

Alice found that she couldn't talk to Jeremy about the new problem with the bank. His ranting and raving over the loan would only make the threat seem more real. Instead she kept it to herself and became even more withdrawn and uncommunicative. She was aware that he was worried about her and becoming daily more frustrated by her silence. She also knew how dependent on his company she'd become, but somehow she couldn't find the words or opportunity to tell him.

One day in early November, the pair were driving out to Hazelbrae paddock to 'pull' a windmill that had been failing to pump properly for some months. They took a detour on the way to check a troublesome new solar bore in Summerlea. In June this large paddock had been divided into three smaller paddocks. Unfortunately, the only watering point in Upper Summerlea was proving to be less than reliable.

With the bore in sight, Alice took a sip from her water bottle, only to discover that Jeremy had stealthily filled it with gin that morning. He looked sideways at her as he drove, obviously hoping for a reaction, but after a small splutter she merely emptied it out the window without saying a word. Jeremy turned away and glared at the track ahead.

Shortly afterwards they arrived at the trough. The tank's overflow pipe was dripping, which meant the bore was currently working well. There was no need to stop, but Jeremy had clearly lost his temper. He slammed on the brakes, got out and walked around to Alice's door. After wrenching it open, he grabbed her arms and pulled her out of the vehicle. Looking up in bewildered surprise she met his stormy frown. She quickly looked away, twisting her wrists free of his grip. But Jeremy grabbed her again, this time by the shoulders, and shook her until she looked him in the eye.

'Bloody hell, Alice!' he exploded. 'Even if you blubbered and whined every day for months it couldn't be as bad as this silent caper.'

Alice winced a little at the frustration in his tone and tried to pull away again, but his grip was too firm.

'Look at me, Ali. You can't keep up this sulky act forever. What's the matter with you anyway?'

Alice became haughty. 'Let go of me.'

'Haven't seen you shed a single tear yet. Why can't you just have a damn good bawl like a normal girl?'

'You're hurting my shoulders.' Alice's tone was icy now.

Jeremy released her immediately, then, grabbing a tin bucket from the ute, he filled it with sun-warmed trough water. Before she realised what he was intending he'd doused Alice with a heavy cascade. She stood bedraggled and gasping, strings of green algae draped across her head and shoulders and water dripping from the ends of the little curls on either side of her forehead. Jeremy looked at her expectantly, but still she said nothing.

He growled. 'I can't work you out at all. Never met another girl as cold as you are. Must have a hide like a bloody rhinoceros. Have you even cried at all for your old folks yet?'

Alice was angry now. She heard herself shouting, 'I don't see how it's any of your business the manner in which I choose to grieve!'

'Oh yeah, righto,' Jeremy shouted back. 'I'm just the bloody lackey. The paid hand.' He spun around, flinging the bucket back into the ute in disgust. It made a satisfying clang. He began to pace back and forth. 'Don't think of me as a mate or anything, will ya? And whatever you do, don't let on to me about how you're feeling. I'll just keep putting up with this bloody grim treatment then, will I? Maybe I should turn all quiet too.' He halted and glared at Alice, waiting for a response, but she looked away.

He began to stride towards her again, his features taut with rage, but Alice ran at him and pushed him in the chest with both hands. 'You don't understand any of this!' she screamed into his surprised face. Then her body crumpled and she squatted down, hugging her legs and burying her face in her knees. She began to sob uncontrollably. The dogs, who had scarpered when Jeremy threw the bucket, gathered around her in concern.

Jeremy kneeled down beside her and put his hand on her shoulder; however, she soon calmed herself, wiped her face and stood up.

'Oh, Jeremy, I'm so sorry.'

'C'mon, Ali, you were getting angry there a second ago. Having a good old yell. That was a big improvement.' Jeremy's tone was pleading. 'Don't go all quiet on me again.' He poked her shoulder hopefully.

She sighed and reached for the ute door handle. 'Oh no ya don't, Ali Baba! Not so fast!' Jeremy squeezed himself between Alice and the ute. 'How do you know I wouldn't understand? I might be a bit of a dull sod, but I have had a bit of rough luck myself on and off over the years. Plus I'm stronger than you and I'm not letting you back in there till you spill the beans.'

'Jeremy, I wish I could explain myself.' Alice looked into Jeremy's bright blue eyes, willing him to understand.

'I reckon you just need to slow down a bit, Alice. Let up on yourself, learn to relax. You shouldn't have tipped out that gin. It would've done you the world of good.'

For the first time in weeks, Alice felt comforted. Jeremy's face was so full of compassion. The tears spilled over again and began to course down her cheeks.

'Will you let me give ya a bit of a cuddle? Just a matey one, you know the kind.' When she didn't demur he put his arms around her dripping, forlorn little form and held on firmly. Alice felt the tight ball in her stomach begin to loosen.

'Heck, I had a soft spot for the old digger too,' Jeremy said quietly. 'But life goes on. It's got to, otherwise we'd all better shut up shop here and now.'

Alice cried for several minutes more, her sobs muffled by Jeremy's stained work shirt. At last she was still. She looked up and smiled at him, hoping that the relief she felt was showing on her face. He grinned back.

'That's more like it. But does that mean I have to let you go now? Bugger.' He gave her a last squeeze before releasing her.

'Thank you, Jeremy,' she said, wiping away the last of her tears. 'I'm so sorry for being difficult. I wouldn't blame you if you packed up and left me at Redstone by myself.'

'Yeah, well, no need to harp on about it. Good thing I'm big and tough. If that's all the hugging I'm getting for today, we'd better go and start on this mill.'

§

During the days that followed, Alice made an effort to be brighter, more positive and talkative. But thoughts of the bank plagued her night and day. She began to feel swamped by all the tasks that needed to be done, and the idea of losing Redstone was becoming more real by the day.

Then comfort arrived from a most unexpected source. Lara began to telephone, not regularly, but often enough to let Alice know she wasn't forgotten. One of these phone calls followed hot on the heels of a conversation with Carl Trent, who'd indicated that he intended to visit Redstone again in the next week. To her own surprise, Alice found herself confiding in Lara, who listened quietly.

A few days later, Carl Trent called back. But rather than arranging a meeting, he told her that the bank was prepared to renew the loan. Alice was taken by complete surprise, no less so when he explained that the loan had been re-evaluated because she now had the backing of the Harradines.

In amazement, Alice rang Lara immediately. She discovered that her mother, furious about the bank's treatment of Alice, had told Conrad, who was even more indignant that someone could have so little faith in *his* stepdaughter's capability merely because of her age. He'd wasted no time in contacting Carl Trent and severely dressing him down. He accused the bank manager of discrimination and insisted that he himself had so much faith in Alice's ability to run Redstone that he wouldn't hesitate for one moment to go guarantor for the loan. (This measure of support had come as a surprise even to Lara.) The bank had taken up the offer, and Conrad and Lara were now officially behind Redstone.

Alice was overjoyed: Redstone was safe for the moment, but the act of love and support from her mother and Conrad was what moved her most. She told Jeremy the whole story when he came in for smoko.

'Holy hell!' He shook his head in disbelief. 'You're a good one for keeping a fella in the dark. But Lara – Jeez! And old Con . . . Who'd have thought it? You could knock me down with a feather.'

'You just never know what's under a hat.' Alice laughed, and had a sudden notion that her grandparents were sharing her joy.

§

After that, Alice began to sleep soundly again at night and her appetite returned. In the first week of December the rain arrived and the land was renewed. The regeneration of the landscape boosted Alice's own healing, and as Christmas approached, she found that she was able to savour once more some of the simple joys of life.

Midway through December, she made a suggestion to Jeremy at dinner. 'Now that it's rained, there's no need for you to be here over Christmas, Jeremy. You missed out on going home last year because of the dry. You deserve to take a break and spend some time with your family.'

'Thanks, Ali. I haven't been home for Christmas in years.'

'Really?'

'Must be nearly ten years since I first left home, to work at Sandy Hills. I'd dropped out of school and came home, see, but found out pretty quick that I wasn't welcome there.'

'And you haven't been home for Christmas in all that time?' she asked, struggling to take it in.

'I think there was one year I went back. But there weren't too many laughs that day, so after that I opted for the pub again. Mum was at me about the same thing a few days ago – you remember she rang. But I don't wanna leave you here by yourself. How about coming with me?'

'Does that mean you'll introduce me properly to all your lovely brothers?' Alice quickly stopped laughing when she saw the look of distaste on Jeremy's face. Perhaps he'd misunderstood her. Was he worried about his ruthless brothers assuming they were a couple? She decided to let him off the hook. 'You're not obliged to look after me, Jeremy. I'll be fine here, honestly. It'll be very peaceful.'

'You don't wanna come, then?' Jeremy asked, a little aggressively.

'Oh . . . it's just that you seemed a bit . . . reluctant. If I came, I suppose you could always explain to them that we're not, you know, a couple. That way we can make sure none of your brothers get the wrong idea.'

She'd been trying to reassure him but he looked crestfallen.

'Yeah, be a bloody disaster if anyone thought we were together,' he snapped. Alice looked at him in dismay, unsure what she'd said to upset him.

'Well, I already told Mum you're coming,' he went on, huffily. 'Like a duffer I assumed you'd want to. I guess I'll just have to tell her you'd rather be here alone for Christmas than with *my* family.'

Alice bit her lip. 'Oh Jeremy, of course I'll come if you'd really like me to.'

'Only come if *you* want to. Let me know what you decide.' He finished his last few mouthfuls in silence, then disappeared sulkily out the door. Baffled, Alice watched him stride across the yard to his cottage.

Chapter 40

'Does he still fall off his horse every ten minutes?' Greg asked.

Jeremy's father and brothers roared with laughter at Greg's question. Alice was seated at the O'Donnell dinner table just after noon on Christmas Day. When she and Jeremy had arrived before lunch, Mrs O'Donnell had introduced her to everyone. Greg, the eldest of the six O'Donnell boys, had been trying his best to embarrass Jeremy ever since. Now they were all waiting for Alice to reply to his question. Jeremy looked at her apologetically. She answered calmly, looking at Greg.

'No, I haven't seen Jeremy come off a horse yet. As you see, he's a big boy now.'

Greg looked less than satisfied with Alice's polite response. His neck went slightly red and he swigged on his beer.

Greg was seated at the right hand of his father, Brian, who sat at the head of the table. Alice was familiar with Brian's square, clean-shaven jaw and stern features from church. On Brian's left sat the second eldest of the O'Donnell boys, Brent, who had been enjoying all Greg's digs at Jeremy. Brent's wife Belinda was close beside him; she giggled occasionally, and darted curious glances at Alice, but barely spoke. The next in line was Roy, the cleverest and laziest of all the brothers. Alice was seated beside him and he looked sideways at her on and off as he chewed large mouthfuls of food.

Jeremy was next to Alice, at the foot of the table. Having his father directly opposite, in his line of vision each time he looked up, seemed to be interfering with his appetite and he was pushing his food around his plate. Mrs O'Donnell was sitting on Jeremy's other side, across from Alice, and she patted her youngest son's forearm lovingly at regular intervals. Alice looked at her kind blue eyes and wondered how she'd survived living with all these males for so many years. The other two seats were occupied by Clinton O'Donnell, closest in age to Jeremy, and Clinton's girlfriend Janine. Janine seemed to be there under sufferance and made no effort to be cheerful. Alice warily met her gaze at one stage and was surprised when she received a wry, good-natured smile from the tall brunette. Alice had been disappointed to discover the absence of John, the only one of Jeremy's brothers whom she'd ever heard him speak of with fondness. John was spending Christmas with his girlfriend's family in Emerald.

Greg finished his beer, and reached for another. 'Jerry, how're Brandi and all those rough sheilas coping with you being stuck out at Redstone? You've toned down a bit, eh? Haven't been getting as many girls lately, or so I've been told.' Greg glanced at the grinning Brent for support. 'King Jed losing his touch?'

'I don't see any girls falling over themselves to get to you either, mate,' Jeremy pointed out.

'Still as much of a smart-arse as ever.' Greg turned to Alice. 'Not so cocky when he's had a good flogging, though. Had plenty of them, haven't you, little Jerry?' The brothers and father laughed again.

Brent added his two cents' worth. 'Used to beat the crap out of him when he got too clever. Hey, Jerry, remember when I broke your nose for swearing at Dad?'

'Is that really true?' Alice asked Jeremy quietly. She was beginning to fume inwardly.

'Hey, Jerry, heard on the grapevine it's a dry camp out there at Redstone.' Now Roy was having a go. 'Been wondering how you've been getting on. Never much good for anything unless you're half cut, eh?'

Jeremy gave a small chuckle.

Brent picked up again where Roy had left off. 'Yeah, been meaning to thank you, Alice, for taking the useless bastard off our hands. Just before you took him on, he was talking about coming back to work out here! We wanna know how you put up with him.'

Once again all eyes were on Alice. This time she looked at Brian O'Donnell, her frank gaze challenging him to restore some order and civility to the occasion. She spoke quietly but confidently. 'Mr O'Donnell, Jeremy has probably been too modest to tell you this, but he has been invaluable to Redstone. Before my pa died, he said we would never have managed to get Redstone back on track in time to satisfy the bank if it hadn't been for Jeremy.'

Greg snorted disbelievingly and Jeremy stared miserably into his dinner.

'Must've grown a few brain cells since he lived here then,' was Brian's unenthusiastic reply.

The brothers laughed again, but Alice continued to look Brian in the eye. The big man squirmed a little. Sue O'Donnell smiled valiantly, overcoming the discord, and said proudly, 'Sam said as much to us, several times, Alice.'

But Alice was still looking at Brian.

'Sam was a good man,' he conceded at last. It was Brian's attempt at offering an olive branch.

'Your father passed away recently too, didn't he?' Sue asked kindly, clearly hoping to navigate the conversation away from Jeremy.

'Guess it's a good thing *his* lot left you alone,' Brian said.

Sue winced, but Alice could see that Brian hadn't intended the comment as an insult.

'I met my dad's family just after he died,' she said. 'I went to Cairns and spent some time with them.'

At this point Greg piped up again. 'Bet you're glad you weren't raised with those fellas. Would've ended up like all those abused Murri kids. Child bashing, drinking and molesting – always going on in those blackfella communities.'

'You mean like older brothers beating up younger and weaker ones?' Alice asked innocently. 'I didn't see anything like that. I found them to be lovely, actually. I didn't see any abused kids, just lots of happy ones.'

Greg was a little subdued for several minutes after that exchange.

Over the next half hour, other topics were raised for discussion and Jeremy and Alice enjoyed a reprieve. Greg became progressively drunker and began to bicker with Janine. Sue O'Donnell seemed to be on tenterhooks throughout the meal, and Alice noticed that she barely ate. All her energy was focused on making tactful and well-timed comments, attempting to defuse potential arguments and soften the insults that were traded between the brothers.

Jeremy spoke softly to his mother and Alice, and occasionally to Roy or Clinton, but he was quieter than Alice had ever seen him at a social gathering, seeming to prefer to fly under the radar. Alice also observed that he'd refrained from drinking more than a couple of beers, she supposed to make sure he had full use of his wits.

After lunch, everyone moved outside onto a paved area shaded by two monstrous tamarind trees. Alice helped Sue and Janine serve bowls of plum pudding, jelly and ice cream. Belinda, who had been drinking steadily during the meal and was now very tipsy, set up a CD player in the window and put on a country dance mix. Grabbing Brent, she dragged him out onto the paving and coerced him into a shuffling dance. Clinton, who was also very drunk, came over to where Janine was sitting talking to Alice and pulled her to her feet. Laughing raucously, he spun her into a lurching kind of waltz.

Jeremy and Brian were making a wary attempt at conversation, both endeavouring to choose uncontroversial topics for their stilted small talk. Their mutual effort was being gratefully observed by Sue, who sat nearby.

Seeing Alice sitting alone, Greg approached and grinned into her face, saying loudly, 'Must be rotten living all alone out there at Redstone with Mr Dick-for-a-Brain Jerry. Does he ever leave ya alone?' He sat down beside her.

Jeremy and Brian paused in their conversation and looked over at Greg. So did an unhappy-looking Sue.

'Greg, you're horribly drunk. Alice doesn't want to hear your silly rambling.' She looked threateningly at her eldest son.

But Alice said calmly, her voice full of conviction, 'It doesn't bother me, Mrs O'Donnell. It's clear to me that no one here has any concept of what Jeremy is capable of. That is, except for you.' She added then, looking back at Greg, 'I'm afraid it's your loss and my gain, Greg.'

He snorted, and drained the dregs out of his bottle.

Sue managed to draw Jeremy and Brian back into conversation with one another and Greg took the opportunity to question Alice further.

'So let me get this straight, you two are just workmates?' he said sceptically.

'That's right.'

'Well, Mum did say you were brainy.' Greg heaved himself to his feet and set off to get another beer. He passed by Jeremy; giving his youngest brother a hard shove, he called back to Alice, 'I guess you're too switched on to get tangled up with a cocky loudmouth like our little Jerry.'

Jeremy ignored him and continued to talk to Brian, but his face flushed. Alice stood up and went towards Janine, who had convinced Clinton to sit down and drink a glass of water. The two women chatted for a while, enjoying the relative coolness under the tamarind tree.

But then Greg was back, a new drink in his hand. 'How about a dance, Janine?' He grabbed her arm.

'Yeah, good on ya, Greg, just not today, okay?' She pushed him away.

'Aw, c'mon, I really feel like dancing. What about you then, Alice?' Without waiting for her response, Greg grabbed Alice's elbow in a vice-like grip and wrapped his arm around her waist. She pushed his chest with her free hand, but he only leered and laughed, blowing hot beer breath all over her face.

'She doesn't wanna dance with you, get it?' Janine pulled Alice free. 'She thinks you're disgusting, same as I do!'

Suddenly Jeremy was beside them. Alice wished he'd stayed away.

'Oi, look out!' Greg slurred his words. 'What's Jerry gonna do?'

Alice took Jeremy's arm. 'Come on, let's go back and sit down.'

But as they turned, Greg put himself in Jeremy's way. Jeremy's face was unreadable as he looked at his older brother. Gently, he pushed Alice aside.

Greg laughed and shoved Jeremy's shoulder with the bottle in his hand. Jeremy tried again to walk past him. Greg's smile disappeared and he swung a punch at Jeremy's face. The younger man ducked easily.

'Still know how to get out of the road, eh?' Greg put down his bottle on the ground. ''Bout time I gave you a good flogging. It's been too long.' He swung another punch at Jeremy and missed a second time.

Sue hurried over. 'What in the world is going on?'

'Nothing to worry about, Mum.' Jeremy smiled at her and once again went to walk around Greg. At that moment, Greg swung a third punch, which hit Jeremy hard on the side of the head. He staggered, but regained his balance in time to block yet another hit from the drunken man.

'Go and sober up, you sad bastard.' Jeremy spat the words at Greg.

'*Come on,* Jeremy!' Alice pulled insistently on his arm, but once again he moved her aside and spun to face the older man.

Greg jeered. 'Now I get to beat the hell out of little Jerry, just like I used to.'

He swung hard and Jeremy stepped lightly aside. Then with one ruthless blow to the jaw, he flattened his eldest brother. Greg lay moaning on the gritty surface of the paving stones, his hands over his face.

'I've grown a bit since then,' Jeremy said. He wiped his hand on his shirt and went to stand beside Alice. Sue looked down at Greg and began to cry.

Brian, who had remained seated and watching from a distance, now stood up and came over to his wife. He put his arm around her and looked down at Greg with distaste. 'Go and clean yourself up, boy.' He glanced towards Jeremy, hostility written on his face.

'What did I tell you, Sue? Didn't I say that if he came here he'd ruin the day for all of us?'

'Greg bloody deserved it,' said Janine. 'I would've given it to him worse than that!'

'You stay out of it, you interfering cow!' Brian glared at Janine.

Alice looked at Clinton, waiting for him to jump to his girlfriend's defence. But the tall, strong young man did nothing, just sat looking exceedingly uncomfortable.

'You ready to make tracks, Ali?' Jeremy asked.

She nodded. Jeremy gave a half-hearted wave at his family and headed back into the house. Alice ran to Sue and grasped her hand. 'Thanks for having me, Mrs O'Donnell. And I'm so sorry.'

'You're welcome any time, darling.' Sue smiled sadly. 'None of this is your fault. It's been going on for years.'

§

They had intended to stay the night at the O'Donnells' property and it was late in the day to be setting off for the long trip back to Redstone. They drove into the low afternoon sun, and neither of them spoke for the first few kilometres. A few things about Jeremy were suddenly beginning to make sense to Alice. No wonder he had no desire to be a father.

Then Jeremy looked across at Alice's serious face. 'Sorry about my family, Alice. Not much to be proud of, eh? They're a bloody basket case.' He shook his head. 'I reckon you knew what you were on about when you said you wanted to stay at home by yourself.'

'There's no need for you to apologise, Jeremy. It's not your fault. And they're not all bad. It's not as though my family's perfect either.' Alice smiled at Jeremy in commiseration.

'Oh yeah. Too true. When you look at it like that . . .' He smiled back at her, his blue eyes catching the rays of the setting sun.

Chapter 41

Valentine's Day passed without a mention from Jeremy. That was one mistake he wasn't going to make a third time. He went to bed early that night and lay awake wondering whether Alice had taken note of the date.

The last weeks of summer flew by in a busy blur, and Redstone was blessed with mild weather and regular rain. Then, in April, Jeremy had his wish: he was going on the bush run with only Alice. At last he'd be travelling alone in the national park with the mysterious goddess of the Brumby Spring and the rustling yellow box trees. Alone with this creature of earth and spirit, at a time when she'd shed her disguise as the quietly spoken girl that most people knew her by.

For the first time years, Jeremy was seriously nervous. Alice was such an enigma; would he blow this opportunity? He could feel that this year, the bush run was going to be a test and a turning point in their relationship. Alice was about to turn twenty-one. It was time to find out how she really felt about him. They couldn't continue as they were; over the last year in particular they had done a lot of living together and their paths were well and truly merged. He'd yearned for this chance, but now that it had arrived, he felt a sudden uncertainty and a reluctance to lose what they already had. But the change was hurtling towards him at a frightening speed, a velocity which prevented his detection of whether the alteration was going to be for the better, or worse.

Once they were out on the bush run, though, the time passed in a happy haze of activity. The days were golden with filtered autumn sunlight, the air humming with the drone of late cicadas. The birds chattered and tiny scaled and furry creatures scurried away unseen at the sound of cattle moving in the bush. The cattle and the dogs seemed to feed off the harmony that existed between the pair of humans. It was a unity that was almost tangible as they rode along side by side in the scrubby wilderness. In this atmosphere even Carmen and Rose decided to bury the hatchet and were behaving almost like friends.

Each day this harmony seemed to expand, until it had drawn everything into its immense, interconnected web. The sky, trees, rocks, animals, birds and microscopic crawling things all became part of the one huge colourful tapestry.

In the evenings Jeremy and Alice spoke in low tones by the fire. Alice had brought along her old battered copy of *Pride and Prejudice* so that they could read the second half of it, picking up the story from where it had been left in hibernation since last year. As she commented to Jeremy one night, it seemed incredible that while Mr Darcy had been waiting patiently in that closed book for Lizzy to come around, her own ma, then pa, had left them for the next world.

The mob of cattle swelling each day was the only indication that the end of the run was approaching. To the man and woman it felt as though they had entered a timeless country. They were nomads, free to wander through it until the end of time, needing no further sustenance than that of their unique companionship. Jeremy found it so satisfying that he needed nothing more. He forgot his mission. Forgot that he was supposed to be seducing Alice.

And then suddenly the last night was upon them. *Pride and Prejudice* was finished, and Mr Darcy had won his girl.

Alice handed Jeremy a tin plate of rehydrated vegetables, pasta and salami, and he found that all at once, he wasn't hungry. He put it down beside him and looked at Alice, who was pensively sipping her tea.

'Do you reckon Darcy and Lizzy'll live happily ever after?' he asked.

Alice considered the question solemnly. 'Yes, I think so. They found stimulation in each other's minds and intelligence. They genuinely respected each other and lived by the same high principles. They were truly a match made in heaven.' She laughed.

'Would you want a bloke like Darcy, Alice?'

'Well, I think we might be in the wrong century. And the wrong country too, for that matter.' Alice's eyes twinkled in the firelight. 'Imagine Mr Darcy striding around Redstone.'

But Jeremy was serious. 'You know what I mean. A man with – what did ya call it? – high principles and morals. A gentleman.' He wondered where this conversation would take them and asked himself what he was hoping to hear.

Alice sipped her tea thoughtfully before answering. 'I *would* like to marry a gentlemanly man. Someone who truly respects others.'

'Does it matter if this fella's had a bit of a past?' Jeremy was sitting up straight now. 'You know what I mean, a bit rough around the edges, but trying his best to turn over a new leaf?'

'I've always found it so unfair that some men seem to think they can do whatever they like when they're young. Be as wild as they want and then, when they've had enough of all that, expect to marry someone really good.' Alice was looking at him insistently but she clearly hadn't realised he'd been referring to himself. 'A man should have to earn a good wife, just as she has earned the right to a good husband.'

Jeremy looked away from Alice and into the fire. He felt as though he was falling. Alice had just described her ideal man, and he was well aware that he was at the other end of the scale. He felt furious at this upright little woman sitting opposite him. But even angrier with himself. So she didn't want to marry him. She hadn't even considered the idea of being with him. Why should that worry him? He wasn't the marrying kind. How many times had he told her so?

Jeremy had admitted to himself long ago that he wanted Alice. But marriage? That was an entirely different ballgame. King Jed would always be free to do as he pleased and would never make himself a slave to that kind of old-fashioned commitment, least of all to someone like Alice. But now, for the first time since meeting her, he was considering the prospect of life without her. And it seemed unbearable.

And why did he feel so foiled, so betrayed? Alice had never encouraged his affection. With a sickening wave of horror, Jeremy suddenly realised that he didn't just want this girl, he was deeply in love with her. Why did this have to occur to him now, at the same time as finding out that he'd never have her? And why did he, a bloke who never wasted a thought on tomorrow, have to realise tonight that all his vague visions of the future contained Alice? And Redstone?

Then she was speaking again. 'What about you, Jeremy? Who's your ideal woman? Brandi?'

Horrified, he realised she was serious. 'That slut?' His bitterness sounded in his answer and Alice looked startled. 'She throws herself at anything male that moves.'

'Jeremy, that's hardly fair. You're not in the habit of denying yourself of any opportunity to be with a woman either. Why is it so much worse in a girl?'

Jeremy couldn't believe his ears. Alice was defending Brandi.

She went on, 'Brandi worships the ground you walk on. What's the difference between what *you* do and what *she* does, apart from your gender?'

Jeremy slammed his tin cup down on the ground and stood up. 'Full of compliments tonight, aren't ya?'

At his sharp tone Alice straightened up and looked at him in surprise. Jeremy glared at her. He wished he felt like shouting at her. Insulting her as he usually did when someone upset him. Exploding to let off some steam. But this was a different kind of hurt. And he respected her too much now. He stood there feeling the blood rushing through his brain. He felt dizzy and disoriented. He drew in a huge breath of air and sighed it out again.

'So now I know what you think of me,' he said quietly.

She blinked up at him and her eyes had the dazed look of a small owl startled from sleep. Disorientated. The curly wisps of soft hair framed her face like downy feathers. 'Jeremy, I didn't mean—'

But he cut her off. 'If you think ya gonna find another bloke like your old pa, you're dreaming. You're a few bloody generations too late.'

'So I've often thought.' Alice's voice was barely audible and she looked away from him and into the flames.

Jeremy spun around, knocking over his uneaten dinner, and retreated from the light of the fire. He clambered quickly into his swag and was hidden from view before the full weight of the realisation hit him. He felt strangely numb and lay still, afraid to move. His ever-persistent sense of humour tapped at the edge of his consciousness with a ridiculous thought. He now knew how Mr Darcy had felt: all the chicks he could have had, and the only bloody woman he wanted . . . Bitterness swallowed up the end of the thought, and any amusement fled, leaving him cold. Frozen to the bone, he curled up and wrapped his arms around himself.

He'd just started to drift into a miserable sleep when another chilling wave of awareness broke over him: he'd have to leave Redstone. As soon as possible – as soon as they got back from this surreal, idyllic bush run. The thought of going from Redstone back into the outside world filled Jeremy with terror. What had happened to him? He must have stayed too long. The place had got under his skin, permeated his soul, just like the girl. They were in league with each other.

He lay tensely, repositioning his internal compass. He now had to confront his hidden hopes. Secret plans that had been so deeply embedded that until now his conscious mind had been able to overlook their existence. All at once these dreams had been painfully exposed in a harsh bright light. Now he was forced to look at them and acknowledge them, before discarding them forever.

§

Alice had turned in for the night too. Wide awake and confused she listened alertly to the night; for what, she wasn't sure. Her heart seemed to be beating in her ears, and her breathing was faster than usual. What on earth had Jeremy been getting at? Initially she'd believed that his interest in her was simply as a difficult conquest. She was well aware that 'getting a virgin' was a bigger notch on the belt for that type of man so she'd always remained out of reach to Jeremy. She was sure that if she'd ever given in to him, his interest would have died as soon as the novelty wore off. Purpose fulfilled. She'd always believed that she was so serious and straight in his eyes. A party dampener.

Odd, in an interesting kind of way. He'd told her so himself, many times. As time passed though, she had recognised in him a deep insecurity and hurt, masked by humour and foolishness, and she had come to believe herself a trusted friend to him. He appeared to relax when he was with her, and seemed truly comfortable to be himself. Being quite alone in the world, he seemed able to draw strength from her, just as she did from him. This, she had believed, was why he had stayed by her through all those bleak months after the death of her grandparents.

But through all this, one aspect of his behaviour had appeared consistent; he was not interested in a serious relationship, with her or anyone. His continued weekend trips to town to see 'the girls', and his absence of comment on the most recent Valentine's Day, had convinced Alice that he had ceased to view her as fair game. And she hoped he respected her more than that now, but only as a dear friend.

So why the wounded look in his eyes when she'd described her ideal husband? Why the crushed body language when he'd walked away to roll out his swag? Husband? Could he possibly think...? No, there had to be another explanation. Marriage couldn't be further from the mind of any individual than that of King Jed's. The rodeo clown. Legendary party man. Lovable bad boy. Not the 'marrying kind'. He had told her so himself. How easily she could have loved him otherwise.

And for Alice, not quite twenty-one, marriage had only ever been a vague hope for the distant future. Marriage and children, with some mystery gentleman she'd not yet encountered. Jed O'Donnell just didn't fit the picture. And she still felt so young, had so many things she needed to do first, so many more immediate claims on her attention.

Now she listened for Jeremy's familiar slow breathing and

intermittent snore. She'd always envied his ability to fall instantly into a deep peaceful sleep, regardless of the events or emotions of the day. She'd complained to him about it on several occasions. 'Clear conscience,' he'd said by way of explanation. But tonight he lay silently, and Alice realised that he must be lying awake too.

§

Quite a while later, Jeremy climbed quietly out of his swag and crept over to Alice's side of the fire. He gently poked the coals and added a few sticks. The fire flared up and the flickering light illuminated the side of Alice's sleeping face. He stood looking down at her. The fringe of lashes resting on the smooth curve of her cheek reminded him of a sleeping infant. He kneeled down and then lowered himself to lie beside her. He reached out and began to stroke her hair. She opened her eyes and turned to look at his face but the firelight was behind him. Her eyes searching for his face in the shadow reminded him of clear dark pools. There was no surprise or fear in those eyes.

'What is it, Jeremy? Are you alright?'

'I have to leave Redstone. As soon as we get back.'

'I know.'

Alice moved over to make room and he drew closer. She threw the canvas of her swag over him. Lying together, they treasured each other's warmth and precious companionship as something that would soon be lost. The fire quickly died down again and they both remained silent so neither of them knew that the other was crying. After a time, soothed by the shedding of tears and lulled by the crackling of the fire, they both fell into a deep sleep.

Chapter 42

After returning from the bush run, Jeremy stayed on for another three weeks, busying himself with checking and tidying-up work around the station. He made sure that all the machines were serviced, cut three hundred wood posts for fencing and welded up some spare gates. He also told Alice that before he left he needed to be sure she'd found a trustworthy replacement for him. 'You might end up stuck out here with some sort of sleaze,' he said in genuine concern.

Then an idea occurred to him. After struggling with himself for a day or so, he did the honourable thing.

'Ali, are you still in touch with Troy?' he asked over morning smoko.

'Yes, every now and then. Why?'

'Because I reckon if you let on to him that I'm leaving Redstone, he'll be back in the country before you can scratch yourself, to snap up my job.' Jeremy looked at Alice searchingly.

She sat quietly for a moment, her eyes downcast.

Jeremy went on, 'Troy'd do the right thing by you here, Alice.'

'Of course he would!' she agreed earnestly. 'But I could never forgive myself if he wasted the opportunity he's been given overseas to rush back home. He's only just starting to settle in over there and make a name for himself. No, best not tell him. We'll have to think of someone else. I have a few more phone calls to make yet.'

Involuntarily, Jeremy felt a rush of relief at Alice's words, then cursed himself inwardly. He had no right to be feeling possessive towards her. Why couldn't he get it through his thick skull that Alice didn't want him? After two-plus years of being with her almost every day, he'd had more than a fair go. And why shouldn't Troy have her? There weren't too many better fellas kicking around.

In the end, it was decided that Arthur and Beryl Sawtell would come to Redstone to help caretake and assist with the odd jobs. A few months ago the old couple had sold Serena Downs and retired to town, none of their children being interested in returning to work the place. Beryl had been lamenting the situation to Alice at church one day: she herself was thoroughly enjoying the social activities in town, but Arthur was very unhappy, 'cooped up and impossibly cranky'. Consequently, the Sawtells had jumped at Alice's offer.

Jeremy telephoned the elderly couple on the sly, to make sure they were going to do the right thing by Alice. He spoke to Arthur and explained how reluctant Alice always was to ask anyone for help. 'She won't wanna put you out. She thinks she can do everything by herself,' Jeremy warned. 'If it looks like she's struggling you need to keep a bit of a tab on things. You might have to dig your heels in a bit and make her let you help.'

'My oath I will,' Arthur assured him. 'Can't wait to get my hands dirty again. They've gone all pink and soft like a townie's. Anyway, Sammy Day was one of my best mates. You can trust me. I *am* a Rotarian, after all.'

'Oh well, in that case . . .' Jeremy tried to sound serious.

'And Beryl will enjoy having someone to fuss over again. Like a mother hen she is, and not a single grandkid within cooee.'

§

A few days before Jeremy was to leave, it was Alice's twenty-first birthday. She was awoken before dawn by soft, stealthy sounds coming from the kitchen. She lay still, listening, wondering whether a possum had found its way into the house. Next came a clatter and a clang, followed by the sound of Jeremy swearing. Then the noises ceased abruptly and the pre-dawn stillness took possession of the house again. But sleep had fled for Alice, so she climbed out of bed and pulled on some clothes.

The kitchen light revealed an odd arrangement that had been placed carefully at the centre of the old wooden table, in the spot usually reserved for the teapot. Placed neatly side by side on the checked tablecloth was a pair of exquisitely crafted old-fashioned riding boots. The tops of the boots had been crammed full of gumtips and an unusual assortment of weedy bush flowers. A tin mug and spoon that Alice had left after a bedtime drink were lying on the floor: the intruder must have knocked them off the table.

She walked closer. The leather of the boots was decorated with a delicate embossing of leaves and swirls. There were several solid brass studs around the top edge and the soles were also made of thick, dark leather. Scrawled on a pale blue envelope that had been placed beside the boots were the words, *Happy 21st, Alice. Love from Jeremy.*

The words suddenly blurred as Alice regarded the familiar messy handwriting. She picked up the envelope and turned it over. It was empty; it must have simply been something Jeremy had found in his cottage to write on. Alice smiled. The soft shade of blue was her favourite, and she wondered if he'd chosen it on purpose.

Alice gently removed the foliage and flowers and put them into a vase that had been sitting empty on the windowsill, dormant since her grandmother's death. Then she pulled on the boots. They were a perfect fit and soft with use. It was clear that the former owner of the boots had taken exceptionally good care of them, oiling them regularly as the leather had a supple sheen.

Stepping lightly out onto the veranda through the open door, Alice savoured the soft thud of the leather soles on the old timbers. There she stood for a time, watching the orange glow that was kindling in the east and listening to the first birds heralding the birth of the day. Looking down at the boots in the dim light, she suddenly recognised them for what they were. Jeremy had once told her about a precious prize he'd won in a calf-riding competition: these boots Jeremy had named as the pride and joy of his early teens. Alice had never imagined he'd still have them, or that they would still be wearable. She felt humbled and undeserving, as though he had given her a small wedge of his own flesh. How would she ever thank him?

'Look, Jeremy,' was all she said, glancing down at her feet when he came over for breakfast. Then, smiling up at him, she hoped her gratitude was written on her face. Unspeaking, he smiled back and she could see that he was well pleased.

§

Jeremy's last days slid by, and all at once the time of his departure was upon them. By six o'clock in the morning, Jeremy had packed his few belongings into the tray of his ute. Alice stood by sadly as he tied down the load.

'Hop in, Ace!' he commanded, in as bright a tone as he could muster. Then he turned to Alice. Their eyes met briefly before she lowered her lashes to hide the tears that threatened.

Her voice trembled. 'Jeremy, how can I ever begin to thank you for everything you've done?'

'It's no big deal, Ali,' he said, with forced lightness. 'Just give me something to remember you by. A kiss'll do. I promise ya, you won't catch any diseases from a little old kiss.'

To Jeremy's surprise, without hesitation Alice put her arms around his neck and kissed him on the lips. Then she buried her face in his chest. He put his arms around her and held her tightly, planting a few tender kisses on the top of her head. Then he released her and turned quickly away, climbing into his ute.

He tried to sound cheerful as he waved casually out the window. 'I'll see ya when I'm looking at ya.' But his voice cracked and the last word came out sounding more like a sob. He looked away from Alice, who was crying in earnest now, and accelerated away in a cloud of dust. He slowed down a little at the grid and Ace took the opportunity to jump out and lope back towards Alice and the Bennet sisters, who were still standing where he'd left them. Jeremy halted for a moment, watching his dog's desertion in the rear-vision mirror.

'Bugger him, he might as well stay. No place for a dog where I'm going.' Then he sped away down the Redstone road.

Chapter 43

Alice decided to let the Sawtells live in the big house and she moved into Jeremy's cottage. She knew that her grandparents had lived in the tiny building for a few months after they were married, while much-needed renovations were performed on the big old Redstone homestead. The simple, rustic slab cottage had well suited her grandfather and had retained some of his essence for all these years. Alice somehow felt closer to him there, and she thought the absence of him and her grandmother might be less painfully obvious there than it was in the main house where all three had lived together. Also, though she'd never have admitted it, being in the cottage made her feel that in some way she was still connected to Jeremy.

A few weeks after he'd left Redstone, Alice found out from Sue O'Donnell that Jeremy had gone to the mines. She felt deeply sad for him, knowing how he'd feel about himself for 'selling out' and doing something he had despised even the thought of. Sue gave her his address, and she wrote to him every now and again, telling him all about the day-to-day happenings at Redstone; about her small achievements, and sometimes about the setbacks that came all too often.

She wrote to him when his heifer, Olive, had a snowy bull calf. She wrote when she saw brumbies at the spring with two leggy foals. But when Ace was bitten by a taipan and died, Alice didn't write. She supposed she'd tell him one day, when the time was right. He never replied to her letters and she wondered whether he even read them. Still, she continued to write to him, telling herself it was just in case he needed something to think about outside the big black hole where he now spent his days. But the letters also allowed her to maintain a sense of connection with Jeremy, and this was more vital to her than she liked to admit.

For the first time in her life, Alice now had to struggle to derive the simple pleasure she once experienced from the most mundane of tasks. Her beloved dogs and horses were no longer sufficient companionship for her. Everywhere she went, she could see the ghost of Jeremy, stepping out of the shed, carrying a saddle to the rail, whistling as he crossed the yard from the cottage to the house, or pulling a wire. And things didn't seem to work so smoothly anymore on the station: she seemed to be continually hitting obstacles. Jeremy had taken his streak of cocky luck with him.

Then there was the nagging worry of the debt. Putting her plans into place seemed to mean only cost and, so far, no gain. She had been prepared for this, but nevertheless it weighed her down like a lead collar. The financial year was coming to an end and she was still afloat, but only because the season had been good. She dreaded the onset of the next extended dry, which was bound to come sooner or later.

§

Jeremy did read the letters. They were his lifeline, a small ray of light in his dreary new world. He read them slowly, soaking in the words, seeing Redstone again through Alice's eyes. A place of simplicity and beauty upon solid ancient earth. Her words reached him through the haze of interminable shifts. Sitting in the cabs of machinery, working levers. Back and forth, round and round.

For the first six months, he ached for Redstone. Lying awake at night in his tiny fibro box in the single men's quarters, he'd squeeze his eyes shut and picture the rough old timber slab walls of the cottage and hear the squeak of the slow-turning ceiling fan. He'd listen for the rhythmic throb of the crickets and the trill of the cane toads. One of Alice's dogs would jangle on its chain and bark at an invisible rustle in the bushes. A warm breeze would steal into the room through the open window and cool the beads of sweat on his face; the huge stars would be hanging low and bright outside, and he'd see them peering at him through the branches of the old box tree.

But there was no breeze here. The tiny cell was air-conditioned and quite cool, and he sweated not from heat but anguish. He'd open his eyes then and take a shuddering breath. Rolling over and holding on to his pillow, he'd try not to listen to the muffled monotony of the television through the wall. Then the tears would come and soothe him off to sleep.

But as the months went by numbness stole over him. One night, in a terrible panic, he realised he could no longer picture the once-comforting scene. And the warm subduing tears wouldn't come anymore. From then on, alcohol and sleeping tablets came to his aid. Then there were the benders that occupied his time off. He stopped going home. He stopped going anywhere but the nearest town. He worked out how many hours it took him to sober up enough to pass the pre-shift urine test. And this was his new timetable.

His reputation was soon established. King Jed was resurrected. He still possessed the knack of ensuring that all the other drinkers had a good time. Laughing along to his antics and jokes, they could all pretend they were having the time of their lives. But King Jed had become more reckless and heartless.

He longed to be able to hate Alice. To have the strength to trash her unopened letters without a thought. He tried to blame her, be angry with her. This was easier than trying to forget her, but still futile. It was like trying to hate the scalding heat of the sun, or the power of rushing rapids. She was guilty only of truly being herself, and how he wished he could have been the kind of man she deserved.

§

Alice was starting to realise how much she'd taken for granted about Jeremy. With him as her offsider, cattle work had always been straightforward and enjoyable. He'd needed no instructions or supervision, and any job he undertook was always done well. Alice's trust in him had been complete.

Mushgang still came for the musters, but Dan had mostly retired, and the other ringers she hired only wanted to get the job done as quickly as possible. They were in short supply and costly, expecting to be paid a day's wage that equalled mining money. She began to rely more on her dogs to do the cattle work, and they rose to the occasion admirably. Kitty had delivered a litter of pups to Darcy, and Alice had kept one, selling the others. So including the two short-haired collies Troy'd given her before leaving for the States, Alice now had six grown canines and the young one coming on.

Darcy was beginning to truly shine and Alice leaned on him more and more. He was more assertive than the bitches and amazingly instinctive. He cast out wide, easily covering the ground on his long legs. He had an uncanny ability to anticipate the movements of the mob and was worth at least two men, or so Alice often told herself.

Darcy also became her main companion, shadowing her everywhere. His only vice was his tendency to take an instant dislike to some people. His hackles would rise at the sight of the unfortunate individual and he'd stand between Alice and the offender. Then, with teeth bared, he'd growl threateningly until she called him to 'come behind'.

One of these people was Arthur Sawtell, and it was something of an ongoing problem for the Redstone folk. Arthur would have loved to solve it quickly and cleanly with a bullet, but he'd seen the dog work and knew that this course of action was out of the question. Overall, the Sawtells were a great help to Alice. Their assistance was just enough to keep things manageable for her. However, the old couple were in no way a replacement for Jeremy.

A few weeks after their arrival, Arthur accompanied Alice on a checking drive, offering to help her lug the heavy dry-lick bags. After driving for most of the morning they were approaching a long shallow gully in Pandemonium paddock. Pointing to the wide area at the base of it, Alice said to Arthur, 'I've been thinking of putting a dam in there. Do you think that sandy soil will hold?'

When he didn't answer, she looked across at him and was horrified to see a look of undisguised animal lust on his face. In a flash, Arthur reached across with his hairy, age-spotted hand and placed it on Alice's thigh. She slammed on the brakes and plucked at his hand all in one moment, flinging it away as though it were a rotten fish.

The next instant she was out of the ute. The dogs, sensing that something was amiss, jumped out of the tray and pressed against her legs on full alert. Arthur climbed out too, looking sheepish; all the fire seemed to have gone out of him and once again he looked like a harmless old man. Darcy began to snarl, and for once Alice refrained from silencing him. Instead she glared at the old man, waiting for him to explain himself. Arthur stayed on the other side of the ute and rested his freckly forearms on the side of the tray, remaining silent.

Alice quietened Darcy, then glared back at Arthur. 'I'd like to know just what you thought you were doing in there.' She waved a small brown hand in the direction of the cab of the ute.

'I'm sorry, pet. It was worth a try.'

Alice was flabbergasted; her mouth dropped slightly open.

Arthur went on, 'Only you're the first real gin I've ever had much to do with, and I've heard tell of 'em.' He looked up and met her astounded gaze. Then he lowered his eyes again self-consciously and studied the switch on the generator.

Alice looked at his neatly ironed work shirt, his tidily shaven face and thick-rimmed glasses. 'You should be ashamed of yourself.' She spoke quietly but her tone was deadly. 'Poor Beryl. She deserves better.' Rather than looking stricken with guilt at the thought of his wife of forty years, Arthur answered matter-of-factly, 'If you're not that way inclined, pet, we'll just pretend it didn't happen.'

Alice felt an angry rush of loyalty for Beryl and her disgust showed on her face. She wanted to forbid him from calling her 'pet'. Instead, and without knowing why, she added an afterthought.

'Fine Rotarian *you* make.'

This seemed to hit a nerve. The old man's shoulders caved inwards and he put his head in his hands and mumbled, 'Please don't think less of me over this. It'll never happen again. God's honest truth.'

Alice nodded once, shortly. They climbed back into the ute, finished the run and returned home in silence.

§

After that occasion, Arthur never stepped over the line Alice had drawn for him. They both pretended his advance had never happened, but neither could forget that it had. And Alice had never felt more alone.

Bustling, hard-working Beryl took on the milking and revived Olive's vegetable garden, which was thriving in no time. By winter, she'd crocheted colourful blankets for all the Redstone beds, and little ones for each of the dogs. But she was clearly concerned about Alice, seeming to sense her physical and mental weariness. She fussed over Alice and tried to mother her, but the girl found her attentions stifling. Every few days Beryl would bring a meal over to the cottage, but it was always so rich and strongly flavoured that the chooks and dogs were the main beneficiaries. Alice, like her grandfather, had always preferred simple food.

One evening, Alice came back late to her cottage. She'd been out searching for Lydia, who was on heat and had been missing for nearly three days. Finally, tonight, with the help of the other dogs, Alice had discovered the little kelpie inside a hollow log not far from the yards. It looked as though Lydia had encountered some dingoes in her wanderings, and she had been lucky to escape alive. The little bitch's back was a swollen mess of deep puncture wounds, from teeth; they had partly closed, trapping an infection under the skin. Using a syringe, Alice had flushed out the wounds with salty water and gave Lydia a large needle of penicillin, but the little dog was exhausted and dehydrated, and Alice knew it would be touch and go.

As she trudged up the steps onto her little veranda, Alice met Beryl coming out of the cottage with a mop and bucket.

'I've just done a little tidy-up for you, dear,' said the old woman brightly. 'And there's a hot bath waiting. I knew you couldn't be far off now.'

'Thank you so much, Mrs Sawtell, but I wish you wouldn't go to all this trouble.'

'No trouble at all, lovie, I like to help out where I can.' Beryl gave Alice a kiss on the forehead and scurried off, her bucket clanking.

Stepping into the cottage, Alice looked around at the spotless living room and then cringed when she remembered the state the toilet had been in. Two frogs had set up residence in it and she hadn't had the energy to relocate them. In the bathroom she undressed and hopped obediently into the bath, to which a strong, fruity-smelling foam had been added. She lay back, closed her eyes and tried to relax, but the scent was so overpowering that she soon opened them again.

The warm bath had been a kind gesture and the heat certainly soothed Alice's tired muscles. But the ever-present ache of loneliness only became stronger with every attempt Beryl made to cheer her. Nothing could replace her grandparents' love. And no one else could provide the companionship she'd found in Jeremy. Without her loved ones, every victory seemed hollow and every task a trial. Maybe Carl Trent had been right after all: perhaps it wasn't worth it. Was it just her exhaustion that was colouring her thinking or was she losing heart?

She watched two geckos stalking insects on the ceiling. Suddenly one of them must have trespassed into the other's territory. There was a brief attack. Locked in combat, they fell into the bath and disappeared beneath the bubbles, leaving a long indentation in the foam that gradually closed over again.

'That's my cue to leave.' Alice spoke out loud, her voice echoing in the emptiness. She pulled the plug and left the geckos to fend for themselves.

Chapter 44

Out of loyalty to Olive, the well-meaning Beryl encouraged Walter Lonergan, assuring him that she'd observed 'the signs' in Alice's apparent reluctance to return his interest. He became a frequent visitor to Redstone, and Alice grew to be quite fond of him. He was thoughtful, good-natured, polite and practical, and he didn't put any pressure on Alice to return his feelings. For this last she was grateful, although she suspected that it was because he was so sure of his own excellence that he had no doubt she'd come around to him in time. She reminded him on regular occasions that she'd never be interested in being anything more than a friend to him, but his phone calls and visits continued nonetheless.

He induced her to go on outings away from Redstone; to her own surprise, these refreshed and cheered her somewhat. He could talk books and history and shared all the refined ideas that were so important to one facet of her nature. But he lacked an earthiness, a rock-solid strength that Jeremy, despite all his apparent instability, had possessed. Everything Walter did was so controlled, so moral, so calculated to please. She felt that he was entirely a product of his environment, as no strong substance of his own shone through. She also sensed something patronising in his manner; sometimes a stray comment revealed that he believed he was making an admirable concession by choosing to associate with someone of 'mixed blood'.

His frequent insistence that her Aboriginality didn't bother him was such a contrast to Jeremy's occasional teasing and mock derogatory comments about her race. And much more offensive. That her blood and connection to the land was a deep source of pride to Alice was a possibility that never occurred to Walter. Jeremy had never put her in any category, delighting in the fact that she fitted none. He'd never analysed her suitability for him, he'd just savoured her company as though it was an unexpected discovery, and one that he wanted to learn more about.

Walter gave her well-chosen gifts that were simple, graceful and useful. Other than the little riding boots, the extent of Jeremy's gifts had been the odd bush flower or rock, and once even a wild baby budgerigar that had proved very troublesome to care for, and had subsequently died. On a few occasions, Walter took her to his home, where she was warmly welcomed by his family. He showed her all the innovations he'd added to their operation and then demurred modestly when she praised him. She was bewildered to find that Walter's constant demonstrations of humility annoyed her far more than Jeremy's egotistical self-praise ever had. And she now believed that both were equally insincere.

In many ways, she thought, Walter was a baby. He'd never struggled in life, always being so comfortable in the bosom of his family. Alice was amazed to discover that she found him immature in comparison to Jeremy, complete with all his larrikin, irresponsible antics.

In short, Walter, on the surface, was everything she'd ever thought she wanted in a man. But he wasn't Jeremy.

The weeks flew by. Rounds of mustering punctuated the work with the fencing contractors and the setting up of new watering points for the cattle in the smaller paddocks. Alice seemed to be forever checking, overseeing and directing. These were skills which didn't come naturally to her. The job of recording and analysing stock numbers and predicting production and costs was a constant juggle, but it was necessary in order to maintain the support of the bank.

Alice continued to make the two-hour trek into town for church some weekends. But seated in her usual pew one Sunday, she was terrified to discover that she could no longer pray. Her prayers in the past had been more like chats with God, and usually occurred when she was out in the paddock or at the yards. Since Jeremy had gone, she'd been so busy that she hadn't noticed the end of these spiritual conversations. She'd always taken for granted her awareness of the supernatural, and prayer had flowed from this as naturally as a talk with her grandfather. Now, it seemed that even God had deserted her.

Bonnie came faithfully to visit every few months and tried her level best to brighten Alice's mood. But Alice found even Bonnie exhausting; her jokes and wild stories seemed out of place in Alice's sombre new world.

The first summer of Jeremy's absence, Redstone enjoyed a bountiful season of frequent gentle rain. The land exploded with growth, and all the legumes Alice had planted finally began to colonise the paddocks; the improved fertility was evident in the deep bluish-green of the grass. The rotational grazing was beginning to pay off. With the higher concentration of cattle in smaller areas, the grass was properly chewed down for short periods. Then it was ready to be spelled again and the cattle were moved. Also, as Alice had hoped, with the grass being properly utilised, the risk of fires was greatly reduced.

The April bush run came and went. Alice persuaded Mushgang and Dan to accompany her, but their ageing bodies protested at extended outdoor living. This, combined with Alice's powerful nostalgia, meant morale on the bush run was unusually low. Evenings around the fire were quiet and desolate, with the crackling of the flames the only sound. And each night, Alice was painfully aware of the ghosts dancing on the edge of the firelight.

Winter was mild, with very little precipitation of any kind. Then over the three months of spring in the paddocks where she and Jeremy had introduced seasonal mating, most of the calves were born, with a few stragglers closer to Christmas. This meant less mustering and calves of a more uniform size, exactly as she'd hoped, and would also make selling much easier down the track. She now intended to extend the breeding program across all the other breeder paddocks as well. But for the lonely girl, all of these successes were bittersweet without Jeremy and her grandparents there to see the results of all their hard work together over the years.

Eighteen months after Jeremy had left Redstone, Alice ran into Sue O'Donnell in the general store. They had seen each other on the occasions that Alice had made it to church, but had avoided the necessity of anything more than a friendly greeting. Now, though, they found themselves side by side in an unusually long queue of five at the cluttered little counter. Gladys Hogan, the owner of the general store, was chatting at length to each customer in turn.

'Alice, how are you?' Sue asked quietly.

'I'm fine thanks, Mrs O'Donnell. How are things with you?' Glancing at the older woman's thin face, Alice noticed she looked tired and drawn.

'Oh, we're getting along alright really. A few too many chiefs and not enough Indians at our place though.'

The two women looked into each other's eyes. Pale blue met warm brown and simultaneously tears started up in both pairs. Then, to her amazement, Alice found herself crying.

'Oh, my dear!' said Sue, impulsively hugging Alice. 'It's so hard, isn't it?'

Alice nodded her head over the older woman's shoulder, not quite sure which of life's difficulties she was referring to; perhaps just life in general. Alice's frame shook with a final sob. She hurriedly wiped her eyes and prepared herself for Gladys. It was unlikely that her tears would have gone unnoticed by the talkative shopkeeper.

Once she'd bought her few items, she waited for Sue to finish at the counter then walked outside with her. Without mentioning his name Alice could tell they were both thinking about Jeremy, and they looked at each other in commiseration.

'I hope you'll be okay, darling.' Sue squeezed Alice's arm.

Alice felt the warmth travel up through her shoulder and into her body like an injection of strength and comfort. 'You too, Mrs O'Donnell.'

§

When Alice arrived home that afternoon she decided it was high time she brought the Arab colt back in from the Brigalow paddock. For many months she'd been functioning on sheer determination. To direct the activities of her days and weeks as they hurried by, she'd clung to the plans that were already in place, plans that she'd made in happier times. And while they were her own ideas, they had been built on the foundation of love and support that she'd been fortunate enough to have at that time. She now realised how much she'd taken it for granted. Since her grandparents and Jeremy had gone, she'd felt keenly the absence of the usual creative energy she'd thrown into her work. The energy from which new ideas were born.

However, her talk with Sue O'Donnell that morning had awakened a faint stirring of enthusiasm in her frozen little soul. A kindling warmth inside of something distantly related to happiness. So she decided to put a saddle on the colt while the feeling lasted. She'd been avoiding even the thought of the chestnut for months, aware that her frame of mind had not been conducive to handling the highly strung creature. But now with this new-found confidence, Alice thought she would be able to catch the colt in the paddock and load him into the truck rather than tailing him on the motorbike all the way back to the yards.

She set off at once, afraid to pause lest she lose the momentum of her new conviction. She drove quickly along the rutted track to Brigalow and parked the truck at the roughly constructed earth ramp. Hopping out, she climbed up on top of the truck crate to see if she could locate the colt and the pack ponies. She saw some bullocks in the distance, camped in the afternoon shade, but the horses were nowhere to be seen in any direction. For some reason she'd assumed they would be in sight; the first part of her plan had already failed. She sank down and sat cross-legged on top of the crate.

Such a small knockback, but enough to sap her of a large part of her rediscovered inspiration. It was just as she'd feared: this feeling was fragile and would only be short-lived. What had she been thinking? Why on earth, in a paddock so large, should the horses have been right here? She decided to go home and forget the whole thing. But then Alice was gripped by a sudden panic. Having been temporarily lifted from her state of numb automation, she was terrified that if she let herself slide back into that condition, the awareness of her discomfort would be so much greater than before.

She jumped to her feet again and desperately scanned her surroundings for any sign of the horses. Nothing. She called wildly to the colt, waited then called again. But there was no response, just a warm breeze playing with her hair and stroking her cheek.

And then a miracle occurred. From out of a gully thickly grown with casuarinas, only a few hundred metres from where she stood, the two stocky ponies casually appeared, followed by the glossy colt. Their ears were pricked and they were looking in Alice's direction, curiously seeking the source of all the noise. She felt like crying with relief – was this a sign? But then she reminded herself, the colt hadn't been handled in months. Why had she imagined she would be able to catch him? She climbed down and went to get the halter from the front of the truck, wondering if he would have disappeared again when she looked back towards the gully.

Halter in hand, Alice stood by the truck and watched in humble gratitude as the colt, with the pack ponies following, walked towards her. He stopped a few metres from her, his head up and his nostrils flaring slightly. She hadn't thought to hide the halter behind her back, and there it was in her hands clearly visible to the colt. They regarded each other for a while, then Alice took a step towards him. He whirled and cantered away, the ponies still with him. But he didn't go far before stopping and turning to look at her again. She sat down on the ground, her mind hopelessly blank; her usual instinct with animals seemed to be dormant or gone. But after a time the colt walked back towards her.

Alice was in no hurry, she had no wish to be anywhere, so she simply sat. Ten minutes later, the colt was sniffing the top of her head. She reached up slowly and put her hands on his velvety neck, then, talking to him quietly, she wrapped the lead rope around his neck and slipped the halter over his head. She leaned against his tensely poised body and stroked him. She could feel his sinewy strength, his buzzing energy. She suddenly thought of her father and was comforted. Tingling with excitement, she led the colt in a circle, a figure eight and then up onto the truck.

Just before dusk, standing in the yard, Alice saddled the colt; then, without hesitation or any strategy, she mounted him. She rode him slowly around the yard until the light faded. He felt tight beneath her, like a wound-up spring, but he carried her without complaint.

'Knightley.' Alice breathed the word and the colt was named.

After she'd unsaddled him and rubbed him down, she released him into the night paddock. She stood and watched him as he walked into the twilight with his head lowered. He stopped a short distance away and half turned to look at her before dropping his head to graze. Without thinking, Alice murmured a simple prayer of thanks.

And so began their daily dusk ritual, and the beginning of Alice's return to the land of the living.

Chapter 45

Alice had suffered a summer of losses. A pack of mongrel dingoes were systematically working their way through the calves in the paddocks closer to the national park. They looked and hunted more like dogs than normal dingoes, mauling and injuring the weaker cattle and using them as playthings.

Alice hadn't been vigilant enough when it came to vermin control since Jeremy had gone. She hadn't realised quite how effective his occasional baiting and shooting expeditions had been in controlling the dog numbers. Now there was a new generation of pups, and they had developed a taste for the blood of the calves. Alice had begun to bait some of the calf carcases and had even allowed Gyro and his hunting cronies onto Redstone a few times, but she'd left it too late and the numbers of feral animals were now well and truly out of control. The adult dogs were wary of the baits and usually too cunning to be seen by people in a noisy vehicle.

Early one morning towards the end of a particularly unlucky fortnight in late February, Alice returned to her cottage after her usual dawn duties at the yards. It was already steamy and the insects were out in force. She intended to head out to the back country to check the calves again, so she slapped together a cheese sandwich and took an empty water bottle from the windowsill, planning to fill it. But lying in the base of the bottle was a tiny withered frog that must have become trapped inside. With a sorrowful murmur Alice went to shake it out of the window; as she lifted the bottle into the light, she thought she detected a tiny movement. So, more gently, she tipped the frog out onto the palm of her hand. It was yellowish and dry, every tiny rib and vertebra visible through the stretched amphibious skin. However, it wasn't yet stiff.

Telling herself it was futile, Alice nonetheless put a splash of water in a coffee mug; reaching out the window, she picked a small leaf off the hibiscus and placed it in the cup. Onto this, so that it was half in the water, she sat the limp, wrinkled little amphibian. She put the cup on the sill, grabbed her lunch and was heading back out again when the phone trilled.

'Alice, is that you?' It was Sue O'Donnell. She sounded worried.

'Mrs O'Donnell? Is everything alright?'

'No, not really, Alice. Jeremy's ill.'

'Ill?' Alice felt a leaden sensation in her chest.

'He's conscious again now, but he's still in Intensive Care in Brisbane. I'll be heading down later this morning.'

Alice's throat tightened with panic. 'What happened?'

'It's called acute pancreatitis. He left it too late to go to hospital and his kidneys failed. He nearly died, they said.' Sue's voice quavered. 'They're afraid of another attack, but at least he's in the right place. His blood results improved immediately after dialysis but his kidneys may be permanently damaged.'

'Oh, Mrs O'Donnell . . .' Alice choked up mid-sentence.

'I'm so sorry to worry you, darling, but the nurses said this morning that he was saying your name through the night.'

Alice found that she couldn't speak.

'Alice? Are you there by yourself? Go and find Beryl.'

At this Alice pulled herself together. 'No. I'll be alright. I should go to Brisbane.'

'Just wait till I get down there and see how the land lies. They said something about transferring him to Emerald if he picks up. I'll ring you again tonight. I'm so sorry to upset you, darling.'

'No! I mean, thanks so much for letting me know. If Jeremy wants me, I'll come.'

'I knew you'd say that, Alice darling – thank you.'

Alice hung up the phone and stood staring at it, wondering what to do next. After a few minutes, she decided that it was best to carry on as normal until further notice, so she gathered her things and drove out to the back country as planned.

The mob of cows and calves appeared happy enough, feeding outwards from the camp of sally wattle trees where they had spent the night. The air was already stifling, and as she scanned the rest of the paddock through the shimmering haze, Alice spotted the red hide of a cow lying on its side some distance from the others. With a sinking heart, she bumped the ute over the clumps of buffel grass until she was quite close to the cow. The animal remained unmoving apart from the slight rise and fall of her ribcage.

As Alice opened her door, the dogs jumped out; the cow, suddenly aware of their presence, began to heave and struggle, her eyes bulging with terror. Alice commanded the dogs to get back into the ute while she walked around to the back end of the cow. She'd been fully prepared to see a stuck calf, but an even more gruesome sight met her eyes. The front legs of a large calf were protruding from below the cow's thick tail, but the nose wasn't showing. The calf's legs had been chewed down to the bone, and the soft tissue of the cow's rear had also been cruelly torn by canine teeth. The cow struggled again, thrashing her legs and trying to gain her footing. She lifted her head and scrabbled hopelessly before flopping down onto her side again.

Alice turned away from the bloody mess and retched repeatedly, beads of sweat breaking out on her forehead. Then, steeling herself, she wiped her mouth and turned back to the cow. Alice spoke to her soothingly and, after a few attempts, was able to get down close to the calf without the cow struggling. The unfortunate creature was spent. First Alice had to push the calf back inside the cow and try to feel for its head. It took all of her strength to force the creature's legs back inside, as the lubricating amniotic fluid had all but gone. She felt around and found the calf's nose inside, tilted backwards and stuck at the wrong angle; this was the cause of the problem. As Alice pulled on the calf's nose, the cow writhed and bellowed, and the movement helped Alice to jerk the head around. But she'd detected, even before seeing the nose, that the calf was horribly bloated in death. It was possibly too swollen to come out, but it was worth a try.

Alice drove the ute closer to the anguished creature and took from the toolbox the wire strainers, usually used for tensioning the barbed wire when fencing. She attached one end of them to the bullbar and the other to the front feet of the calf. As Alice pulled back and forth on the ratchet lever, the chain became tight and the cow began to bellow again. The calf's nose was now protruding, puffy with fluid. Alice continued to work the handle until the handle became too stiff and the calf would budge no further.

She unhooked the strainers and tied a rope securely around the calf's bloody hocks. The other end of it she tied to the bullbar of the ute. She climbed in and, as gently as she could, began to reverse, inch by inch. The cow writhed again in agony and was almost dragged bodily herself, but the calf stayed put. With another shuddering bellow the cow began to scrabble again with her feet in the dirt.

This was the final straw for Alice. She'd been keen to save the cow, a young, square-framed Brahman of a very nice type. According to the year number of her brand this was only her second calf. But now she'd suffered enough. Her chances of recovery weren't good, even if Alice had been able to extract the calf. She'd most probably have calving paralysis and be almost certain to develop septicaemia, the bites from the wild dogs adding to the likelihood of infection.

Alice knew what she must do. She'd faced this kind of scenario many times before, but until this year, there'd always been someone else with whom she could share all the grisly discoveries. Now she had to handle it alone. She gritted her teeth and unzipped the rifle case. The subtle noise of the zip was enough to send Darcy leaping from the ute and scooting away to a clump of shrubs a few hundred metres away.

Alice tried to focus on a tuft of hair above the cow's eyes to avoid looking at the eyes themselves, so mournful and pleading. The single shot rang out across the paddock and echoed in the hills of the nearby national park. The animal's suffering was at an end. It was a task that Alice despised at the best of times, but today she had no emotional reserve. She dropped to the ground and sat, rifle across her lap, crying bitterly. The discovery of the unlucky cow had been the final, fatal thrust on the floodgates that had been creaking and groaning for several days.

All at once, through her misery, her grandfather's most frequent prayer rang in her mind, as clearly as though he'd spoken it into her ear: 'Thy will be done.'

How many times over the years had she heard the old man say it, even in the face of great adversity? Alice tried to repeat it, to simply accept and survive, but her lips wouldn't form the words. She couldn't do without Jeremy. She no longer wanted to protect herself from him, because nothing could be worse than being without him. Redstone, everything she'd ever wanted, paled into insignificance beside the loss of him.

'Give him another chance,' she sobbed. 'Give me another chance. I swear I'll try harder not to judge people.'

The dogs were pressed against her, distressed by her uncharacteristic outburst. Darcy had even overcome his fear of the gun to creep close and rest his big ugly head on her foot. Alice wiped her eyes and nose on her sleeve, reassured her dogs and was calm. Feeling a little foolish, she climbed back into the ute and finished her checking run.

When Alice returned that evening, Beryl was sitting at the table on the little veranda of the cottage. She looked as though she'd been patiently waiting there for some time, working industriously on her patchwork.

'Hello, dear,' she greeted Alice gently, putting her sewing aside on the table, beside a bunch of garden flowers she'd arranged in a vase. She examined Alice's face closely. 'Thought they might brighten things up a bit.' Beryl motioned towards the vase, but Alice wasn't listening. She wanted only the news that Beryl must be bearing.

'Mrs Sawtell, have you heard . . .'

'Yes, dear, Sue rang and Jeremy seems to be out of danger. They're sending him back in a day or two.'

'To Emerald?'

'No, to Sue's. His kidneys are coming good. He should recover quite well provided he stays away from the drink from now on.'

'Oh.' Alice sank into a chair. 'Thank God.'

'Yes.' Beryl nodded knowingly. 'He's a very lucky young man, by all accounts. Saved by an iron constitution and nothing else. He needs to take a leaf out of your Walter's book and try his hand at some clean living. Can I make you a cuppa?'

'No thanks, Mrs Sawtell, I've got a few more jobs to do yet.' Alice stood up again.

'Well, there's some dinner in the fridge for you. Just zap it in the microwave for a minute or two and it'll be ready to go.' She smiled sympathetically at Alice.

'Thank you, Mrs Sawtell, for everything you do for me.' Alice gave the surprised old woman an impulsive hug and kiss before skipping lightly down the stairs and heading for the yards.

§

Just on dark, Alice came back into the cottage and sank down onto a kitchen chair. The coffee cup on the windowsill caught her eye. She stood up again and peeped in doubtfully, then exclaimed out loud in amazement at the sight of an apparently healthy, tiny green tree frog, his soft throat pulsing and his large glossy eyes looking back at her. Alice's skin tingled with goose bumps and she was filled with awe. Life. Such a fragile, fleeting thing.

Her sudden appearance having disturbed the tiny creature, he leapt onto the rim of the mug and poised there gracefully, turning his head to regard his rescuer for a moment, before launching himself into the night and the sheltering leaves of the hibiscus. Alice smiled to herself. She knew exactly what she had to do.

Chapter 46

Alice walked through the half-open door into one of the old timber bedrooms of the O'Donnell homestead. The French doors at the other end of the room were flung wide open, and a light breeze was playing with the curtains and an old cobwebby set of wind chimes outside on the veranda. Jeremy was stretched out on the bed, asleep on top of the covers, the bottom of his bare feet facing her.

She looked at his face. It was grey and drawn. There was no sign of the mirth that usually hung about the lines of his eyes and mouth. Instead, anxiety had carved new grooves in his forehead and his cheeks were hollow. Her first sensation was overwhelming guilt that he'd suffered so much and she hadn't been there for him. But then, finding herself near him again after all this time, she felt an undeniable sense of rightness. He'd clearly been through the mill, but every detail of him was so familiar, so dear to her. How had she ever imagined that she could do without him?

She made no sound as she stood there, but Jeremy must have sensed her presence, as he stirred and opened his eyes. As he focused and realisation dawned, his face was transfigured. It reminded Alice of sunlight breaking through clouds onto a sombre colourless landscape, transforming it. They smiled at each other for a minute or so in silence. She could feel the tears on her cheeks but couldn't remember shedding them.

Jeremy spoke first. 'That angel's here again, Lily. She's just walked into my room.' He brushed away tears of his own and reached out for her like a child wanting to be picked up. Alice went to him and, sitting herself on the bed beside him, held him for a long time. She tried not to tremble, but she was fighting to contain her happiness. She felt as though she'd just awoken from a long and dreary dream, the confusion was over and she was safe at last.

'Are you going to be better soon, Jeremy?' she said, her arms still around him. 'I can see you've been terribly sick.'

'That pancreatitis wasn't much of a laugh. I really thought I was buggered for a while there.' Jeremy pulled her a little closer. 'Thought I was having a heart attack or some bloody thing. Could've died too, they reckoned. They said alcoholics get it. Alcoholics, Ali!' Jeremy drew back and looked earnestly into her face. 'Put the wind up me that did. I told 'em I was no damn soak. But then they told me I'd have to give it away for life and I couldn't face it. Life without bloody booze.' He sank back into Alice's arms and stifled a deep sob. His voice cracked as he forced himself to go on. 'Even a week without a drink seemed unthinkable. Then I knew I was in strife. A first-class bloody wino.'

Jeremy buried his face in Alice's shirt. She stroked the back of his head gently. He lifted his face towards her again. 'Do you understand what I'm telling you, Alice? That's how bad I'd become out there in that stinking black hole. Couldn't even sleep unless I was half cut.' Tears were coursing down his face now. Tears of shame, sorrow, joy and relief – relief that he'd been given a second chance.

'Come back to Redstone, Jeremy.' It was a command.

'What for? So I can be head stockman for you and Wingnut? Sorry, Ali, no go.'

'No, because I love you and don't want to be at Redstone without you any longer.'

Jeremy jerked free to sit up and examine her face, his blue eyes wide with astonishment and his eyelashes damp from tears. 'You fair dinkum? You're asking me to tie the knot?'

Alice felt a flicker of surprise, but she replied without hesitation, 'If you're willing.'

'Willing? You're bloody barking mad. Let's quit all this small talk and get onto a serious matter. You're being too light-hearted. Tell me about the weather or something, I haven't seen you for a lifetime.'

'Does that mean yes?'

'Willing? I've been willing ever since the night we caught poddy-dodging Fuzz and I tried to wipe the dribble off your cheek.'

Alice laughed and shook her head. How she'd missed him. There would never be anyone else like him.

'Heck, speaking of that . . .' Jeremy quickly ran his fingers around his mouth. 'Phew. Can't accept a proposal of marriage with slobber on me gob.'

At this point Sue O'Donnell knocked quietly on the door frame and after a moment poked her head around the door. At the sight of the pair on the bed the worried tension evaporated from her face and it was flooded with relief. She quickly withdrew and hurried away.

Jeremy grabbed both of Alice's hands and looked hard into her face. 'Are you really fair dinkum, mate? Have you thought this through properly?'

'I really haven't thought about much else since you left.' Alice's face glowed as she smiled at him. Joy was flowing into all the corners of her small form. Jeremy swung his legs to the floor; wrapping his arms around her, he stood up, pulling her to her feet. He looked down into her face in wonderment. She looked into his blue, blue eyes and knew that she'd truly loved him for a very long time. Then he overwhelmed her by the passion of his kiss and the power of his arms holding her. She could feel his bones through his shirt and was overcome with sympathy and remorse. Reaching up, she put her arms around his neck, and suddenly, she was kissing him back.

With that one kiss, Alice and Jeremy made up for all the kisses they had never shared.

Then Jeremy buried his face in her hair and sagged a little in her arms, his legs shaking. She helped him back onto the bed and held his hands again. His face was serious while he rested for a moment. Then the grin returned.

'Bloody women these days, the cheek of them. Can't even wait for a fella to propose. Have to jump in first and catch him off his guard.'

Alice smiled, and he went on, 'Was gonna come out to Redstone when I was a bit more presentable. But then I got back here yesterday and heard that it was all on with you and Wingnut, so I gave that idea away. I thought to myself, who's she gonna choose, a cashed-up church boy, or a drunken clown? My chances weren't looking too flash. Hell, I reckoned you'd probably even gone out with him on Valentine's Day.'

Alice gave a teary laugh, shaking her head.

'I felt bloody sorry for myself then, I tell ya. I even wished the pancreatitis had taken me out. But after a bit, I decided, what the hell, I had nothing to lose – I'd try my luck, Wingnut or no Wingnut. Was even prepared to lie in the dirt at your feet and grovel.'

'Jeremy, stop!' Alice interrupted. 'What must you think of me? I can't believe I made you feel like that about yourself.' She hung her head.

'Keep your shirt on! Was the best thing that ever happened to me, meeting a girl with the guts to boot me up the ar . . . backside. I'll make it worth your while, Ali.'

Alice looked at Jeremy's animated face. His cheeks were flushed and his eyes were a little too starry. She said firmly, 'I'm going to go now so you can calm down and get some rest.'

'Calm down!' he exclaimed, clinging to her arm. 'A snowflake has a better chance in hell! Where are you going, to break the news to Wingnut? Poor bugger – just think, I wanted to kill him a couple of days ago. Twist his top off. And now he's out on his ear.'

'Jeremy! You need to be quiet and rest now.'

'No, seriously, makes me feel like a right bastard when I think of the poor fella.' Jeremy was still gripping Alice's hand.

She sat back down. 'Walter will get over it.'

'Jeez, Ali, that's bloody heartless, that is.'

'No, you misunderstand me. He doesn't love me. He doesn't even really know me. I just fitted the description of what he's looking for. Almost. If he wasn't so sure of himself, he'd have worked out long ago that I was in love with someone else.'

Jeremy went to speak again but she silenced him with a finger on his lips. 'I'll come and sit with you tomorrow. I'll bring Henry and Banjo and even Jane if you want her.'

'It's *you* I want, not Jane blooming Austen.'

Alice gently unhooked Jeremy's fingers and stood up.

'Alice . . .' His face was agitated again and his eyes were pleading. She had never seen him look so vulnerable. 'Now that I've seen ya, I'm scared to let you go . . . in case you up and disappear on me again. Once you're gone I'll think I dreamed the whole bloody thing.'

Alice bent over and kissed him again. She put her hands on his cheeks and he became calmer. 'It's no dream, Jeremy. I'll be back first thing. I promise.'

He smiled and settled back on his pillow. 'Righto, beautiful. I'll be waiting.'

Alice's heart was singing as she turned and walked from the room.

Epilogue

They had pulled up the cattle for the night at the head of the usual gully. Alice drove Jeremy mad while she meticulously nightlined Rose and Carmen and set up camp. Seeing his look of reproach, she spoke to him encouragingly. 'You've waited this long, Jeremy. Another few minutes can't hurt.'

Six weeks before, driving home to Redstone after her initial reunion with Jeremy, Alice had been engulfed by a wave of happiness so overwhelming it had seemed that if she didn't share her feelings with someone, she'd surely drown. On arriving home at Redstone, she'd run past a curious Beryl with only a joyful wave. Back in her cottage, she'd picked up her phone and dialled. She told Leilani the news all in one breath.

'That's deadly, sweetheart,' said Leilani. 'Wait'll I tell your Mary. The silly old fish might even smile. But your white folks might have a fit if all us blackfellas blew in for your wedding,' she'd exploded with laughter at the very thought, 'so make sure you bring your man north to our place soon.'

Then in early April there had been the wedding. Lara and family had driven up from Brisbane and joined the group of locals who gathered in the church for the occasion. On greeting Alice before the ceremony, Lara had kissed her softly on the forehead and clasped a fine string of milky baby pearls around her throat. They had been Olive's, and Lara had worn them on her own wedding day.

Father Callaghan had come out of retirement, driving up from Toowoomba especially for the day. Bonnie had been vibrantly present in a shockingly bright, lime-green wrap-around dress, and the O'Donnells had filled their traditional family pew and were generally docile and respectful, as was their custom in church. Sue's pretty eyes had been full of tears, but without the sorrow that usually resided in them. Instead they had twinkled with a clear blue contentment.

Hammerhead, Mushgang, Dan and Stretch had rolled up looking unusually tidy. Beryl Sawtell had cried, while Arthur held her hand affectionately. Ellen had wheeled Mr Collins into the church and he'd dozed throughout the ceremony, opening his eyes just long enough to make a muttered observation to his invisible comrade Cedric. The smiling Mesiti family, with a precious Keira in their midst, had commandeered a whole pew, and the ruddy-cheeked Fred Campbell had beamed from the front seat with Heidi clasping his arm. A grinning Ewan Webber, who had drifted into town for the weekend, sat with Jeremy's old drinking buddies. They hadn't anticipated a churchy wedding like this one for their King Jed; in fact, they had never expected a wedding at all. And Brandi was nowhere to be seen.

Swept up by the excitement of a wedding in the town, the Country Women's Association ladies had overcome their feelings of disapproval towards the youngest O'Donnell and decked out the hall with leaves and flowers from their gardens. They had covered the trestle tables with crisp blue and white tablecloths and an afternoon feast.

When at last the newlyweds found themselves alone together, driving the dusty road out of town towards their home, Alice had given Jeremy some less than welcome tidings. There was to be no 'wedding night' at Redstone. She'd insisted they wait for a few more days until their first night out on the bush run.

§

They'd taken a tent, as rain was forecast for the week. It would be a tight squeeze with all their saddles if the sky did choose to open, but Jeremy was looking forward to cuddling up. He climbed inside and waited impatiently while Alice did some final jobs outside and checked on the loose ponies one last time. But when at last she lifted the flap and poked her head in through the door, it was to reach in and take his hand.

'Not in there,' she said, pulling on his arm. 'Out here, under the evening star.'

Jeremy was suddenly anxious. She'd need some careful handling, this one. 'Just like that touchy little Arab mare,' he thought to himself. All at once he found that he was no longer in such a hurry. His nerves made him hesitant, so he was gentle and tentative with Alice. But after a few moments she took his hands and let him know that there was no need to be. He knew then that Alice was no longer afraid to love him. She'd truly given herself to him and was holding nothing back.

At long last King Jeremy had won his Queen. Sex with love. It was something new for Jeremy and it took him by complete surprise, someone who had believed he'd tried it all.

Finally he understood: 'Making love,' he sighed one night, lying in one of the old slab huts, the arms of his new wife wrapped tightly around him. Then another thought occurred to him. Before Alice, he too had been a virgin in some ways, never having really entered into the spirit of the thing. He was about to say so to Alice, but decided that she might have trouble seeing it from that angle. And was it any bloody wonder? No, he'd keep quiet for once. Warts and all, she loved him, even with full knowledge of what he really was. And she was the only person in the world to truly possess that.

§

Then, once again it was time to return to the real world. Their honeymoon bush run was over. Yet as they rode closer to the Redstone boundary Alice felt none of the usual regret. Instead her heart was full of anticipation. The medley of bush and cattle sounds combined, and the earth seemed to be singing with the same joy that the two of them were feeling.

They rode side by side behind the mob, content to let the dogs do all the legwork. The pack ponies were following loose, also happy to be on the home stretch. Alice and Jeremy rode along so close to one another that occasionally their knees brushed. A glossy willy-wagtail flew from tree to tree, staying just ahead of them, seeming to tease the young lovers with his cheeky swinging dance. At each new perch, he'd turn to look at them, taunting them with his grating chirp and insolent, stuck-up tail.

Their knees touched again and Alice looked across at Jeremy. She felt a sudden powerful thrill at the sight of the intense emotion in his eloquent blue eyes. For the first time, she experienced no hint of her usual hesitation or shyness. Instead she felt alight with pure, passionate love and desire for him.

Jeremy seemed to read her expression. He jerked impulsively on the reins and Carmen came to an abrupt halt, throwing her head up in indignation. The next moment he was off the big grey's back and lifting a protesting Alice out of her saddle. Despite her show of annoyance, Alice wrapped her arms around his neck as he lifted her down. Rose skittered sideways in alarm; then, seeing that Carmen had dropped her head unconcernedly to graze, the dark mare followed suit.

Jeremy held Alice up off the ground triumphantly, like a treasured prize, squeezing her so tightly that the air was forced from her lungs. Then he lowered her a little so that her head was only slightly higher than his and grinned up into her face. But Alice was serious and thoughtful. She'd nearly lost him. How thankful she was to have him here with her now. Her husband. She stroked his cheek softly, and tears of joy sprang up in his eyes.

Neither of them noticed the cattle disperse a little and begin to crop the grass. The willy-wagtail wagged and scolded insistently from a branch above them, outraged that they were paying him so little attention. Darcy and the Bennet sisters lay down in a thick patch of shade and with panting smiles looked on tolerantly. But Alice and Jeremy were oblivious to everything but one another.

Tomorrow morning they would arrive back at Redstone. There was still so much to do, so many improvements to be made. It would take years. Their whole lives. Alice quivered with excitement at the thought of it. She and Jeremy. She could hardly wait to begin.

Acknowledgements

Firstly, I would like to thank all the splendid and inspiring bush people I have encountered since leaving Sydney in 2003. You are truly a special breed and have provided all the substance for the characters in this story. When I lived in Sydney, I only ever saw negative portrayals of people on the land. If they weren't being presented as environmental vandals, they were poor helpless victims, struggling against the cruel elements and asking for a handout. Through this story I have attempted to provide a much more realistic, and positive image of rural communities to convey some sense of the resilience, ingenuity and grit that I have witnessed first hand.

My heroine Alice doesn't just ride around the countryside on a pretty horse, she is a strong, scientific, progressive, ecological food producer, with the courage to adapt and make the changes necessary to be a true steward of the land in her care. I thank my mother-in-law, Ailsa, my cousins by marriage, Nancy and Helen Creed and all my women friends on properties, most particularly, Wendy Lynch,

Shannen Rae, Melissa Miles, Roxanne Olive and Sharon Kingston, who have shown me that women can be superior farmers too.

Thanks always to my wonderful parents and my siblings, for their unconditional love, and for always building me up and encouraging me from afar, no matter what I happen to be attempting. Heartfelt thanks to Cath Wells, Marianne Hiron and Carole Kurz, for being in on the secret that I was writing a book by night, and for egging me on. And to Carole also for the hilarious photo shoot. Thanks also to Inga Stunzner for her great editorial advice just when I needed it, to Hazel Leahy, Danielle Norton, Sally Kirk, Jocelyn Creed, Janice McCamley, Megan Tribe and Leanne Rutherford for your ongoing support and friendship.

Thank you Louise Thurtell, Karen Ward, Kylie Westaway and Amy Milne, for babying and encouraging me throughout the confusing publication process, and for seeing potential in my story in the first place. To Julia Stiles and Clara Finlay for your sensitive, intuitive and meticulous editing and for all that you have taught me about writing. To Wayland Holyfield for allowing me to use the lyrics from 'Could I Have This Dance'. To my faithful furry companions, my horses and dogs who have humbly taught me so much about life, most especially, Murphy, Rani, Buck, Byron and Sue.

Most importantly, thank you to my husband Cedric for his patient faith in all my hare-brained schemes. Without his rock-like support, constant help with the kids, and ability to turn a blind eye to piles of washing and an extremely untidy house, this book would never have come into being. And to Cedric also, for providing plenty of material for the character of Jeremy. Lastly, to my four darling sons, thank you for understanding that 'Sometimes Mum just has to write her book,' and for your constant, hilarious, vibrant and upbeat companionship.